HOME GROUND

HOME GROUND

Cecelia Holland

ALFRED A. KNOPF   NEW YORK   1981

THIS IS A BORZOI BOOK
PUBLISHED BY ALFRED A. KNOPF, INC.

Copyright © 1981 by Cecelia Holland

Library of Congress Cataloging in Publication Data
Holland, Cecelia, [date] Home ground.
I. Title.
PS3558.0348H65   1981   813'.54   80-2710
ISBN 0-394-50405-4

Manufactured in the United States of America

FIRST EDITION

Fiction
Hol

To my mother

HOME GROUND

"Mike," she said, "pull over and let me drive."

"Shut up."

They were climbing Laurel Canyon Boulevard; the Porsche slithered squealing through the curves, lurching from right to left. Mike clung to the wheel, his teeth clenched, as if the car were pulling him along and would leave him behind if he let go. Rose grabbed the sissy bar on the dashboard.

"Mike! For Christ's sake, stop. You're too drunk to drive."

"Ah—wha'd'you know?" He lashed out with his right arm at her, backwards, the blow awkward and harmless. The car's rear end lost its grip on the road and fishtailed violently to the left. Rose, who was also very drunk, felt her stomach mounting to her teeth, her eyes bleary. She screamed. Mike let out a triumphant bellow.

"Gotcha, did I? Gotcha!" He rolled the steering wheel from side to side, putting the car into a rhumba. Rose gulped. The road was narrow and the houses packed along it on the steep slopes, their glowing windows (like spectators) overlooking the chute of the road. She clutched the dashboard with both hands.

Mike roared a wordless drunken howl, a kind of war cry, and punched the gas pedal. The car took off. Rose was slammed back into the seat. She screamed again. Her head was spinning; her eyes could not grip the world ahead of her anymore, and it was sliding wildly around; she was going to be sick.

"Gotcha!" Mike shouted.

It was not her head spinning, but the car. Rigid with fear, she sat bolt upright while the big Porsche whipped around in the middle of the road like a top.

It stopped. She blinked, amazed to see the world stationary again. They were stopped in the middle of the road, near the top of the road where Mulholland Drive crossed over, away from houses and lights. Then suddenly a siren began, down the road.

"Oh, Christ," Rose said. She threw open the door.

"Get back in here," Mike roared. "I'm gonna run for it."

"You stupid asshole!" On the side of the road, the door hanging open, she stood pulling out her pockets, throwing two joints and a tablespoonful of loose marijuana into the bushes. Below them a red light streaked across the mountainside, moving like a scythe blade through the darkness.

"Get back in the car!" Mike beat the wheel with his fists; he bounced on the seat. Rose jumped back into the passenger side and slammed the door. He stepped on the gas.

Nothing happened. The car had stalled. Through the rear window the police light threw its red blaze into the Porsche. Rose covered her eyes with her hands. Her fear was gone, in its place a sickening rage.

"Michael," she said, "this is the end, my friend."

The police car swerved in around them, cutting off Mike's escape. He said, "If you hadn't gotten out of the car—"

The door next to him flew open, and a cop grabbed him out of the car. "I'm coming," Mike cried. "Don't muss my brand-new jacket."

Rose sat still, her heart pounding. The door on her side opened and an arm in uniform shone a flashlight into her face. "Get out." She got out of the car.

"Look," Mike was saying. "You don't have to make this into a big deal, do you? I mean, I didn't actually hurt anybody, did I?"

"Driver's license," the cop beside her ordered Rose.

She brought her wallet out of the hip pocket of her jeans and opened it and fished her license out of its plastic sleeve. The cop asked, "You this man's wife, ma'am?"

"We live together," she said. There was something wrong with her heart, beating irregularly, too hard, unevenly. Her legs were wobbly. Behind her, Mike was still talking, but she shut her ears to the words. She had been drinking and smoking dope all day long. Her mind refused to work and her stomach churned with every move she made.

"Put your hands on the top of the car, please," the cop said.

She did, turning to face the car, and he patted her pockets and sides with his hands. On the other side of the car the other cop stood with his flashlight aimed at Mike, who was trying with no success to walk a straight line down the middle of the road. Rose lowered her head.

"You gonna arrest me?" she said to the cop.

"You weren't driving, were you?" said the cop. He nudged her out of the way with the flashlight and bent to reach into the car.

"No."

"On the other hand, you're too drunk to drive."

She raised her eyes again, watching the cop on the other side pull Mike's arms behind him. Mike was saying, "Look, guys, you really are making a lot more out of this than necessary—" Across his words the click of the handcuffs fell like a blade, cutting him off.

Rose turned to the cop on her side of the car, who was shining his flashlight into the space behind the seats, poking into corners; he picked up a tiny bit of burned paper in his fingers and sniffed it. She said, "I got a friend who lives just down the street. Can I go there?"

The cop straightened. It was a cool, damp night, and he was wearing a leather jacket; he looked very young. "Do whatever you want. We'll take your husband into Central." Lifting his voice, he said to his partner, "I'll call Central and tell them we're bringing in another deuce."

She looked across the car at Mike, who was watching her. Their eyes met. She controlled the urge to spit at him. Silently she turned and walked off down Laurel Canyon Boulevard. It was a long way back to the party, but the walk would help her clear her head, and she had a lot to think about.

• • •

She and Mike Morgan had been together for nearly ten years. Walking along the dark road in the cold and damp, she could not remember anything good about it.

The old song kept on playing in her head. *This is the end, my only friend, the end—*

Of course there were good things about her and Mike. Their house: the old Victorian, condemned by the city of Pasadena, that they had bought for almost nothing and restored. Rescued, she liked to think, revived. Mike had done most of the heavy work himself. Painted the living room pink with green trim, while she screeched and swore at him, until she saw how the colors blended and felt how the room relaxed her.

Even thinking about the house did not ease away the hard knot of rage in the pit of her stomach.

She walked along the edge of the road, where the ground was rough. She stumbled and nearly fell and walked on, wishing she had a joint. She thought of going back for the joints she had ditched, but in the dark she would never find them.

The end.

She shrank from it. She was approaching houses now, with short, steep driveways that climbed up under the houses, clinging to the sheer slope of the canyon on pilings and props. A Mercedes passed her going uphill. Another car came down behind her; it was only after the car had swept on past her, its headlights leaving her behind, that she saw it was the police black-and-white, with Mike in the back seat.

They had been together so long that she had lost herself in him; they had grown together, like the trees in the myth, and she lost her nerve at the thought of separating them.

She walked on, trying to cool off. She had been angry with him before. He was a fool often, Mike Morgan, living in another universe than hers, where it was important, paramount, to be noticed, even unfavorably. He would love this arrest; he would milk it for years, telling and retelling it. Already she could imagine what he would say. Making it the ultimate battle, Himself, the hero; the police, great sneering, snarling villains.

Now inexplicably there were tears in her eyes.

She scuffed her shoes against the rough ground under her feet. What a fool she was. Shivering in the stiff breeze coming up the canyon, she tried to conceive of her life without Mike and could not. She would not leave him. She could not think even how to tell him. He needed her. The tears rippled down her cheeks. God what bullshit, she thought. What a fool I am.

A car was coming toward her; she stepped closer to the side of the road, blinking in the dazzle of the headlights, but it did not roar on past. It stopped. The window rolled down. A head stuck out toward her.

"Rose? What're you doing down here?"

It was her friend Felice, who had also been at the party. Rose moved toward her like a moth to the flame. "Felice," she said, "Felice, Mike's been busted. Can you give me a ride home?"

Her friend's eyes widened. "Sure." The door opened, and Rose slid into the warmth and shelter of the seat beside her. She cradled her head in her hands.

"Hey," Felice said, touching the back of her neck. "What's wrong?"

"What was he busted for?" asked the driver, Felice's lover, Jerry.

"Drunk driving," Rose said, straightening. Her head spun.

"Ooh," Felice said. "Well, the way he was at the party, you know, he's lucky he didn't get the cops called on him there."

Rose said nothing. At the party Mike had danced and sung, climbed on the furniture, and challenged all the men to duel. Jerry drove the car on up Laurel Canyon. They passed the Porsche, parked on the side of the road at the Mulholland intersection.

"Hey," Felice said. "Isn't that your car?"

Rose nodded. The hard anger would not go away. It was her car. She had paid for it, most of it, but Mike had driven it. Architects needed to impress their clients, he said. And it ate too much gas just to drive to the store and back.

The end. She pried open her jaws and said, "I'm leaving Mike."

"Hey," Felice said again, softly, and put her arm around Rose's shoulders. "You better go home and sleep it off."

Now again the tears spilled down Rose's cheeks. I am leaving Mike. Not for the car's sake or the sake of the house or the drunk or whatever, but because of this knot in my guts that won't go away. It will never go away, this rage, and like the philosopher's stone it will transmute everything—me, and my relationship with Mike, and Mike himself—into its own image.

"Is she crying?" Jerry said, taut.

"It's okay," Felice said, her arm around Rose. "It's okay. They fight all the time, her and Mike. It don't mean nothing."

Jerry said, under his breath, "Guy's an asshole." They were going downhill now, down into the valley, toward the freeway.

The end.

When she woke up, she felt no different. Mike was still gone. She had slept not in the big waterbed in their room but on the cot in the solar where she worked. She got up feeling as if she had not slept at all. Her head throbbed. She went into the bathroom and took a shower.

When she had dressed, she went around the house, from room to room, looking at everything. It was a wonderful old house with lots of rooms; usually they had people living with them, but all their friends had lately gotten settled in their own places. Felice had lived with them for years, in this room off the stairs; she had painted it this pale blue and made the chintz curtains. At the top of the stairs was a wide hall lined with bookcases, so many shelves, ceiling to floor,

She did not move, recognizing the sound of the motor, the slam of the car door. Familiar footsteps crossed the porch to the front door. Her hands in her lap, she watched the door open, and Mike came into the room.

"God," he said and dropped into the big soft chair by the fireplace. "I never want to go through that again." He gave her a sideways look. "Thanks for coming down and picking me up this morning, Rosie."

"You're welcome," she said.

He looked very hung over, his eyes bloodshot. His clothes were rumpled. Across the sleeve of his new wool jacket there was a black, mucky stain. Rose fisted her hands together in front of her.

"Mike," she said, "we got to do something. We can't go on like this."

"Not now, Rose. Go make me a cup of coffee. I got to go to work."

"I'm leaving," she said.

He appeared not to have heard her. He sprawled in the chair, his feet on the grate in front of the fireplace, his arms flopped over the arms of the chair. Eventually his hands moved, making limp little gestures in the air.

"They threw me in the drunk tank. Took my clothes and gave me this thin uniform. They wouldn't even let me keep my socks on. It must've been forty degrees in there. I didn't sleep a wink."

"Did you hear me?"

"I heard you. Jesus." He rolled up out of the chair and trudged off toward the kitchen. "I heard you. You're going. Leaving everything on me, right? The house, the car—"

She was following him through the dining room. She said, "Sell the house. Pay off what we owe. Give me half of what's left."

"Sure," he replied. "Just like that."

Leaning over the sink in the kitchen, he turned the hot water on full blast. He got a cup out of the dish drainer, dumped a spoonful of instant coffee into it, and stood waiting that even Rose had not been able to fill them up with books.

The room at the end of the hall was Mike's workroom. In the curtainless window, where the morning sun glared through, was a pyramid of beer cans. The drafting table was empty. He worked for his father, who lately had been insisting that Mike come into the office, where he could not drink or smoke pot. Rose pulled the door shut.

She went on through the house, her hands in the pockets of her jeans. How could she leave this house? The kitchen with its slate floor, its porch full of creeping Charlie and wandering Jew. The dining room they never used. Mike was building a curio cabinet into the corner. She had always meant to find really great draperies for this room, to go with the old-fashioned cabbage-rose wallpaper. She stood trapped in the middle of the room, in the memories of the room. How they had struggled with the great sticky sheets of wallpaper; Mike would have settled for having the edges meet, but she had insisted on matching the pattern exactly. Glue in his hair. In her hair. Moments she had thought would bond them together forever.

The books alone were too much to move. The plants she could not move. The weeping fig in the living room that she had just coaxed into robust leaf. She could not move the weeping fig even into another room without sending it into shock.

She sat down heavily in the chair by the fig. She could not leave this house. Yet without Mike and Mike's income she could not afford to keep it. She had always made money writing, short stories mostly, reviews and articles, now and then a screenplay treatment or a rewrite, but they had been profligate spenders, she and Mike, buying everything they wanted in the confident expectation of paying for it when they had more money, later. She had been delighted to discover that they could refinance the house, once it was restored.

She might get him to pay her some kind of support, perhaps. If she went to his father. The thought of that revolted her.

Somebody was coming up the driveway.

for the tap water to get hot enough to melt the coffee. Rose leaned against the kitchen doorway watching him. She had expected more from him, shouting, arguing, maybe even pleading. She pushed herself away from the doorjamb. It didn't mean anything to him, either.

She went upstairs to their bedroom. While she was taking her clothes out of the drawers, he came in behind her.

"So you're really taking off," he said loudly. "Cutting and running, hey, Rose? A real sticker, you are."

"Oh, come on, Mike." She put her three pairs of jeans into the suitcase and went to the closet. Most of the clothes hanging there were Mike's; she had never gone in much for clothes.

"Yeah," Mike said. He fell backwards onto the water-bed, which sloshed and flowed beneath his weight. "Good old Rose. When times get tough, Rose starts packing."

She took down her shirts on their hangers and wrapped the tails up over the hangers and stuffed them into the suit-case. Socks. She had always worn Mike's socks. She opened his sock drawer and began to take out all the unmated socks, to pack them.

"This is the best thing for you as well as for me," she said over her shoulder. "We're not making it together."

"I don't know that. I liked it fine. Who says we aren't making it?"

She said nothing. She was going to cry again. As a child she had wept under any strong emotion, humiliating tears she could not control; she remembered sitting on a boy in the playground, weeping and weeping while she slugged at him with both fists. Crybaby, he yelled. Crybaby. She put back the unmated socks and took out three pairs of new socks, still in their wrappers, that she had gotten Mike the week before. She placed them in the suitcase.

"You're really going to leave me, hunh?" he said. "After everything we've been to each other."

"Yes," she said, and the tears rolled over the brim of her eyes.

"Why? Because I got drunk? Because I got busted?" He bounced up off the bed. "You been drunk. You been busted."

"Because—" Her mouth open, she hunted for the words, but there were no words for what she felt, remembered feeling, the night before, when he nearly killed them just to hear her scream. The hot core of temper was burning again, taking over her mind; when Mike came up face to face with her, she had to force her arms down to her sides, the urge to hit him almost too strong to control. She sobbed. The tears in her eyes blurred her vision. She backpedaled away from him and went to the bathroom for towels.

"Rose!"

"God damn you," she shouted. "I've had it with you!" She slammed the bathroom door, sat down on the toilet, and cried, not from sorrow but from red rage.

He banged on the door steadily while she wept, while she mastered herself, wiping away the damp on her cheeks, and washed her face. He was still pounding on the door when she opened it; he nearly hit her in the face with his knocking fist. She went by him into the bedroom, threw the towels in, and shut the lid.

"Go," he said. "Go on, get out. Who needs you? Running out on me—" He threw something across the room. "Who needs you?" His voice was rising to a bellow. She went to the stairs. Her heart was beating hard in her chest.

"Go!" he was shouting. "I don't need you. I can make it without you. You were just a drag on me anyway! You and your prissy schoolmarm East Coast jive—"

Her feet were carrying her down the stairs. Like a spectator she watched herself hurrying through the house to the back door. This was happening, really happening. Panicked, she wondered if she were doing the right thing after all.

"Go on," he roared from the stairs. "Get out! I never want to see you again. At least this will give me some excuse for being late to work. Get the hell out of my life!"

She opened the back door. At the end of the driveway, by the hedge, the Porsche was parked beside the little old yellow VW she had been driving for eight years. The VW she owned outright. The Porsche, in both their names, carried with it two years of payments, two hundred dollars a month. Its long, clean lines fascinated her. She loved to drive it. She had wanted a Porsche since she was five. It seemed to her now that she had wanted this house, this life, as long as she could remember.

"Rose!"

It looked like a back step in front of her, but it was an abyss, a warp through which she walked into nothing, not even another life, but into no life at all.

"What about your books?" he was shouting. "What about all these goddamned plants?"

"Sell the car, too," she said, going down the back steps. She walked out to the VW and got in and drove away.

"Kinda scary, you know?" Felice Kaffa said. "I always thought you and Mike would be together forever."

"So did I," Rose said.

She began to think she had loved the relationship more than she had loved Mike. Maybe that was where she had gone wrong.

She was sitting in Felice's kitchen. The day was ending. She had spent it going to the bank, to a motel, where she had rented a room, to a lawyer. The lawyer had sent her on to a newspaper office, where she had put a notice in the classifieds disclaiming any further connection with Michael Raines Morgan. Now suddenly there was nothing to do. Usually she would have been helping get the dinner together, making a salad while Mike, performing a monologue on the perfection of his art, composed a sauce or struggled with a crepe. She had meant to get him a chafing dish for his birthday.

"Can I help you?" she asked Felice.

"Naw. You just sit there and take your mind off things."

Felice was chopping onions at the counter between the sink and the stove. The countertop was of yellow Formica.

The knife beat a tattoo on the wooden cutting board. Felice used the blade to sweep the onions into a bowl. With her olive skin and high cheekbones she was sometimes mistaken for a Chicano. Actually she was Arab. At nine years of age she had moved from a Tunisian village into the East L.A. barrio, crossing half the world and seven hundred years in the space of two days.

She glanced over her shoulder at Rose. "You okay?"

"Yeah," Rose said. "Sure."

"Yo, ho," a voice called from the front of the house. "Anybody home?"

"Angie," Felice said in a glad voice. "In here."

A tall, skinny girl of fourteen walked into the room. "Hi."

"Hi, Reina," Rose said.

"Where's your mom?" asked Felice. She put up both hands to fix her hair, which was coming loose from the leather butterfly that pinned it in a coil to the back of her head.

"I'm here." Angie Darrezzo came in behind her daughter. Her wild bush of red hair stood out around her head like an aura. She wore a white tank-top undershirt and jeans. Rose had always thought she was beautiful, but she wore so much makeup that it was like looking at a dead face, only the blue eyes shining with life behind the smeared black mascara and the powder.

She came across the kitchen to Rose, her arms out, and silently embraced her. Rose got to her feet and hugged her back.

"I'm sorry," Angie said. She went backwards around the kitchen table to the other chair and sat down. "I'm very, very sorry."

"I'm not," Rose said.

"What are you going to do? You keeping the house?"

Rose shook her head. "I don't know." Suddenly she was exhausted. Everything seemed old to her, suffocating her in her old life. She had been in this room thousands of times. There seemed to be nothing to do, nowhere to go, except back to Mike. She would not go back to Mike. "I told him to sell the house. I got to get out of here. Maybe I'll go up and stay with my brother a while."

In unison their heads turned toward her, fixed her with their stares. "You're leaving L.A.?"

"Oh, I don't know. Maybe." She had some money, saved up over the past year. At her brother's she could live very cheaply.

"Can I go watch television?" Reina said. She had been watching all the women from one side of the room.

"Sure," Felice answered. She stirred the sauce bubbling on the stove and with a cloth wiped red splatters of tomato from the splashboard. She was meticulously neat. Rose lowered her eyes. Even this habit of her friend's had become painfully familiar to her, like a rope rubbing in the same place, burning the skin.

"You gonna date other guys?" Angie asked. Her long, nervous hands fussed with her purse, getting out her cigarettes, fumbling for a match. "Got a light?"

"In the drawer." Felice was rolling out the pizza dough with strong motions of her arms; she put her body into it, pushing and tugging the dough out flat. Her big round backside swelled her purple jeans. Felice had owned those same pants for as long as Rose had known her, six or seven years; they were faded and worn and patched and mended, a tribute to Felice's conservative Arab instincts.

"Where does your brother live?"

"Up north."

"Near Mendocino? That's beautiful up there." Angie had found matches in the table drawer and was lighting her cigarette.

"No, farther north than Mendocino."

Angie's eyes popped open. She puffed at her extra-long cigarette. "You leaving California?"

Rose laughed. "No. I'm not that bad off yet."

"What's farther north than Mendocino and still in California?"

"Is this a test?" Rose stretched her arms along the table-top. She wished she had a joint. "Humboldt County. Del Norte County. My brother lives in southern Humboldt, near a litttle town called Springville. His place is up in the hills."

Reina came back into the doorway between the living room and the kitchen. "Can I play a tape?"

Rose said, "He has a big place, my brother. A ranch." She grinned at Reina. "He even has a horse."

The young girl turned toward her like a puppet on wires. "Where? Where's there a horse?"

"My brother has a horse. I think it's a pet, mostly. Peter doesn't ride." Rose tipped her chair back on its hindlegs, her gaze on Reina Darrezzo. Angie's daughter, half-grown, had all Angie's beauty fresh and unpainted and unpaid-for in her face and her lean, long-legged body. Like her mother, she looked straight into people's eyes; she had magnificent green eyes, notched with brown. In Angie this direct look had something tragic in it, as if she already knew she would not see what she wanted.

Reina's eyes blazed with expectation. She said, "Where does he live? Can I go there?"

"My brother? He lives seven hundred miles from here. Sorry."

The girl's shoulders slumped. Dejected, she dragged herself back into the living room.

"Horse-crazy," Felice said. She was spreading the sauce on the pizza; as her arms worked, she glanced at the clock above her on the wall.

Rose said, "Well, so was I, at her age." She regretted having raised Reina's hopes, just to tease her; she felt corrupt with age. In the next room the stereo came on, playing disco music. On impulse, Rose turned to Angie and said, "Could she come up there with me?"

"What?" Angie bobbed up off her chair and went to the refrigerator.

"Let her come up to my brother's for the summer. If I go." As she spoke, the desire grew stronger in her to do this, to give Reina a horse, at least for a while: carry through on the promising tease. "Come on, Ange. Just for the summer."

"Are you serious?" Angie took a beer from the refrigerator and pushed in the press-top with her thumb.

"Sure, I'm serious." In Pasadena the summer heat reached 100, 105, too hot to leave the house, and the outdoors for Reina was a stifling, dusty alley, a concrete lane between apartment buildings and cars rusting away on blocks. Rose laid her hands on her thighs. She saw something taking shape ahead of her in the featureless, empty time.

"You're really going, then," Angie said.

"I want to get away," Rose said.

Felice said, "You ain't going for good. Nobody leaves L.A. forever." She put the pizza in the oven.

Rose laughed. Leaning out, she swatted Felice's backside. "A Felice-ism."

"What would your brother think?" Angie asked.

"Peter? Peter doesn't think. Peter emotes. Haven't you ever met my brother?"

Angie shook her head. "Is he handsome?"

"Yeah, as a matter of fact, he is."

"Maybe I'll come up and leave Reina down here." Angie released a gust of laughter and stamped her foot.

The front door slammed. Felice looked up, sharp-eyed and smiling. "That's Jerry."

Her old man came into the kitchen, an attaché case in one hand. He wore a three-piece gabardine suit and brown shoes. Rose did not know him well, although she was one of Felice's closest friends; he worked full-time and went to school at night. Once, cautious, they had talked about books. He liked nonfiction. He put the attaché case on top of the refrigerator.

"Hello, Rose." Bending forward, he kissed Felice's cheek.

"Hi, Jerry."

He said nothing to Angie; he kept the side of his face to her. Pulling out the chair between her and Rose, he sat down and stretched out his legs.

"Make it up with Mike?" he said to Rose.

"Not exactly," she said. "How was work?" She had no idea what a law clerk did. Angie had just crossed her legs away from Jerry. Inside the dark, cracking circles of her makeup her eyes were clear blue, the brighter for the hard disguise around them. Between her and Jerry Burnham the air seemed dead.

The doorbell rang. With an air of enormous surprise, Felice said, "Somebody's at the door." She went out.

Jerry said to Rose, "We have a big case. I been on my feet all day long going through books."

Felice came back. "Pizza's almost done," she said and, as she passed, gave Jerry a quick, fluttery touch on the shoulder.

Behind her came a fat young man in a T-shirt. Angie straightened in her chair like a spring and put out her hand.

"Hey, how you doin'?" she grabbed the fat man's hand and wrung it. "You looking for Reina?"

"Looking for Reina?" Rose said, startled. Beside her, Jerry Burnham sat bolt upright, his chin set like a cement slab.

"You remember Miller, don't y'?" Felice was telling him. "You met Miller."

Rose leaned back, one arm on the table, looking curiously over this developing situation; Jerry obviously did remember Miller and did not like him; and Angie was still clinging to him, saying, "I think Reina's out in the living room listening to records."

Jerry shot up out of his chair. "You let that kid play with my stereo?" He strode out to the living room, and Felice muttered something and rushed after him.

Rose sniffed at a new scent in the air. Somebody was smoking pot. Abruptly the newcomer thrust a joint at her.

"Thanks," she said. "My name's Rose."

"Miller," he replied.

Angie finally let go of him. "Didn't you ever meet Rose? She just broke up with her old man, and now she says she's going away. We had some good times." She gave Rose a look heavy with remembrances.

"Yeah," Rose said. "Sometimes they were good."

She toked on the joint. Almost at once, her head ballooned, her heartbeat began to race in her ears. Warm all over, she let out the smoke in a gust. "This is pretty good weed."

Miller recovered the joint. He was tall as well as fat, his fair hair crinkled like Brillo. He put the joint to his lips.

"Can I buy some of that?" she asked.

Reina came into the room, her cheeks red, her eyes snapping. "Fuck him," she said, not loudly, and flung herself into a chair. Angie leaned over her, solicitous as a lover.

"What happened? Whatsa matter?"

Miller gave Reina one quick look and dropped his gaze. Rose saw that Angie was right; it was Reina he had come to see; and seeing her, he hunched his shoulders, shifted his feet, his whole body reacting to her presence. He wasn't that young, Rose thought, twenty-five or twenty-six, nearly twice Reina's age.

"The pizza," Rose said suddenly and got up and went to the oven.

When she opened the door, the hot, sharp smell of burning cheese flooded the kitchen. She grabbed the pot holders off the counter and hauled the pan out of the oven. The crust was charred, the cheese dark brown and blistered. Angie cried out in dismay. Rose stood uncertainly holding the pan. The heat seeped through the thin pot holders, and she put it down hastily on the counter.

"Fel! The pizza!"

Felice dashed back into the kitchen. "Oh, my God. My God." She put both hands up to her hair, holding her head on. "You made me wreck the pizza!"

Jerry strode into the room, his arms crooked belligerently. "*I* made you do it! I suppose now I don't get any dinner?"

"How much do you want to buy?" The fat young man moved over closer to Rose.

"I don't know." She put her hands in her pockets, keeping Jerry under watch; he and Felice were shouting at each other. "How much is it?"

"Forty an ounce."

Jerry lunged between them suddenly, pushing past them to Angie, and shouted into her face. "You keep that kid off my stereo, you understand?"

Reina cried, "I wasn't touching your fuckin' stupid—"

"Shut your filthy little mouth!"

"Are they good ounces?" Rose asked Miller.

"Yeah, they're okay; they weigh out."

Felice charged across the kitchen, her body at an angle. "These are my friends, Jerry. You can't talk to my friends like that."

"I think we'd better get out of here," Rose said.

Nose to nose with Felice, Jerry cried, "I don't want to hear it. Either they go, or I go, Fel—that's my last word!"

Angie and Felice were staring at him, their mouths slightly open. Jerry wheeled, poking his finger under Angie's nose.

"You stay away from my girl, you understand? She's not going bar hopping with you, she's not going anywhere with any of you—" He twisted his head to include them all in this. "She's mine now, and you get the hell out of my house!"

"Jerry!" Felice got between him and Angie. "You can't say that. You can't talk to me like that." She reached out to Angie with one hand, but she was facing Jerry, and Angie moved away from her outstretched hand.

"Out," Jerry roared.

Miller was going, his hands in his pockets, the stub of the joint between his lips. "Come on," Rose said to Angie. "I'll see you later," she said to Felice.

"Not too soon," Jerry shouted.

"Oh, don't worry about that." Rose followed Angie and Reina out the dark hallway to the front door.

"Why does she have to live with him, anyway?" Angie cried. "Why does she gotta have anything to do with the schnook? Schnook," she said again, with special force.

They were sitting crammed into Miller's VW, at the curb in front of Felice's house. Rose was in the front passenger seat, with Miller behind the wheel, smoking another joint.

"Ma," Reina said, "Ma, let's go home, hunh? Ma, come on. What're we waiting around here for?"

Angie leaned over the back of Rose's seat. "Why's she living with him anyway?"

"She wants to be respectable," Rose said. "Maybe she loves him." Felice still lived, in her heart, in the Arab village where she had been born. The barrio worked well on her and gave her more room, but in the end the village ruled her. "I'm sorry, Angie."

"You want to buy dope or not?" Miller asked.

"Sure. How much?"

"I told you. Forty an ounce."

"What'll you do me for a hundred?"

"Two and a half ounces," Miller said. "Forty an ounce."

"Oh, come on, give me a break. I'm buying a quantity, aren't I?"

"Ma," Reina was screaming, and Angie reached around her to pat Miller sharply on the shoulder. The street lamp ahead of them shone into the car, and when she leaned forward out of the cavelike darkness of the back seat, her face was chalk white in the lamplight. "Give us a lift home, will you? Todd drove us here, but he went to play pool."

"Two and a half ounces is *a* quantity," Miller said, ignoring Angie, his eyes fast on Rose's. "You want a real quantity? I'll do you a pound for four-fifty."

"Give me three ounces for a hundred."

Angie prodded him again. "I'll buy y' a milk shake if you take us to McDonald's."

"Two and a half," he said to Rose. He started the engine.

She grunted. She decided she disliked him. "I guess it's not my day," she said.

Angie tapped her on the head. "At least you got days that are yours. I never get my own days. They're all somebody else's days." She laughed at that, and Rose turned and put out her hands to her, and they hugged each other.

"You got a car?" Miller asked her.

"Back at the motel where I'm staying. I walked up here."

"You got the money, at least?"

"Oh, yeah."

He pulled his car away from the curb. Rose sat straight, her hands in her lap. The pot had brightened her mood. Everything would work out. Nothing good or bad but thinking made it so. For a while there, she realized, pleased, she had forgotten all about Mike.

They turned down Lake Avenue, into the sea of lights, the shopping center parking lots blasted by forty-foot stadium spots, the amber street lamps, the red and white lights of the cars, the red and yellow and white store signs. Overwhelmed by the radiance, Rose sat like a hick, staring out the window. They passed Der Weinerschnitzel, the Pizza Hut, the Taco Bell with its bonfire leaping and crackling out front, the Pup 'n' Taco, customers streaming through its doors. Miller wheeled his car in a broad curve into the parking lot beside the McDonald's.

"Two and a half," he said to Rose. "Take it or leave it."

She inhaled, her hands cool and tingling. It was very fine marijuana, and forty, she knew, was the going price. "Okay," she said. "It's a deal."

"Come on," he said to Reina and got out of the car.

"Get me a Big Mac," Angie said, stuffing money into her child's hand. "And fries. And a Coke. And get Miller a shake. Anything he wants." She sank deeper into the back seat as Reina left it, her feet braced up against the seat in front of her. Miller was halfway across the parking lot, his hands in his pockets. Reina ran after him. The car door swung nearly shut. Rose blinked, stranded in the abrupt silence.

"Who the hell is he?" she said.

Angie chuckled. She put her feet up on top of the driver's seat. "That's Miller Tarn. He's a friend of mine. He says he's in love with Reina."

"Reina is fourteen."

Folded in angles on the seat, Angie adjusted herself slightly in a shrug. "Before this he was always telling me how much he loved Caroline Kennedy. It's okay. He's cool. He don't come on to her or nothing."

"You've got some weird friends."

"Not as many as I used to have," Angie said. "Now you're going, too."

"I don't know. Maybe I won't."

"You'll go." Angie took a Silva Thin out of her purse and lit it. "Keep an eye out for Miller. He don't like me smoking in his car."

"He'll smell it."

"He won't say anything if he don't catch me doin' it." Angie puffed on the cigarette. "What happened with you and Mike?"

Rose was shaking her head again. "I don't know, Ange. He got drunk, we both got drunk, and he was driving like a wild man, just to freak me out, and a cop hauled him over. Everything just clicked. Or unclicked." She raised her eyes, looking into the shadows where Angie was. "I can't take him any more. He's fucked up, Ange. He's past thirty and he acts like a twelve-year-old."

"I always thought, you know, that was part of Mike's charm. You know?" Angie's cigarette glowed like a red eye in the dark.

"Yeah," Rose said, suddenly almost in tears again. "It used to be."

There was a light, warm touch on her shoulder, and Angie's arm slid awkwardly between Rose and the seat back. Rose turned. They embraced again between the seats.

"Hey. You're on fire."

Laughing, they put out Rose's hair.

"Here they come." Quickly Angie snuffed out her cigarette, rolled down the window, dropped the butt onto the concrete, flapped her hands at the dense, sharp smoke. Miller was coming toward them, a white paper sack in each hand;

he had sunglasses on, and the brilliant overhead lighting glared off the dark plastic lenses. Reina came after him with another sack.

They crowded into the car, Reina climbing into the back seat again with Angie. Miller gave Angie a yellow Styrofoam box and a red package of french fries and piled blue boxes and bags of french fries between his seat and Rose's.

"You didn't say what you wanted," he said to Rose, "so I didn't get you anything."

She warmed with a burst of irrational temper. "Gee, thanks ever so much just for thinking of me."

He took off the sunglasses and put them up behind the sun visor over the windshield. His blue eyes stabbed at her. Tearing open a Filet-O-Fish box, he crammed half a sandwich into his mouth; he put his other hand between the spokes of the steering wheel, turned the key in the ignition, and spun the little car around and out of the parking lot onto Lake Avenue again.

"Take you home?" he said to Angie.

"Take her home," Angie said, meaning Reina. "Take me down to the Handlebars." She plucked at her bristling aureole of hair. Tufts of hair poked out of her armpits. Her breasts were so small that they hardly swelled the ribbing of the white tank top. She burrowed into her purse for a comb.

"You can't leave her alone all night," Miller said. "You go down to the Handlebars, you'll be out all night."

"Richard is there," Angie said. "Todd will come back sometime."

"Richard is younger than she is."

"Okay. Okay." Angie threw up her hands in a gesture of defeat. "Okay. Take me to the liquor store at the end of the alley and I'll get a six-pack."

"I'll come back after I score for her," Miller said. "I'll keep you company." He was maneuvering across Lake Avenue to turn left; he slipped the VW through the heavy traffic like an ace into a deck of cards.

The crowded avenue fell behind them. They took a cross-street that dove down through the shadows of the trees. Where the alley opened onto the street was a liquor store, lit up like a bomb, a handful of boys loafing on its high, concrete steps. Miller pulled into the curb in front. Angie got out of the car and went in to buy beer; as she climbed the steps, the boys drifted to either side out of her way.

Her mother gone, Reina lunged for the door. "Let me go. I'm going home."

Miller got out of the car. Fat as he was, he moved fast sometimes. He flipped the seat back forward to let Reina out and jumped back behind the wheel. "We'll be back in half an hour. Your mother can walk."

He raised his voice to reach Angie, silhouetted in the door of the liquor store, her six-pack under her arm, a pack of cigarettes in her hand, and her mouth going hard on a piece of beef jerky. She waggled her fingers at Miller. Dropping her cigarettes, she leaned down to retrieve them and dropped the jerky. While she was fumbling for that, Miller backed his car into the street and drove away around the corner.

Rose braced herself against the seat, one hand on the door. Her spine cracked against the seat; her head snapped back painfully as the car shot forward into the traffic on Lake again, this time going north. She settled back into the seat, crossed her arms, her temper climbing. He reached down between the seats for the second blue sandwich box, and driving sometimes with one hand and sometimes with his knees, he ripped apart the box and ate in great choking mouthfuls.

"You got this money now, I hope, in your pocket?"

"Yes, now, in my pocket. You drive like this normally or are you out to prove something?"

He gave her a stare focused somewhere behind her head. "I'm a good driver," he said and put both hands on the wheel. Another look probed at her. "You're the writer. Angie told me about you. She and Felice think you're pretty intelligent."

"Do they," she said, pleased.

"Not that they know much about intelligence," he continued, "being women."

"What do you mean by that?"

He shrugged; he took a joint from his pocket and lit it. "It doesn't take too much intelligence to impress a woman, that's all."

They had turned off the well-traveled street onto another shadowy cross-street lined with houses. They passed under a street light and she saw him smiling. She swallowed down the angry arguments mounting in her throat. He was baiting her. It was the same old game, only with a different player. She turned her face away, staring out the window, unhappy again.

They were rolling along the darkened side street. He passed her the joint and she toked on it, thinking again of going up to her brother's place. She had not seen her brother Peter or heard from him in over a year. It was unexciting up there, and the weather was often very grim. Maybe she would stay here after all. Her friends here loved her. Maybe she should stay where she had friends, where she knew the turf.

Miller was parking at the side of the road. "Come on," he said, and they left the car.

They walked down the sidewalk past a row of trash cans and turned into the walk up to a huge apartment building. The cinderblock front, like a great fortress wall, climbed up through four ranks of identical balconies, each with an iron railing. The entry was dark. Rose went up closer to Miller, just being cautious. He thumbed the elevator button a few times impatiently, looked up frowning at the numbered panel that showed which floor the car was on, and made for the stairs. Rose followed on his heels.

They went up to the second floor; when they passed through the glass door that separated the stairwell from the building, a wall of rock music met them. Miller led her into the first apartment. The door stood open and the music was pouring out of it.

At first there seemed to be no one in the apartment, only the blaring music, so loud that the tones blurred and she could not make out the words. She went after Miller through the middle of a dark living room. Halfway through she realized that there were people sprawled across the furniture around her, not moving, not speaking. They might have been dead. She hoped they were only nodding off.

Nobody said anything to Miller. He pushed open a swinging door into a kitchen.

In here the light was dazzling. The walls and the refrigerator door and the cupboard doors were plastered with posters of Kiss. A pot of coffee was boiling furiously on the stove. A man sat at the table with his belt wrapped around his upper arm; a woman in a halter top bent over him with a needle made of an eyedropper.

Rose's stomach rolled over. She blinked, trying to clear the dazzle from her eyes. Miller said, "Where's Jimmy?"

"In the back," said the woman.

Miller turned to Rose. "You got the hundred?"

She put her hand into her pocket, wishing she had used foresight and separated the hundred from the rest of her money before coming in here. While she was stripping twenties from her roll, the man at the table gave a low sound, almost a sob, and the woman stepped back; she loosened the belt for him. Rose thrust the money at Miller. It made her sick to her stomach to watch people fix.

"Wait," Miller said to her and left. She went out into the darkened front room again.

She stood at the side of the room, every muscle tensed. The record came to an end. The music faded, letting up the little sounds buried under its roar. A glass clinked somewhere across the room. Someone mumbled, "What time is it?" The needle swung back across the turntable and dropped to the beginning of the same record and started off again through the ear-shattering blast of music.

Miller reappeared, a paper bag under his arm, and walked past her, saying nothing, going straight to the door. She trailed after him, making no effort to catch up with him, out through the hallway and down the stairs and out to the car.

"Come on," he called from the car. "You want to hang around here all night?"

She did not want to hang around there at all. She got into the car.

He gave her the paper sack, and she put it on the floor by her feet. "Thanks," she said. She was thinking of her brother's place, the rainy, windswept meadows and the silence.

"You want me to drop you off someplace?" he asked.

She said nothing for a moment, unable to think of anywhere she wanted to go: Felice's was out, and obviously he did not want to take her back to Angie's.

"Well?" he said. "Jeez, you slow or something?"

She swiveled her head toward him. "You got a big fat mouth, you know that?"

"I don't like hanging around in front of dope houses."

She had to admit that was sensible. "I'm staying on Colorado Boulevard. Can you take me there?" She would pick up her car and go to someone's house, some friend's house. Even as she thought about it, she knew she would go nowhere; her mood closed in on itself, like the motel room closing in around her.

"Anything you say." He started the car.

"I'm sorry," she said stiffly. "I've had a hard day."

"I guess so," he said.

Something in his voice was like a spur to her temper. She forced herself quiet. He had scored the marijuana for her, and now she could get away from him. They were cruising through darkened streets, past the big old houses of northern Pasadena, once elegant and now sinking into slums. The will to leave hit her again.

Just running away. She should stay here and work things out.

They drove along Colorado Boulevard. She found her motel, whose name she had forgotten, by the big yellow sign in front.

"Fourteen," she said. "Over there." She pointed to the space beside her own VW, parked under the light. She reached down for the paper bag of pot. "You want a pinch of this? For transportation."

"It's cool," he said. He shut his car off and let it roll on its momentum into the parking space.

"No, really," she said, determined to be just. "I'll give you some. You got a Baggie?" Something moving under the light caught her gaze. "Oh God," she said and opened the door.

Mike lunged forward toward her, his arms folded over his chest. "It's about time you got back here." He was drunk. He weaved back and forth as he walked.

Rose got out of the car. She stuffed the paper bag under her arm. "Get away from me, Mike."

"Who's this you brought back with you?" He stooped to look into the car she had just left.

"He's just—"

"That's what I thought." Mike whirled around, grabbing her by the arms. She dropped the paper bag. He said, "There's some other guy, isn't there? You got some other guy, don't you?"

"Hey," Miller said. "What's going on?"

He got out of the car and stood looking across it at Mike. Rose thrust off Mike's hands.

"You idiot," she said. "You don't know what you're talking about. Leave me alone."

"Some other guy," Mike said loudly. He barged around the VW toward Miller, his face cranked up into a scowl; the light glared on his face. "Jesus, you coulda done better than this, couldn't you?"

"Mike—"

"What is this?" Miller said, backing away.

"This guy's a fat slob," Mike roared. He shoved hard at Miller.

Rose went around the car and got between them. "Mike, you're wrong. You don't—"

"You whore," he shouted at her. He breathed beer fumes

into her face. Her temper burst. She swung her arm around with all her strength and slugged him in the side of the head.

He swayed, lost his balance, and fell backwards. Rose backed up. Her hand hurt. Mike rolled onto his face, groaning. She hovered near him, still caught in his act, afraid she might have hurt him. He groaned again, theatrical. He was playing. She turned and started toward her motel room.

Miller Tarn got in front of her. "Get him away from my car!"

She glanced behind her at Mike, now writhing on the concrete, his legs stuck in under the car. "I'm not going near him," she said to Miller and went around him, toward the bag of pot on the ground.

"Move him away from my car!" Miller dodged between her and the pot. Through the electric glare of the lamplight, his eyes blazed, his face caught tight. "I don't know who he is or why he's on me. Just get him away from my car!" His arm swung hard toward Mike.

Rose put her hands on her hips. "Move him yourself."

"You got me into this!"

She grimaced, knowing he was right, angry at him for being right. She glared at him, contemptuous. For all his macho he was afraid to go near Mike. She took a step to one side, toward the pot, and he barged violently into her path.

"Okay!" She turned and went back to Mike, grabbing him by the jacket, and dragged him off across the concrete.

"Rose," he cried. "Hey—Rose—" His hands grabbed at her. She dropped him. Miller walked straight to his car and got in and backed the car in a quick arc across the parking lot. She found the paper bag of pot, let herself into her motel room, and slammed the door.

"Rose!" Mike hammered on the door. "Rose, let me in. Let's talk. Rose!"

She sat down on the bed and picked up the phone to call her brother.

· · ·

She drove through a blazing summer day all the way to San Francisco. Gum wrappers and red Coke cans accumulated on the floor of the car. She stopped once to stretch her legs, walking up and down the side of the road, while semis thundered by on the freeway, shaking her little VW in their backwash. At dusk she crossed over the Golden Gate Bridge into a damp fog that hung like cotton lace in the stream of the oncoming headlights. The traffic slackened as she passed through Marin County.

In Novato she pulled off the freeway again for gas. On the broad four-lane surface street where she found an open gas station the brilliant overhead lighting drowned the headlights of the cars and blotted up all colors into a black and white and silver world. As she was pumping gas, a light rain began to fall. She stood with her money in her hand while the teen-aged attendant filled out a credit card blank for a man in a white Lincoln. In the street the tires of passing cars hissed on the wet pavement.

"What's the weather like up north?" she asked, when the attendant took her money.

"Wet," he said. "Going north on one-oh-one? Where you headed?"

"Eureka."

He whistled at that; his eyes widened in surprise. "Pretty wet," he said. "It rains all the time up there." He gave her four dollars in change.

She got back on the freeway. The rain was so light at first the windshield wipers squeaked on the glass and she turned them off. She smoked a joint. She could not keep it lit; with only one person toking on it, the stick went out at once every time she let go of it, and finally she got tired of trying.

The rain fell harder. The traffic thinned. The freeway ended, and she drove on two-lane blacktop through a dark town.

The freeway began again. There were no lights, no towns, only the road swinging on black and empty into the north. Through the beams of her headlamps the slanting rain danced on the pavement. She remembered once, a long time before, driving from New York to L.A.; she had gone straight through, nonstop, with one other driver, knocking back amphetamines every time they stopped for Cokes, until somewhere in the Rockies, late that night, she yielded to a speed-induced paranoia and imagined the road slippery as black glass. She would go no faster than thirty-five, although her friend fumed and swore and demanded the wheel.

At the end of the trip she crashed off the speed on a stranger's couch in a living room in Venice, reading Kazantzakis and drinking orange juice. The next day, looking for a place to live, she had met Mike Morgan.

The freeway was ending again. An enormous arrow of orange reflectors blazed through the rain and dark ahead of her. She followed a line of red cones down to the surface. There were no other cars; she tried the radio, but found only static. The narrow road wound up and down hills. She could see little of the countryside, stretches of open pasture studded with manzanita and live oak.

The rain stopped. The sky cleared enough to let the moon shine through. She drove down into the gorge of a river, where the road and the river ran side by side. On the slope above her, trees filled in the open grasslands. A pickup truck with its brights on soared up behind her and flew past, the dry whine of its tires singing in her ears. She smoked half of another joint.

Before midnight the clouds closed over the sky and the rain began again. The road turned into a blacktop ribbon twisting and winding around the feet of enormous trees. She had come into the redwood forest. She passed a coffee shop and rental cabins, huddled beneath trees as wide as the road. A sign advertised, far ahead, a tree you could drive through, a tree you could get married in, souvenirs, owl clocks, smoked salmon.

She began to think of Mike. Smoking dope did not help. You needed a friend to smoke with, if only to keep the joint going. Maybe the Chinese were right: a person alone was not a whole thing, but only a lost piece, a stray. She pushed Mike out of her mind, set herself to think of something else. She had been reading Wallace Stevens, pleased with his opacity: his phrase "fretful concubine" came into her mind. Loving *Hamlet,* she recognized the source: was it an accident? Insurance men left nothing to accident. She tried to expand the pun. Quilts upon the. Thrills upon the. Thrills within.

This game kept her mind busy. Reassured her in her aloneness.

Ahead of her, red taillights appeared on the road, winking between the trees. She came up fast behind a truck that carried a huge camper shell and lurched inward on every curve. In the deep curves the truck slowed to ten miles an hour. There was no place to pass. She crept along behind the teetering camper, through the subterranean darkness of the redwood forest.

The freeway began again. She drove up the ramp with a sensation of taking to the air, free again, and had the car going seventy before she let her foot up off the gas.

Only a little while on was the exit for her brother's place. She left the freeway and followed a narrow country road back into the hills. The rain was falling in a steady downpour. She slowed, watching for the turnoff; the headlights' glow seemed trapped in the rain, glancing off the falling waterdrops, showing nothing but filmy gray. She began to wonder if she had missed the turn.

Ahead, something huge lumbered along the road, a moving mountain of bristles. Startled she swerved, giving it half the road. Toward the ditch waddled an enormous porcupine, as calm as if Rose were only another animal.

A moment later the car clattered onto a bridge. She had come too far.

She crossed the bridge and turned around again. This time she found the way, a dirt road, climbing slantwise up the hill, its ruts already flooded to overflowing. She got one front wheel up on the center strip and the other on the edge of the road and gunned the motor. The car scrambled sliding and slipping up the hill. The headlights' beam sliced through the dark, across the trunks of trees, the ferns under the trees, the raw mud of the road. The road climbed steeply into a hairpin turn. She threw the car into second gear and put the gas pedal to the floor. The VW jumped like a deer. It roared into the turn and slid sideways, bumped the rear fender into the bank, spun its wheels a moment with a banshee whine, and bounded on up the hill again.

At the top of the hill, in the drenching rain, she came unexpectedly to a gate.

She stopped. It was a big aluminum gate, hanging on a post with a guy wire to support the free end. A chain with a padlock held it fast to the fence on the other side.

Rose turned off the ignition. Switched the headlights off.

She sat for a moment listening to the rain. Every drop hit the roof of the car with a different sound. It was warm here, in the car, and cold out there in the rain; maybe she would spend the night here. She leaned forward to search the ash-tray for a roach to smoke.

When she did that, she caught a glimpse of a light through the trees, off to her left and beyond the fence. She opened the door and went into the rain.

It was warmer than she expected. And louder, the rain crashing and dripping through the trees, the trees stirring in the wind. She tramped across the muddy road and up to the gate for a better look at the light.

The glow burned with the steady brightness of electricity, and it was only a few hundred yards away, in the lower meadow of Peter's ranch. She climbed through the gate and walked across the grass.

As she approached the light, it took on an odd shape, twenty feet tall, much wider at the base, and darker at the top. Slowly she recognized it as a teepee, with a light shining through the canvas walls. A pole beside it supported the wiring and a television antenna.

She went slowly around the teepee, looking for a door, and tripped over a tent stake. She fell. The tug on the tent fabric brought someone out at once.

"Who's there?"

"Hello," Rose called. "I'm harmless." She got up off her knees, wiped her hands ineffectively on her pants, and went toward the voice. "I'm Rose McKenna." She walked around the flank of the tent, into the light, and came face to face with a stark-naked man.

"I'm Jim Wylie," he said. "You're Peter's sister?"

"Yes," she said. If being naked didn't bother him, she would be damned if it bothered her. "I'm down at the gate. Is there any way I can get in?"

"Peter has the key," said Jim Wylie. He put his hands on his hips. The light was nearly above him, hooked on above the teepee door. The rain speckled his shoulders. His chest and arms were shaped with long muscle, smooth and hard; his ribs were like a washboard under the plate-sized muscles of his chest. She wondered if he were alone. He had been watching television; she could hear the tiny voices inside the tent.

She asked, "I don't suppose you have a telephone in there?"

"Sorry. Go back to Springville and come up in the daytime."

"Unh-uh. I'll walk up and get Peter." She looked away from him, into the rain. "You're one of the settlers here?"

"You mean is this my property? Yes."

"And you don't have your own key to the gate?" She faced him again. "I'm just curious. Don't take it personally."

Cheerful, he smiled at her. "We decided it was safer if there was only one key."

"What the hell is going on? There's never been a gate on River Ranch before. We left the house wide open, the keys in the cars—"

He said, "Talk to Peter. I'll walk you up there."

"I know where it is. I've been here before. I own forty

acres of this place." She was still hoping he would give in and produce a key to the gate, but he only shrugged.

"Yeah, I know. Just a second while I put my clothes on."

"Oh," she said. "Not on my account, I hope."

His smile grew broader by an inch, his eyes narrowing. "I'm getting cold. Or do you want to come inside and warm me up a little?"

"Unh-unh. I'm going to find my brother."

"Just a second." He went into the teepee.

Rose started away, back toward the road that led up the hill; it was a good half-mile to the old ranch house on the top, where her brother lived. She was crossing the ditch by the road when Jim Wylie caught up with her, his shirt flapping unbuttoned, and his shoes in his hand.

"Wait," he said and got her by the arm and held her. He looked all around them. They were standing at the side of the ditch, with the meadow rustling in the rain around them. He stared toward the gate. "That's your car?" He slipped on his shoes.

"The Volks."

"Come on."

She started up the road, and he walked along beside her, buttoning his shirt. The road was streaming with watery mud. She angled over to walk on the grass beside it; the calves of her jeans were already soaked through, wrapped like clammy arms around her legs. She lifted her head a little, to feel the rain falling on her cheeks.

"I called Peter before I left L.A. and he didn't say anything about a gate."

"It's only closed at night."

"Somebody's ripping you off."

"What are you doing up here, anyway?" he asked. "I thought you lived down south."

"I did. I just broke up with my old man. I had to get away."

He laughed at that. "Well, you picked a good place to get away to. This is about as away as you can get."

Short of breath, she laughed obediently at this humor. The backs of her knees hurt. The road was turning steeper again, but ahead it leveled off for a few hundred yards, swinging out past the end of a line of eucalyptus trees that blocked the west wind. She could hear the rain crashing and rattling on the fallen bark and leaves of the trees. As she and Jim Wylie approached the trees she thought she heard another sound, under the racket the rain was making, heavier and more even, like footsteps.

Something brushed her side. Startled, she saw that Wylie had come over closer to her, and she said, "What's going on?"

"Hold it," a rough man's voice bellowed, from the eucalyptus trees.

Rose stopped in her tracks. Wylie, beside her now, took hold of her arm.

"It's me," Wylie shouted. "It's cool."

"Coyote?"

"Yeah."

"Okay, man. Take it easy."

Rose was staring into the rain-shrouded trees; she could see nothing, but again she heard the tread of feet in the eucalyptus debris. Jim Wylie's hand left her arm.

"Oh, yeah?" she said to him. They started up the road again.

He said nothing; he walked with his head down. She turned her eyes back toward the gaunt trees. The bark shredding from their trunks and branches swayed out in the rainy wind. She had thought, all this time, that Wylie was protecting the ranch from her.

If she asked him anything more, he would only fob her off again. She hunted for some neutral subject.

"Do you live in that tent all the time?"

"Only this summer. I'm selling off some of the timber on my section here so I can build a house."

She made a sound in her throat, taken aback by the prospect of a summer spent to the accompaniment of chain saws. "Who's gonna cut it?"

"I am."

"Oh, yeah? You're a logger?"

"When there's work."

That explained the hard beauty of his body. She thought of his naked body again, a fresh interest lively in her stomach; in over nine years she had slept with no one but Mike Morgan, and she had forgotten how to start with someone else. They climbed the last few yards to the bench of land where Peter's house stood, and she stopped.

"Good God, what is that?"

"That's Peter's rhinoceros."

Another exclamation escaped her, unworded. In the gloom she could make out only the general shape of the thing, which stood in the grass beside the road, ringing faintly in the rain. It seemed to be made of pipes and fittings. That made sense: Peter had been a plumber, on such occasions as he worked. She went on toward the house.

It stood back on the meadow grass that covered the bench; behind it the next stage of the mountain loomed into the sky. The house was a low, sprawling structure that blended into the dark, its wide, roofed porch like a mouth, its string of windows lidded in wooden shades. Only one light burned, in the back. The kitchen. She broke into a trot around the side of the house, where Peter's several battered cars were parked, and to the kitchen door.

The light shone through the window onto the tiny, wooden porch. She ran up the steps to the door and flung it open. Taking three steps into the kitchen, she paused to get her bearings, drawn by the warmth of the old black woodstove in the corner. She put out her hands and took a step toward it.

"Stay right where you are!"

She yelped. Something hard jabbed her in the back. She reached around behind her and felt cold metal. A gun barrel.

"Put your hands up," the same voice said.

"Look, I'm—"

"Put 'em up!"

"This is—"

"Put 'em up!" The gun barrel poked her hard enough to hurt. Rose turned around, to face a girl in glasses and a bathrobe, aiming a lever-action .22 at Rose's middle.

The back door swung wide again. Wylie-Coyote came in.

"Gimme that." He snatched for the gun in the girl's hands.

"No!" She recoiled away from him, yanking the gun up out of his reach, almost over her shoulder. "I'll do this!"

"You're doing it," Wylie said. "That's Peter's sister."

"Oh." The girl blinked. The thick lenses of her glasses made her eyes bigger. She was very young, only eighteen or nineteen, her dark blond hair mussed from sleep, the bathrobe falling open in front. She clutched it closed in her fist.

"Peter," she shouted.

"I'm coming. Gotta get my fuckin' pants on."

Rose laughed. She moved away from the girl and her gun, over into the dry heat around the woodstove. "Yeah," she said. "This is River Ranch."

Buttoning the fly of his Levi's, Peter McKenna walked into the kitchen. His face was still coming out of sleep. He blinked in the bright light of the kitchen, saw Rose, and tramped across the kitchen with his arms outstretched. Wordlessly they embraced. Peter thumped her several times on the back. He stank of beer and dirt and sweat. His luxuriant dark hair had grown nearly a foot since Rose had last seen him. She held tight to him; they had been very close all their lives.

"You weren't supposed to get here until tomorrow," he said.

"I never said that. I need the key."

"Takes two days to get here from L.A. I figured you'd show up for dinner tomorrow. I got a turkey and everything." He gave her a wounded look for ruining his welcome feast.

"Peter, I have to have the key."

"Oh, Christ." He turned to the girl with the glasses and the .22. "This is Patty. That's Coyote."

"I've met Coyote."

"This is my sister Rose."

"Hi," Patty said, putting out her hand.

Rose shook the girl's long, skinny hand. "Where were you when I came into the house? I didn't even see you."

"Scrunched down by the cupboard there." Patty gestured toward the other side of the kitchen, where the old wooden counter ran along the wall. She grinned, proud of herself. "You walked right by me."

"Let me have that," Peter said and took the .22 from her. "God, Patty, you're nuts." He shook his head. "Come on and let's smoke a joint."

"I'd like to get my car," Rose said. "I need the key, Peter. Will you get it together?"

Her brother looked vacantly around the kitchen a moment, hitched up his Levi's, and turned his gaze to Coyote. "What'd I do with it?"

"You said something about putting it in the lock box."

"Oh, yeah. I'll be right back." He started out of the kitchen again, into the depths of the house. Over his shoulder he said, "You better go fire up my truck. No sense in walking all the way down there."

Rose followed Coyote out of the house again. After the warmth of the kitchen the rain seemed like ice. Patty called, "Wait! I'm coming with you." She bounded barefoot down the steps and came up between them. "I'm not staying in the house alone."

"God," Rose said, "what the devil is going on here?"

Jim Wylie laughed. "Never mind about Patty. She's crazy all the time."

They tramped through the rain to the side of the house, where Peter's cars were lined up in a row between the house and the shed. A few minutes later Peter came out with a flashlight in his hand and the key to the gate.

"What is all this?" Rose said, when they were rolling down the road, all four of them together jammed into the front seat of the pickup. "What's with the guns? Why is she afraid to stay alone?"

"She's always afraid to be alone," Coyote said.

"I am not," Patty disagreed hotly. "Just at night."

Rose nudged Peter, on her left, driving. He said, "I'll tell you when we get back."

He aimed the truck down the rutted road, past the rhinoceros. The road tossed them and bumped them from side to side, the engine whining so loud that they had to shout to be heard.

"You have a good trip?" Peter shouted.

"Yeah, fine."

"You bring that fancy car of yours?"

"No."

"Gave it to the jerk, hunh?"

"Don't call him that."

The windshield wipers slopped back and forth across the glass, sweeping the rain aside. They were coming to the gate. Rose got out and went to her car, and Coyote and Peter opened the gate and held it while she drove through. In her rearview mirror she watched Coyote lock up the gate again; he gave the padlock a shake, to make sure it was closed.

She followed Peter's truck up to the ranch house. The gate confounded her. Peter still left his house open, still left all the keys in all his cars. He had lived on River Ranch for twelve years now, since the time when on his last-known full-time job his boss had dropped a pipe wrench on his foot. They settled out of court. Peter got enough to buy the ranch, and since then he had been selling off forty-acre chunks whenever he needed money. In all that time, in all his life, in fact, Peter had turned a trusting face to the world, and putting up gates seemed foreign to his nature.

In the rainy beam of the headlights the rhinoceros looked like a plumber's nightmare, a tangle of pipe four feet high and six feet long. She drove by it and parked in front of the house, close to the front door.

Coyote had stayed at the bottom of the hill. Peter rolled the pickup truck back into its space beside the house; he and Patty came out onto the front porch just as Rose was dragging her suitcase and her new sleeping bag out of the back seat of the car.

"Come on in," Peter said. "You can stay in the bunkroom. I was meaning to clean it up a little before you got here but you came early." His voice was reproachful, as if he might actually have gotten around to making ready for her. She followed him into the house and through the dark front room to the hall that connected all the rooms in the house.

The bunkroom was at the far end of the house from the kitchen. Peter went in ahead of her and turned on the lamp that hung from the center of the ceiling.

"I been storing stuff in here."

The room was piled up with boxes. On the right and the left a set of bunkbeds stood against the wall; a huge old dresser, painted green, stood between them under the window. The floor and the bunkbeds were heaped with magazines and empty milk jugs and old, dented aluminum cans. Peter never threw anything away. Rose went to the bunk on the left and with her arm swept the junk off the bottom bed.

"This is fine," she said. "I'll clean it up." She grinned at her brother. "Might even take some of this crap to the dump."

"Talk to me first," he replied swiftly. "I need some of this."

She laughed; she put out her hands to him, Peter, who valued everything, even an empty can. He slipped his arms around her. The embrace warmed her. She felt as if some missing piece of herself had moved back into place.

They went down to the kitchen and Rose lit one of her joints. "Wait 'til you taste this stuff, man. This'll put the fear of God into your lungs."

Peter went out into the rain and returned with an armload of wood. With a stick he pried open the round belly of the woodstove. The bed of red coals inside sent up a shimmering veil of heat. He piled wood on top of them.

"Scared you, did I?" Patty asked, passing the joint to Rose.

"I didn't see you," Rose said.

"Didn't think you would." Patty smiled, pleased with herself. "I just scrunched down there behind the counter. Man, you walked right by me."

"I sure did." Rose leaned back in the old, uncomfortable chair. Peter lived in this kitchen. Half of it was given over to the refrigerator and the sink and the countertop with its shredded linoleum; two big couches filled up the other end of the room, around the woodstove, each couch burdened with stacks of magazines and newspapers and crumpled beer cans and bundles of wire and tools. It was all filthy; the dishes in the sink, even the dishes in the drainer beside the sink looked dirty, the floor unswept in days and unmopped in months, the refrigerator door black with fingerprints. Rose hung her arms over the back of the chair. Peter's house-keeping always reassured her of her own.

"Peter says you're a writer," Patty said. She toked on the joint, her little finger crooked like an old lady sipping tea.

"Yeah," Rose said. "On some occasions."

"What d'you write?"

"Science fiction. Screenplays. Whatever I can get paid for."

Peter put the coffeepot on top of the stove and sat down in his rocking chair. He grabbed Patty by the hand, pulling her toward his lap; shrieking, she resisted, and he let her go.

"What's she gonna think?" Patty cried, recoiling, her arm held back out of his reach.

Peter laughed. "Oh, God." He stretched his arms up over his head. "Where's that joint?"

"Right here. Now suppose you tell me why the guns and the gate and all this other foofooraw."

Peter rubbed his hands together. "You know why the gate?" He nodded to her, his eyes gleaming. "Because we got twenty acres of pot planted on this ranch, that's why."

Rose turned her head to stare at him. "Acres?"

"That's right."

"Twenty acres? That's a hell of a lot of weed, man."

"You damn right." Peter nodded his head. He grinned

at Patty, who was glowering at him. "What's the matter, sweetie?"

"You talk too much," Patty said darkly.

"Oh, come on. She's my sister. Besides, she lives here, too."

"She just got here!"

"She's staying. You are, aren't you, Rose?"

"Until I leave," Rose answered amiably.

"Hey," he said, frowning. "Don't talk like that. You're staying."

"I don't know, Peter. I like a little excitement in my life now and then. I don't know how long I'll be able to handle living here."

"It's exciting around here," Patty said.

"The last time I was here the biggest event that took place was a doe raided Peter's corn patch and he shot her and we ate venison for two weeks," Rose said.

Peter exhaled a plume of smoke. "Well, that was when that goofball you were—"

"Don't call him names."

"Yeah, well," Peter said, "as I was saying, that was when Mike Morgan was here with you."

"I'm going to bed," Patty said. "Good night."

When she stood up, Peter palmed her backside briefly. "Good night. I'll be right up."

"Good night," Rose said.

Patty went out. Rose and Peter passed the joint back and forth a while longer in silence. Finally Rose tossed the last scrap of the joint into the woodstove. She leaned back.

"Now. What's this about the dope?"

"What?" he asked blandly.

"Come on, Peter. Just growing pot on the place doesn't constitute a reason to throw a gate up."

"Oh, yeah?" He got his cigarettes out of his shirt pocket and, bending down, took a redwood splinter from the pile of wood beside the stove. "Think you got it all figured out?" He thrust the splinter into the belly of the stove, withdrew it flaming half its length, and lit his cigarette with a flourish.

"No," Rose said. "I have nothing figured out. Who's that girl?"

"Patty. She lives down on the flat. The guy she's with is a trucker and she's afraid to stay down there when he's out on the road, so she came up here."

Rose stretched, tired, letting all this impress itself on her mind. Slowly, she said, "Then you aren't, unh—"

"Oh, yeah, we are, unh," Peter said.

"Oh."

They stared at each other in silence, Peter daring her by his look to say anything and Rose fighting the nasty impulse to do so. Eventually she said, "Well, about the gate."

"Ummm—" He looked away, fidgeting suddenly. His beard grew down into a dandified point; he had the habit of stroking it down when he was nervous. "It's hard to explain," he said, and his hand went up to his beard. "The pot—the twenty acres—that's a community project, more or less. We all went in on it. Everybody helps with the work. Everybody's in on the payoff."

"Who's everybody?"

"All of us on River Ranch, you know, me and Coyote, Patty and her old man, and the other people on the flat, and the people living in the woods, you know."

The flat was the valley just beyond this bench, including half the ranch, and nearly all the usable ground, where lay most of the parcels he had sold off. The last time she had been here, two years previous, there had been four families on the flat. She said, "How many?"

"Still the same houses," he said. "Only the Baxters, you remember them?"

"No."

"Anyway they sold out to some people named Vigg. They got lots of kids."

"I'm happy for them." The heat from the stove was overpowering her; drowsy and stoned, she struggled against sleep. She yawned. "How tall is your pot?"

"Just babies." He held out his hands six inches apart.

"You mean," she said, "you just got these plants to grow,

and already you're so paranoid you're going around with guns? Jesus. I don't want to be here when the field's ready to pick."

"They'll settle down," he said. "That's another good reason for you being here. You can vote in the meetings."

She said, "Hunh."

He was getting up, yawning, stretching. "Think I'll go give Patty a pat. You okay now? You need anything?"

"I'll find it," Rose said. "I'm going to bed."

"Give me another love."

She stood up and took him fast in a hug, her head on his shoulder, his arms around her, her arms full of him. Her brother slapped her back.

"Good girl, Rosie," he said in a voice that quivered. "Good girl for shaking that shit off your shoes."

"Don't talk about him like that." She did not want to see that she had made a mistake, going with Mike.

"You did a good thing, anyway," he said. He went heavily out of the room. His footsteps scraped in the hall. Rose stood listening to him tramp down to his room, midway between the kitchen and the bunkroom. The door opened and shut. She looked around the kitchen. There was a lot to do here, a lot of work. She would get to work in the morning. She went down the hall to the bunkroom, unrolled her sleeping bag on the bottom bunk on the right, and lay down to sleep.

"God, Peter," she said, "it's hideous."

"Hey," he said, injured.

She walked through the drenched knee-high grass, circling the pipe monster. Unable to form curves, Peter had shaped the rhinoceros's vast head in a series of right angles, and it looked more like steps to nowhere than a beast with two horns. Rose shook her head, grinning.

"You ever make the buffaloes?"

"Someday." For years he had been saying that his masterpiece would be a life-size granite statue of two buffaloes fucking.

Rose reached out her foot and nudged a square, pipe hoof. She jammed her hands down into her pockets. The rain had ended during the night and the sky was a clear, deep blue, without a cloud. The sunlight gleamed on the wet grass, on the rusting pipe animal. Steam rose in clouds from the roof of Peter's house. The air smelled of pine. She turned around, her gaze sweeping the tree-shrouded mountain behind the house.

"Tell you what. I'm going to take a crack at your kitchen and them I'm going for a walk."

"Feel free. You seen a crescent wrench around here anywhere?" Peter walked around his beast, swishing the high grass aside with his feet.

Rose went into the house. She washed Peter's dishes; opening up the cupboards, she got out the dishes stacked there and washed them, too. She wiped the countertops, scraping off the encrusted mess with steel wool. While she was scrubbing at the black fingerprints on the refrigerator door, Patty walked into the kitchen, her feet dragging over the floor, and collapsed into the rocking chair by the woodstove. Her face was puffy; she looked only half-awake. "Hi," she said. "At least the rain stopped for y'."

"Yeah," Rose said, looking obediently out the kitchen window. The forest began only twenty feet behind the house. By contrast to the brilliant wash of sunlight on the grass, the dark under the trees looked impenetrable. She wrung out the rag she was using and hung it on a nail under the sink. "Peter still has that horse, doesn't he?"

"What horse? That old white nag? God, I haven't even seen it for months. Is there any coffee?"

"On the stove there."

"Are there any clean cups?"

Rose took a white mug out of the heap of dishes in the drainer. "Here." She tossed the cup in a high arc to Patty, who caught it in both hands, looking startled.

"Listen," Patty said, pouring coffee from the pot into her cup. "That horse is gone. I haven't seen it in maybe a year. Is there any sugar?"

Rose brought her the box of sugar. "You come up here a lot?"

"Well, you know, so does everybody else." Patty looked suspiciously at her. Her blond hair was streaked with darker color. "Got any cream?"

"If you come up here a lot," Rose said, "then you must know where everything is, and you can get it for yourself."

"Hey," said Patty. "That's not very friendly."

"I'm busy," Rose said, although she had done all she intended to do for one day. She went down to her room for her jacket.

The rain had soaked everything. She found a well-worn path that led back over the shoulder of the mountain behind Peter's house and down across the slope beyond. It was cold under the trees; she was glad she had brought her jacket. Most of River Ranch had been logged off, sixty or seventy years before, and the second-growth redwoods had grown up close together, the ground under them matted with needles and dense with fallen branches. Yellow toadstools sprouted on the wet flanks of the trees.

Under her feet the earth turned sticky and sucked at her feet. She skirted the edge of a black marsh.

Just beyond that the trail forked; she went off to the left, which looked less traveled. It led her down a short, steep decline and along the foot of an embankment. The runoff from the rain streamed down the path with her. She had to walk on the edge to keep from getting her shoes wet. At the bottom of this slope she came on a house built in a tree stump.

She stopped, wary of these crazy people here. The stump was huge, as big as a good-sized room; it had burned a while ago, and the outside was blackened. The roof was of redwood planks. Two little windows and a door opened out toward Rose. There were little white curtains in the windows. As she stood there getting up the courage to go closer, she heard the bleating of goats, somewhere behind her, and turned.

Three big brown and white goats came trotting down the path toward her, saw her, and stopped. In around their legs were two kids; as soon as the big ones stopped, the kids turned and butted their heads up under a flank and began to nurse. Behind the herd walked a woman in a great, floppy hat.

"Go on," she cried, waving the long stick in her hand. "Go on, Molly, Maggie, go on!"

The goats bustled down the trail. Rose moved quickly out of their way. Their sour smell enveloped her as they passed. The woman in the hat smiled at her.

"Hi. Isn't this a beautiful day?"

"Sure is," Rose replied.

The woman herded her goats toward the house in the tree. They disappeared around behind the stump. Rose lingered, her hands in her pockets, her curiosity high. Instead she went around the stump on the other side and fought her way through brambles and swamp back to the trail.

The slope flattened out, and the trail met a creek and turned to run along it, following the narrow, twisting canyon it had formed. In some places the creek flooded the whole floor of the canyon and she had to pick her way over it from stone to stone and log to log. Ferns grew up over the walls and hung like curtains in her way. Climbing around a fallen redwood, she jumped down into a high patch of nettles. Her hands burned and stung from the contact; she licked them, adopting the child's remedy for such things.

The canyon widened. Ahead, beyond the tall trees, the sun shone down clear to the ground. A meadow, perhaps, or the river lay there. Rose stopped to drink from the creek, cupping the water up in her hands; it was cold enough to numb her fingers. She sat on a log, looking around her. Slowly she grew aware of the sounds around her, the in-

sistent ringing call of a bird off to her left, the gurgling of
the stream, a branch creaking in the wind. In a backwater
of the creek where the surface was quiet, water-skaters
scooted busily from side to side. She roiled up the stream
with her finger, clouding it with dirt, and the current swept
the muck away.

A flurry of motion caught her eye, up on the hill opposite
her, and she sprang to her feet in time to see a great gray
bird launch itself outward onto the air from the dark green
shelter of a tree. The huge wings beat slowly through the
air; the bird soared across the creek and curved its path
around, swinging out through the mouth of the canyon, its
long legs trailing below it.

"Egret," she said. "Heron." She sat up, watching the way
the bird had gone. She must be close by the river. She
wiped her hands on her jeans. Just across the creek, the
ground tilted up steeply into a little peak, topped by a few
small trees. She went across the water, careless now of getting
wet, and climbed through the brush toward the crag.

It was much steeper than she had expected; she had to
grab handfuls of the brush to pull herself along. She climbed
over a fallen tree and through tangles of thorny brush. A
spider web wrapped itself over her face. The ground broke
and slipped away under her, and she paddled madly with her
feet to keep her place. Halfway up, she stopped for breath,
one arm crooked around a little tree that grew from the side
of the hill. The creek looked far below her. She raised her
eyes to the top of the climb and went on.

Panting, scratched, her legs heavy with exhaustion, she
reached the top, or near the top; now she saw another ridge
ahead of her, just behind the file of battered trees. She
walked on trembling legs out across the summit.

There was the river, far below her, only one curve visible, a flat stretch of water turned the color of cocoa by the
rain. She let out a low sound, seduced by the wildness. The
heron was flying over the water, its wings steady in a glide;
it sliced through the air and turned and dipped and landed
on the river bar.

Turning, she went up through the trees along the highest point of the crag. The wind raked across this height, keening over the bare rock. It was hotter here, too, than below. She climbed up through the thinning brush and low trees. Sweat formed on her face and she wiped it on her sleeve. Her neck itched. The wind blew through the trees, and they sang, giving tongue to the wind, a thin, high, eerie tuneless call. She stopped, out of breath again. Her gaze went to the trees, moving in the wind. She heard other sounds now, squeals and bumps, gasps and whimpers. On the nape of her neck the hackles stood on end. She looked quickly all around her, expecting to see something—animals, demons—watching from the shelter of the trees. It was the wind, banging the trees together, that made the racket, yet she heard it as voices, whispers and murmurs. Right over her head suddenly there was a shrill scree-scree; she jumped. It was only the tree, rubbing one branch over another in the wind.

She wiped her face on her sleeve. Slowly she circled around the height of the crag.

At the top the wind smacked her in the face and roared in her ears. She walked out onto the peak, where nothing grew, and there suddenly opened before her, almost at her feet, a little green bowl of a meadow, tucked into the high shoulder of the crag.

The rock outcrop Rose was standing on sheltered it from the wind. At one end the ground was wet and black where a spring broke out of the ground. She went down into the grass. The wind spread her hair across her cheek, and she brushed it back with her fingers.

From where she stood now she could see across the river, over the forest on the other side all the way to the mountains; and turning, she brought under her gaze the forest along the bank of the river, and the broad meadow half a mile away where the little creek she had followed here emptied into the bigger water, and another meadow beyond that, and more trees; and wheeling again, she saw the way she had come, trees marching in rank on rank back toward the horizon, until sheer distance blurred them into indeterminate dark hills.

The wind began to low again, down in the forest below her, seething through the trees, growing louder, rising, roaring up around her, from all around her, the voice of the wind swelling until it filled up the whole world, a vast hollow cry, an endless song.

She sat down where she stood, got a joint from her pocket, and lit it. The wind died, then began again, raking through the trees until they sang like harps.

She wondered whose land this was. It was part of River Ranch, she knew, because the river was the eastern boundary. Her forty acres had never been marked off on a map, it being left that she had forty acres, somewhere, and she determined to have this place on her land. As she thought that, a certain happiness welled up in her, an idiotic delight just in being here, being herself, now.

She could grow pot here. That would make it hers.

The joint finished, she stood up again and looked over the meadow with a new purpose. She walked down into it. The ground was still very wet, perhaps just from the rain, or maybe the spring, running stronger in the winter, filled this hollow up with water. The grass was dense and matted. She would have to dig it up. Cut the grass at least. The amount of work involved dampened her delight a little. There was no way to get anything bigger than a shovel or maybe a pick up here.

Still, there was water, there was good sun, and the crag was hard to get to, which would keep down the losses to deer and hikers. She wandered over close to the far edge, where the hillside fell off in a sheer cliff. Pleased, she walked along the entire perimeter. Nobody would find this by accident. She could put caps over the baby plants to keep the birds off.

It would take time. But there was nothing else to do.

She stopped at the place where the crag reached highest, where the ground was bare, wind-scoured rock. Pleased with herself, she looked out across the forest again. The sun was sucking the rain water from the ground, drawing up the vapors in long, ragged mists that lifted like wraiths among the trees. It was beautiful here, beautiful and empty of people, and she would make it hers.

Her gaze sharpened. Down there, in the farthest meadow she could see along the river, something moved, something white, something large.

She yelled. It was the horse. She had completely forgotten that she was supposed to be looking for the horse, but there he was, half a mile away, grazing in the meadow by the river. She scrambled away down the side of the crag, down to the creek bank.

"Somebody named Angie called for you," Peter said.

"Oh. Good." She cupped her hands into the water in the sink and bathed her face.

"Everybody's coming up here tonight, just sort of a walk-through, to see you."

"Peter, for God's sake." Her face dripping, she put out her hands blindly into the open air, and a towel was thrust into them; she pressed her face into the towel. "Thanks."

"Everybody's got to know everybody else," he said, "or this won't work."

"What won't work?"

She raised her head from the towel; her brother leaned against the bathroom door, looking out to the hall. He was frowning, not as if he meant it, but as if he had been frowning a while before and had forgotten to straighten his face out.

"What's the matter?"

"Oh—" He waved his hand by his face, shooing away something. "Oh, it doesn't matter. You gonna come out and mingle?"

"Sure, Peter. If you want me to."

" 'Cause I know how antisocial you are sometimes."

"Sure, Peter."

He was looking at her now, and the frown was smoothing into a smile. He asked, "Where'd you go today?"

"I walked and walked and walked."

"Find the horse?"

"I saw him, at least. It was a ways from where I was." Thinking of the horse reminded her of Angie. She hung her arm around his neck and hugged him, "How do you feel, Bub?"

"I feel fine," he said, in a guarded voice. "What's up?"

"What makes you think there's something up?"

"Yeah. Well, I know you. What's up?"

"My friend Angie, who called me?" Her arm still around his neck, she squeezed a little, talking into his ear.

"Yeah?"

"She has a fourteen-year-old daughter and I asked her if she wanted to send the kid up here for the summer, and that's probably why she called me."

She watched him closely, his head gripped in the crook of her arm. He grimaced, of course, but only face deep; underneath, she saw, he did not mind. "What d'you think I'm running here, a summer camp?"

"No," she said. "Just the most beautiful, quiet, clean, and peaceful place in California."

He smiled at her. His wide cheekbones made his eyes seem slanted; he grinned like an elf in his beard. "You sure know how to get to a guy."

"Get out of here. I'm taking a shower." She pushed him away.

"Oh, sure. Now that you've got what you want from me, cast me off like dirty socks."

"Peter," she said, unbuttoning her shirt, "dirty socks at least I can wear." She whirled around, pretending to tear open her shirt and expose her breasts to him, and with a gasp of shock he darted out the door.

She made a sound in her throat, amused. She felt much older than Peter, although he was thirty-six and she only thirty-four. Taking off her clothes, she climbed into the shower and shivered and danced in the thin trickle of water from the spout. All the water came from an old well that Peter had been claiming for years was running dry.

Her suitcase still stood open on the green dresser in the bunkroom. She pawed through the jumble of clothing to find a clean shirt. When she was dressed, she sat down on a cane-bottomed chair by the window. She could see the light on the kitchen porch, illuminating the barred railing of the porch, the trash barrels, the front of Peter's pickup, and the clapboard wall at that end of the house, the clapboards extending toward Rose, into the darkness. She could hear people walking in front of the house, coming up the road from the flat. A woman's voice; a child's.

She knew none of these people. In a few months she would be gone again. No sense in getting interested in anything here. She touched the window sill; the paint had worn off; the grain of the wood showed. She wondered what Mike was doing.

Not thinking of her.

Her marijuana was in a cigar box in the old dresser against the other wall, and she went and got it, sat there by the window with the box on her knees, and rolled a joint. More people were walking by outside, unseen, their voices louder as they passed; there was an abrupt cackle of laughter. She smoked the joint, thinking again of Mike Morgan. She did not love him. Why did she miss him? Just habit, left-over feelings.

She pressed the heels of her hands to her eyes; she had the sensation of teetering on the edge.

The joint was getting short. She got up and rummaged through her things again, looking for a roach clip. That led her, being stoned, into putting things away. Most of the furniture had come with the ranch and was as old as furniture could be without becoming more valuable; the dresser was overlaid with sheet on sheet of ancient cracking paint, and the drawers stuck, and the newspaper that lined them was yellowed and dry and said things about Eisenhower and Stevenson. She took out the paper gently and unfolded it on the table to read it, fascinated.

Beyond this room, somewhere in the house, an opening drum roll crashed into a boom of rock music. Rose unfolded the edge of the crisp newspaper with her fingers, reading about the missile gap.

The door opened. Peter said, "Damnit, Rose, are you going to fink out on me? Come out here and meet everybody."

"I will." She stood up. "Just gotta put my shoes on."

He leaned in the doorway, glaring at her, and she waved at him. "See? I'm just putting on my shoes."

Peter said, "Hurry." He went out, but he did not shut the door.

The music poured in, working out its four-four beat. She sat down to put her shoes on and listened to the crash and roll of drums. This music had lost her, somewhere around 1974. She knew few of the bands anymore. It made her feel old to listen.

She had loved rock in the sixties, when the music had come on like an underground newspaper, bringing in the news, hot and urgent, telling what at the time had gone for deep truth, big new ideas of power and who had the power; and she had listened with her whole body, the music joining her to everyone else who listened, joining everyone who listened into a single, vast, inchoate being, the Movement. Exactly what the Movement was, nobody bothered to say. It was unsayable, anyway. The panicky non-Movement called it a revolution and cleared for action, and in great glee Rose and her friends assumed revolutionary poses, looked out for barricades, said threatening things, but only to goof on it, which was what you did anyway when you were stoned.

"I'm going to Canada," a boy had told her once, long ago, in a ramshackle cabin in the Colorado Rockies. "There's nothing doing here."

"What about the Revolution?" Rose had asked, at the time being a victim of the mass delusion.

"When the Revolution comes," the boy said, "I'll come back."

That was when she saw how far they were from any real revolution. Later on that night the boy had fired up a massive dose of heroin, nearly cooling himself out for good.

Led Zeppelin filled her ears. This music seemed isolated to her, superficial, speaking of nothing but the pulse in its steel heart.

Mike liked the Zeppelin. He was younger than she was. He felt the difference in their ages as a change in her, a shift he would come to someday, in his own time. Maybe then. . . .

She knew she would never go back to him. Even so, there was something in her that wanted to think about it, to fantasize about it. Or maybe she was just horny.

She thought of Woodstock. It was at Woodstock that she had picked up her dislike for crowds. Yet she had loved Woodstock. Her life had disintegrated the year before that, in 1968, when she began questioning the war, and she had drifted from one place to another, staying with friends, with people she met on the way, in Connecticut, New York, California, and the spaces between where people got high. In the summer of 1969 she went to Woodstock.

She had dropped five or six tabs of acid a day at Woodstock. Her memory of the weekend flowed like an irresistible tide whenever it came into her mind—the ditches ankle-deep in garbage, watermelon rinds, and wine bottles; the naked man, a blissful smile curving his lips, who walked past her as she sat by the side of the road; red mud everywhere. The great field, jammed edge to edge with bodies undressed in the heat, handing on a continual stream of wine and marijuana, acid and speed, while the enormous speakers drowned them in rock music, a music that was like bathing in their own blood, the conductive agent of the nourishment and knowledge of a single being.

It was not the music she remembered from Woodstock. The people she remembered with an intensity that roused her even now. She had had a big canteen, which she carried full of water over her shoulder; there was no water in the field in front of the stage, or on the wooded hill behind it, or the little field behind that. As she wandered around, restless on the acid, people came to her and asked for water and she stopped and gave them the canteen to drink from. That sometimes made her cry, that she had something to give these people who were like her, who were her people.

After Woodstock she went to California. She got a job turning a story she had written into a screenplay. She found a place she liked to live in. She stopped doing acid. She met Mike Morgan.

Now I'm back where I started from, she thought. Back before Mike.

She attached a roach clip to her collar and went out to meet Peter's friends. At the threshold between the hall and the front room she stopped, dismayed: the room was crowded with strangers. The music was coming from the end by the pool table, where Peter and two men were shooting pool.

> *Gonna fly like an eagle, to the sea*
> *Fly like an eagle, let my spirit carry me*

One of the men was Jim Wylie. Interested, Rose started in that direction, but before she had gone three steps into the room, she came face to face with the goat woman.

"Hi," the woman said. "Did you find the horse?"

"Oh, yes," Rose said. "He's down by the river."

"I'm glad for you."

She was wearing a shapeless dress or sari made of burlap feed bags. The powerful, sour smell of the goats was making Rose sick to her stomach.

"You're Peter's sister, I know," the woman said and put out her hand. "I'm Hal."

"My name's Rose." She shook Hal's hand, smiling at the firm, calloused grip.

"Everybody's dying to meet you," Hal continued. "Peter's told us so much about you."

"Good old Peter." Rose put her hand to her shirt pocket, which was flat. She would have to go back to her room and roll a couple of joints.

"Do you drink milk? I'll have to bring an extra quart when I bring Peter his milk," Hal said.

"Goat's milk," Rose said faintly. "Well, I'll give it a try. Is that your house? That stump?"

"You know," Hal said, "most people respond just that way to the first thought of goat's milk, but it's really quite delicious." She smiled at the thought. She was not pretty; she had a big nose and bad acne, but her looks were honest, and her open friendliness was honest, too. Rose grinned at her.

"Sure. I'll try it."

"I make cheese, too," Hal said.

"Oh, really. I've always wanted to make cheese. But I hate feta cheese. Is that what you make? I'm sorry. Is that what you do? Farm goats?"

"Well, not really. I'm a secretary at a bank in Oakland. I just took a year off and came up here, well, you know—" Hal made a small self-belittling shrug. "To find myself."

"You must be my age," Rose said. "I haven't heard that expression since I was at college."

"Rose." Peter swooped down on them. "It's about time. God, what a party pooper. This is Hallie. Hallie—" He slipped his arm around her waist and squeezed her, and Hallie emitted a gurgly squeal. "Hallie is my favorite goat." He still had the cue stick in his hand. He planted a wet kiss on Rose's temple and rushed away back to his pool game.

"God, is he drunk already?"

Hallie was looking steadily up the room after Peter. She said, "He's marvelous. He's so talented."

Rose put her hand up to her mouth. "Talented?" Alerted, she looked keenly at Hal, who was smiling after Peter, and thought, She's in love with him. My brother the romantic. She took Hal firmly by the elbow.

"I don't know any of these people."

"I'll introduce you," Hal offered, in tow. She gave Rose a quizzical look. "You're a writer, Peter says."

"Oh, yeah."

"I'd like to read something you've written."

"What do you like to read?"

They talked about science fiction and fantasy, walking slowly through the room to the fireplace.

The big stone fireplace took up the whole end wall of the room, and the hearth reached out six feet into the room. People had set dishes of food out along the semicircular rim of the hearth; several children sat cross-legged on the floor there, eating from paper plates. Beside Rose, Hal clicked her tongue.

"Paper plates," she said. "God, what fools." She turned suddenly on Rose, her face burning with enthusiasm. "Did you know that Coyote is going to cut trees on his land?"

"Yeah, he told me." Rose went over toward the food, her stomach growling.

"Well, what do you think about it? Are we going to sit by and let it happen?"

"His land," Rose said. "His trees. I don't like the sound of a chain saw myself, but—"

"Those trees," Hal said firmly, "are like gods."

"Hear, hear," said a man behind them. He was sitting on the floor with his back to the hearth, eating a handful of nuts.

"Hal," Rose said, "what are you talking to me for? Go talk to Coyote."

"He won't listen." Hal turned her hands up. "The trees don't need us. We need them. They convert the radiant energy of the sun into a chemical energy we can use. Without plants—"

"I love trees," Rose said. "I hope they never cut another tree in California. I voted for the Coastal Commission. I used to be a member of the Sierra Club—"

"Then help us," Hal cried. "We need all the votes we can get."

A couple of other people were coming closer to listen to the discussion. Rose was hungry; she glanced at the simmering beans beside her, bits of onion and bacon in the bubbling sauce. Something Hal was saying connected with something Peter had said recently, and she straightened, more interested in this.

"Vote? On what? You got some way you can vote to keep Coyote from cutting his trees?"

"We can call a meeting," Hal replied, "if we can get enough votes."

Rose touched her shirt pocket again, remembering she had meant to roll a joint. She glanced at the people around her, a young man and a young woman, and the black man who had been sitting by the hearth and was still eating nuts out of his hand while he watched her. She looked at Hal again.

"What does Peter say?"

"Oh, Peter," Hal said, exasperated. "He's so bourgeois sometimes."

Rose grunted in her throat. "Then if Peter's against it, I don't see what good it would do to call a meeting, since Peter's got all the votes."

"Peter only has one vote," countered the young man beside her.

"Peter owns seventy-five percent of the place," Rose said.

"We decided," the black man said, "that Peter should only have one vote."

"He agreed, naturally," Hal added. "I mean, Peter is very together in a lot of meaningful ways."

"Some of him is together," Rose said. "Some of him is nowhere. Who decided this place was a democracy?"

The black man smiled at her; he put nuts and seeds into his mouth and, chewing, said, "Well, you know, we figure we ought to do it right. Who are you, sister?"

"I'm Rose McKenna," said Rose.

"My name's Johan," he said, extending his hand. He had thin, bony hands, cool to the touch, and a limp handshake. He pronounced his name as it was spelled. He continued, "We're making a new world here, Sister Rose. We're midwives here, bringing forth a new community." As he spoke this, a sermonizer entering into his pet theme, his voice grew louder and clear. "You don't believe in democracy, Sister Rose?"

"I believe in as little as possible." She smelled marijuana. A familiar face, hung with glasses, came toward her; she had forgotten the girl's name, until suddenly Peter's pun from the night before leaped into her mind. The girl held out a joint.

"Hi."

"Hi, Patty." Rose took the joint and toked on it, and immediately her hunger doubled. She scanned the hearth methodically for plates. On a table by the wall was a stack of paper plates. She went that way.

Hal pursued her. "You've got to help us. He'll start cutting trees in a week unless we can call a meeting."

"I'm sorry, Hal. As far as I'm concerned, he can do as he pleases with his own trees." She grabbed a plate and a plastic fork and started back to the hearth.

"But the trees are like gods," Hal cried.

"So gods die all the time." Rose paused, waggling the white plastic fork under Hal's nose. " 'Man comes and tills the earth and lies beneath, and after many a summer dies the swan.' "

Hal looked indignant. Perhaps she was not a fan of Tennyson. Johan said, "What does that mean?"

"I don't know," Rose answered. She bent over the crocks lined up on the hearth, a casserole with ham and hard-cooked eggs in sauce, a pot of brown rice and carrots and celery, the steaming and mellifluous beans. She reached for the spoon in the beans. "I'm tired of taking everything so seriously."

"Well," Hal said. She clasped Rose's elbow a moment. "Welcome home, anyway." She went to a chair nearby and sat down to talk to someone else.

The black man wore bib overalls. He slid one thin hand into the bib pocket and took out a Baggie of nuts. "Rose," he said, "life is very serious."

"You think so, do you?" She shook her head. "I'm sorry. I've had it up to here with anything requiring commitment. Besides, my brother always ran things around here, and nobody ever complained. Why change it now?"

"We all decided," Johan said. "Don't you write things?"

"Yes."

"Ever get anything published?"

"Yes, every now and then." That graveled her; nobody was a writer who didn't get published. She stuck her fork into the mound of baked beans on her plate.

"Good for you," Johan said placidly. He popped a handful of nuts into his mouth and chewed.

The girl with the glasses edged toward her again. "Hey, unh, if you talk to my old man," she said in a low voice, "don't tell him I was up here last night, will you?"

Rose replied, "Don't worry."

"Thanks."

Rose dug her fork into the beans, which were delicious. A cluster of children had gathered by the hearth to her right; in their midst two little towheaded boys began to argue over a slingshot. Wary of the slingshot, Rose backed away, toward a big bowl of lettuce on the table near the wall.

A woman in a halter top stormed down the room toward the little boys, yanked the slingshot away from them, and drove them angrily out of the room. Because she was very fat, she looked too young to be the boys' mother; a broad band of dark roots showed along the part of her lank, yellow hair. She went back up the room toward the pool table.

Rose stood eating salad and beans, the paper plate supported on one hand. Peter came up to her, smiling, a can of beer in his hand. "Hi. Having a good time?"

"Oh, super. Point out Patty's husband to me, so I can remember not to let him know where she was last night."

Peter's smile slipped. He looked her over carefully, glanced around, and said, "The guy by the door with the ponytail. Are you going moral on me?"

Rose widened her eyes into an innocent look. "Me? You

have a guilty conscience." She scooped up a forkful of beans. "Open your mouth."

He opened his mouth; she fed him, by way of showing him she still loved him. She said, "The goat lady thinks a lot of you."

"Hallie's okay," he said fiercely.

"Why don't you do a number with her?"

"I said she was okay, not terrific."

"Speaking of numbers, I'm going to roll some dope. I'll be right back."

"Don't go in there and crawl into the corner with a book."

"I'll be back."

She went down the hall to her room and sat at the table and rolled up all that was left of her stash. The moon was up; she switched off the overhead light and worked by the moonlight through the window. The wind was blowing in the trees outside. When she had done up all the marijuana into cigarettes, she sat still in the dark, the moonlight lying over her lap, her hands in her lap, and listened to the wind blow.

These people irritated her. She could see nothing in them but vanity and stupidity. That unnerved her. She felt herself going sour, turning bad, like a fruit cut from the branch. There was something seriously wrong with her if people like Hal and Johan pushed her off.

She had rolled fifteen joints. She put five in her pocket and stepped into the hall. As she was going toward the main room, the door to Peter's room suddenly opened.

Rose stopped. A man she had never seen before was coming out of Peter's room. Her thoughts flashed at first to Patty's husband, whom she had not bothered to look at, but this man had no ponytail, and anyway he was smiling at her.

"Just trying to find the bathroom," he said and bounced out through the next door into the bathroom door.

Rose watched the door close. She wondered if he were drunk. Opening the door to Peter's room, she put her head inside and looked around. All the lights were burning; the room was stifling hot from the fire in the little Franklin stove against the outer wall. The bed obviously had not been made in months. Piles of boxes stood all along the walls and the tops of the boxes were buried under sheets of paper covered with Peter's sketches. There didn't seem anything worth stealing. She went down the hall to the main room again.

As she went over to the hearth to find some dessert, a man with black hair and beard, a red bandanna wrapped Indian-style around his head, came up and got in her way.

"You're Peter's sister, aren't you?"

"Yes. Rose." She put her hand out.

"I'm Dave Preston. Billy Vigg's brother."

"Brother," she said. "I haven't had the honor yet of meeting Billy Vigg."

"Never mind about Billy," said Dave Preston. "Can I talk to you about something?"

"Sure," Rose said uneasily.

"I mean, I seen everybody else come up and lay their sob story on you."

"Sure."

Dave's dark eyes were bright; he was small and wiry and moved quickly, like a squirrel. He said, "You know about our pot field."

"Yeah. Peter told me. I haven't seen it yet."

"Nothin' to see yet, just a couple baby plants."

"Sure."

"The thing is," he said, "all those little plants gotta be watered, and weeded, and all that. We all do it, you know. But there's some people—" He nudged her. His voice dropped to a conspirator's murmur. "Some people around here don't do their share."

"Oh, yeah?"

"I'm not naming names," he said, but looked pointedly down the room at Hal, standing in her bulky burlap clothing under the lamp in the center of the room.

"Maybe she isn't interested," Rose said. She took a joint from her pocket and lit it.

"Hey," Dave said, in genuine admiration.

She took a toke and handed the joint to him. "For instance," she continued, "I have no intention of working in your pot field."

Dave looked at her, round-eyed, his lips pursed to suck on the joint and tendrils of smoke floating around his head. He lowered the joint.

"Our," he said earnestly. "It's ours. We all work; we all take our cut."

"Yours," Rose said. She took the joint from his fingers and started off across the room, toward Hal.

Dave walked along beside her, leaning forward to talk to her face. "You hill-toppers sure stick together, don't you."

"Tight as Andronicus," Rose said to him.

He stopped; she walked away from him and paused beside Hal. The odor of the goats shortened her breath.

"Hi," Hal said, smiling. "Having a good time?"

"Sure." Rose held the joint out to her.

"Oh no," Hal said. "I don't smoke. It's really bad for you."

"Is it really," Rose said. "I'm sorry to hear that." She moved away, on down the room toward the pool table.

Jim Wylie was chalking up his cue; nobody else seemed to be playing, and Rose said, "Shoot a little pool?"

He looked up. Tonight he was wearing clothes, soft, worn jeans and a faded shirt. His curly red hair reminded her of the hair on Greek statues. He said, "Any game you want, lady. How you like it here?"

"It's okay," she said. She went to the rack on the wall for a cue stick.

Wylie fit the balls into the triangle. "The weather certainly got better when you showed up." He rolled the filled triangle around on the table, centering it for the break. The table was old and falling apart, the pockets sagging out of the corners, and the felt worn here and there to the bare slate.

"Peter oughta buy himself a new table," she said, circling the table for the chalk. "You want to break, go ahead."

"Ladies first," said Wylie.

She chalked up and moved the white cue ball over to the right to get an angle on the pocket, handed the joint to Wylie, and stroked the cue ball hard. Under its impact the triangle of balls exploded off in a Brownian movement over the table.

One of the solid balls fell in the course of the break; she knocked in another on the next shot, but missed the third. Wylie gave her the joint and bent with his stick over the table.

"What the hell is going on here?" Rose asked. "People keep lobbying me. How'd Peter lose control of the meetings? He used to run things; he called a meeting once a year, to tell everybody what the taxes were."

Wylie shot; he drove the cue ball on a long curving roll down the table to tap in the purple stripe. "Who's been on your case? Hallie, about me cutting trees, I'll bet." He moved around to the far side of the table, studying the lay of the balls.

"She's not the only one."

Neatly he banked the red-striped ball off the side bumper and into the corner pocket. "Oh, you know," he said, "nobody around here ever knows when to shut up."

As he leaned down over the stick, his eyes moved, looking across the room, just for an instant. Turning his gaze to the pool table, he tried a combination on the twelve and the thirteen that missed. With her eyes Rose followed his glance up the room; the only person she saw there was Dave Preston.

Patty was coming toward them, pulling a man along by the hand, a stocky, bearded man whose shaggy, fair hair hung down his back in a ponytail. He grinned cheerfully at Rose.

"Sam," he said and put his hand out.

"I'm Rose McKenna." She shook his hand and gave him the joint.

"Well, what'd'you think of the place?"

"It's beautiful," she said. "A little wet, though."

He laughed; he passed the joint to Patty, now clinging to his arm. Rose moved around the table to shoot. Sam turned to Jim Wylie, leaning on his pool cue beside him.

"Hey, you ol' Coyot', where you been keeping yourself?"

"Working," Wylie said.

"Got us a sauna, man."

"You did? Good news. What is it?"

"Mason's gonna give me his old chicken house, man. It's little, but it's solid. We can move it in the back of my truck, stick that old stove in there, and cook, man."

Rose bent down, putting her eye close to the stick, and knocked the cue ball down the table; it veered slowly off course, and she twisted her whole body trying to English it back. Groaning, she watched it rebound uselessly off the bumper and bang a few other balls around.

"You met this lady?" Wylie said to Sam. He held the joint out to Rose. "Last hit." He had the quarter-inch of roach nipped between his fingernails. She pinched it carefully away by the very edge of the paper.

"We just met," Sam said.

Rose lit another joint. "Your shot," she said to Wylie and turned, her eye catching on someone coming into the room from the hall. "That guy, there," she said to Sam. "Who's that?" It was the black-haired man she had seen coming out of Peter's room.

"That?" Sam said. He sucked noisily on the new joint. In a rasp, holding his toke, he answered, "That's Billy Vigg."

"Oh," Rose said, her curiosity keen.

Billy Vigg was coming toward them. In the wiry nest of his beard his mouth curled in a toothy smile. "Hey, man, how you doin', man?" He shook the blond man's hand. "Is that a joint, man?"

"What'y'up to?" Sam said.

"Nothing much, man. Collectin' unemployment." Billy looked at Rose. "How do?"

"Fine, thanks," Rose said. "I'm Rose McKenna."

"Bill Vigg. That's my old lady, down there, Glory."

Rose's head swiveled; he was pointing to the fat woman

with the dyed yellow hair, who was down by the hearth again, shooing her children around. "Well," she said, "pleased to meet y'."

"Pleased to meet anybody who's got dope, man," Billy Vigg said and laughed. He lifted the joint to his lips; as he inhaled, his eyes met Rose's, and he winked at her.

She grunted, unwilling to be amused. She turned away from him, to watch Wylie shoot.

Behind her, Sam said, "Hey, man, what's this about another meeting?"

"What?"

"Dave wants to call another meeting, he says, to get some rules laid down about the pot."

Billy Vigg snorted. "Dave just likes to keep things stirred up, man. Forget him."

"Good. I'm getting tired of these meetings."

"How do, Patty?" Billy Vigg said. "Say, where was you last night?"

Rose straightened; her gaze followed the white ball rolling over the felt, but her ears strained to hear behind her. Patty said, "What d'you mean by that?" in a shrill, angry voice.

"Well, I came over there for a match, and you wasn't home."

"I went for a walk," Patty said.

Wylie came around the table, and Rose turned back to watch Patty. Billy Vigg was grinning ear to ear, delighted with what he was doing; he said, "Well, you oughtn't to go for a walk then at two in the morning, Patty. In the rain?"

Sam said, "What is this?" He reached for the joint that Billy Vigg was holding, his head turning toward the woman beside him. "Where were you?"

"I was asleep," she cried, indignant. "I don't answer the door at two a.m. I don't care who it is."

Wylie suddenly bent down for a shot; as he drew his stick back, the butt end banged hard into Billy Vigg's ribs.

"Hey, watch out." Billy jumped to the side, his fingers fluttering over his shirt.

"Where were you?" Sam asked Patty.

"In bed," she said. She glared at Billy Vigg.

"Yeah?" Sam said. "With who? Up here, I bet. Or down with the Coyot'. Hell," he said, raising his voice, "I don't care." He looked from Billy Vigg to Jim Wylie, speaking loud enough to reach every ear in the room. "I don't care what she does. She don't mean nothing to me. I didn't invite her; she just showed up and moved in. I don't care what she does."

Patty's face was red with embarrassment. "You don't have t' be like that," she said. Everybody was looking at her. She backed up a few steps. "Why d'you have t' be like that?"

Sam was staring at her, a very hard look, for not caring. He turned suddenly and walked away from Patty. Behind the lens of her glasses Patty's dark eyes shone brightly with tears. She ran out of the room.

Rose let her gathered muscles relax. She put her cue stick in the corner with a dozen others and walked across the room to the front door and out onto the porch.

Peter was sitting on the porch railing. She went up beside him and lit a joint and they smoked it together, Rose leaning against the rail and Peter sitting on it.

"Nice night," he said finally.

She made a noncommittal noise in her throat. The new moon was dipping down the sky; midway between it and the horizon was the blue-white blaze of Venus. The air smelled good, sweet and clean.

"Peter," she said, "I want to go someplace else."

He lurched up onto his feet. "Away from River Ranch? You just came."

Rose shook her head. The scene between Patty and Sam had raked across her nerves. Mike Morgan crowded into her mind. She did not want him or love him, but she was still bound to him somehow, Francesca to his Paolo.

"Rose," Peter said. "I need you here. I need your vote in the meetings."

"Oh, for God's sake." She turned her back to him, clasping her arms across her breast against the chilly air.

"Rose, come on. You can't go. You told me you'd stay."

"Look, you lost it here, that's not my—"

"What about that girl?" he cried, triumphant. "You gotta be here for her."

She had forgotten about Reina Darrezzo. She lowered her eyes.

"Look, Rose," he said. "It's not so bad here."

"These people are feeding on each other. I don't go in much for cannibalism." Her stomach hurt.

"Hey," he said sharply. "It's not that bad. People get a little excited sometimes—"

"There's too many people here. I can't hack it."

"Couldn't you go camping?"

She had not thought of that. The crag she had found returned through her memory, the wind crying in the forest, the long, slow glide of the heron. She drew the sweet air into her lungs. "Okay," she said. "Maybe I'll do that."

"I'll loan you my tent."

"No, no, I'll just take my sleeping bag. Have you got a ground cloth?"

"Sure. My tent."

"Okay."

He threw one arm around her and hugged her. She let herself be wrestled up against his chest.

"I guess we're a couple of losers, Peter."

"God, you are in a bad mood."

"Aw, Jesus."

"Why, because of that asshole Mike? Rosie, the best thing you ever did—"

She broke out of his grip, putting room between them. "I don't want to talk about it." If Mike were an asshole, what was she for living with him so long? A fool. A mistake. I made a mistake. A ten-year-long mistake.

"Are you staying here?" Peter said.

"I'll go camping. I found a place in the woods today I like."

"Thanks, Rose."

She drew close to him again, her arm slipping around his waist. "I'm sorry I called you a loser." The warmth of his body reached her through his thin T-shirt. She remembered climbing trees with him once; he had gotten stuck, and she had had to help him down. Walking to catch the school bus in the morning, the sun hardly risen, and the damp chill of a New England autumn roughening their skin. She hugged him against her, grateful for this continuity.

"Where did Patty come from?"

One of his shoulders lifted in a shrug. "Ask her. She has about twenty answers. She makes a new one up every time you ask. She ran away from home a couple of years ago, bummed around, ended up here."

Rose turned away wishing she had not asked; she did not want to know so much about Patty. "Ended up, or just passing through? I'm going to bed."

"Good night, Rose."

"Good night, Bub."

"Leave me a joint?"

She had one left in her pocket, and she gave it to him. She went in through the main room, still noisy and crowded, and down the hall to her room.

With a toothbrush and a towel she went back down the hall to wash. When she came back from the bathroom, her gaze fell on the row of joints she had left on the table. Two of them were missing.

"Aw, Christ," she said, furious. She remembered that Billy Vigg had been in this part of the house for a long time after she saw him go into the bathroom. There was no future in confronting him over it. She put the joints away in the back of a drawer.

She turned off the light and opened the window. The clean, sweet wind swept in, clearing out the musty smell of a room long unused. As she undressed in the dark, the passing air raised bumps on her skin and sent a thrill down her spine. There were blankets stacked on the top shelf of the closet, and she ran to get them. Pile them on, she thought. Like guilts upon the fretful concubine. She laid the blankets over her sleeping bag on the bottom bunk, slipped beneath the weight, shivering, and went to sleep with the clean wind in her face.

In the morning while she was cleaning up her brother's kitchen, she thought of Angie in Pasadena and called her. It was Saturday morning, and Angie would be home from work.

"Hello?" Heavy with sleep, Angie's voice answered.

"Ange, it's Rose. What's happening?"

"Oh, yeah," Angie said. "Rose. God, what time is it?"

"It's after nine, Ange."

"Oh, God, what a night."

"Oh, yeah? Tell me all about it."

"You don't want to know. I don't want to remember." Angie laughed. "I can't remember." She laughed again, delighted, as if she had succeeded at something. "Oh, God, what a night."

"Yeah, Ange. Look, is Reina coming?"

"Reina. Oh, yeah, that's right. Gee, I'm glad you called."

"Atta girl, Angie."

"Miller Tarn's gonna bring her."

Rose's mood cooled down. "That guy? Is he still hanging around?"

"It's the only way I can get her up there, Rose. Jeez, d'you know what it costs to fly up there?"

"A fortune. Yes."

"And the bus takes so long."

"Yeah, I know. That Miller guy, you know, he and I did not hit it off too well."

"He wants to stay a little while. He says he'll pay for his food and everything else and he'll help out."

Rose said nothing, remembering, not Miller Tarn, who was only a fat shadow in her memory, but Mike Morgan, shouting at her. Her eyes ached suddenly with tears. She swallowed, shaken again by the looseness and violence of her feelings.

"He's not a bad guy, Rose. You just got to know him better."

"Oh, yeah," she said, "let him come. If Reina can come. When will she be here?"

"Next week sometime. School gets out the twelfth and then I gotta go get her some stuff, clothes and all, and she has to go to the dentist."

"Okay."

"So how's everything?"

"Everything's . . . fine, actually, I guess."

"How's your brother?"

"Oh, Peter, he's the same. He's such a teddy bear. He made this huge rhinoceros out of iron pipe; it's out in front of the house. You wouldn't believe it. You seen Felice?"

"No. I don't see Felice any more."

"Oh."

"That's the breaks, I guess."

Rose said nothing for a moment. She was thinking of herself, Angie, and Felice, how long they had been friends, how little she had made of leaving them, how now they were separated, the thing just coming apart somehow, unnoticed under the fireworks of her separation from Mike. She was glad again that Reina would be here, a root back into a life that now seemed to her as distant as the center of the earth.

"Ange, don't get her anything fancy, just some jeans. Some shoes to ride in."

"Don't sweat it. I just got two hundred dollars back from the government, I got plenty of money." The last of this was said over a smothered yawn.

"What does she like to eat?"

"Oh, she eats anything. Rose, lemme go back to sleep, honey."

Rose searched for something else to say, to hold Angie to her, but she could hear the drowsiness in Angie's voice, falling like a veil between them. "Okay," she said at last.

"I'll give her some money," Angie said. "I'll send you a couple bucks whenever I get paid."

"Okay."

"G'night, Rose."

"Good-by, Angie."

She hung up. For a moment she stood there, alone in the kitchen, looking around her at the woodstove, where the coffee simmered, at the peeling yellow linoleum on the floor and the yellow walls turning brown to black over the stove; it all looked strange to her, as if she had just been transported here from somewhere else. Slowly she took the broom and swept the floor.

When she had finished with the kitchen, she packed to go camping, opening out her sleeping bag on the floor and rolling it up again with clothes, pots and spoons, and a spatula. This was going to be a long hike, she realized and was pleased. She needed to try something hard, to find her limits, to bring herself all back together.

When she had her pack ready, she unearthed a frame in Peter's room and lashed everything to it. There were other things she needed, an axe, maybe a fishing pole, and something to read. Tools to work her pot field. She went looking for her brother.

In the bright sunshine in front of the house Peter was at work on his rhinoceros, banging it with wrenches. He sat on the peaked back and leaned down over the shoulder to get at some inner part of the head, so that he seemed to be wrestling with it. Rose strode through the tall grass toward him.

"I'm going to need an axe, man. Or a hatchet. A small saw."

"Got a little camp hatchet you can use," Peter said. "Here, hold this."

She held one wrench while he fit another over the joint. "That rain sealed everything up tight. I can't get the goddamn head off." He heaved his whole weight down on the wrench, his face beet-colored with effort. Rose gripped the handle tightly in her hands; its edge pressed into the flesh of her palm. Slowly the two wrenches strained apart. Peter sat up straight and quickly unscrewed the joint.

"Okay."

"Where's this famous hatchet?"

"I think I loaned it to Billy Vigg. It must still be down at his place."

"Oh, Christ."

She went off down the road past the house; the dirt track rolled on across the bench and down into the valley beyond, so-called the flat, where most of Peter's settlers lived. Rose went to where the road turned down and stopped. From here she could see the whole south end of the valley. The creek that had worn this cleft into the hillside rambled down one edge and under the county road, just barely visible through the row of silver-green eucalyptus that marked the far boundary of River Ranch. The road ran down the other side of the valley. Three of the four houses were clustered together halfway to the gate; the other house was set up away from the road just by the gate. A huge old weeping willow filled its front yard. Right now there was a red semi truck parked under the willow tree. Patty's Sam, she remembered, was a trucker.

She did not want to go down there even to get an axe. The Viggs' house would be the one on the left side of the road. It looked more like a prehistoric mound than a house, swarmed over by berry vines, its chimney thrusting up just clear of the encumbering growth. The Vigg children were playing on a wrecked car in the front yard.

Not now. She turned abruptly and walked toward the forest.

She walked back into the forest on the trail she had followed the day before. The backpack began to weigh heavily on her shoulders, and she shifted it and held the straps with her hands to keep them from pressing into her flesh. Reaching the crag where she meant to grow her marijuana, she turned east, to find the river, and plowed through the thorny underbrush until she came to the rushing water's edge.

Still full from the rain, the river coursed along in a brisk, muddy surge, its little waves splashing over into the murk. Here it was a hundred yards wide; just upstream it narrowed to half that. As she stood there admiring its race, a large branch came down the stream, dragging on the bottom and tumbling over in its passage.

She walked upstream along the overgrown riverbank. Brambles choked it. She fought her way through them, climbed over a fallen tree, and waded a little creek that fed into the river. Ahead of her, in the brush, something crashed and crackled through the branches. She stopped. But the sound faded, without her ever seeing what had caused it. A deer, maybe.

Some way on, she came to the edge of a meadow. Here the river curved, and the grassland lay along the curve. Stands of poison oak and rushes and small shrubs were invading the meadow, the advance guard of the forest, but broad stretches of rye grass remained, bending in the wind. At the river's edge there was a big white horse, drinking.

Rose sighed, glad to see him. She started toward him, thought of the backpack, which would surely frighten him, and slipped it off her shoulders and let it down.

The horse raised his head to watch her approach. He was not white all over; his ears and neck and lower legs were red roan. Black streaked his long white tail. Ten feet from him, she stopped, to keep from frightening him off, and as soon as she stopped, the big horse snorted and turned and walked slowly toward her.

"Hey," she said, delighted at his friendliness. "Hey." She put out her hand, and he sniffed it, licked it, and pushed his head against her.

She ran her hand along his neck. All down the groove in his neck where the big vein ran, blue ticks and tick bumps poked up the hair. She pulled out the parasites, breaking them up between her fingers and talking all the while to the horse.

He pushed his head against her again. His eyes were

strange. The sclera of most horses were brown, but this horse's were white, like a human eye's, giving him a look of startled attention. She stroked him all over, looking for ticks, and scrubbing the matted dirt on his flanks and barrel with her fingertips. His mane was thin, but his tail hung to the ground, snarled with burrs and long strips of blackberry vine. She picked it clean.

When she had touched him all over, making them friends, she went back for the pack, lugged it down to the river, and walked along the bank looking for a good place to camp. In the bight the river had already receded from the inside of its bed, the current flinging it deep into the curve; a broad stretch of sand lay exposed below the bank. She jumped down to it. This part of the bar was well above the river, and the bank sheltered it from the wind. She put her pack against the riverbank and went for wood to build a fire.

The horse grazed near her, his tail swishing occasionally across his flanks. She started a fire and put on a pan of water, to heat for coffee, then went up and down the river shore gathering more wood. The water boiled and boiled and boiled away. She piled the wood in heaps along the edge of her camp and went off to the woods to cut green boughs.

Peter had given her his tent, which she opened up and spread across the sandy bar for a ground cloth. The bank made one wall. Up and down the river, she found long sticks, redwood limbs, the bark still hanging like remnants of fur to the sleek wood, and tilted them up against the bank to make a lean-to. She spread leafy branches over the frame, layer on layer of pine boughs, holding them all down with stones. She thought of Mike only once, the whole afternoon, and had no trouble sending him out of her mind.

As she worked, and the lean-to took shape, there grew in her a simple pride, a satisfaction, and a kind of peace.

In the afternoon she called the horse, looped the rope around his neck, climbed onto his back, and turned him around toward Peter's house. At the far end of the meadow was an old logging road that led into the forest and seemed to promise a shorter path back to her brother than the way she had come. She urged the old horse toward it.

It was a long ride. Unused to riding and bareback on a bony horse, she was sore and aching before she was halfway home. Her fingers were cut from grabbing the mane to stay on. The horse knew where she wanted to go; he kept straight on, through the woods on the logging road and then up through a series of meadows that climbed the shoulder of the mountain. At the top they came on the county road, just below the dirt road to Peter's.

She would have to ride by the Viggs' anyway. She resolved to stop and get the hatchet.

She rode up past the house where Patty lived and the red box of the truck cab parked by the willow tree. Long and narrow, the valley stretched away from her. Three or four cattle were grazing across the ditch, and there were sheep on the grassy slope beyond them. She stretched her legs cautiously, peeling her jeans away from the insides of her thighs, which felt like ground meat. Ahead was the Viggs' house like a barrow by the road.

Billy Vigg was in his front yard, chopping wood with a full-sized axe. He wore red suspenders; his shirt hung on the rusting truck hulk that dominated the yard. Rose drew up the horse across the fence from him.

"How do?" he said, rather formally, and she smiled tentatively at him.

"How do. You got my brother's hatchet, there, man?"

"Hatchet," Billy said vacantly and furrowed up his forehead. "He say I have his hatchet?"

The door behind him opened, and Glory Vigg, his wife, filled the space above the threshold. She smiled cheerfully at Rose. "Hi, there."

"Hi," Rose said. "You make those beans last night?"

"Sure did."

"They were sensational."

Glory beamed at her. Her face went pink with the compliment. "Why, thank you. You come on in and have a beer."

"She's looking for Peter's hatchet," said Billy. "You remember us ever having a hatchet of his?"

"Loaned it to Johan," Glory replied. The smile still dimpled her face. She nodded cheerfully to Rose. "Come have a beer some time." Turning away into the kitchen, she shut the door behind her.

"Over across the way," Billy said.

Rose looked where he was waving; on the far side of the road was a garden, a house on either side of it. She said, "Which? Suppose you come with me and help me find it."

Billy swung the axe in his hands around into the chopping block, took his shirt, and vaulted nimbly over the fence. "I don't even remember—oh, yeah, now I remember." He snapped his fingers, smiling up at her. They went down the road, she on the horse and he walking beside her. "Was years ago, maybe. Where'd you find this old fellah?" He slapped the horse's shoulder. From that his hand traveled six inches backwards and patted her thigh.

Rose drove the horse off sideways, pressing her leg to its side. Billy was walking on as if nothing had happened. Maybe he hadn't meant it. She knew he had meant it. She wished she had kicked him, instead of moving away from him; she could have kicked him over.

"Right here," he said, opening a gate. "Better leave Trigger here, I guess." He laughed at his humor. Rose slid stiffly down from the bony back and let the rope trail.

They went through the picket gate into an orchard of half-grown trees, none taller than Rose. Little green leaves like ears sprouted all over their branches. Through this miniature forest they walked on a slate path up to a redwood house.

A deck ran the length of the front; on the deck was Johan, sitting in a full lotus, eating nuts, and reading. Rose went toward him, curious to see what the book was. Billy hung back, to let her go by, and as she passed him, he palmed her backside.

Startled, she jumped away from him and turned to glare at him. He winked at her.

"Hello, there, Sister Rose," Johan said.

She faced him, her hands on her own ass, her heart thumping. "Hi," she said, trying to collect herself. Johan was watching her calmly. The book was in his lap.

"Kahlil Gibran?" she said. "Well, that's too bad. I'll bet you loved *Jonathan Livingston Seagull,* too."

He blinked at her, looking insulted. Probably he had a right. She slid her hands into her hip pockets. "My brother says he loaned this—" She gestured with her head toward Billy Vigg, beside her, slipping him a poisonous look as she did—"a hatchet. Now he says he loaned the hatchet to you."

Johan asked, "When was this?" He looked at Billy a moment and brought his solemn gaze back to her. "There was a lot of truth in *Jonathan Livingston Seagull.*"

"Yes," she said, ashamed of attacking him. "I'm sure there was. If you liked it, then there must have been something in it I missed."

That brought his ready smile. "Very smooth, Sister Rose," he said. "I think I gave the hatchet to Reid, once when he was cutting stove wood and his chain saw broke."

"Reid," she said, unhappy. "Don't they live all the way back up on the hill?" She nodded toward the mountain.

"That's where they are, Sister Rose. However, they have a phone. I'll call and find out." He went into the house.

Rose turned to Billy Vigg. "You know, you are a real turkey."

"Hey, man," he said, wiping his hand on his chest. "I didn't mean nothing." He offered her a nervous smile. He had his shirt in his hand, and slipping his arms like snakes out of the suspenders, he put the shirt on and undid his pants and stood there vigorously thrusting the tails of his shirt into his pants, saying, "I don't mean nothing. It's just me, that's all. Just being me."

The greasy smile returned. Over it his eyes gleamed with a wicked humor. A wise pup who knows when to cringe. She snorted.

"You are a genuine three-barrel turkey."

"Aw, come on. I ain't that bad." Billy snapped his suspenders into place. "In fact, you get to know me, I'm a right nice guy."

"I think," she said, "the more I get to know you, the more I am confirmed in my original suspicions."

"Oh, yeah?" he said blankly. "Did you say something good or bad?" His irrepressible laugh started up. Johan came out onto the deck, and Billy turned to him.

"Hey, man, tell this here lady I'm just harmless ol' Billy."

Johan sat down again beside his book. "Reid says he thinks Dave Preston's got that hatchet now." He favored Billy Vigg with a searching look. "He bothering you?"

Rose shook her head. "He just thinks he is. Who's Dave Preston?"

"M' brother," answered Billy. "M' half-brother, actually. Come on, it must be back at my place somewhere."

"Thanks," Rose said to Johan. "Sorry I bad-mouthed your book."

"Have a good day, Sister Rose."

She and Billy went back down the walk to the road; this time, going back to the Viggs', she walked, leading the horse, her legs throbbing with every step. There was an old black Ford Fairlane coming up the road from the gate, and she nudged the horse with her shoulder, pushing him toward the ditch.

The car turned into the Viggs' front yard; it was Dave Preston himself. He got out of the car, scowling at Rose, and folded his arms over his chest. His jaws ruminated on a wad of gum.

Billy said, "You got that old red-handled hatchet somewhere?"

Preston eyed Rose a moment longer. Apparently it took very little to get on his bad side. Rose smiled falsely at him. He turned away from her with a sneer. To his brother, he said, "I think I left it up in that pickup of Pete's, that time we went to the beach."

"Oh, Christ," Rose exclaimed, then burst out laughing.

She wheeled the horse around, banging her elbow into his ribs to turn him. "Well, thanks," she said to Billy. "I can take it from here."

"Come down and be friendly," Billy said. He reached for the axe in the chopping block. Preston grunted and strode abruptly across the yard toward the house.

"I don't think your brother thinks very much of me," Rose said.

Billy said, "He don't like anybody, the first six months he knows 'em. Come on in."

"No, thanks," she said. "In six months, if I'm still here." She swung the horse around again and started up the road to her brother's house.

"Found him, did you?" Peter said. He went up to the horse and patted his neck. The horse blew a sustained snort through his nostrils.

"He found me," Rose said. "He's the genius of the forest. We're going to get along just fine."

"What do you need that for?"

Rose put a shovel down on the tarp, the pillow, and the sack of food she was taking back. The hatchet was already lashed to the backpack. "You have anything around here to read?"

"Sure. What d'you think I am, illiterate? There's a whole box of books in my room."

"Where's the saddle and bridle for this horse?"

"In the shed somewhere."

She went past the row of cars to the shed where Peter kept his tools. Her brother followed her.

"Rose, there's going to be a meeting tonight."

"So?" She went into the dark of the shed. The redwood planks of the walls had shrunk with age; blades of sunlight shone through the cracks into the dusty room. The smell of creosote made her sniff. She stood still a moment. Something here, the tools, or perhaps the creosote, reminded her forcefully of a long time before, being with Peter at the family's beach house, and the little tool room where they had gone to play some guilty game.

Her brother said, "Rose, you got to come."

She glared at him, angry. "What's it about? This pot field?"

"Oh, I don't know," he cried, spreading his hands. "Preston wants a schedule for people to work in the pot field, and Hal and Johan want to vote on whether Coyote ought to cut his trees or not—"

"Peter, do you want this meeting?"

"No, for God's sake, Rosie, I feel like there's a revolution happening, and I'm the king."

She laughed, tired; it was a long way back to her camp, and Peter needed her here. Maybe she would stay the night at the house. Another part of her grew angry at that and longed for the river. She shook her head.

"No, Peter."

"Rose. I thought at least I could count on you. My own sister."

On a wooden frame on the far wall there was an old Mexican saddle, layered over with dust. She plowed toward it through the clutter of tools and sacks of fertilizer and seed. "Peter," she said over her shoulder, "why should I take you off the hook? This is your problem. You let it happen. You take the consequences." The bridle hung over the huge, flat horn of the saddle. She took it gingerly by the crown piece and held it out at arm's length, inspecting it for spiders.

The door slammed. Peter had gone.

Relieved, she coiled up the reins and slung the bridle over her shoulder, freeing both hands for the saddle. Peter would do anything to avoid fighting with people. He would handle the meeting better than anyone else, letting it run leaderless, working off its energies in meaningless rushes in all directions, until everybody was tired and bored and ready to go home. She lugged the saddle down off its frame and out to the open air and the horse.

There was indeed a box of books in Peter's room, paper-back and hardbound all jumbled together, many of them stamped YALE UNIVERSITY, where Peter had spent a disas-trous freshman and only year in college. She dumped the box's contents into a pillowcase and slung it on top of the saddle, already piled up with gear, and led the horse away to the woods.

She opened her eyes into the dawnlight. She thought at first that the light itself had wakened her, piercing and clear as it never was at noon; she lay still, and an instant later noticed the steady crunch-crunch of something eating, just outside the lean-to. The horse must have wandered into the camp.

She put her head out of the lean-to. A deer stood a few feet away from her, its rump to her and its little black-edged tail flipping back and forth. It had dragged a loaf of bread out of the box of food by the fire and was eating a slice at its feet.

"Hey," Rose said, and the deer bolted away down the river bar, sprang to the top of the bank, and vanished into the meadow.

Rose crawled out of her sleeping bag. The damp chill that greeted her brought every nerve tingling awake. Swiftly she pulled on her jeans and sat down to put her shoes on. All over the ground by the fire, pieces of bread and crumbs lit-tered the sand.

Guess I better stash the food, she said. She would leave some bread out at night to draw the deer.

She lit the fire; while her coffee was heating, she dug a hole into the bank, stuck the box of food inside, and piled rocks over the opening. The pillowcase filled with books she put carefully in under the lean-to. She reached into the pillowcase, just to see what was in it, and took out a biology book. Sitting down cross-legged in the mouth of the lean-to, she started reading about evolution.

She read all morning, drinking coffee, smoking dope, and

eating the dusty bread that the deer had left behind. The biology book gave her good news and bad news. The good news was the incalculable complexity of life, which, like the salmon swimming against the current, fought upstream against the relentless disintegration of the universe into entropy. The bad news was that anything so complex as a living body was certain to break down eventually.

She envisioned herself as a colony, not an individual but a mass of them, microphages, neurons, mitochondria, *E. coli*. Her personality seemed fragile as a soap bubble and strangely peripheral, an envelope of habits and manners to enclose the world inside.

Everything came from there, anyway, she thought. When she left Mike, it seemed to her now, she had been working up to it for months. Her conscious mind was the last to know what she had intended. For months she had been planning it, in oblique ways—that was why she had hoarded up nearly two thousand dollars, when usually her money was spent even before she got it. Even selling her typewriter, two months before, now seemed to her to have prepared for the moment of flight. But she had never thought to herself, until the very last, that she was leaving Mike. She would never have been able to do it, had she known.

She had read about a woman with sixteen discrete personalities, none of them invented, representing different aspects of the victim's life. She knew herself to be sixteen people at least, constantly negotiating new imbalances, ascendancies and détentes, which the broad abstractions of her reason played on like an uncertain light, wiping out detail and throwing a confusion of shadows. She wondered if the number of people in her life reflected the number of her selves: if each friend or lover were attracted, like hormones, to a different receptor. Then of course the friend or lover would have other connections. A great mass of interrelated positions. A sudden rush of marijuana good feeling gave this thought the resonance of an idea in a dream. What she needed was something to take her mind out of fast forward. Something to eat.

She made herself a sandwich. When she had eaten, she went back into the woods toward the crag where she would grow her marijuana. The shovel and pick from Peter's tool shed rested over her shoulder; she followed the riverbank to the creek and turned upstream along the creek, looking for the path she had taken the day before.

She could not find it. She walked below the familiar hill, fighting through the berry bushes and nettles up to her armpits, but she could find no trail. Finally she went back where she had begun, between the sheer hillside and the creek, and holding the tools awkwardly against her body with one arm, she struggled up where there was no trail, up the face of the hill. Halfway to the top, the pick fell from her grasp. Her fingertips bled from the rough clinging to the rocks. She heaved herself up over the edge of the cliff and lay on the flat rock, panting, the sun on her face.

She searched around the top of the crag, looking for an easier way down, but found none. She had made up the path in her memory somehow. Of course the hard climb up made this place all the better, for her purposes. She would have to arrange some kind of lift. She went back to her camp for some rope.

The rest of the day she spent on the crag, rigging the rope so that she could get up and down without killing herself, and then digging up the meadow with the pick and shovel. The meadow covered about a quarter of an acre. Its broad-bladed grass, bearing soft, fine, silvery hairs like fur, grew knee-high, and the soil under it seemed to be mostly decomposing leaves. Wet and loose from recent rains, it came up in clumps when she picked it over and broke into steaming clods under the shovel. Every shovelful turned up a couple of worms.

It was too acid, this soil. She had never grown pot, but she knew it came from high, dry, mountainy soils, and this rich humus would burn it to death. She would have to get some lime and dig it in.

The sun was hot, and her sweat turned sticky on her skin as she worked. She began to wish she could take her shirt off. When the thought poked through into her conscious mind, she laughed, buoyant, and peeled off all her clothes and worked naked.

She sat down under the scrubby trees on the high side of the crag and smoked a joint, looking across the canyon at the next ridge, a line of redwoods like spines along its crest. In the chapter on evolution the biology book had mentioned the simultaneous and independent invention of the theory by two men on either side of the world; she wondered if there were a story in that, somewhere. It was certainly a very odd event, unsettling, suggesting the domination of culture over personality. You could know only what your culture let you know. Of course that implied that the knowledge existed before the knowing. She puffed on the joint, enjoying the feel of the wind on her naked body. The wind was there whether she thought of it or not. In the mind of Yours Faithfully, God.

At sundown she dressed and went back to her camp. The horse was standing to his knees in the river, drinking. The sun had just slipped below the mountain. Its glow faded along the rim of the world. She dropped the tools on the ground near the bank and picked up the hatchet to chop wood for a fire.

In the morning she went back up to Peter's house. The back door hung open, and there was a beer standing on the railing of the little porch, the dew still weeping down the side of the can, but she could not find her brother. The whole house was quiet. In the distance a chain saw screamed, like an accent to the silence.

She drove up the freeway to Springville, the nearest town of any size, half an hour north of River Ranch. Eight thousand people lived in Springville, the largest town between Ukiah and Eureka. Rose had been there last almost four years before. It looked much the same, although there was a lot of construction going on, even a new shopping center at the edge of town. The rusty, buckling cone of the incinerator at the mill was still the tallest structure for miles. Along the main street there were private houses side by side with the wooden false-fronted stores and cattle grazed in open fields in the middle of town. A banner hanging across the street advertised the local rodeo.

Rose stopped her car to let two girls on ponies cross the street in front of her. She drove on slowly through the town, looking for the lumberyard. Springville reminded her of the town in New England where she had grown up, not because of any real physical likeness, but because it seemed thirty years behind the times: instead of a McDonald's, there was a soda shop, and the only movie theater in town was playing *Snow White*.

At the lumberyard she bought two sacks of lime. They weighed 100 pounds each, and she began to think out how she would get them up to her field without anyone else's learning she had them. As she drove out of town, she passed a dozen hitchhikers with their backpacks and dogs and signs, waiting by the on ramp of the freeway. Most of them were going to San Francisco.

She drove back up to River Ranch, planning how to take the lime in. If she packed it in on the horse, someone might see her; for reasons she did not bother to sort out, she knew that would be disastrous.

The company road ran by the ranch for some distance in two separate places, on the northeastern edge at the front gate, and on the southern line at the back gate. She was vague about the distances, but because her camp was by the river, it had to be somewhere near the place where the county road crossed over the bridge, just past the front gate. She could leave the lime there and lug it down the river on the horse.

She rounded the curve toward the bridge and nearly ran into a deer, dead in the middle of the road. She wrenched the wheel over. The VW plowed off the side of the road into the bank, bumped, and stopped. Out in the road, half a dozen great bare-headed birds flapped their wings and struggled grossly to escape into the air.

Rose got out of her car. The vultures shambled off across the road and labored into flight. Its neck twisted, the deer sprawled across the pavement. The birds had torn open a bloody hole in its side to feed from; a rib stuck out, horribly white.

The carcass was still warm. It had been killed only a few minutes before. Her stomach churned; she did not want to touch it; she had a superstitious dread of dead things. But she had to move it, before some other driver piled up his car because of it. Grasping the deer by one leg, she pulled and wrenched and hauled it over the pavement to the ditch.

A slimy red trail followed the carcass across the blacktop. She put her hand on her stomach. A shadow glided over her, and she startled, half-crouching. Raising her eyes, she watched the vulture soar slowly past, just above the trees, its curved wings like scimitars.

She went back to her car, wondering if that were the same little deer she had found in her camp that morning. A bad omen.

Right at the far edge of the bridge a dirt road passed under it, leading down to the river bar. She left the lime there, under the bridge where no one would see it from the road. Her arms hurt from dragging the heavy sacks. She got back into the car. Her hands were shaking. Her mind kept slipping back to the deer sprawled over the road, and the red gaping pit the carrion birds had torn in its side.

In a grim mood, she drove the car back up onto the road; she turned to the right, to go the long way back to River Ranch. She did not want to cross that smear of blood that lay the other way. She went around through the forest, past a little cluster of houses in a clearing a mile on, and then back to the south gate of River Ranch.

Just inside the gate, she drove up on Johan, walking along the road, and was glad for the chance to have company. She stopped the car.

"Want a ride?"

He came and got into the car. He wore his bib overalls without a shirt, and he was eating nuts and seeds from a Baggie. "Hello there, Sister Rose," he said. "Where you been?"

"Down to Springville," she said and drove on. Johan held out his Baggie to her. She shook her head. "I'm carnivorous."

He presented her with his smile. "You leaving the ranch?"

"Me? No, not quite yet. Why?"

"Well, you weren't at our meeting."

She said, "Unh." They were coming up to his house now, and she pulled the car over on the grass by his fence and stopped. Johan made no move to get out.

She said, "Look, Johan, I am not into this. I feel like being by myself for a while. The meetings and common work and telling everybody else in the kingdom what to do, that I can't handle. Sorry."

He put sunflower seeds in his mouth and chewed, looking thoughtful. Impatiently she wondered if she would have to ask him to get out of the car.

Finally he swallowed the seeds; he said, "That's what a community is for, Sister Rose, isn't it? To help each other out."

"Maybe."

"You don't want to work in our field." He nodded at her, his face childlike and grave. "I can accept that. I'm not trying to make you do anything. I want you to be part of us, that's all." His fingers digging into the pouch of nuts, he smiled at her, looking very young. "We need good people like you, Sister Rose."

"How old are you?" she asked.

"Twenty-three," he said.

That explained his monolithic certainty. She said, "What kind of community are you looking for, Johan?"

"I'm not looking for one, Sister Rose. It isn't even here yet. But it will be. We are going to build it, Sister Rose, you and I and everybody else."

As he spoke, his dark intense eyes burned. Rose turned

sideways in the driver's seat, her arm across the back. "I have the feeling you can't plan communities. They grow from some other source than the human intellect."

"Like the Mormons, Sister Rose?" he said.

Obviously he had all his arguments ready. She grunted, amused, beginning to enjoy the clash. "I was thinking of Brook Farm. Jonestown. Things like that. You're right about the Mormons, but historically speaking utopias have a depressing track record."

"I don't believe in history, Sister Rose," he said.

She smiled at him. She had majored in history. "That's rather like not believing in the law of gravity, right? You may disagree with the explanation, but you're still going to fall."

He said serenely, "Well, we'll see who's right."

"I hope you make me wrong. I—" She stopped, her ear catching a sound she realized now she had been hearing off and on for a long time: a chain saw. She sat up straight. "At the meeting, what did you decide? About Coyote and his trees."

Johan blinked once, his mouth losing its accustomed good-natured curve. "We voted that he can't cut the trees."

"But he's doing it," Rose said.

"Yes."

"Good for him."

"I don't think so," he said, and for the first time she thought he might be getting angry. "When I bought my place, those trees were here, part of my idea of what River Ranch is, and if they're cut, even if I never see the stumps, River Ranch will be less than what I want it to be."

Rose turned forward in the driver's seat. "I'm leaving, Johan. Hop out."

He did not move, his gaze on her; abruptly he gave a little shake of his head. He reached out and slapped her soundly on the knee. "I want you with us," he said, opening the car door. "I'm not giving up on you, Sister Rose." Sliding out of the car, he slammed the door shut and thumped the roof of the car, adding more emphasis. He walked away to his house.

Rose drove up the hill to the ranch house. She decided she liked Johan. She remembered the slap on her knee. Billy Vigg, touching her on the leg had put her on the high boil; Johan's touch meant something entirely different, giving instead of taking. Amazing how much in human relationships went on below the influence of reason. That alone condemned utopias; they were reasonable, but life was not. Yet Johan radiated like a lighthouse with the vitality of his idea.

Peter was not home. The horse had gone as well. She left her car parked beside the house and walked back through the forest to her camp.

She finished the biology book late in the afternoon and reached blindly into the sack of books for another. Her fingers closed on a paperback. She pulled out *Mansfield Park* by Jane Austen. She had read it once, long ago, and not liked it; she was tempted to throw it back. She had begun taking the books by chance, though: better to stick with the plan. She settled down to read it.

Slowly the light faded. She kept reading, falling deeper and deeper into the world of the book. When she began to have trouble making out the print, she got up and built a fire, but she did not cook a meal. She lay down in the firelight and read.

The situation of the book delighted her. She had always loved ugly ducklings, and the book was about the triumph of a plain, honest woman over a brilliant but superficial beauty. What fascinated her more was the moral structure that gave the story its deeper resonance. Most of the characters could not see beyond themselves; it was Austen's craft to make their self-centeredness attractive at first, with the prettiness of high spirits. In the process, she made the hero into an impossible prig; Rose could not bear him. And it irritated her that the heroine, Fanny Price, should love him. Fanny, the little samurai whose moral vigor got much of its power by contrast to her physical feebleness—unable even to canter her horse!

She stopped reading only long enough to put wood on the fire. Late that night she finished the novel. She lay in her sleeping bag, thinking about *Mansfield Park*. Those people would have loathed her, a woman like her, smoking dope, living unmarried with a man, mouthing off whenever possible.

The fire settled and cooled. She snuggled down into the sleeping bag, drowsy. One hundred and fifty years lay between her and Fanny Price. She yawned, contented. Suddenly it occurred to her that for hours and hours she had not thought of Mike Morgan once, not even now when she had thought of their long relationship. Warm with that triumph, she went to sleep.

In the morning the horse was there, in the meadow, and she walked him along the river, where the shrinking stream was leaving long stretches of the gravel bar exposed, down toward the bridge to get the sacks of lime. The sun had just come up. The air was still sharp from the night's chill. Over the calm water where the river was widest, swarms of small insects hovered, moving slowly over the water. Under the furious whirling cloud, fish jumped, feeding on them, and in the air above them, half a dozen birds wheeled and dove and circled.

She heaved the sacks up on the saddle and led the horse back across the river and over to the crag. While she was trying to haul the lime up the cliff, her rope broke.

She rode back up to Peter's to get another. Once again, Peter was not there, but Patty was sitting on the front porch railing, eating ice cream from a quart container with a spoon.

"Hi," Patty said. "Come to see the circus?"

"Actually I'm looking for a rope. What circus?"

Patty smirked. Ice cream whitened her upper lip. "Hallie's chained herself to one of Coyote's trees."

"Goddamn," Rose said. She turned to stare off across the valley; the eucalyptus grove blocked her view of Jim Wylie's homestead. She swung back to Patty again. "Why?"

"She's crazy," Patty said, around a mouthful of ice cream. "Like everybody else around here."

The chain saw started up, across the valley. Rose swiveled in that direction again. She was eager to go back to the river, to work in her field; yet the idea of Hal fastened to a tree, a burlap dryad, drew her irresistibly. She wheeled the old horse around and clapped her heels into him.

At a canter he took her down the road past the rhinoceros and turned out over the meadow, going straight toward the sound of the chain saw. The hillside turned steep. Sheep trails threaded back and forth over it. The horse slowed to a walk picking his way downhill at the slant.

They skirted the eucalyptus grove; the wind lifted the trailing leaves like streamers. The pungent smell reached her. Ahead the slope flattened out into the upper part of the valley. A stand of redwoods covered this side of it; for a while, coming down the hill, she could see Coyote's teepee, beyond the trees.

The chain saw's howl came from these trees. As she rode up to the edge of the redwoods, the saw stopped. Cautious, Rose drew rein. On the far side of the grove there was a ripping, splintering crash. A tree falling. She urged the horse in among the redwoods.

The trees were very close together, and it took her and the horse a while to find a way through them. The saw started up again. Its high scream tightened all Rose's muscles; she wondered how Wylie could bear listening to it all day long. The note suddenly fell a couple of octaves. The blade was meeting wood.

Ahead of her, through the trees, she saw a patch of red. She steered the horse toward it and came out onto the edge of the meadow where the teepee was. The last tree between the woods and the meadow was a giant, twice as big around as the others. To this tree, Hal was attached by several lengths of chain wrapped around her waist and the tree trunk.

The patch of bright color Rose had been following was Peter's red jacket. He was sitting on the ground next to Hal, smoking a joint.

Rose stopped the horse. She looked toward the sound of the chain saw, now deafeningly close; Coyote was just a hundred feet away, his long body braced against the three-foot blade in his hands, slicing into the trunk of another tree.

Rose dismounted. On foot she went up to the tree where Hal was chained. "What's happening?" she said.

Hal lifted her moon-shaped face toward her. "He's not cutting this tree," she replied.

Startled, Rose saw the stains of tears on Hal's cheeks. She sank down on her heels beside her brother, who handed her the joint.

"How long are you staying here?" Rose asked Hal.

"Until he promises not to cut this tree."

"Oh, Hallie."

Peter said, "You know, some very bad things get started because people put themselves into positions they can't back out of." He glanced over his shoulder at Rose. "Right?"

"Sure," Rose said.

She held out the joint to Hal, whose arms were free of the chain, but the goat woman shook her head. "No, I don't smoke dope."

Rose put the joint to her lips. Beyond this tree, the meadow invaded the wood, and the sun shone down. Past the sunlit stretch of grass the trees grew up again, and there Coyote was standing, his back to Hal and her redwood. He pulled his saw out of the tree and went around to the other side to cut. The chain saw shrieked.

"You're going to stay here all day long listening to that?" Rose asked.

Hal said, "Yes." She spread her arms out, her palms turned to press against the bark.

Rose handed the joint to her brother. She had come prepared to find this funny, but now some sympathy toward Hal moved in her, a feeling old and unused for a long time. She envied Hal's courage. Risking ridicule, Hal put herself beyond it somehow. Or maybe the tree gave her some of its power.

"God," Hal said, even as Rose thought this, "you know, I wish I were a tree."

"If you had to be a tree," Peter said, "it'd be good to be a redwood."

Rose turned her gaze on the tree, straight and solid, its bark riven into great red plates like scales. Unlike most trees, the redwoods did not waste their substance too much on branches. They went straight up, putting everything into the climb for the sky, their thrust so intense that they always seemed to be moving upward, bringing the earth after in their clutch of roots.

Rose said, "Hallie, can I get you something? Something to drink?"

Hallie shook her head. "Peter brought me a thermos." She laid her dreamy smile on Peter for this benevolence.

"I'm going," Rose said, "if you don't need anything I can do for you."

Hal said, "Thanks for coming, Rose."

Rose did not move. She thought of the sacks of lime, of the crag and the pot seeds she had to plant today. Before her, this woman leaned against the tree, part of its course, her face soft and vaguely disfocused, as if her human consciousness yielded to some tree-ish way of being.

"Good-by," Rose said.

Nobody answered, as if she were already gone. She went back to the horse and rode away through the woods.

She worked all morning. The sun grew hot and strong. From the height of the crag she could see down the river, where a strange car had driven out onto the riverbank; half a dozen people lay on the river bar or frisked and swam in the water. A dog bounded back and forth after sticks thrown for it to retrieve. The sounds of this gathering, fragments of voices, reached her sometimes, when the wind turned a little. She dug the lime into the turned earth of her field, whitening the soil.

At noon she stopped to smoke a joint, and while she smoked it, she shook the Baggie of seeds out onto a piece of paper and used a matchbook cover to winnow through them, shaking out the last bits of leaf and twig. The seeds were dark and fat; they looked potent.

She made furrows with a stick and dropped the seeds in, an inch or two apart, smoothing the soft, crumbling dirt over with her foot. There was water in the little spring at the foot of the field, but she had no bucket. She tried for a while to carry water in the empty lime sack but the paper soaked through and fell apart. So she went down again, caught the horse by the creek, and rode back to her camp, circling through the woods to avoid the swimmers. She left the horse in the meadow to graze and took the bucket back up to her field.

By midafternoon she had planted and watered every seed. The long, soft mounds of the furrows reached from one end of the field to the other, taking up all the space. She gathered the dead grass she had pulled up when she cleared the meadow and spread it over the field, to help keep the water in the ground; the sun was so hot she had to take her clothes off again. She sat down at the lip of the crag, her legs hanging off the edge, and smoked another joint.

The swimmers had gone. The wind was rising and the trees swayed and boomed in its currents. It still amazed her how many different sounds the trees made: she sat trying to separate them with her ears. The colors, too, were far more various than they seemed at first, every green a shade different. The bark of the redwood by the creek was brown in the shadow but rust, almost dark orange, in the sun. Perhaps the pot made her see all this. She drew one knee up to her chest. The touch of skin on skin surprised her. She had forgotten she was naked. At that, something came together in her mind; she felt herself back on her axis again, at the still center around which everything whirled.

In the afternoon she rode back to Peter's house; this time she went around, to come in through the south gate and pass by the field in the flat where the community marijuana was growing. She had some trouble finding it; they had laid out the field in a long strip behind a stand of redwoods, across the creek. A fence of green poles and branches surrounded it. She rode up to it and stood in her stirrups to see over the fence.

There were people working, Glory Vigg stooped over, another woman hoeing the ground on the far side of the field, and a few children. They were weeding down the long rows of young plants. Their plants were already nearly a foot high, their stems dividing at the top into two sets of many-fingered leaves; near the ground the trunks already looked a little woody. Her plants were going to be runts.

Glory straightened suddenly, palming her long yellow hair back off her face. Her nose was bright pink from the sun. Her free hand on her hip, she glared at Rose. Hastily Rose reined the white horse away from the fence and cantered back to the road.

She went up between two corn fields toward the redwood grove, where now suddenly the chain saw began to screech again. When she rode through the trees where Hal was, she found a crowd there, getting ready to remove the goat woman by force.

"No," Hal cried; she sounded exhausted, and she clung to the tree like a child to its mother, with both arms. "No, don't take me away." Leaves clung to her hair, roughened and snarled from the constant contact with the bark.

Peter had his chain cutters in his hands. He said, "Hal, you got to use some sense."

Rose glanced around her at the other people watching this. Johan was there in his bib overalls, and Dave Preston, and two or three others from the flat. She turned her attention again to her brother, who was now trying to get the blade of the chain cutter between the chain and the tree, while Hal hauled on the chain with both hands, to keep it taut. Rose slipped down from the horse.

"Peter," she said. "What are you doing?" She went up to him and grabbed his arm. "What are you doing? Let her do what she wants."

"Rose," Peter said, "she's an idiot. She can't do this too much longer."

"She has to go milk her goats," called a girl in the crowd.

Dave Preston stepped forward. His black hair curled around his ears, and the ends of his mustache and his full black beard curled, too. He looked like Billy Vigg. She wondered if they were really only half-brothers or if David Vigg were a poisoned identity.

"This is just an ego trip for her," Preston said, half-shouting; the chain saw had broken in on them again, its dry whine coming from the trees just past them. Preston marched forward another few strides, putting himself between the crowd and Rose.

"She's just on an ego trip," he said again, angry, or perhaps his shouting voice just made him seem angry. "She's not doing anything productive. Pretty soon she'll have to leave, and then he'll cut the tree. For Christ's sake—" He thrust his arm at Hal like a weapon, like a blow across the air at her. "How long's it been since the broad took a crap?"

Rose let out her breath in a snort; she put her hands on her hips. "So? If she's got to quit pretty soon, why not let her do it herself?"

Under the wiry, vigorous mustache Preston's lip curled. "You hill-toppers, you all stick together."

"That's the second time you've said that," Rose said.

Johan came forward, rubbing his hands up and down his bare arms. "Sister Rose, she's not accomplishing anything. She is being unrealistic."

"So what?" Rose replied. She licked her lips, struggling with her feelings, all tangled in her mind; she caught Peter's eye as he stood there with the chain cutters in his hands.

Peter said, "All in favor say Aye." The screech of the chain saw fifteen yards away stopped halfway through his speech, so that "say Aye" rang like a bell through the silence.

"Aye," Preston shouted, and others echoed him in a chorus. Johan said nothing. He was watching Rose, his brown forehead corrugated with thought. She put out her hand to him.

"Say I," she said. "That's what she's doing, Johan; she's saying I. I. Are you with me? Please, Johan."

He stared at her a moment. She wondered if he understood and searched for another way to say it. But then he turned to Peter and said, "Maybe we should talk through this again, Mister Pete."

Grateful, Rose patted his bare arm, turned, and at a jog trot went off through the trees in the direction of the saw.

Downed trees lay across her path; she climbed over a red-scaled trunk and swerved to go around the next, whose topknot of branches hung in bridal arches four feet above her head. The sun poured in through the gaps in the forest roof and filled the woods with a glaring light. Coming on a tree that had already been limbed, she struggled up over the fat trunk and slid down the other side, landing almost on top of Jim Wylie, who was kneeling over his chain saw and pouring gas into the tank from a red coffee can.

Rose stopped, out of breath. Wylie looked up. He was filthy from the work and sweating, naked above the waist, his muscular chest and shoulders coated with the dust and dirt.

"What's happening?" he asked.

Rose looked around her; she could see at least three more downed trees lying among the standing redwoods on crushed mats of fern. "You do good work," she said. "It must be hard to keep them from hitting the other trees."

"It takes a little thinking," he said. "What's—" He nodded toward Hal.

"They're trying to take her off bodily. Look, do you have to cut that particular tree?"

He smiled at her. His eyes looked bluer for the redwood

dust that powdered his lashes and eyebrows. "That tree's worth a lot of money."

"Can't you cut another?"

"That's the biggest one. Besides, there's good young trees around it. If I cut it, they'll grow much faster." He folded his arms over his chest.

"Preston's over there getting ready to drag her off," Rose said. "Preston and my brother."

"She's got to go sometime."

"Why not let her have what she wants," Rose asked, "if somehow you can get what you want, too?" She thumped him on the chest with her fist. "Come on, Jim. Us hill-toppers got to stick together."

His smile broadened, crinkling the skin at the corners of his eyes. She clasped her hands in front of her. He nodded at her. "Okay, lady. I got three more trees to cut. I'll give her two if she lets me take that one. The other two are small anyway. I'll get 'em in a couple years."

"Come on," Rose said. She started back toward Hallie's tree, breaking into a lope; she stopped to scramble up over a fallen tree.

Jim Wylie followed her more slowly. By the time she reached the little mob beside Hallie, he was far behind her. Preston and Peter were trying to get the chain cutters on the chain, or rather Peter was trying and Preston was standing there, shouting, "Do it! Just fuckin' do it!" his face red and his hands fisted.

Rose trotted up to them. The other people were gathered in a knot, listening to Johan, who suddenly walked halfway to Peter and called, "We are leaving. You're making a mistake doing this." At once he marched off, taking the others with him in his train.

Rose went up to Hallie and bent to whisper to her. "Coyote has a deal for you."

Hal was clutching the chain in both hands, pulling it tight against the tree so that Peter could not fit his chain cutters around it; she raised her head, her expression abstract, all her effort bent on keeping the chain taut. She said nothing.

"He has three more trees to cut. He'll give you the other two. This one is the best one."

Hal blinked at her. "The best."

"But the others are younger and smaller."

"Two of them?"

"I've got it," Peter said.

"Peter," Rose cried, "if you cut that chain, I'll break your fucking neck."

Preston roared, "Stay out of this!"

Peter stepped back from the tree and glared at Preston. "Don't you talk to my sister like that, motherfucker."

Coyote walked up among them, his arms swinging at his sides, and looked at Peter, but did not look at Preston. He went by them all to Hallie.

"God, lady," he said, "you're crazy. Beautiful but crazy. Come on, we'll call it even." He put out his hand to her.

Hal smiled at him, her face soft with exhaustion, and took his hand. "You're beautiful, too," she said in a little voice. She raised her other arm, and he bent and hugged her.

Rose stepped back, caught in a sudden rush of feeling. She looked down at the ground. They unchained Hal from her tree. Preston said loudly, "Now all this fuss for nothing. What a waste of time."

Peter stood coiling up the chain, a heavy, flat-linked length, still shiny and new. He would not meet Rose's eyes.

"What's the matter with you?" Rose asked him.

"You keep jumping down my throat that I'm losing it," he said under his breath, "and then when I do something, you come along and cross me up."

"Peter, come on."

Hal was getting to her feet. "It was beautiful," she said. Her voice quavered. "All day long, with the tree—I just felt such things with the tree—"

Peter said to Rose, "I thought all these hassles up here were getting you down. Why don't you do what you said you wanted and stay away from us?" He slung the coil of chain over his shoulder. With a pointed look at Rose he began to walk away.

Preston said sharply, "Who's that?" and pointed.

Everyone turned to see. Even Hallie paused, midway through her monologue. At the edge of the trees, where the sunlight began, a man was standing in the shadows, his hands in his pockets.

Rose walked three or four steps toward him, recognized him, and stopped. "God, what are you doing here? I didn't expect you for another week. Where's Reina?"

"I wanted to be sure that I was in the right place before I drove in through that gate," said Miller Tarn. He nodded behind him. "Reina's in the car."

"I have to go milk my goats," Hal said and started slowly away through the trees. As she passed each tree, she put out her hand to touch it.

Rose turned, looking for Peter, and said to him, "This is the guy I told you about, who's bringing that girl I told you about, you know?"

Peter grimaced, his shoulders hunched up, and gave her another needle of a look. "For a writer you have wonderful powers of self-expression." He turned to Preston. "Come on up and shoot a game of pool."

"She's worse'n a wife," Preston said, falling in beside him. They marched away through the trees.

Rose's temper nudged her; what Peter had said made her uncomfortable, because she saw that it was true. Another the in the garbage. Behind her, Jim Wylie said, "I think I'll cut this tree tomorrow."

She faced him. "Thanks."

"I'm getting tired of cutting trees," he said; he was going away, too, his lean back mottled with peeling sunburned skin.

Rose walked over to the tree, where the old horse was standing with its reins trailing, and led him back toward Miller Tarn. "Welcome to River Ranch."

"What's going on?"

"It would take me a year to tell you. Let's go liberate Reina."

They started into the meadow, leading the horse. Rose cast a cautious sideways look at the man walking beside her. He was wearing blue tennis shorts; under his T-shirt his stomach bulged out in a soft mound. He was taller than she remembered. His hair was short and wiry, exposing his neck above the round collarless neck of the shirt.

"Have a good trip?" she said. She remembered not liking him, the last time they had met; but he was still a stranger to her.

"It was okay," he said, his head down, his eyes lowered, talking to the grass.

"Where'd you spend the night?"

"I drove straight through."

She had driven the trip in one day, but it surprised her that someone else had. They crossed the meadow toward the gate, passing the teepee on the left; Coyote was there chopping wood for his fire. The tall grass hissed past her legs. She looped the reins up over the saddle horn and let the horse walk along between them.

At the gate his old white VW was pulled off into the weeds by the fence. Even before they reached it, the door popped open, and Reina slid out.

"Is that the horse?" She raised her arms a little, her eyes fastened on the horse, but came no closer. Rose and Miller walked up to her.

"Yeah, I guess he's a horse."

"Oh." Reina laid her palms against his neck. "Oh. He's beautiful."

The horse's nostrils expanded in an almost soundless sigh. His ears drooped; he was tired.

"The house is right the top of the hill," Rose said. Now she began to see some difficulty in this; she chewed on her lip, her gaze meditatively following the upward curve of the road to the eucalyptus grove. "Here," she said to Reina, holding out the reins. "You ride up there and we'll meet you."

Reina flung her arms around the horse's neck. Quickly,

as if Rose might change her mind, she threw the reins over the animal's head and climbed up into the saddle, her legs dangling down above the stirrups, and pulled on the left rein. The horse turned his head, but his body remained in place.

"Go," Reina cried. "Go."

"Kick him," Rose said.

Reina slapped her heels tentatively against the horse's sides.

"Harder."

She kicked harder, and the horse groaned and moved slowly away up the road. Rose laughed.

"Come on," she said to Miller. "Drive up there." She got into his car.

It smelled strongly of marijuana smoke. Empty Coke cans littered the floor in front of the passenger seat, and there was half a Snickers bar stuck to the dashboard. Miller slid behind the wheel.

"At that rate she's never gonna make it." He started the car.

"Go on. She'll get there."

He drove through the gate and onto the road. The horse was trudging along the side of the road, his head down and every stride deliberate, as if it took a separate act of will every time he lifted a hoof. Reina was kicking him now with every step. Rose leaned back in the seat.

"We got a small problem."

"Oh, yeah?"

"Nothing insurmountable. My brother's pissed off at me."

"Meaning what?"

"Meaning I don't know. It's nothing serious, as I said, but don't be surprised if he starts shouting at me and he orders everybody off." She shook her head, thinking about that. She did not want these people down in the woods by her camp, by her pot field.

Miller drove past Reina and gunned the car up the hill. The VW engine roared; the rough road shook a thousand rattles out of the body and the frame. A rock spun out from beneath a wheel and whacked the floor under Rose's foot. She bounced halfway out of the seat and grabbed the sissy bar.

"Where else is there to stay?" Miller said.

"Naw, it's okay," she said. "He has lots of room. He'll just fuss a little." She hoped.

They roared past the eucalyptus tree and onto the bench. Rose put her head back. It would not do to seem too concerned about having them near her camp.

"Did Reina's mother tell you I'd like to hang around up here awhile? I mean, it's a long drive back," Miller said.

"Yeah, sure," she said. "Angie said something about that."

"I'll pay for my food and help out and all that."

"It's fine with me if it's okay with my brother."

"Thanks," he said.

They pulled up in front of the house. The head was off the rhinoceros, which, lacking the weight in front, was sitting back on its tail. The grass bent under the incoming sunset wind.

Rose got out of the car. Far down the road, now, Reina was just passing the eucalyptus trees. The horse was trotting. The girl straddled his back as stiffly as a piece of wood, bouncing with each stride, one hand clutching the saddle horn and the other holding the reins up awkwardly in the air. As she came closer, Rose could see her face, rapt in furious concentration, her lips between her teeth.

The horse shied at the headless rhinoceros. Reina squealed; she fell off.

Rose laughed, seeing herself at that age, remembering that she'd felt the same way about horses, and her heart lifted suddenly. This would be fun. Miller was hurrying over to help Reina onto her feet, but the girl thrust him off.

"I can do it!"

Rose walked up the steps to the house. She wiped her feet on the mat before the door and walked into the front room.

At the end near the windows, Peter was shooting pool

with Billy Vigg and Dave Preston. Rose went down toward him, wondering how to manage this. She paused by the sideboard, where a line of empty beer cans marched over the scarred wood.

Peter was chalking up his cue. Billy Vigg stooped to line up a long, easy shot to the side pocket. Screwing the blue cube down over the end of his cue stick, Peter scowled across the table at Rose.

"Now you want something, hunh? Now you want me to do something for y'."

"Well, sort of," she said. "Can these people stay the night here?"

"No!"

"Look, I'm sorry," she said. "You know I'm very managing."

"You're just like Mom."

"Come on, Peter. Don't get nasty."

Billy Vigg shot a look at her; he was still bent over the table to shoot, and all she saw was the gleam of his eyes under his black eyebrows. Dave Preston was watching her from the corner by the windows. Suddenly the front door banged open and Miller came in with Reina.

"Look, Peter," Rose said. "They drove all the way up here from L.A.—"

"Hell, no," Peter cried. "Take 'em down to your place! I'm not your puppy dog, woman. I don't do whatever you say." He cast a look around him, at the brothers, gathering support; Dave Preston grunted loudly in agreement. Billy Vigg stooped lower over his cue slide, one arm extended down to the green felt.

Miller said, "What's the matter? Is there a hassle?"

"Take 'em with you," Peter said and waved his hand at her.

"Miller Tarn and Reina Darrezzo," Rose said. "This is my brother, Peter McKenna, who is really a very nice guy when he isn't trying to prove something."

"Take 'em with you! What d'you think I am, a babysitter? You invited 'em up here!"

Miller turned to her. "Where do you live?"

"I been camping out down by the river," she answered. "It's a long walk. Peter, come on. They just drove for twelve hours straight—"

"I don't mind walking," Miller said. "Come on."

"Can I ride the horse?" Reina jumped up and down in place, her hair flying.

"Sure," Rose said.

"Whoopee!" She flew out the door again, clapping her hands. Miller went after her as far as the door, stopped and looked back toward Rose. She gave up. With a shrug she followed him outside onto the porch.

"He'll forget about being mad by tomorrow," she said.

"If he doesn't want us here—"

"No, no," she said, "he's just pissed off at me, that's all. He'll like you tomorrow. He likes everybody, Peter does." She started down the front steps. "Come on, we got a long way to go, and the light won't hold."

Miller's car was stuffed full of baggage. They loaded sleeping bags and jackets on the horse, behind the saddle, and tied it all fast with rope. Reina rode the horse, and they started down the trail behind the house. At first Miller walked behind the horse and Rose in front, but he had a long stride and the path was clear. Before they had reached the fork in the path, he was out in front by ten feet. The horse followed on Rose's heels.

Ahead of her Miller stopped. "Where to?" He had reached the split in the trail.

To the left ran the path that would lead them eventually to her crag. She said, "Go right."

They turned right. The horse tried to go left, but she pulled him along by the reins.

The light was failing, and the trail here was very faint. She had come by this path only once before and from the other end, and she began to worry about losing the way. Miller was walking with much shorter steps than before; he slowed until he was walking just behind her, there being no room on the path for two people side by side.

"Is this all your place?"

"I don't know whose place it is," she said. "The owner-
ship arrangements up here are arcane." The ground squished
under her feet. She swerved around the edge of a swampy,
open meadow. Out across the clearing, bats swooped and
dove through the deep twilight. There were no stars yet,
only Venus like a pinprick through to the empyrean. "I
think my brother still owns the whole shebang, on paper,
thirty-four hundred acres, thirty-six hundred acres—"

"He owns it?" Miller said. "That much?"

"Yes, it's all Peter's, fur, feathers, and all. Then the rest
of us have rights, all sorts of legal bullshit, one list of rights
for the whole ranch, another list of rights for the particular
property we each own. Oh, it's very complicated. My brother
loves grand designs." She stopped, unsure where she was. The
open meadow lay behind them and under the trees the
gloom seemed almost palpable, like a wall. "I think I am
lost," Rose said.

"Shit," Miller said. "You told me you knew where you
were going."

"I do." She looked up overhead. Beyond the black leaves
and branches of the trees a patch of sky showed, still pale
with the last feeble sunlight. Here under the trees she could
not see much past arm's length. She peered back behind
them, trying to orient herself by the meadow. The horse
nudged her with his head.

"Do you know where you're going or not?" Miller said.

"What's the matter?" Reina asked. "Are we lost? Oh!"
She ducked down, flattening her body to the horse; a bat
shrilled in the darkness.

"It's nighttime," Rose said. "I know where I'm going.
I just don't want to get lost on the way there."

"I shoulda known better than to go out in the woods with
a woman," Miller Tarn said, a fine note of sarcasm in his
voice.

"Look," Rose said angrily, "I know where I'm going.
I—"

"Oh, yeah? Then why aren't we moving?"

"I just—"

The horse put his head against her back and shoved her forward a step, and with her mouth open to protest again she realized, with a relief that took all the tension off, that the horse would lead them home. "Come on," she said. She took hold of the bridle, moved to one side, and clicked her tongue, and the horse stepped off at a brisk walk into the darkness.

"You know what you're doing?" Miller asked from behind her.

"Seldom if ever," she said, one hand on the bridle.

"Are we lost?" Reina asked. "God, it's so dark. Don't you have a flashlight?"

"Relax," Rose said. "There's a better trail up ahead."

"I'm hungry."

"When we get to my camp, I'll make something for dinner."

The darkness now seemed to be closing over them, the sky disappearing into the omnivorous shadow. Rose put one hand out in front of her to ward off branches. Her feet banged roots on the path. The horse slowed once, and she clicked her tongue and he picked up his long, swinging stride again. She had to smile at that; usually he walked as slowly as possible. Now that he was going home, she could barely keep up with him.

"I'm hungry," Reina said in a cranky, young voice.

"Here," Miller said.

Rose glanced over her shoulder; he was poking around in the jackets packed on the horse behind the saddle. "Don't knock everything loose."

"Just get us wherever it is we're going," Miller said, "and don't worry about anything else." He took something from his jacket and handed it up to Reina.

"I told you, I don't like—"

"Eat it anyway."

Abruptly the trail dropped off in a steep bank. The horse

stopped, but Rose missed her footing and fell. She let go of the bridle and flung her arms out into the darkness, hit the ground where it slanted down away from her, and rolled. There would be water at the bottom of this—she scrabbled with her hands and feet to stop her downward slide and came up hard against a stump.

"Hey," Miller called, above her head. "You all right?"

"Yeah." She got up, one ankle throbbing and her side sore from the rough contact with the stump. "I think the trail goes to the right up there. See what the horse thinks." She put her hand up, groping over the top of the bank above her head, and suddenly felt her wrist grasped hard. He pulled her up onto the bank as easily as if she were a child. She was glad of the dark, to hide her embarrassment; gracelessly she muttered, "Thanks."

"Going places at night with you is a real thrill," he said. "I remember that from the last time." He turned and smacked the horse on the rump, and the horse started off along the side of the ravine, to the right.

"Hey," Reina cried. "Hey, where's he taking me?"

Huge and white, the horse moved through the woods like a ghost. Rose followed him at a trot. The waning moon was shining brighter now, and ahead the trail widened into an old logging road.

The horse stopped. She caught up with him and patted his neck and took hold of the bridle again.

Miller came up beside her, where the wider road allowed it, and took a joint from the pocket of his T-shirt. He lit it and handed it to her.

"Not bad," Rose said. She toked deeply on the joint and held it out to him. "You remember that other time, back in Pasadena, well, I had nothing to do with that. I don't know what you think was going on."

He shrugged, taking the joint back; their fingertips brushed together. "Forget it." The joint was burning faster along one side than the other, and he spat on his finger and wet the paper to slow down the run.

"I'm still hungry," Reina called.

"We're almost there." Rose pointed ahead of them, where the road reached the meadow. "See, there, ahead, where the trees stop? That's the clearing where my camp is. The river's just over the horizon."

"What river?" Miller asked.

"The Eel River."

"Are there eels in it?"

"I guess so. I've never seen one. There's plenty of fish."

They walked out of the woods onto the meadow, and the wind came and blew the grass down ahead of them in silvery sweeps through the moonlight. The road led over the rolling height of the meadow.

"Christ," Rose said under her breath. Her eyes searched the low ground ahead of them for her campsite; it was gone. Long streamers of paper lay twisted and rucked in the grass and over the low brush by the river. "Somebody's trashed my camp." She ran off through the grass toward the riverbank where her camp had been.

The lean-to was scattered all over the river bar. Her blankets were gone and her camp goods strewn around, pots and pans, cans of food, firewood, and over everything, in streamers and loops and fluttering white bows, an unrolled roll of toilet paper.

"You know," Miller said, "you're a pretty bad house-keeper."

"Shut up," Rose said. She walked off in a widening circle around the camp, moving fast, her gaze sweeping the ground on either side. Most of her belongings seemed to be here, scattered everywhere. Something white caught her eye. With a yell she pounced on her pillowcase of books lying in the grass.

"What happened?" Reina asked her. "Was it a raccoon or something?"

"No," Rose snapped. Reina looked worried, tired, and unhappy; Rose put her arm around the girl's shoulders. "It's all right. Just a gag. Here, he's been particularly lazy about the firewood; it's still all real close to the camp. Let's get a fire going. Oh, he took the labels off all the cans. Isn't he funny?"

While she was making the fire, Miller squatted down on his heels beside her. "You know who did your place in? What the hell is going on here? Why did you have that girl chained up to a tree?"

Rose laughed, beguiled by his version of it. "Well," she said, "we were going to sacrifice her to the spirit of the wood, but he turned out to be a vegetarian."

"You're never going to get this fire going. Let me do it."

"Oh no. I'll do it." She stooped down and struck a match and held it to the shavings in the middle of the fire. "Actually, Hal chained herself to the tree. The man who owns that piece was cutting his timber and she didn't want him to." The shavings caught a tiny flame. She fed it bits and chips of wood.

"Jesus, what an asshole," Miller said.

"Who, Hal? Actually it was quite an interesting thing, very moving, I like people who do what they believe. Are you a lucky person?"

"Right now I'm an extremely hungry person."

"Good. Let that guide you. There's cans all over the place. Go pick out three or four. The big cans are probably meat and the little ones are fruit and vegetables."

"I'll keep opening them until I find something good," Miller said, walking away into the darkness.

Rose built the fire. Reina huddled by it, her jacket buttoned up to the collar. "I'm so cold. When are we gonna eat?"

"It's not that cold," Rose said, surprised. "Of course you've been down there in the tropics. How's your mom?"

"Okay, I guess."

"She ever see Felice now?"

"Unh-unh."

"How was school?"

"Aw, school sucks. I hate school."

Miller shouted, "Hey, instead of sitting around over there, what about digging up some pots? I got ravioli and a chicken."

Rose got up and cruised off through the grass where she had seen some of her cooking things scattered. She stepped on an aluminum lid, bent in half. Picking it up, she held it in her hand a moment and dropped it again. Preston probably hadn't done this; she could not see where he had had the time, for one thing. Somebody else, some kid. The Viggs had lots of kids.

"Hey," Miller yelled.

She found a pot and a frying pan, two spoons, the coffee-pot, and several cups and took them back to the campfire, now burning warmly and brightly enough that Reina was unbuttoning her coat; she held out her hands to the blaze and smiled. Rose emptied the can of ravioli into the frying pan and the chicken into the pot and pushed them around on the fire until she had each one cooking.

They ate; afterward Rose found a box and went around the meadow picking up her goods and lugging them back to the camp. Miller helped Reina lay out her sleeping bag. The girl crawled into it, complained bitterly about the hard ground, and was asleep in minutes.

"You know, this is not bad," Miller said. He sat down by the fire, wearing his jacket, and took another joint out of his shirt. "This morning in L.A. it was a hundred and ten and the smog was incredible." He took a twig out of the fire to light his joint.

"So far the weather's been pretty good," she said.

"I keep waiting for you to explain to me what's going on here."

Rose shrugged. She was avoiding looking at him; her mind kept slipping back to the moment on the trail coming here when he had taken her by the wrist and pulled her up the bank.

"Well, I don't exactly know how to tell it. Some of these people have a huge plot of marijuana they're growing, and they're very paranoid about it, possibly with reason, since some of them are a little, I don't know—" She scratched her nose. "Flaky."

"So why does somebody wreck your camp? You aren't growing any pot, are you?"

"No," she said smoothly and hurried his attention on. "They don't like me. They've got my brother pretty much over a barrel; he does whatever he's told, my brother, pretty much. I'm not into their games, and that pisses them off. Authoritarians. You know. It's all or nothing with the godhead."

"I thought you admire people who do what they believe in."

Rose grunted. "No generalization is wholly true, including this one. How long you planning to stay up here?"

"Why? You want me to leave?"

"No, it's fine with me; stay as long as you want. I was just curious. Most people can't just take off into the wilderness for indefinite periods of time. Don't you have a job or anything important like that down in L.A.?"

"Nothing's more important to me than Reina."

That startled her. Somehow she had expected him to avoid talking about Reina, as if he should be ashamed of his love. She thought about his hand on her wrist again and the effortless strength of his arm.

"There's a meteor." He pointed up toward the sky.

The moon had set; the sky was all stars. Rose put her elbows on her knees. "What's your sign?"

"Aquarius," he said and gave her a quick, oblique look. "You believe in that?"

"No," she said.

"Then why'd you ask?"

"Just curious. I'm a Capricorn."

"I thought you didn't believe in it."

"I don't. Do you?"

"No, for Christ's sake, it's a colossal piece of bullshit."

Rose laughed, remembering that he had wanted her to

believe; he was looking for a fight. She livened to it. It would help anyway to placate the sexual interest in him that she was struggling to ignore. "Well," she said, "Aquarians are supposed to be skeptical. What's your rising sign? I'll bet you have planets in Virgo."

"I thought you didn't believe in it."

"My ex–old man was big on astrology."

"Your ex–old man strikes me as a complete loser."

"He was an Aquarian," Rose said. "He came by it naturally."

"We go to the extremes," he said. "The complete losers and the epitomes of perfection, like me."

"God, your modesty proclaims you. I'm glad you warned me ahead of time, so I'll be prepared for the dazzle when it starts."

"Don't worry," he said. "I know how hard it is for ordinary people to accept perfection, so I make mistakes now and then, just so you won't feel bad." He was lighting another joint. Rose lay back on her side in the warmth of the fire.

"This is pretty good dope."

"Where's this pot these people are growing?"

"Back in the valley on the far side of the house. It's huge. They must have brought a tractor in to plow it. They must have tons."

He passed the joint to her; they smoked a while in silence. Rose was tired and began to think of sleep. She would get up early and go water her pot before anybody else awakened. She would have to be careful. Stoned and sleepy, she told herself that Miller Tarn seemed to be dangerously interested in the pot fields.

"Tarn. What kind of a name is that?"

"Tarananovitch," he said.

"Oh, yeah?"

"Yeah. That's why I shortened it. Miller is my grandfather's name." He laid the runt end of the joint down on a rock by the fire. "I think I'll go for a walk."

"Feel free," Rose said. "I'm going to bed."

"Good night," he said.

In the morning she left the camp before the others were awake and walked up the river bar to the creek that ran below her crag. She climbed the steep side of the hill, using the handholds now so familiar to her. The day before, she had used all the water in the pool around the spring. Slowly the spring was filling the pond up again, but there was still only about a bucket's worth; she left it to encourage more and hauled the water up from the creek. Under the layer of dry grass she had spread over the field the ground was still moist, and she needed only a little water to soak it down again.

When she returned to her camp, Reina and Miller were standing just beyond it in the meadow, putting the saddle on the horse. Rose went to the campfire, which was still cold and, kneeling, began to stack kindling in the center.

"Rose," Reina called, an exasperated whine edging her voice. "Come help me, please?"

Rose struck a match and set it to the chips and twigs tented up in the center of the fire ring. "What's wrong?"

Reina ran toward her, holding out a tangle of leather and metal in both hands. "How do I put this on?"

It was the bridle. Rose let the budding fire die. "Hold it like this." She took the crown piece of the bridle and lifted the tangle off Reina's hands; the weight of the bit dragged everything straight. Rose pulled the reins free. Walking up to the horse, she passed Miller, standing with his hands in his pockets.

"Back under your bushel again?"

"He doesn't know from nothing," Reina cried, scornful.

Rose slipped the bridle over the horse's head. "This horse will do anything he can to keep from moving around a lot. He's what you might call a real lazy horse. You just got to take him in hand. Get a stick and beat hell out of him until he does what you want."

"What's his name?" Reina put her arms around his neck and nuzzled his cheek. The horse groaned.

"Unh—I don't really know. He was here when Peter bought the place, and I don't know if Peter ever gave him a name."

"You going to make some breakfast?" Miller asked.

"Sure. I'll make pancakes." She went back to start over again on the fire.

She made pancakes twice: Miller Tarn ate one batch, and she and Reina ate the other. Reina rode the horse around the meadow, kicking and clucking to him, hitting him with sticks. Now and then he broke into a loose, un-connected trot, but most of the time he walked, as if he knew that Reina could not force him to do anything more taxing. Rose washed the dishes in the river, scrubbing off the sticky syrup with the fine black river sand. There were many more dishes, now that there were three people eating.

When she had done that, she settled down to her next book, a collection of philosophical essays that nearly put her to sleep. An idea for a story was coming to her, and she lay on the ground and drew doodles and made notes for the work on the endpapers and margins of the philosophy book.

Miller went around putting the camp back together, its wreckage being strewn from the road to the river. Rose ig-nored him. The story was coming to her in great snatches, whole sentences and pieces of action and character traits rushing up from the depths faster than she could note them down.

Reina rode over to her. "Rose, I can't make him do any-thing."

"Keep trying," Rose said. "Take him out in the woods. He likes to move out a little better on the trails."

Reina turned the horse, who trudged hoof by hoof across the meadow. Rose dipped into the pillowcase for another book, needing more space to write on. The story ended with a delicious quirk, the protagonist learning at the very end that the mysterious saboteur wrecking his every plan was none other than himself, misinterpreting everything and reacting badly. A Möbius strip. The story had to be set up very carefully, so that when the new interpretation came in, at the very end, it would work its changes back through every event of the story and turn it into something utterly different.

Miller stepped over her, carrying something that shadowed her book. She glanced up just long enough to see that he was putting the lean-to back together and returned to the construction of her syllogism.

Reina came back. "Rose, he won't go on the trail."

"Sssh," Rose said.

"Rose, please?"

Rose's temper surged; she snapped her head up, ready to drive the kid away, but the pleading look on the girl's face stopped her. She took a grip on her anger.

"Look, give me about half an hour, and I'll come help you. Okay?"

"Okay, Rose."

She looked down at the book, her mind blank now, the thread lost, the whole structure gone. Miller was setting the poles of the lean-to back in the holes they had made when she put them up; she moved away, down closer to the water's edge.

"I'll help you," Miller said to Reina.

"You don't know anything about horses."

"I know a little. How do you know she knows anything? Come on, I'll help you."

"Get away from here and let me do this," Rose shouted, furious.

Miller took the horse by the bridle and led him off down the gravel bar to the trail up to the meadow. Rose stared at the page. Suddenly the shape of the thing came into her mind again, and she scribbled notes in the margin and across the words of *Mansfield Park,* turned the page, wrote and wrote and wrote.

It worked. It was very artificial, but it enchanted her. She would worry about the artifice later. She got up, stuffed the books back into the pillowcase and the pillowcase back into the hole in the bank, and went up onto the meadow.

She spent the rest of the morning teaching Reina how to make the horse obey her. Miller disappeared soon after the lesson started. Reina had ridden a little in the past, but not enough to be confident on the horse; Rose made her go in circles and figure-eights and three-leaf clovers, walking along behind Reina through the grass, shouting until her voice was hoarse.

"There, you see?" she cried, when Reina finally guided the horse at a trot through the last maneuver. "It's not that hard."

"I'll never do it," Reina said. "I'll never be able to do it." She slumped in the saddle, her arms drooping. Rose patted her knee.

"Yeah, that's what I always think, too. Let's go get something to eat."

"It's too bad there's not another horse, so we could both ride."

Rose laughed. "Yeah, it's the truth. And if there were two horses, it'd be too bad there wasn't three, so Miller could ride, too."

"Not Miller," Reina said promptly. "He's a creep."

"Hunh. You didn't mind him when he was bringing you up here all that way."

Reina shot her a look of surprise. One hand lifted to brush back her curly dark hair. "I didn't ask him to. He asked me did I want him to, that's all."

"What don't you like about him?"

The girl shrugged. "He's a creep, that's all." *La belle dame sans merci.* Rose studied her a moment; she could see that it meant nothing to Reina to be beautiful or even to be loved.

They went back to the camp, and Rose fried some bacon and cut up a tomato and some lettuce that had survived the attack. "You want toast?" She threaded slices of bread on a green twig and held it out to Reina. "Toast the bread."

"How?" Reina said.

"Just hold it up where the heat will brown it." Rose dug into the back of the hole in the bank, searching for the mayonnaise; she screwed the lid off the jar and sniffed it warily, wondering if it had spoiled yet.

"I don't know how," Reina said, making no effort to try.

"Learn." The mayonnaise seemed good to her, and she put it down by the other sandwich makings. Reina was still staring at her, the twig with the bread held distastefully in her hands. Rose said, "Do it, Reina. I want toast."

The girl's eyes widened a little. Gingerly she held the bread out over the fire. Rose kept watch on it, to make sure it did not burn.

While they were eating, Miller came back up the river. He had his shirt and his shoes in his hand, and his hair was wet; he had been swimming. He sat down silently on the log at the end of the lean-to and put his shoes and socks on.

"Want something to eat?" Rose asked him.

"I'll take whatever you're having," he said.

"Make it yourself. There's something left of everything."

He came over to the fire and made himself a sandwich. "Is there a town around here somewhere?"

"Springville. That's the nearest town of any size. There's a couple of wide spots in the road that are closer. Souvenir stands and country stores. What do you want?"

"Just scouting out the lay of the land. Where can I get some mail sent?"

"There's a mailbox out on the road for the ranch. I don't remember what number it is. I'll ask my brother." It sounded as if he meant to stay for a while. She watched him assemble his sandwich. Reina had gone back into the meadow to play with the horse. Rose wandered restlessly through the campsite. When she was alone here, she had never been bored; now, in the company of these strangers, she suddenly found nothing to do. She wished they were both gone. At loose ends, she went down to the river to skip stones.

. . .

"You like Led Zeppelin, do you?" Rose asked. The music blared out of the stereo speakers on either side of the car, so loudly that she had to raise her voice to be heard.

"That's the greatest rock and roll band in the world," Miller Tarn said.

Rose made a disparaging sound in her throat. "The greatest rock and roll band in the world is the Rolling Stones."

"Not any more," he said.

Showing her age. She suspected he was right, at least about the Stones; she had not liked a Stones album since *Gimme Shelter*.

They were roaring up the freeway to Springville. The freeway here was built on the side of the slope, overhanging the valley of the Eel River; the asphalt ribbon seemed suspended among the soaring upper reaches of the redwoods on all sides. It had rained that morning; now the sky was blue again. Reina was supposed to have come with them, but had backed out at the last minute to ride.

As if he read her thoughts, Miller asked, "Is she gonna be safe on that horse?"

"For God's sake," Rose said. "You've seen that horse. Is he a threat to life and limb?" They were crossing the river again. Ahead the valley opened up into a broad expanse of fields and pastures.

"It's not the horse who bothers me," he said. "Reina can get into enough trouble on foot. She's got very poor judgment."

"Well, God, and she's all of fourteen."

The ditches along the road were filled with hawkweed and wild mustard. They passed a yard of redwood logs stacked up for a quarter-mile along the road. A truck hauling logs pulled out onto the freeway, and Miller eased his car into the passing lane. Ahead of them lay Springville. On the tree-darkened hill beyond the town there was a stand of eucalyptus, taller and more open than the redwoods around it, like a crown over the little city.

Rose bought a notebook and some pens and groceries. While she was putting oranges into a sack, Miller came up with a candy bar, which he dropped into the basket.

"For Reina," he said.

"Don't give her that," Rose said. "Get her something good for her."

"She likes candy."

Rose gave him a sharp look. "So? She's a kid. Who says she gets what she likes?" She rolled the basket into line behind the checkout stand.

"She likes me when I give her candy," he said.

Rose slipped a look sideways at him. He believed what he wanted to believe; Reina certainly gave him nothing to hang his hopes on. Like the knights of Languedoc, perhaps he wanted someone unattainable.

The checker in her pink store coat rang up the items in Rose's basket. While she was digging in her pockets for money, Miller handed a twenty-dollar bill to her. She was glad to see it; she was running out of money.

A little knife of guilt stabbed her. She liked him when he gave her money. She reminded herself that he ate a lot, that he was eating her food and sharing her camp. Silently she took the money and held it out to the checker.

The rain brought her seedlings up. Under the layer of decaying straw, rows of little green shoots appeared, at first only the curl of the stem breaking through the ground, then the first round leaves, some with the seed cover still clinging to the edge. They came up in clusters. After a few days she thinned them down to a plant every foot.

Their secondary leaves appeared, now recognizably marijuana leaves, long and thin with notched edges. She gave each a good splash of water.

It was hot. She had begun coming here at different times during the day, to throw off any suspicion, and today she had arrived in the late afternoon. She peeled off her clothes and lay down in the sun near the edge of the crag and smoked a joint.

She thought over her story, thinking through one of the double meanings, which seemed not to fit into the general flow of the story. She saw a way to do the same thing more simply. She wished she had her notebook; she drew idly in the dirt beside her with her finger, making X's and drawing O's in the angles. Something moved behind her.

She rolled over onto her stomach. Miller Tarn was climbing up over the edge of the crag.

She yelled. She lunged for her clothes. "Who the hell invited you here, anyway?" She hated being seen naked; she poked her legs into her pants and flung her shirt around her.

Miller climbed onto the flat rock ten feet from her. "Yeah," he said. He stood looking down over her marijuana field. "I had a feeling it was something like that."

"What are you doing up here?"

"Well, you kept disappearing—" He went down toward the plants; she rushed after him, buttoning her shirt. "So I thought I'd find out why."

"Get away from them."

"You're getting a late start."

"I'm sorry. If I'd known you'd take such an interest, I'd have consulted you." She got his arm and pulled, trying to turn him away from the field. His upper arm was much bigger than she expected and hard with muscle; it hardened even more under her hand, as he refused to move. He smiled down at her.

"What a sneaky female you are. I guess it's true about women, isn't it, how you are none of you to be trusted."

"How'd you find me?" She took her hand off him, now that he was looking at her and not the field.

He put his hands on his hips. His eyes were the blue of worn denim. "The first time we came here, at the fork in the trail, the horse wanted to go one way, and you went the other. And then you got lost. Obviously that wasn't how you usually came. I just walked down that other fork. Then I smelled the pot."

"Such a Sherlock."

"Why don't you cut me in? You need help. I'll split it with you."

"Help," she said. "What help do I need now? Where were you when I was digging it up, and lugging the lime up here—"

"Lime," he said, laughing. "You need help. What do you know about growing pot?"

Wary, she shut her mouth. She knew very little, not even how much there was to know.

"Can you tell the difference between a male and a female?" he asked.

"No," she said.

"You need help. Besides, how are you going to sell it?"

"I don't want to sell it. I want to smoke it."

"Oh, yeah?" He spread out one hand toward the field. "There's going to be twenty, thirty pounds worth of marijuana here in a couple months. You must smoke a lot of dope."

"Twenty or thirty pounds?" She was amazed.

"Provided you didn't dig in too much lime." He folded his arms over his chest. "I'll help you do the work, and I'll sell it for you. Fifty-fifty split."

She was looking at his body. His arms were wrapped in hard muscle; around his middle he wore the great fat belly of a sloth. She said, "What if I say no?"

"Then I'll come back in the fall and just take it," he answered. His smile curled up toward his ears.

"You'd have to stay the whole summer if I agreed, though," she said. "Or else how would you do your share of the work?"

"Unh-unh. After a couple weeks these plants can go with just some water now and then. The real work comes when they start showing their sex."

Her eyebrows lifted; she sucked on the inside of her

cheek, thinking. He was right. She had no idea how to culti-
vate marijuana. Maybe he was bluffing and knew no more
than she did. At any rate he was certainly not to be trusted.
She said, "All right. Fifty-fifty."

"Good deal." He turned toward the field again. "Let me
take a look here."

"The lime was a bad idea, hunh?"

"I don't know. Depends on how much you put in." He
pulled the straw away from a row of plants. "Marijuana's
pretty hardy stuff. How deep did you dig?"

"A foot, a foot and a half."

"Good." He put his face down to inspect a plant with a
red stem. "Where'd you get the seeds?"

"From that dope you sold me in Pasadena."

"Oh, yeah?" He laughed, straightening, wiping his hands
on his thighs. "You see, it was always my pot." Covetously
he looked around him at the field. Rose watched him, her
hands on her hips. Months would pass before the plants
matured, months when some chance would come to get rid
of him. His gaze swung toward her.

"You can take your clothes off again, if you want."

"Hunh." She went off across the edge of the crag, to the
place where she usually climbed down the side. Miller followed her, talking.

"I mean, anytime you want, just peel. I'm a very natural
kind of guy, if you follow me."

She kept her back to him. She knew that if she looked,
she would catch a broad smile on his face. He was baiting
her; sex was too risky a matter to let him draw her into a
game over it. She went down the rock hand over hand, foot
after foot, down into the trees.

"Put your head down," Rose said. "I have you—I have you—
I won't let you go."

Clinging to Rose's arms, Reina leaned slowly forward,
sinking down into the water. They had found a quiet pool

upstream from their camp, deep enough to swim in; Rose was trying to teach the girl how, but Reina refused to put her face into the water.

"It's cold," she cried. "Oh, it's cold." Her face screwed up tight, she lowered herself, still braced on Rose's arms, down to the surface.

"Put your face in the water. Hold your breath."

"I can't. I can't."

Rose fought off the urge to put her hand on Reina's hair and push her under the water. She made her voice soothing. "It's okay. Just relax. Try to float."

Reina lay in Rose's arms, and Rose lowered herself down until she was just barely holding the child up in the water. Gasping, Reina cranked her head back as far as it would go.

"Reina, look." Rose stood up, and Reina stood up. "Watch." Rose put her head down into the river and blew bubbles. The water was warm enough, once she was in it. Bringing her head up, she whipped her wet hair back out of her eyes. "Watch." She sprawled awkwardly out across the surface of the water; it had been years since she had swum. She dog-paddled vigorously around the pool, came back to Reina, and, putting her face down into the water, let herself float there, motionlessly, until the need for air drove her up again.

Reina was watching her uncertainly, her arms clasped over her and her legs wound together, as if she stood in an arctic blast. Rose reached out her hands to her.

"Come on."

Reluctantly Reina took her grip. Rose drew her gently forward. The girl resisted at first, until Rose was at a full arm's length from her; then suddenly Reina leaped forward into the water, her face squeezed tight.

"Good girl! Good girl!"

Reina gasped. Holding her head up as high as she could, she struggled with arms and legs for a few yards.

"Good!"

"Am I swimming?" Reina cried.

"Yes! Yes! Keep going!"

Now, bolder, Reina took longer strokes with her arms; her head lowered. She kicked up a thunder with her feet and chugged around the pool.

"I'm swimming," she shouted. "I'm swimming."

"Well," Rose said, walking up onto the beach, "I suppose you could call it that."

Reina reached out one arm after the other in a sort of crawl stroke. She would not put her face in the water, but at least she was staying up on the surface. Rose jumped back into the pool with her.

"Keep your legs stiff. That's right. Good."

"I'm swimming," Reina cried. She stood up to her waist in the water, the water sluicing down over her body, and flung her arms around Rose. "I'm really swimming."

Rose hugged her back. "Keep on practicing."

They swam a while longer, until the cold drove them out. Miller had left that morning, saying nothing about where he was going. Rose made herself and Reina each a sandwich.

"I wish there were another horse," Reina said, "I wish I had somebody to ride with."

"Go find someone," Rose said.

"How?"

Rose chewed a mouthful of meat and lettuce and bread, eying Reina thoughtfully. When she had swallowed, she said, "Reina, for God's sake, are you going to spend the rest of your life waiting for somebody to come along and show you how to do everything? Go find somebody. Just go look, and somebody will turn up."

"Where?" Reina asked blankly.

Rose shook her head. "I give up."

"Can I ride anyway?"

"Sure."

Reina went off to the horse. Rose hung their bathing suits on the bushes near the river and sat down with her notebook. Her mind still caught on the young girl, she could not work; she drew doodles on top of the clean white page, circles in circles. Put flower petals on the circles, a stem on the flower, a pot at the end of the stem. A window around the flower in its pot. A room behind the window. She wanted to protect Reina, to shelter her beauty and youth and freshness. Finally she set to work.

Miller came back; she did not notice him until he was right next to her.

"Hi," she said. She had done nearly half the story, writing it out from the notes she had made in the margins of books.

"Where's Reina?" he said.

"Out riding."

He went off, moving around the camp; she heard him rummaging through the food box. She read back through what she had written, dissatisfied.

"Why do you do that all the time?" he asked, eating a sandwich. He sat down on the log by the lean-to.

"Because I enjoy it," she said.

"There's nothing in books. Nothing except what some other person thinks."

"Well," she said, "there's more than that."

"Real life is out here, you know."

"Real life," she repeated sarcastically.

"You're wasting your time in those books."

That spurred her anger, and she sat up, ready to argue. Her eyes met his. There was a gleam in his brilliant blue eyes. He wanted to argue; he wanted attention. She leaned back, on her guard. With one hand she shut the notebook.

"You go to school?"

"Sure," he said. "Even college. That's how I know there's nothing in books."

"What did you major in?"

"Economics."

That surprised her; she made a sound in her chest. "Why, for God's sake?"

"Everything comes down to money, in the end," he said, fast, as if he were reciting a truism. He took another bite of his sandwich.

There was a candy bar in the pocket of his T-shirt. She said, "God, you eat like an elephant."

He looked where she was looking and put his hand over the candy. "For Reina."

"I told you, I don't want you giving her candy all the time."

"So what? You don't run my life."

"I'm standing in for Reina's mother," she said. "So I'm running Reina's."

He stared at her a moment, chewing, and swallowed and said, "I got you something, too."

"Oh," she said, intrigued. "What?"

He reached down beside him and tossed her a paper sack. "I'm tired of canned ravioli and canned chicken."

Inside the paper sack was a steak. She took it to the hole in the bank to store it, asking herself what right she had to be disappointed.

"Here comes Reina," he said much later, while she was fixing the dinner.

Rose looked over her shoulder. He vaulted onto the top of the riverbank and stood waiting, while the white horse crossed the meadow toward the camp.

"You were gone all day," he said. "Did you have a good ride?"

"Rose," Reina shouted. "Watch this!"

Rose stood up, the knife in one hand and the potato she was cutting up in the other. "Yo."

The girl waved her arm at her. She had a long stick in her hand. She reined the big horse away from the camp, and beating him around the flanks and shoulders with the stick, she forced him into a reluctant trot out across the grass. "Go," Reina shouted. "Go!" She doubled the blows of her stick and her heels. The horse raised his head, his ears back, and rocked into a canter.

Reina screamed with triumph, bouncing high out of the saddle with each stride; she had to grab for the saddle horn to stay on. As soon as she stopped hitting him, the horse dropped back into a trot.

Reina's cheeks glowed. Smiling with pleasure, she steered the horse back toward Rose. His trot flagged steadily down to a walk, and he put his head into the grass to graze.

"I made him gallop!" Reina shouted.

"So you did," Rose said. "The first of many triumphs, I'm sure."

"Where'd you go?" Miller asked. He put one hand out to the horse.

"Just out there, on that dirt road." Reina waved her hand toward the forest. Standing by the horse's shoulder, Miller ran his fingers lightly back and forth over the red roan neck.

"What did you do?"

"I just rode," Reina said, indifferent to him. She raised her voice, calling to Rose. "Can I give him a name?"

"Sure. Why not?"

The girl slipped down from the saddle and crossed the campsite to her. "I want to call him Windfire."

Rose smiled at that; in her childhood she had filled notebooks with the names of her imaginary horses, their lineage and colors. "You having a good time?" She went toward the horse, whose shoulder was rough with dried sweat.

Reina trailed after her. "I wish I was a good rider," she said under her breath.

"Keep doing it. You'll learn."

"I fell off."

"Oh, yeah? Nothing hurts, I hope."

"No, I landed in the grass." The girl laughed and raised her eyes quickly to Rose; her eyes were mottled green and brown, fascinating in their brilliance. "One thing he always does really well is stop."

Rose laughed too, delighted with her buoyant spirits. She suppressed the wish to touch her. "You'll learn. Just keep trying. You're doing really well."

"You think so?"

"Sure. Now go find me some firewood before the fire goes out."

"Firewood." Reina looked helplessly around her; her arms drooped and her back curved, as if all her strength were draining away. "Where do I find firewood?"

"Out in the woods," Rose said. "Go on. Good, sound pieces of dry wood."

"Do I have t'?"

"Do you want to eat?"

Reina stared at her a moment longer, sighed, and wandered away across the meadow toward the trees, moving as slowly and spiritlessly as the old horse did sometimes. Rose watched her until she was gone from sight into the trees.

While they were eating dinner, Miller said, "Is there any place to rent horses up here, you know, for a couple weeks?"

"I don't know," Rose replied. "I doubt it. You might be able to lease a horse, but I wouldn't know where to look. What's the matter, you don't like this horse?"

"I do," Reina cried.

"I just thought, if we had another horse, I could ride with Reina."

Reina's fork scraped busily over the dish, gathering up the last of the steak, the fried potatoes, and corn. "You ride any better than you put on bridles?" Her face split into a wide smile. "You're so fat, if you fall off, you'll bounce." She guffawed, leaning across her plate to throw this humor in his face.

Miller said defensively, "I can ride."

Reina's eyes snapped with good humor. She smiled widely at him. "You're so fat, if you had a Santa Claus suit, it'd need alterations." Overwhelmed by her own wit, she roared with full, round laughter.

His eyes lowered, Miller picked at a hole in his jeans. Rose reached for his plate. "You want some more?"

"He's so fat," Reina shouted, "he needs a horse girth for a belt!" She fell over backwards, releasing peals of laughter.

There seemed more malice than pleasure in the laughter. Miller got up and walked away from the fire, his hands in his pockets.

Reina sat up again, her mouth tipped into a smirk of triumph. Her eyes shone. Rose was scraping the dishes and stacking them in the bucket. Working gave her a sense of power, a place to start from with Reina.

"Don't tease him," she said to the girl.

"He teases me," Reina said indignantly.

"I don't think—" Her gaze went toward Miller, who was walking down by the river. It was none of her business. He had gotten himself into this.

"He's a creep," Reina said.

"He loves you," Rose said. "He loves you."

The passion in her voice unnerved her. She felt she was letting out something long kept secret, best unseen, and she bit the words off and stood, reaching for the bucket. "Come help me wash the dishes."

"But—" Reina's face fell open in shock, the eyes wide, the mouth distressed. "But I got wood."

"Come on, I need some help." She found the soap and a handful of rags and started toward the river.

"Why do I have to do all the work?" Reina followed her, shouting as if Rose were fifty feet away. "Get Miller to do it."

"Miller does lots of work," Rose said. She took a tight grip on her temper. Angie never made her kids do anything.

"But I don't want to!"

Rose stopped and turned to face her. "I'm not asking you to want to. I'm telling you to do it. Now come on and shut up before I slug you."

Reina's beautiful eyes flashed with bad humor, and her mouth twisted into an angry scowl. She strode off toward the river. Rose followed after her at a leisurely pace.

Reina stopped bitching when they set to work. Rose showed her how to scour out the pans with sand. The water was cold, numbing her hands. Silvery scratches gleamed in the dull metal of the frying pan, and she thrust it into the current to sweep the sand away. Reina worked hard, in spite of her complaints. They stacked up the dishes on the grass.

"He's such a neat horse."

"You mean Windfire?" Rose asked.

Reina smiled at her, looking down. "You think that's silly."

"No. I think it's great."

Miller was walking down the bank toward them. The sun had set, and the deep twilight sky was behind him. She saw him only as a flat black shape.

"I'm going up to your brother's house and shoot some pool," he said.

"Oh, yeah? Well, watch out for Peter. He'll shark you." Rose rubbed her chilled hands together.

"I'll beat him," Miller said.

"Peter's pretty good."

"I'll beat him. You want to bet on it?"

"You ever play my brother before?"

"No."

"Sure, I'll bet. Twenty dollars?"

His shoulders lifted and sank again in a careless shrug. "Sure."

Rose turned away. She had hoped a bet that size would scare him off. Peter would win. She could not afford to lose twenty dollars.

"Can I come?" Reina said.

"Sure," he said again, in an entirely different voice.

"That's a long walk, up there in the dark," Rose said. She pointed to the dishes. "Here, help me drag this stuff back to camp."

"My car's down under the bridge," Miller said. "Fifteen minutes' walk along the river and five minutes' drive."

"The gate's locked."

"I have the key from Peter."

That rattled her, to find him so well prepared. She stooped and picked up a stack of dishes and a pot and started away toward the camp. With a clatter of metal, he poured

the forks and spoons and the smaller pots into the big one
and came on her heels along the gravel bar.

"You can't think ahead of me," he said to her, smiling.
"Don't try." Walking at his best speed, he went on past her
to the camp.

"Wait for me," Reina called, running after him.

When Rose reached the lean-to, they were rooting around
for their jackets. She stood watching them; pulling on her
jacket, Reina said, "Does this guy have a television?"

"Yes," Rose said, "But they only get two channels."

"Oh, goody!"

"Candy for the mind," Miller said, looking at Rose. When
he caught her eye, he smiled at her. Stooping, he pulled
the blue-striped case off his pillow and stuffed a mass of
dirty clothes into it. "You got anything you want washed?"

"Yeah," Rose said. "While you're at it."

She went back into the snug, dark corner of the lean-to
and got out her dirty clothes.

They left. They left her alone, sitting by the fire. She
put another log on; she got up and rolled a joint, moved a
sleeping bag in behind her so that she had something to
lean on, and sat there and smoked.

She thought of Miller and his passion. He seemed to get
very little out of it; she wondered why he persisted. There
was something she liked in his persistence. Reina's dislik-
ing him was more understandable. He was always there, always waiting; she could not ignore him, and yet she could
hardly give him what he wanted. Rose had read somewhere
that girls loved horses because managing the big beast was a
safer analogue of a woman's dealing sexually with a man.
She wished men were as easily dealt with as horses.

She took out her notebook and worked on her story,
which was not coming out well. She drew more doodles.
There was something compelling about Miller's love, though.
Everybody assumed in a relationship so uneven that the child
would be the one exploited, but Miller gave and gave and
got nothing.

She missed them. When she had been alone down here, before they came, she had enjoyed the solitude. But now when she was used to company, she felt the chill of loneliness. She sat looking into the fire a while longer and got up to put the clean dishes away.

All the marijuana plants had grown up above the level of the straw; they raised two and three sets of leaves into the sun. Rose sat down in the little patch of grass at the side of the crag, where she had used to sunbathe. She had brought a couple of empty cans with her to make some sprinklers, and she got out her pocket knife to punch holes in the bottoms.

While she was doing that, Miller climbed onto the crag. "Hi."

"Hi," she said, poking holes in the aluminum.

"Why didn't you wake me up when you left the camp? How long have you been here?"

"Just a couple of minutes." She threaded a piece of string through a hole in the side of the can to make a handle.

"You owe me twenty bucks." Miller went past her, down to the plants, and walked along the rows, looking them over.

Rose lifted her head, surprised. "You beat Peter?"

"Six times. He beat me twice."

"Hunh." She was amazed. Peter always beat her at pool. I am the standard of the world. She lifted the two cans, one in each hand, and went to the spring and dipped them into the water. Raising them full and dripping, she walked quickly down the first two rows of plants, holding a can over each row. The water sprinkled over the plants as she passed.

"See?" she said, pleased with herself.

"Great," he said. "Don't get water on the leaves in this bright sun; they'll burn. You're better off pouring the water onto the ground under the mulch."

Rose ignored him, carrying her sprinkler system to the

end of the row. The water gave out and she went back for
more. Miller was using the bucket; he went from plant to
plant, watering around the stem. She began to think that he
was right. She paused, unwilling to give in.

"Go on," he said, still bent to water a plant at his feet.
"Get the other bucket."

She stood there a moment longer, faced with the choice
between doing as she was told and doing it wrong. The effort of choosing cooled her off. She went for the other bucket.

When they were done, they sat on the grass and smoked
a joint. Miller lay on his side, braced on his elbow, his shirt
soaked dark with sweat. His beard was growing out, a blond
stubble fairer than the hair on his head.

"Do you cut your hair?" she asked.

"No. It just stopped growing."

"Well, that's convenient." His hair was a mass of springy
curls, which made it seem much shorter than it was.

"Yes, I thought so," he said. "But then perfection is always convenient."

She smiled at that, seeing through this front now, down
to the man who had slunk away like a dog under Reina's
teasing.

He lit the stub of the joint again, holding it by the edge
of the paper. "I'm running out of dope. You know where I
can score around here?"

"Peter will know."

He held out the roach. "Last hit."

Carefully she pinched it away from him and sucked the
last stream of smoke into her lungs. Crushing out the coal,
she rubbed the paper to nothing between her thumb and
forefinger. Miller said nothing; he was staring out over the
field, his hands between his knees. He was a very quiet man,
she realized, saying almost nothing on his own. Not like Mike
Morgan, whose pyrotechnic conversations had kept her
amused for years. Of course Mike had not been fat, either,
or in love with a little girl.

She wondered what Mike was doing. She thought of calling him and recoiled, aghast at her mind's turning traitor to her. I won't go back. Yet she longed for the fullness of her life with him.

"I'm going," Miller said suddenly and got up and walked away. Rose let him go. She leaned back on her arms, her face lifted to the sun, wishing for the solitary peace she had found here once. Now that there were other people sharing her camp, the silence was only a space waiting for a human voice. She put her arm over her face, to shield her from the sun.

"Where's Reina?"

Rose looked up from her notebook; Miller was standing at the mouth of the lean-to, drying his shoulders and chest with a blue and white towel.

"She hasn't come back yet," Rose said. "Where did you go swimming?"

Miller rubbed the towel briskly over his hair. He wore nothing but shorts, his belly overflowing, soft and huge.

"It's five o'clock. She ought to be back by now."

"She doesn't have a watch. She'll be back."

He grunted at her. Stooping, he went into the lean-to, and Rose turned again to her notebook. She was trying to work on her story, but as hard as she pushed, she could not make anything happen in it.

"Can't you keep your face out of a book for five minutes?"

She looked over the rim of the notebook. Miller had put on gray corduroy pants and a frayed T-shirt. His hair, still damp, looked like a snarl of fine gold wire. She met his eyes. "Fuck off, Miller," she said precisely.

"Yeah, sure," he said bitterly. "That's all you care about her. What if she's lost?"

"The horse will bring her back."

"God, you act as if that horse were some kind of infallible machine."

The image arrested her attention; she had a superstitious mistrust of machines. With a glance at the sun, she lowered the notebook to the ground. It was late, time to start dinner. A few coals still glowed in the charred remnants of the fire. She took the hatchet to chop some kindling wood.

"I'm going to look for her," Miller announced.

"Be my guest."

He left. Rose opened a can of stew and dumped it into a pot to cook.

The daylight faded. She went up on the edge of the meadow and looked around, but there was no sign of Reina or the horse or even Miller. The meadow stretched away in a rippling carpet of dry grass. Along the edge of the forest, innumerable cow parsnips lifted their lacy, white parasols six and seven feet above the ground. The wind was rising. Rose cupped her hands around her mouth.

"Reina," she shouted. "Ray—na!"

There was no answer. She went back to the camp.

The stew was bubbling. She cut up the few fresh vegetables she had left and threw them in, then opened a can of beef and chopped it and put that in. Mixing up a biscuit dough, she dropped spoonfuls of it onto the surface of the stew and set the pot on the hottest part of the fire. Reina did not come back. Miller did not come back. When the dumplings were done, she ate a little of the stew, put the lid on the pot, and moved it over to a cooler spot.

Maybe Reina had gone to Peter's house. Rose put on her jacket and went up the trail through the woods.

Peter was watching television. Hallie banged and clanged around the kitchen making an elaborate soup. Reina was not there.

"Did you see her at all today?" Rose asked.

Her brother propped his feet up on the empty chair beside him, his can of Rainier ale cradled in his lap. "I haven't seen her since last night. Have a seat. *The Great Escape* is coming on after the news."

Peter was a habitué of escape pictures of all kinds. Rose

sank into the chair, leaving room for his feet. "You like me again, hunh?"

"When did I not? The Springville Rodeo is next week. We're all going in. Are you coming?"

"To a rodeo? That's not my style."

"Rodeo schmodeo. The actual rodeo isn't much. Rodeo week in Springville is the biggest bash in southern Humboldt. We'll camp on the beach and party all week long."

She thought of the beaches she had loved in the South, Zuma Beach, Leo Carillo, the soft white sand, the gentle blue-green ocean waves. "Okay—that'll be fun. Provided I can find Reina."

From the kitchen Hallie called, "The dinner's ready, Petey."

Peter said, "Stay and eat."

"No—I have to find Reina. I'll see you tomorrow."

She went back to her camp, hoping to find the horse in the meadow, the girl by the fire. The meadow was empty. Only Miller sat there in the glow of the fire.

"No luck?" Rose asked.

"I don't even know where to start." He poked at the fire with a stick. The yellow light licked at his hair.

"I see it hasn't affected your appetite." The stew was gone, the pan scraped clean of all but the grease.

"Where could she be?"

"I don't know." Rose gathered the dirty dishes. "We can't look in the dark. We'll have to wait until tomorrow." She looked down at the little heap of dishes. At the thought of the mean, cold work of washing them she lost heart. For the first time a tinge of fear sprang alive in her mind.

"Maybe she's up at Peter's."

"I thought that was where you just went."

"I mean, maybe she's come since I was there."

Miller faced her across the fire, the light glinted on his bristling, electric hair, and his eyes were wild. He does love her, Rose thought, startled again by the intensity of his feeling.

"Come on," she said. "We'll go up to Peter's."

"What if she comes back here?"

"Well, then, you go to Peter's and I'll stay here."

He nodded to that, lowering his eyes; they seemed to dim, a little, as if he were drawing his passions back from the surface. "I'll go." He went to the lean-to for his jacket.

When he was gone, she got her notebook out again, but the block was worse than before; the story on the page was lifeless and contrived compared to the problem of Reina. Giving up, Rose took another book at random from the pillowcase. It was a history of America up to the Civil War. She settled down with that, and when the fire burned low and the night chill crept in, she got into her sleeping bag and read until she fell asleep.

She woke in the opalescent moments just before dawn. A bird was calling in the trees on the other side of the river, three off-key, haunting notes. She changed her clothes. Reina had not come back. There was no sign that Miller had been there, either, but when she walked toward the woods a little, she could see him under the trees, wrapped up in his sleeping bag.

She went over to him, walking quietly, to keep from waking him. He had a blanket around his head and face so that nothing showed except the tip of his nose. By this mummy's head was an array of small objects: a ChapStick, a lighter, his radio, a green-capped bottle of Sinex. She stopped, unwilling to wake him.

The head moved. "What do you want?" he said, surly.

"Did you find Reina?"

"No." The blanket heaved and Miller poked his head out. His cheek was red where it had pressed against the ground. Across the river the bird cranked out its weird, mournful cry. Miller sat up and wiped his hands over his face.

"I guess we'd better go look for her," he said.

"I'll make some breakfast." She went back toward camp.

While they were eating scrambled eggs and bacon, Reina galloped up.

Miller leaped to his feet. "Where've you been?"

"Over at her house," Reina said calmly, gesturing behind her. On a buckskin mare was a plump blond girl, who smiled cheerfully at Rose.

"I'm Bonnie Morrison," she said. "We live up on Watson's Flat."

"What the hell were you doing down there?" Rose said. "We were looking all over for you."

Reina shrugged her shoulders. "I met her—" a gesture at Bonnie Morrison—"yesterday, and they asked did I want to spend the night." She looked from Rose to Miller and back again. "What're you so steamed about?"

"Get off the horse," Miller said.

Reina glared at him. "I came by to get some lunch. We're going riding."

"No, you aren't," Miller said. "Get down off that horse!"

"Shut up," Rose said to him. She went a few steps closer to Reina, near enough to touch her, and laid her hand on the horse's shoulder. "We were scared stiff. If you're going to be away, anywhere off River Ranch, I want you to tell me first."

"My mom doesn't—"

"I don't care what your mom does or doesn't do. You tell me, you understand?"

Reina shrugged again. She wore a plaid shirt, nipped in at the waist, with little puffed sleeves; there was straw in her hair. "Sure," she said. She looked around at Miller and back to Rose. "I stay over my friend's house all the time at home. My mom doesn't care."

"I care," Rose said.

Miller strode up to her. "Tell her she can't ride for a week."

Rose gave him the briefest of looks and returned her attention to Reina. "Where are you going today?"

"You're not going to let her go off again, are you?" Miller shouted.

"Shut up," Rose said to him. "Where are you going, Reina?"

"Down to Cutter's," Bonnie Morrison said. "You know where that is?"

"Cutter's Bend? The swimming hole? Okay. Take some lunch."

Miller shoved her. "You can't let her get away with that!"

"Leave her alone," Reina cried and lifted her fist.

Miller drew back; he stared from one to the other of them, his eyes hot with temper, and abruptly wheeled and walked away, down the riverbank. Rose watched him until he was out of sight in the trees. She turned back to Reina.

"Get some sandwiches. Take some money to buy milk. There's a store down at Cutter's, I think—isn't there?" she asked of the blond and jovial Bonnie.

"Yes," Bonnie said. "Sure."

Rose dug change out of her pockets and gave Reina fifty cents. "If you get stuck and can't be back by nightfall, call my brother. His number is in the phone book. Peter Mc-Kenna."

"Thanks, Rose." Reina slid down from the saddle. Rose caught her by the arm.

"I was scared something had happened to you," she said in a low voice. "Miller was freaked out of his nest. Don't you do that again to me, you hear?"

"Okay," Reina said. Her cheeks turned ruddy with embarrassment. "I don't see why you're so steamed. I can take care of myself, y' know." She marched away, back toward the riverbank, where her new friend waited. "I can take care of myself," she said loudly to Bonnie Morrison. "Come on, let's make a couple sandwiches."

They went into the lean-to together; Rose heard them rummaging through the box of food. She picked up the dirty dishes around the fire and stacked them in the frying pan.

The two girls made sandwiches and packed them in a bag, which Reina tied to her saddle, and they rode away. Miller came back to the fire.

"Wha'd'you think you're doing?" he asked and kicked

at the rocks around the firebed. "You think she'll like you better if you let her do whatever she wants?"

"No," Rose answered. "I just don't think punishing people does any good. It only makes them emotional."

"Emotional," he said. His arm swiped violently through the air, knocking down her idea. "Who d'you think you're dealing with here, Albert Einstein?"

"Get off my back."

He kicked a rock down the cobble beach to the river. "If you loved her, really loved her, you'd make her behave."

"Leave me alone!" Furious and half-convinced, she flew at him. "Don't take it out on me that she can't stand being around you."

That shook him; he stepped backwards away from her. They stared at each other a long moment, close enough almost to touch. Finally he looked away. He said, "I'm going for a walk." He kicked another rock down into the water, slid his hands out of sight in his pockets, and walked off toward the woods.

Rose took the breakfast clutter down to the river to wash. How had she gotten into this, now, with a crazy girl and her lovesick swain? She broke a fingernail scrubbing out the frying pan, heavy with bacon fat that the cold river water hardened into gluey lumps. Her mood darkened as she worked. She was sick of this place, sick of these people, tired even of herself, out of phase with the whole universe. She had to get out of here.

What Mike had said rang in her mind. "When the going gets tough, Rose cuts out." She had run from Mike; she had run from the mob at Peter's house. Now she wanted to run away again. She rubbed the sticky plates with sand. She would not run away again. She had to make a life for herself somewhere. River Ranch was as good as anyplace. The place didn't matter anyway.

She straightened up, kneeling on the gravel of the river bar. What did matter? She had no answer for that one. Maybe there was no answer at all, except the hard, small, trivial ones, like washing the dishes and eating the right food. To be happy seemed impossible. To love somebody. But that was so desperate, she thought, as Miller came to mind. As for being loved, that was not to be trusted. Never to be trusted again.

Around her the sun shone, burning through the last of the damp early-morning fog, and the water danced in the new light. The edges of the shadows of the brush behind her sharpened suddenly against the sunlit rocks of the cobble beach. Out on the river a fish jumped with a little splash. Her mood yielded slightly. If nothing really mattered, then that did not matter, either. The tao that is the tao is not the tao.

There was always work, that remade the world. She finished washing the dishes.

She walked up to Peter's house. On the way she came on Hallie, striding along in the midst of her goats.

"Going up to Peter's?" Hallie asked brightly. "So are we."

Rose stood aside to let the first two goats pass on the narrow trail. These were the nannies, with long flopping ears and eyes like yellow marbles. She fell into step with Hallie, walking at their backs; their bulging udders made the goats walk slightly spread-legged.

"God, these are odd animals," Rose said. She looked back at the three kids, bouncing along behind them on their faun-feet, and stopping at every bush and fern to sniff and nibble.

"Don't you love them?" Hallie said. "They're just darlings."

Rose scratched her cheek, eying the big black goat's udder. "I like horses, myself. You've been up at Peter's a lot lately. D'you think he'd mind if I moved back up there? I'm real tired of washing dishes in the river."

"Oh, I'm sure he'd love to have you. You know Petey."

They reached the open grass on the hill below Peter's

house and walked up by the dirt road. Hallie was going to make bread in Peter's kitchen, and she told Rose the whole recipe as they walked.

When they reached the house, Patty was in the kitchen, making coffee.

"Oh, God," she cried, when Hallie came in. "Don't let those goddamned goats in the kitchen again."

Hallie chased the goats off the back porch. She came into the kitchen, frowning at Patty. "I thought you were going home."

"I stayed the night," Patty said archly. "What's it to you?"

"Excuse me," Rose said and went on through the kitchen to the hall and down to her brother's room. As she opened his door, he came out of the bathroom, wrapping a towel around his waist. "Hi. You find your kid?"

"Not my kid," Rose said. "Yes, I found her. Where's Watson's Flat?"

"Oh, you know, those houses out on the county road. She was up there? Morrisons', I'll bet."

"Yeah."

"They got lotsa kids and lotsa horses." Peter went into his bedroom. "Don't come in here, I'm going to be putting on my clothes."

"For Christ's sake, Peter. D'you think I have designs on your body?" She leaned against the wall beside the door. "Actually I have designs on your house. Can I move up here again?"

"You and the kid and that guy?"

"Reina and I, for sure. Maybe Miller will go home."

The kitchen door slammed. Rose wheeled around to see Patty stalk down the hall toward her. Patty swept around her into the bedroom. "Peter? Peter—"

"I'm right here," Peter said. "I'm talking to—"

"Get that woman out of this house, Peter."

Rose leaned her back up against the wall, her hands clasped behind her. She could not see them, but their voices were loud enough to carry through the whole house.

"Look, what's the matter with you? I—"

"She stinks! She smells just like a goat."

"Oh, you mean Hallie."

" 'Oh, you mean Hallie,' my ass! Get her outta here!"

The kitchen door opened slightly inward. Rose looked toward the sound, but saw nothing.

Peter said something too softly for Rose to hear. Patty let out a yell. "I'm leavin'!"

Peter did not answer.

"I'm leavin'!" Patty strode out the door past Rose. She stopped to glare back into the room, stamped her foot, and walked away. At the door into the front room she stopped for a moment, looking back, her face now more worried than angry. When no one called her, she went into the front room, and a few moments later the heavy front door slammed.

Peter came out of the bedroom, buckling his belt. He glanced down the hall and stopped to put his shirt on.

"What's the matter with her?" Rose asked.

"Nothing," Peter said. "She'll be back pretty soon."

"Oh, yeah?"

"She's got nowhere else to go," Peter said amiably as he went down the hall toward the kitchen. "Hallie! You making me some pancakes?" He banged in through the door, leaving it rocking in and out in his wake.

Rose stayed where she was. With her foot she traced a line on the floor, down the worn hardwood plank, her hands still clasped behind her, and wondered if it was worth the hot water, living with Peter's entanglements. She decided it was. Turning as precisely as a soldier, she went down the hall to the bunkroom, to make sure it was fit to live in.

She took her car around by the county road to the dirt track that led onto the river bar and, bumping and jouncing over rocks and sand, drove up along the bed of the river almost to the bank opposite her camp. She waded across the river, which reached her waist in the middle of the stream where the current ran fast, and began to pack up her camp. Although she could not remember bringing more than a few boxes and blankets, there was an enormous amount of things to pack. She carried bundles of clothes and sleeping bags back over the river to her car; while she was collecting her books, Miller came up.

"What're you doing now?"

"I'm moving back up to the house." She straightened, blinking in the hot, bright noon sun. "You can stay here if you want."

"What about Reina?"

"I'm taking her with me."

"Now? Have you seen her?"

"No."

"Then how's she gonna know you've moved?"

"Well, what are you going to be doing for the next couple hours?"

"I'll be here. I can wait for her."

"Good." She nodded at him. "You want me to take your stuff?"

He helped her carry the rest of the camp goods over to her car, and she drove back to the ranch. When she parked her car and walked in the back door, she found Patty there, sitting on the counter, smoking a cigarette.

"Hi."

"Hi." Rose put down the box of food she was carrying. "I thought you were leaving us."

"As long as that goaty bitch isn't here," Patty said. "You moving in up here, Pete says?"

"Yeah," Rose said.

"Good. Then maybe Hallie won't have the excuse of comin' up here and cleanin' house." Patty dusted the air with the hand that held her cigarette. "Ol' nanny bitch."

Rose began putting away the food left over from her camp. "How old are you?" she asked.

"Eighteen," Patty said. "What's it to y'?"

"Nothing," Rose said, putting cans of vegetables up on the cupboard shelf. "Nothing at all."

Peter was working on his rhinoceros. Rose sat on the grass, watching him wrestle with it.

"I've decided it wants to be something else," he said as he pried apart two pieces of the head.

"Oh, yeah? What?"

"I don't know. Something with sharp angles."

Rose snorted at him. She lay back on the grass, staring up into the sky. The wind came along through the grass and brushed her cheek. Peter's wrenches and pipes clanged.

"How do you like this?"

She turned her head. He had reassembled the pipes into a square with a smaller square sticking out on one end and a medium square squatting on the back. "Wha'd'you call that?"

"I don't know. 'Composition with Pipes.'" He stood back, frowning at the thing. Through the network of rusting pipe Rose caught a glimpse of white, moving through the forest beyond the road.

She sat up, her gaze sharpening. It was the old white horse. On his back, Reina was kicking him and beating him with her stick, but he picked his way carefully along the narrow path through the trees.

Ahead of them was Miller. Rose did not see him until he broke out of the woods onto the green meadowland, some way down the road from her. He sprinted toward the house. Without missing stride he bounded over a fallen tree and raced toward the house, his arms pumping. The hard, forceful gasping of his breath reached her. As he passed her, he smiled at her.

Reina had reached the open ground, and now, at last, the old horse was willing to move out. He pricked his ears up and rocked into an easy canter. Reina yelled to him. Her stick thudded on his rump.

"Come on, Windfire!"

The horse slowed to a trot, snorting, to pass the rhinoceros. Ahead of him, Miller had almost reached the house, but he was obviously tiring. The horse broke into a gallop again, catching up with him. A clod of dirt from his hoof flew into Rose's lap. Just before Miller reached the house, Windfire passed him.

Miller veered sharply away from the spray of dust and pebbles spurned up by the horse's hoofs. He dropped to a walk and swerved over toward the people by the rhinoceros.

"I should have won," he said, panting. Sweat streamed down his face and chest. The vein that crossed the middle of his forehead stood up like a rope under the skin. His T-shirt was balled up in his hand, and he rubbed it over his body and dropped into the grass beside Rose.

"I was ahead all the way from the camp," he said, still breathing hard. "I should have won." He flopped backwards onto the ground, his arms outstretched.

Reina trotted the horse over toward them; he slowed at once and put his head down to the grass.

"I won."

Miller rolled up onto his feet. He had caught his breath. Rose watched him covertly, amazed that he had run uphill all the way from the river. His huge, sloppy stomach hung down over his waist; the muscular chest and arms that grew up through the fat seemed to belong to another body entirely.

His eyes shone. He looked more alive, more intense than she had ever seen him. He slapped the horse's neck.

"I won," Reina repeated.

"Yeah, I know."

She was looking past him, down to Rose. "Are we moving up here?"

"Yeah, I think so," Rose said.

"But I like it down there!"

"You'll like it here, too," Peter said. "I don't think this is balanced." He reached for a pipe wrench.

Rose got up and went over to Reina and Miller. "We can stay down there a couple more days. Until we go to the rodeo."

"The rodeo? Where?"

"In Springville. We're going down there for the week."

"Oh no," Reina said. "I'm not leaving Windfire." She leaned down and put her arms around the horse's neck. He was eating steadily, his jaws crunching through the grass.

Miller said, "I'll stay here with her."

Rose said, "Hunh." She gave him a narrow look. She would not let him stay alone with Reina; she said, "It's just for a week. When we come back, you can ride all you want."

Reina wailed. Miller said to Rose, "What's the matter with you?"

"I'm not going! I'm not leaving Windfire!"

Peter came up to them, wiping his hands on his Levi's. "We can take the horse in the back of my pickup." He slapped the white, down-curved neck.

"Really? Really, Rose? Can I take Windfire?"

"Sure," she said. Miller was still staring at her, frowning. Saying, "I'm going in to make supper," she retreated to the house.

On the freeway going to Springville, Miller said, "Why don't you let me stay alone with Reina? What d'you think I'll do?"

Rose said nothing. She looked out the window into the redwood forest. They were in Miller's car, the back seat crammed with camping gear; he was driving. Reina had insisted on riding in the back of Peter's pickup with the horse, whose bony, white rump showed above the wooden railing of the truck.

"I wouldn't hurt her. I love her. I'd never do anything to hurt her."

"You fight too much."

He took a joint from behind his ear and leaned forward to push in the car's cigarette lighter. In the same motion he popped a cassette into the tape deck under the dash. A blast of music, too loud to talk over, filled the car. Rose looked forward again. She didn't want to talk, either. This wasn't her business, anyway.

When the lighter snapped out, he lit the joint and passed it to her. Rose wet her lips and sucked the smoke down into her chest. At once her throat hurt and she coughed up the hit and coughed and coughed until her lungs were clear.

"Where'd you get this dope?"

"From Peter. It's kind of harsh."

"Kind of. There's seeds in it, too." She handed him the joint; a thick curl of smoke was flowing from the burning seed. The sharp smell stung her nose.

Miller took the joint and knocked the cherry into the ashtray. While he was lighting the roach, the music ended and the tape jumped halfway out of the deck.

"Turn it over."

She turned over the cassette. Music thundered forth into the car, making nothing of their voices.

Ahead the sky opened; they were leaving the gorge of the river. The freeway led them out over flat farmlands. Here and there on the checkerboard of fields, a lone house stood— square old houses, each with its huge barn and its windbreak of eucalyptus or pine. Once this whole valley had been a bay; the Eel had silted it in. The long, bald hills that flanked it looked like old sand dunes. On their seaward slopes the wind had worn the trees into wedges, the low end meeting the wind, each leafy branch sheltering those behind it so that they could grow a little higher.

"Where are we camping?" Miller asked her over the music.

"On the beach. Just follow him."

He glanced at her. The joint was gone; reaching above his ear, into the wiry mass of his hair, he brought out another. The crescendo of music reached its climax and stopped in a ringing silence.

"You're the only person I know who likes to smoke as much dope as I do," Rose said.

The music began again, softly, a guitar, a voice singing. Rose was intensely stoned. She felt the music throughout her body, the high tones in her ears, the bass vibrating in her groin.

"What d'you think I'm going to do to Reina?"

She shrugged. "I told you. You fight too much."

"You should see her when we're alone together. She hugs me and kisses me—"

"I think you're seriously demented."

"Really?"

She shook her head. "You're not sick, you're just in love."

"I can't help it. I didn't ask for it. The first time I saw her, I knew I wanted her for my lover someday."

Peter's turn signal flashed. The horse raised his head into the wind; his mane flew.

Rose said, "Well, you're going at it wrong."

"Oh? What do you think I should do?"

"Be friends with her. Stop telling her what to do all the time. Treat her as your equal."

"She isn't."

They rolled down the exit ramp onto two-lane black-top. Rose considered what he had just said: the key to the whole relationship.

They crossed the river on a concrete bridge and drove down to the beach. As Rose got out of the car, the wind whipped her across the face. A big sign in the parking lot warned against swimming and wading, because of the un-dertow. While Miller parked his car and the others helped Reina unload the horse, Rose walked up over the low dune that separated the parking lot from the beach.

The wind sweeping in from the ocean brought tears to her eyes. She gasped at its force. The empty beach stretched away for miles on either side, backed by yellow cliffs to the south and a levee to the north. The waves rolled in with a boom and thunder that stirred a deep, old excitement in her. She went down the sand to the combers. The waves began to break a hundred yards from shore. Wind-driven, they rushed onto the land and spread out, their foaming margins gobbling up the ground. Two waves collided in a fountain of muddy spray. Then the whole sea slid back from the beach with a hiss and a rattle of turbulent sand.

Sea drift marked the high-tide line, dried kelp, bits of shell and seagull feathers, the bubbly carcasses of jellyfish and by-the-wind-sailor. A redwood trunk, its root mass still attached, lay on the beach a little way from Rose; tendrils of smoke curled up from its lee side and were instantly shredded to nothing by the wind. She walked that way. The lee side of the tree was burned hollow halfway through the trunk. The charred innards glowed in the lash of the wind.

"Let's camp here," she called. "There's already a fire."

Peter tramped through the damp sand toward her. The wind lifted his mane of heavy, black hair. "Not here. This'll be Surf-fishing City all week. Let's hike up the beach a little." He never missed a step; as he ended his speech, he strode on by her, headed off down the tide line. Rose followed in his tracks.

There were mobs of people in Springville, roaming all up and down the sidewalks and cruising in pickups and high-powered shorts along Main Street. Every restaurant was packed. Rose and Reina waited half an hour for tacos and beans on paper plates. They went out to the sidewalk and sat down on the curb in a red zone to eat.

"Where do all these people come from?" Reina asked. "Are they all cowboys?"

A lot of these people did wear cowboy hats and boots. They also favored quilted down vests in spite of the heat of the day.

"Rednecks," Rose said. "I guess they all live around here."

"There's a horse!" Reina flung her arm out to point. A

thin, little, long-maned horse with two children on its back was crossing the street a block away. "Oh, I knew I should have ridden Windfire instead of coming with you."

"Gee, thanks," Rose said. "It would take you all day to ride here from the beach."

The horse had gone out of sight down the beach. Reina stood up. "I'm going down to see what's happening. Bye." She started off at a long, striding walk that quickened to a run before she was halfway across the street.

Rose picked up her abandoned plate and ate the cooling rice and beans. While her attention was centered on the food, someone sank down beside her.

"Hi. When'd you guys get here?"

It was Glory Vigg. Rose pushed the plates away. Although she had previously met Glory Vigg for a total of thirty seconds, the strangers all around them made them friends. "We came up this morning. Where are you people staying?"

"People we know back in the hills a little." Glory had a can of beer, which she raised now to drink from.

"What're all these people doing here?"

"Oh, there's a dance tonight. You heard of any dope for sale?"

"I just got here. How much do you want to score?"

"Just a lid."

Rose dumped the stained paper plates into a trash bin. She and Glory walked up Main Street, weaving through the passing mob. Three blocks of the street were roped off to car traffic, and there, in the street and around the empty bandstand, people were gathered in noisy, exuberant, shifting groups. At one end there was a tower rigged of raw lumber. The man building it paused to take a beer from a friend.

"A dance, or a public hanging?" Rose stared up at the tower.

Glory chuckled. "That's for the firemen's races."

Peter swung out of a bar and wrapped his arm around Rose's neck. "Well, well, well, if it isn't my little sister. How you doin', Rosie?"

She braced herself against his unbalancing weight. "What's happening, man?"

"Big dance tonight, Rosie. Big doings."

Rose stood watching the people around her. They were rednecks, cowboys, and loggers, but many of them wore their hair long, and now the man building the tower was stopping work to toke on a joint held up to his lips by a girl in a long skirt and laced boots.

"Rose!"

Reina dashed up to her. "Look who's here!" Behind her, pink-cheeked and robust, came Bonnie Morrison.

"Hi."

Reina was bouncing up and down in place, her hands clasped together. "They're putting up a carnival! There's a Ferris wheel, and a Krazy Kars—" Radiant with excitement, she whirled around and flung out her arms. "Whoopee!"

Rose put her hand into her pocket, anticipating the next question; she had brought only twenty dollars with her. Reina wheeled back to her.

"Can I have some money? Tonight's kids' night. The rides are twenty-five cents apiece—"

Rose took a wad of bills out of her pants and counted five dollars into Reina's hand. "Don't spend it all in one place. I'm going back to camp at ten. You be at my brother's truck at ten, okay?"

Miller was coming toward them through the crowd. Reina started off, side by side with Bonnie, but he stopped them.

"Want to watch me play tennis?"

"Play tennis," Reina said blankly. "Why?"

"There's a little tournament here," he said. "I'm playing my first match in half an hour."

"Oh, yeah?" Reina said. "Well, good luck." She raced off with Bonnie Morrison.

Rose laughed at the expression on Miller's face. "No chance to be a hero today. What kind of a tennis tournament can you sign up for the same day you play?"

"It's just a local thing."

"You'll get slaughtered. I've never seen you play tennis."

"I play tennis," he said defensively. "I play all I can, when I'm home."

"I'll watch you." She enjoyed the prospect of seeing him humbled by reality. "I used to play, when I was a kid."

They walked away down the street, Miller leading. Over the door to a bar was a big hand-lettered sign announcing a wet T-shirt contest at two-thirty. Already two big buckets of water waited against the wall near the door, and as they passed, a man in a bartender's apron brought another pail out and set it by the others.

"If you play, then you can help me warm up," he said. "I haven't hit a ball in two weeks."

"I haven't got a racket."

He moved toward her, heading her across the parking lot behind a row of stores. Here, less than a block away from the crowd, the streets were empty. In front of a beautiful country-style Victorian house a man in red suspenders was sweeping the sidewalk.

"I haven't got a racket," she repeated.

"I have a spare in my car."

His car was waiting in the high school parking lot, next to the tennis courts. A green sign wired to the chain link fence around the courts read TENNIS TOURNAMENT in white letters. Below it, at a card table spread with papers, a woman with a blue name tag stuck to her sweater was still signing people up.

Rose had not played tennis in years. The first swing she took missed the ball by inches and nearly carried her off her feet. Watch the ball, she thought, panting already. Keep your eye on the ball. The next one she sent arching back over the net.

Patiently Miller ran down her wild shots. He hit the ball with a lot of spin, and she kept jamming herself up against it, misjudging the bounce. After a dozen or sixteen swings, her coordination improved, and she hit them back straight and deep.

He returned everything she hit. When she had to stop, out of breath and with a fiery ache in her right elbow, he was barely warm.

A man in glasses and cowboy boots came up to them. "You're Tarn? You play Wilson. You can use this court if you want." He wheeled toward Rose. "How would you like to keep score?"

She went off with him to carry a box of wooden numbers over to the corner of the court, where a green pegboard was propped on a chair. Sitting down with her back against the fence, she watched Miller and Wilson warming up.

Wilson was a slender boy who talked nervously under his breath. "So much for timing," he mutttered once when he missed a backhand. From the beginning she knew he was no match for Miller. In spite of his fat, Miller moved around the court with a loose, confident grace; he hit the ball well, with smooth, clean strokes that drove each shot deep into Wilson's court, leaving him running uselessly after them. Sometimes the ball bit the court with so much spin that it bounced backwards.

They played, and Miller won easily, two quick love sets.

"Well, that was a piece of cake," Rose said, afterwards.

"Yeah. I was lucky. They matched the intermediates against the advanced and let us seed ourselves." He stripped off his T-shirt and wiped his sweating face with it. They were going back across the parking lot toward crowded Main Street.

"You have any dope you want to sell?"

"Not here. Why?"

"I know somebody looking for a lid. If you hear of anything, let me know." She glanced at him, walking beside her, his young beard a mat of curls. "Maybe I can pinch us some decent smoke."

"Sure," he said, unbaited. "Do what you can."

Ahead of them the crowd was cheering and yelling; Rose turned the corner onto Main Street in time to see two men in black, firemen's oilskins scrambling up a wooden ladder to the tower. Each firemen carried a splashing bucket of water. Everything around the tower was drenched, and the ground was a streaming puddle. Reaching the top of the tower, the firemen poured what was left in their buckets into galvanized tubs and raced down again. The screams and shouted laughter of the crowd cheered them on. Two groups of firemen waited in the street; the men coming down handed off their buckets, and the two new men ran to a hose to fill them.

Rose laughed and clapped her hands. "God, look at this!"

Miller was strolling off, his hands in the pockets of his shorts. Rose hesitated, thinking of going with him, but the firemen were racing up the ladders, and the crowd roared with excitement; she went in among them to cheer.

"It's a little messy," said the guy in the cowboy hat, apologetically.

Rose ducked her head to get through the narrow door of the camper. Inside there were two beds and a tiny kitchen, crammed into a space six feet by four feet. The beds were half-buried in clothes and magazines. She sat down on the mess, making room for Peter beside her.

Hustler centerfolds plastered the ceiling. Rose gaped at the beavers overhead.

Peter came in and the woman in the long dress followed him. She and the man in the cowboy hat lived here. With four people inside, there was hardly room to move, and the air heated swiftly; Rose began to sweat.

"Here it is," the guy in the cowboy hat said. Standing on the bed, he reached up into the shadowy recess above the cab of the truck and took out a Ziploc bag full of dope.

"Roll one up," Peter said, putting his beer on the floor between his feet.

"It's hot in here," Rose said. "Could you crack a window?"

Peter nudged her with his elbow. "Do you want everybody in Springville to know we're smoking dope in here?"

Which was true. She resigned herself to the humid heat.

The man in the cowboy hat rolled a reefer and handed her the bag to examine. Opening the top, she stuck her nose in.

"Smells pretty good."

The joint came to her, and she inhaled deeply through it. The smoke was much smoother than Miller's pot.

"How much d'you want for this?" she asked.

"Forty-five," said the woman.

"For Christ's sake." Rose squeezed the bag, feeling through the plastic film. "There aren't even any tops. It's just shake."

"The tops from this dope sell for fifteen hundred a pound," said the woman sharply. She wore a paisley kerchief over her smooth, brown hair.

"Not to me, it doesn't," Rose said. "Besides, it's got seeds in it. It's homegrown and not sinsemilla. And the lid is light. I'll give you thirty."

"Forty."

"Thirty-five."

The woman glanced at her old man, who took off his cowboy hat and shrugged. "Okay with me."

Rose turned to her brother. "Loan me twenty bucks."

He gave her the money. They bought the can and left.

The night had come. From the block dance came the steady banging of drums and, very faintly, the crickety sawing of a fiddle. Rose and Peter walked over to the carnival, looking for Glory Vigg.

"Make sure she pays you," Peter said. "Getting money out of the Viggs is like squeezing blood out of a turnip."

On the way to the carnival they came on Patty. She was smoking a cigarette and blew the smoke out to the side with a nervous twist of her mouth. "Hi," she said and lowered her voice, her gaze full on Peter. "I gotta talk to you."

"Sure. Talk."

Rose said, "I'll get out of your way." She went a few yards toward the calliopes and flashing lights of the carnival and stopped. "Hey, wait a minute. Patty, can I have the cellophane off your cigarette pack?"

Patty gave her the clear envelope from her Marlboros. Rose walked off to the dark shelter of a tree and took out the bag of dope. Carefully she felt through it for the few buds it contained and put them into the cellophane, twisted it shut, and stuffed it into her shirt pocket.

The carnival was set up in the park at the center of town. The children's slides and swings looked drab and forgotten behind the dazzle and uproar of the rides. The Ferris wheel rolled up into the sky like a huge wheel of fortune; nearby, a Tilt-a-Whirl carried its screaming cargo in a giddy sweep through the air. Little kids rushed from ride to ride, their strings of red tickets pulped in their hands. At a stand selling pink cotton candy and soft drinks, Reina and Bonnie Morrison were paying for corn dogs on sticks.

"Rose." They surrounded her. "Come and ride on the Cannonball with us."

She let them tow her along. They passed a booth with a pyramid of little glass bowls in the center, each bowl enclosing an orange fish; a child in a blue and white shirt was trying to throw a Ping-Pong ball into one of the bowls. The barker waved his stick at Rose.

"Just twenty-five cents a try. The perfect pet, never needs walking, guaranteed housebroken. Too bad, sonny." He went to put three more Ping-Pong balls on the counter in front of the little boy. "Try again. Just twenty-five cents—"

The Cannonball was a ride in a closed car; Rose and Reina and Bonnie sat jammed together behind a mesh door, while the long arms of the ride flung them up and rolled them over and let them drop in a sickening plunge toward the grass. Rose clung to the handrail, trying to control her stomach. On either side of her the girls shrieked in terrified delight. This was torture; why did they like it? They loved it. When at last the car stopped tumbling and the attendant let them out, the girls screamed to do it again.

"I'll watch," Rose said.

While the ride was whirling them around, Johan and his pregnant wife came up to Rose.

"Are you having fun?" Johan called through the carnival din.

"Sure," Rose said. She smiled at his old lady. "Hi. I keep seeing you all over but we never seem to meet. I'm Rose."

"Margaret," said the other woman. She stood with one hand on her back, her belly thrust out, so that it lifted her skirt into a shelf.

"Sunshine," Johan said with emphasis.

"Sunshine," Margaret repeated placidly. She wore the calm and inward look of the pregnant, who know that nothing else is important.

Johan took a step closer to speak near Rose's ear. "You know where we can score a couple reefer?"

"Unh—" Rose put her hand to her shirt pocket. "Sure. Come on over here."

They went off behind the Fun House; Rose gave them the cellophane cigarette wrapper full of pot.

"How much?"

"Two bucks. It's not great smoke."

"Have you seen Mister Peter around anywhere?"

"He and Patty were up by the block dance half an hour ago."

He gave her two dollars in coins. She slid the money into her jeans pocket, saying, "Do you need some papers?"

"No—I use a pipe."

"A pipe—how quaint. I don't know anything about the Man here, but there's dope all over the place." She glanced around them into the dark playground. At the far edge a footbridge crossed the little stream. The whirling carnival lights and noise jangled in her ear. Above them all, the trees towered, too big and too quiet to be noticed.

There was a lesson in that, somewhere, maybe in the relative ages of the trees and the carnival. She felt cold; she wished she had brought her jacket.

"Going down to the block dance?" She and Johan and

Margaret Sunshine walked back around the Fun House to the carnival. As they passed the gate, a car full of kids banged out through the Fun House door and swung around hard on the track, back into the waiting line. Through the swinging doors, Rose saw a fluorescent skeleton dancing in the darkness just inside. She parted company with Johan and Sunshine and went off toward the block party.

At nine-thirty, when she went back to Peter's truck, behind the Bank of America, Patty was sitting in the cab crying and banging her fist on the steering wheel. Peter leaned up against the outside of the truck, extremely drunk. Rose had seen him dancing, up at the block party; the violent exercise had brought him down on his knees, flashing into the street. She looked up at Patty, in the truck, wailing.

"What's the matter with her?"

Peter shook his head. "Ask her."

"Patty, what's wrong?"

Patty turned her head toward the open window. There was a mercury street light on the corner, and it threw a green cast over her face.

"I'm pregnant," she said. "And none of the bums will marry me." Shedding tears, she pressed her face into the palms of her hands.

"Why should I marry her?" Peter said. He struggled to focus his eyes; Rose guessed that he was leaning on the truck because he couldn't stay on his feet. "How'd I know it's my kid?"

Rose watched Patty cry. Finally she said, "Well, it's a little hard to have a kid with only one parent."

Patty lifted her head. The tears glittered in the green-purple mercury light.

"I'm not gonna have an abortion."

Peter looked away. Rose put her hand on the window. "Don't make any light decisions. Having a baby is serious."

The girl's head swiveled, her dark eyes huge with tears.

"I was adopted. I never even saw my mother. I won't have an abortion."

Rose could not see any immediate connection, but she nodded anyway. "Need some company? It's cold out here."

"Sure," Patty said. "Climb in."

Rose went around to the opposite door and slid up onto the seat. Patty was lighting a cigarette. She blew out a stream of smoke through her nostrils.

"Fuckin' bastards."

The dope was still in Rose's hip pocket. She took it out and fished around the glove compartment looking for papers.

"What about your folks? Will they help you out?"

"I told you. I was adopted."

"Is that why you ran away from home? Where you from?"

"Nova Scotia."

"My God, you don't look Canadian."

That made Patty laugh. Rose had found a book of Zig-Zags. She took a paper and crumbled marijuana along the crease. She rubbed the paper back and forth between her thumbs and forefingers, settling the weed, rolled the top edge under, and licked the gum. Patty would be better off if she got an abortion. She twisted the ends of the joint and reached for a lighter.

"What am I gonna do?" Patty sat hunched over, her hands between her knees. "Why did this have t'happen to me?"

Rose handed her the joint. They smoked a little in silence. Peter came over to the window and took the joint from Patty.

"You know what I heard tonight?" He poked his head in through the window of the truck, one arm draped down the inside of the door. "You know what's the biggest cash crop in California?"

"Grapes," Rose said.

He shook his head. "Marijuana."

"You're shitting me," Patty said.

"No shit. That's what I heard."

Rose said, "Sour grapes. Here comes Reina." She leaned back against the leather of the seat. Beside her, Patty sniffed and rubbed the tear-slime from her cheeks.

"Why did this have t'happen to me?"

Rose said nothing. She did not want Reina to know too much of this. Opening the door, she called to the girl to get in.

They were camped on the beach below a yellow cliff, which the wind and the rain had scoured into knife-edged columns. Peter had rigged a windbreak out of driftwood. There was no grass, and after breakfast Reina took the horse up the beach to find some graze. Rose stacked the dishes; it made her temper short that she was stuck with the work.

"I'll help you," Patty said.

"I can do it," Rose said stiffly. She was angry enough to enjoy feeling put-upon.

"D'you want to use seawater?" Patty reached for the bucket.

"Sure," Rose said.

They heated the salt water on the fire. Rose washed the dishes and Patty dried them.

"Those bums," Patty said. "They never said no to me when I was putting out."

Rose fought the urge to smile. She watched her hands scrubbing egg yolk off the frying pan. "You can't count on anybody any more. Does it make any difference to you which one's the baby's father?"

"I don't know—God, they're all so nice when they think they're getting to you. What an idiot I was—"

She stopped, on the verge of tears. Rose held out the frying pan to her. For a moment Patty stared away, out over the ocean; her nose was red.

"Maybe you should reconsider having an abortion," Rose said.

Patty's gaze snapped around. "No. No abortion." She folded her arms over her middle. Her mouth hardened into a grim line.

"Then you'll have to do it on your own, I guess," Rose said.

She meant to make Patty see how impossible it was. Instead the girl faced her with a dangerous glitter in her tear-filled eyes.

"Then I will. By myself." She curled her arms around her body. "At least I got somebody now who belongs to me. And I'm not giving him up."

Rose said, "I'll help you. And Peter will." She doubted they could do anything for Patty. Yet she liked Patty much better for this courage. She said, "Everything will come out okay."

Patty snorted. "God, are you an optimist." She got up and walked off down the beach.

Rose put the camp in order and rolled up her sleeping bag and Reina's. Miller appeared, running along the wave line. He had gone up with Reina to find grass for the horse. Now he jogged across the dimpled sand toward Rose.

"Want to play tennis?"

"Sure. Where's Reina?"

"Feeding the nag. Come on, we're going to have trouble finding an open court, and I need practice."

All the courts at Springville High School were in use. They drove on to the next town and found an empty court there.

"When's your next match?" Rose asked.

"Tonight at five-thirty."

They hit the ball back and forth a few times, and Miller called, "Let's play a set."

"Are you kidding? I haven't served in twenty years."

"Come on, you can do it. It's boring just rallying."

Rose shrugged; her temper burned a little; she knew she was going to lose. The trick was not to care. She moved over to the deuce court, to receive serve, and Miller smacked the first one right by her.

Gradually she remembered where to stand, how to watch his racket to see where the ball would go, how to get her racket out just to meet the serve, her wrist tight, her eyes on the ball. Still she lost, point after point, and as she lost, her anger simmered closer to boiling over. By the end of the first set she was tired. Grimly she faced his serve, beginning the next set.

"Get back away from the ball," he shouted. "You're jamming yourself. You can't swing well like that."

She clenched her teeth. She had been playing tennis when Miller Tarn was still sitting on his potty chair.

But he was good, so good that even when she did her best, hitting her hardest and lowest forehands, he hit winners back to her. He made it look easy. She gripped her temper; she reminded herself that he was younger than she was, and a man, but slowly the raging voice in her head crowded out the tennis game.

Playing with only part of her mind, she played very badly. After she hit three straight into the net, he called, "Get under the ball more."

That broke it. She shouted, "For Christ's sake, will you shut up?"

He walked toward the net, his eyes sharp. He had taken off his T-shirt; his fat hung down around his waist like an inner tube around a swimmer. "What's the matter with you?"

"For Christ's sake, don't you think if I could play better, I would?"

"What's the matter? You can't take criticism?"

At that her fury took over completely. She flung the racket across the court and strode toward the car.

"Hey," Miller said. "That's a good racket."

She ignored him; she reached the gate in the fence and stopped to open it.

"You can't leave," he shouted, "until you pick up my racket."

That, unfortunately, made sense to her. She stared at the U-shaped latch on the gate. Her temper had spent itself; she began to feel silly and a little guilty. Now she had to apologize. Let the punishment fit the crime. Turning, she walked down the court to pick up the tennis racket.

Miller walked toward the gate when he saw what she was doing, and she followed him over to his battered VW.

"I'm sorry," she said. "I just don't like to lose."

"Then learn how to win," he said brusquely and opened the door and got in.

Peter was in Springville somewhere; she asked Miller to take her back to the town. All the way there he didn't light a single joint. She realized that he was so angry he didn't even want to smoke dope with her. She regretted her temper. It was always getting her in trouble—that and her assumption of her own superiority over nearly everybody else. She brooded in silence on her failures.

In the parking lot of the Springville Safeway, where Miller let her out, she came on Glory Vigg, leading her children toward the store. Rose said, "You still looking for a bag?"

"Sure. You got something?"

"Can we do this in your car?"

Glory's car was an old Chevy pickup, its grille missing, its fenders and hood patchy with Bondo. While the kids climbed around in the back, Glory and Rose sat in the front seat, smoking a joint.

"Not bad," Glory remarked when the joint was halfway gone. "How much?"

Rose had been thinking of that since she bought the can. She could not remember how many joints Billy Vigg had ripped off that night at River Ranch, but that mattered little. It was the principle that mattered. She said, "Forty-five dollars."

"Let me see the bag."

While Glory inspected the plastic bag of marijuana, Rose looked out the window, over the low roofs of Springville to the pine-covered ridge behind it. The grove of feathery eucalyptus on the crown of the ridge was visible all over the Eel Valley, every day of the year. In Pasadena it had been the red and white television antennas on Mount Wilson that overlooked the town, but most of the time the smog was so thick that the mountains might not have been there at all.

But I got out, she thought, and a surge of elation lifted her humor.

"Is this a weight ounce?" Glory asked.

"I don't know, I don't have a scale. Feels a little light to me."

Glory kneaded the bag between her fingers. "I haven't got forty-five. What will you give me for twenty-five?"

"You got another bag?"

Glory rummaged through the glove compartment and the space behind the seats. When she straightened up again, she had a greasy paper bag in her hand. Rose put half the dope into the bag and weighed the two bags in her hands. In her new good spirits she regretted her revenging impulse. She put another large pinch into Glory's bag.

"Thanks." Glory picked up her purse and opened it on her knees. "Can I pay you some in food stamps?"

"Okay."

"What's the word on Patty? Is she pregnant?"

"I wouldn't know," Rose said.

"Oh, come on. She told Sunshine she was going to the doctor. Only one reason a girl like that goes to a doctor."

"I have no idea, Glory, really."

"Maybe she's got the clap."

Rose grunted, wished now she had taken her revenge. She got out of the car and went into the Safeway to buy something for dinner.

She got a hoof pick at the Springville feed store and showed Reina how to clean the horse's hooves. Rose hadn't used a hoof pick in nearly ten years, but her hands remembered it, cupping the broad sloping toe in her palm and digging down through layers of muck to the grooves on either side of the frog.

"Let me try," Reina said and took the red-handled pick.

Rose stood back, pulling her jeans up by the belt loops; she had lost her belt somewhere.

"Like this?"

"Harder. Don't be afraid. You can't hurt him if his feet are sound."

She showed the girl how to hold the pick so that the sharp edge got the most leverage. The horse had big feet, striped like the hoofs of all appaloosas. The toes were long, with little pieces of the hoof breaking off.

"We should get a horseshoer up to the ranch. At least trim his feet."

Reina put one hoof down and walked back to the hind-feet. Rose showed her how to run her hand down the back of the lower leg and pinch the fetlock, so that the horse lifted his foot.

Reina worked doggedly, grunting at the effort, her face red. Rose stood back to watch. The old horse turned his head to look at Reina. His dark, prominent eyes and pricked ears gave him a look of friendly curiosity. He swished his long tail over Reina's head and shoulder.

"Stop that," the girl cried and struck him on the rump with her open hand. Rose laughed. She held out her hand to the horse, who sniffed it and rubbed his thick tongue over the palm.

"This is the kindest horse I've ever seen."

Reina put the hoof down and straightened. "He's wonderful." She leaned against his barrel, her arms stretched over him. "He's the most wonderful horse in the whole world."

"Give me the pick and I'll do the other leg."

"No—I'll do it." Reina moved over to the horse's far side.

Rose patted the red roan neck. Miller was coming up the beach. She wondered if he were still angry; afraid to find out, she backed off and went away down the beach toward the camp.

She lay on the sand all afternoon reading *Middlemarch*. Reina galloped off down the beach. Miller raced her a little way and came back to the camp. He said nothing to Rose; she said nothing to him. Still, when he left, she wished she had.

She got up, putting the book away. Sand clung to its pages. Her cheeks were stiff from the drying wind off the Pacific. She went through the camp looking for some smoke, found the remains of the bag she had sold to Glory Vigg, but then decided not to use it after all. Pot made her paranoid, got her in trouble, was ruining her lungs. Besides, her fingers were too dry to roll. She stuffed *Middlemarch* into the pocket of her windbreaker and walked up to the parking lot to catch a ride into Springville.

There were some other people camped in the parking lot, where they had a huge Winnebago. The wife took her into town. Rose walked around Springville; the carnival was choked with kids, and at the dusty rodeo grounds behind the park some cowboys were unloading steers from an aluminum stock-truck. She watched two men on quarter horses practicing spins and stops.

She leaned against the fence, thinking of Miller. She missed his company. In spite of his being so difficult, or maybe because of it, she liked being with him. He was a challenge, an adversary, so different from her that it gave being her a higher value.

One of the men charged his horse the length of the ring. The horse was flying by the third stride, its body stretched flat by the effort; when it seemed that it would crash into the fence, the horse sat down on its hocks, its forefeet out straight, and slid to a stop, showering dirt over the fence ahead of it with a rattle like a machine gun.

Rose was almost straight. She thought of smoking a joint, but she had left the pot at the beach. Proud of herself for that foresight, she walked back through the rodeo grounds toward the town. She was hungry, but all she had was seventeen dollars in food stamps and eight dollars in change, most of which she owed her brother. She was running out of money.

Across from the Ferris wheel at the carnival there was a telephone booth. She got inside and closed the door, but then her courage gave out. She wanted to call Mike Morgan in Pasadena and find out what he had done with the house, and when she could expect some money from that, but she would have to talk herself into it first.

A boy wandered by the telephone booth. He wore tennis whites and carried a fancy graphite racket. She remembered the tennis match and called the time-of-day service. It was almost five. She would have to hurry if she was going to be there for the first serve. She tried out a few opening sentences because she would have to call him at the office.

Hello, Mike. How are you—Mike, it's Rose. I'm sorry to bother you—take you away from your work—

She dialed the number. While the phone rang, she moved around a little, to fidget away her nervousness.

"Morgan Burr and Baylor," said the mechanical voice of the operator.

"Michael Morgan, please."

"Mr. Morgan Junior is no longer with us, sir."

"Ma'am," Rose said automatically. "What d'you mean, he doesn't work there any more? Where is he?"

Recognition enlivened the voice. "Is this Miss McKenna? Rose McKenna?"

"Where is he?" Rose said.

"We don't know. Hold on, please, Miss McKenna, Mr. Morgan Senior will want to talk to—"

"What d'you mean, you don't know?" Rose cried. "Where is he?"

"Hold on for Mr. Morgan."

The phone clicked into limbo. Rose ran her tongue over her lips, her mind fluttery with surprise; a beep on the line pulled her attention together again. They were taping the call.

"Rose?" his father said. "Rose, is that you?" and she hung up. She leaned up against the glass wall of the booth. Only a few minutes ago she had dreaded talking to Mike, but now she wanted to talk to him more than anything in the world.

She called the people who lived next door to the house on North Gibson Street. The wife answered.

"He sold it," she said, sounding surprised when Rose asked her about the house. "Sold it the day the sign went up. Nearly a month ago."

"Do you know what he got for it?"

"I don't know, Rose. I'm sorry."

"I'm sorry, too," she said. Mike could not have sold the house without her signature on a lot of papers, but he had, and that meant he had also taken all the money.

She felt as if he had stolen not only money but the whole ten years of their life together, wiped it out entirely. There in the glass booth she broke down crying.

That helped. Crying always helped. She wiped her eyes and walked across the town to the high school tennis courts.

She got there late. Miller was already playing on the far court. She walked around between the courts and the high windowless wall of the girls' gym and sat on the bleachers among half a dozen other spectators.

Miller was serving, his back to her. When he tossed up the ball, he stretched so high to hit it that his feet left the ground. Going to the net, he volleyed the return into the backhand corner.

That won him the game. He tossed the ball over the net and walked over to the base line.

He saw Rose. She could tell by the way he walked, a new strut in his stride.

The other player wound himself up to serve. He was tall, unshaven, the dark beard like shadows on his cheeks. He played in the same style as Miller, serve and volley, attacking on every shot, taking lots of chances.

The points never settled into rallies. One player or the other would put a move on the ball, a spectacular leap, a stabbing volley, an overhead smash, win or lose in two shots. The people around Rose gasped and cheered. She gripped her hands together; when Miller ran back to fol-

low a high lob, her muscles tensed as if she could hit it for
him. When he smashed it into the net, she groaned.

They ended the set at six-all and went into a tie breaker.
Miller moved around the court with the ponderous, powerful grace of a lion. Going to the net, he leaped up for a high
ball, stretching himself, using his weight to drive the ball; he
hit it so hard that it bounced once and soared up over the
other player and hit the backstop fence.

She cheered, clapping her hands; she saw Miller square
his shoulders, his head high, proud of himself.

He won the tie breaker and the next set. After the match
she went over to the scoreboard, which was wired to the
chain link fence by the gate. All the flights in the tournament were tacked up to the green board, and she had trouble finding Miller's name. When she did, she let out a
whoop.

"He's in the final!"

"Hi," Miller said, smiling at her, his blue eyes brilliant.
He came out the gate, his racket in his hand. A towel hung
around his neck. His face glistened with sweat. The thick unruly curls, drenched, clung to his cheeks. "How'd you like the
match?"

"You were fabulous," she said, relieved to find him
friendly again. "You were serving really well."

"Yeah, it felt good." He scrubbed his face with the towel.
"Come on, let's get something to eat."

She walked across the parking lot after him, going to his
car. Shoving her hands into her pockets, she fingered her
money. "You get something to eat, and I'll watch."

"What's the matter with you?" He tossed the racket into
the back of his car and peeled off his sodden T-shirt.

"I'm broke," she said. "Not only that but I been robbed."

While he put on a clean shirt, she told him about the
house. They walked over to the Mexican restaurant on Main
Street; she held open the door for him, saying, "That
bastard. The only thing I don't believe in this is that he
didn't make certain I'd find out about it."

"How much do you think the house was worth?"

"I don't know. We paid twenty-two for it in 1972. Three years ago we refinanced it for sixty. Maybe a hundred twenty, hundred fifty thousand."

He sat down at the counter. "Eat. It's on me. Anything you want."

"Thanks," she said. "When's your next match?"

"Tomorrow at ten in the morning."

"Okay."

"Will you come watch me?"

"Sure."

"Good. I love an audience." He reached for the menu and opened it flat on the counter between them.

Back at the beach, she made hamburgers and grilled them on the fire. The tide was high and the windbreak Peter had made was soaked with spray. There was sand in everything.

When she was putting the food onto plates, Reina appeared. "Can I go to the carnival tonight?"

"How are you getting there?" Rose spooned carrots onto her plate.

"I don't know." Reina sat down by the fire and put her hands to the warmth. Her gaze rested a moment on Miller, who was already eating. "Maybe I'll hitch a ride." Her eyes shifted toward Miller again.

"I'll take you," Miller said.

The girl nodded; she brought her attention back to her hands, warming by the fire, and she said nothing more.

"You have any money?" Rose asked her.

"I got some tickets left."

Rose took the money out of her pockets. "Peter," she said, "can I owe you a couple bucks?"

"You already owe me twenty, remember?"

"Here." She counted out a mixture of money and food stamps to a total of fifteen dollars. "Now I only owe you five." She gave Reina two dollars in change.

Reina stuffed the money into her pocket. "Come on," she said to Miller, "I wanna go."

"Wait until I'm done," he said. "And I gotta roll some joints."

"Well, hurry up."

Miller took his time. Rose had made potato salad, and he took the bowl and finished it, while Reina twitched and jittered impatiently around the beach. Finally he stretched and got up, put a joint behind his ear, and sauntered away up the beach. Reina flew after him, her arms spread.

Rose put the camp in order. Peter was still sitting in the warm, calm space behind the windbreak. Night was falling. She put more wood on the fire. They were nearly out of wood; she would have to collect some before the dark took over the beach entirely.

"Rose," her brother said. "You think I oughta help Patty out? I mean, what if it is my baby?"

Rose coughed. Knowing her brother well, she recognized this for a rhetorical question, to be followed by yards of rationalization.

"Do you think, you know, there oughta be someway to find out, you know?" He hunched forward, his body curled over itself, as if he sheltered some being from the wind. "I mean, blood types or something. There must be some way."

His face was drawn. The light of the coals, shimmering in the twilight, cast its glow over his features.

Rose said, "Maybe you'll never know. What if you could be sure about it? If it was yours, what would you do?"

Peter spread his hands. His eyebrows made arches over his eyes. "Marry her."

"Peter. How bourgeois. Then why don't you marry her anyway?"

His face tensed with panic. "What if it's not my kid?"

Rose looked away. Sitting on the sand, she reached for her shoes and socks and put them on. Peter reached down beside him for the ubiquitous can of Rainier ale. Rose's heart contracted. He had built a life around excusing himself. Now when he needed courage and will, he had nothing down there to call on.

"Wha'd'you think I oughta do, Rosie?"

She said, "I don't know. Start over again, maybe." Getting up, she put her hand on his shoulder and went away down the beach before he could ask her anything more.

"Come on and hit a few with me," Miller said. "Help me warm up."

They went to the tennis courts fifteen minutes early. The trophies were lined up on the stone curb under the scoreboard. Miller stood staring at them while Rose found out which court he would be playing on. Together, they walked onto the near court, where he had beaten the teenager in the opening round.

She had only hit a few shots when a slender, smiling man in a striped shirt and a visor approached them. Rose went over to the corner. Miller shook hands with the newcomer, whose name was Franklin. They opened a fresh can of balls and took the court to loosen up.

Rose sat down with her back to the fence. Even while they were still warming up, she saw that Miller would have more trouble with this one than the others.

Franklin hit the ball with a deceptive, choppy stroke, his elbow bent, not a hard stroke, but consistent, and with perfect aim. Miller returned everything that Franklin gave him; but he could not put the ball away. They rallied back and forth a dozen times on each point, until Miller lost patience and tried to smash the ball past the other man and missed.

Franklin never lost patience. He won the first game, on his serve, and Miller held his own serve, but then Franklin won four games in a row.

Rose clenched her fists. Sitting in the corner, she strained her muscles with every shot, trying to pull Miller's sailing drives inside the line and to push Franklin's out. By the time Miller was down five games to one, she had given up.

But Miller had not given up. He won the next game, hitting the ball deep, rushing the net, leaping so high for one lob that he had to hit backhand at the full extension of his arm; at that one even Franklin cried, "Oh, nice shot."

And he won the next game, and the game after that, so that when they changed courts after the ninth game, the score was five games to four.

As Miller passed her, going to the service line, she called, "Hit 'em deep. He can't handle those base line shots as well."

He gave her a look sharp with irritation and went over to serve. He won the first two points; Franklin won the next two. On the fifth point of the game they rallied back and forth for what seemed to be five minutes, each man dashing around his side of the court, hitting the ball into the corners and down the lines, until Franklin hit a ball deep to Miller's backhand. Instead of crouching to hit it, Miller came in too close and stood up straight and tried to stroke the ball hard. It went into the net.

Rose sighed. It was set point, and she knew he was going to lose.

Again, they fought it out for twenty or twenty-five strokes, playing conservative tennis, keeping the ball on the lines and in the corners. Miller lost it on another backhand, and the set was over.

The second set was all Franklin's, six games to two, as if Miller had lost all his confidence with the first set.

Rose went slowly over to join him at the gate. He was scrubbing his face with a towel. His hair was tangled into a mop.

"I'm sorry," she said.

He looped the towel over his shoulders. "I fought all the way back in the first set, and then when you talked to me, I lost my concentration."

"I'm sorry," she said, feeling inadequate.

"I'm not blaming you. It was my fault."

They walked across the expanse of blacktop. Bits of broken glass littered the parking lot surface.

"Don't you get something for being runner-up?" Rose asked.

Miller shook his head. "I don't want it." They reached his car, and he leaned against it, his arms across the top, and put his head down. "I'm beat. I'm going for a swim. You wanna come?"

"The parade's about to start," she said. If she hadn't spoken to him during the match, he might have won. "I'm sorry, Mil."

He straightened up, opened the car, and dropped his racket and the towel into the back. "Come on, let's go watch the parade."

They walked over to Main Street, where already grown people and children crowded the sidewalks. Balloons floated in the air overhead and bounced lightly down into the street. A little stand near the post office was selling hot dogs and Cokes, and Miller bought them each a soda. A man on ten-foot stilts swayed in his enormous walk along the edge of the crowd. Rose and Miller sat down on the green-painted curb in front of the post office.

"I lost, Rose."

"I know. I'm sorry."

"But I tried so hard, and I still lost."

She said nothing; she was tempted to put her arm around him, but an inner caution restrained her. He had lost because of her, and yet he did not blame her. She watched a green helium balloon soar away over the flat roofs across the street.

The parade began in an unexciting silence, with fire engines that rolled at a walking pace down Main Street. The firemen in their black rubber coats and boots hung off the ladders and sat in the cabs, while pretty girls perched on the fenders threw handfuls of candy into the street. The children in the crowd dashed out to gather the chunks of bright foil. Then after the fire engines came a line of old cars, shining and flawless, as if they had just rolled out of an earlier world, with their spoked wheels, their rumble seats, their accordion-pleated convertible tops.

Miller straightened up, interested, and pointed to a gray sedan. "Look at that old Dodge, Rose—I had a car like that once. But the door was smashed in."

Rose was more interested in the older cars, Model A's and Model T's, an electric Cord, and an early pickup, its shape blithely square and high off the road, ignorant of streamlining. More candy skittered across the concrete toward her, and two little boys, balloons tied to their wrists, rushed out for the sweets.

Now at last the parade began to sound like one. A marching band strutted down the street playing "The Battle Hymn of the Republic." The sun flashed off the polished bell of a trumpet; the drums banged. Right in front of her and Miller, half the band turned left, and the other half turned right, and they high-stepped back and forth across the street, the lines passing through each other, while the instruments blared the old, righteous song.

Two Belgian workhorses clopped along after the band, drawing a stagecoach. More pretty girls sat up on top, in the luggage rack. They called to people they knew in the crowd. More candy. Two clowns on unicycles zigzagged from curb to curb, pretending to be out of control. Then another pack of cars, the chopped hot rods of the teenagers, their pipes now and then venting an earsplitting thunder.

After that there were more horses, the kids' horses, many in costumes, cowboys, Indians, a spaceman, and one girl whose horse wore a set of trousers on each pair of legs, held up by suspenders, and a straw hat decorated with plastic fruit pulled down over its ears. Rose clapped her hands. In her hometown parade, back in Connecticut, the kids had covered their bikes with crepe paper. More handfuls of candy bounced and skidded over the pavement. Rose stared down the street, her eye caught by a horse that looked remarkably like Windfire.

"It is," she cried. "It's Reina. Look, Mil. It's Reina."

The girl did not seem to see them. She rode at ease, looking curiously around her, as if all this were happening for the sole purpose of presenting Springville to her, Reina Darrezzo.

"She is beautiful," Rose said.

Miller said nothing. He watched Reina with an unquestioning adoration.

The parade was ending. She let him watch until Reina was out of sight and then took him away to the hot dog stand.

"It was that tenth game," Miller said. "I tried so hard I blew it."

"That guy Franklin was a hell of a fine tennis player," Rose said. "I thought you did okay."

"I lost," Miller said. "That's all that matters."

The Lombardi school of sports psychology. Rose scuffed her feet over the pavement, thinking of Reina again.

"When did she leave the beach? God, it must have taken her hours to ride here from Centerville."

"I knew she'd do it as soon as she saw the other kids here on their horses."

"You still want to go swimming? I'll go down to the river with you."

"Sure."

They walked through town, following the road that curved down between the lumberyard and the river. There the river was wide and deep, the current invisible. Rose and Miller climbed over the dike and down the rocky slope to the dark water. The wind sweeping upriver from the ocean drove deep ripples ahead of it, slopping over now and then in a tiny crest of foam. Rose sat down on the warm rocks by the water's edge. Some of the water in this part of the river probably spent months here, especially in the summer. Miller was taking off his clothes.

"You gonna come in with me?"

"I'll watch," she said.

"Come on, Rose. Take your clothes off and jump in. I'll turn my back."

"The water's too cold."

"What are you afraid of?"

"I told you, the water's too cold."

"You scared to be naked around me? You ashamed of your body?"

She took a firm grip on her temper. "Just swim, Miller, and stop telling me what I think."

He stood up, stripped of his clothes. Studiously she kept her gaze above his waist. He might have had a good body if he weren't fat, but he was no prize now. She busied herself gathering a handful of stones and tossed them one at a time into the river.

He dove into the cold green water and swam off into the middle of the river. Rose thought about the money she did not have; subconsciously she had been counting on the money from the house to live on, at least for a while. She had to sort out her new problem and decide what to do.

She tossed a stone into the river; the ripples rushed to the shore like miniature surf. It was not a new problem; it was more like the end of an old one. Her last tie to Mike was gone. She was free now.

That lifted her spirits. She lofted another pebble in a high arc over the water. As for the money, it was only that, paper and ink; if she had it, she would only spend it all. Another stone plunked into the still water. In her mind some face of memory had been turned backward to the past; now, turned forward, it blended into the present and was gone.

On the far side of the river Miller was walking up out of the water. He reached the shore and began to run along the water's edge, majestic in his fat. Rose threw the rest of her stones into the river; folding her arms behind her head, she lay back in the sun.

"Let's go for a ride on the Ferris wheel."

Rose and Miller walked through the carnival crowd toward the white and yellow lights rolling up into the night. At the ticket booth Miller bought them each a ride, but

Reina appeared while they were waiting for the wheel to stop and take them on.

"When are we going back to the ranch?" Reina stuffed her hands down into the pockets of her jeans, her shoulders hunched. A tiny scar on her cheekbone caught the edge of a dimple when she smiled.

"Tomorrow," Rose said. "Maybe tomorrow night. Depends on my brother." The wheel was slowing down. The operator came up to unlock one of the swing seats, his expectant gaze on Rose and Miller and Reina. Miller was smiling, his eyes on the girl, his face eager. Rose stepped back.

"Here. Take my ticket." She poked the cardboard bit into Reina's hand.

"Aw, no, I—"

"Go on. Ferris wheels make me dizzy."

"Thanks." Reina took the ticket from her; at the last moment she lifted her eyes to Rose's, her smile returning, as if they shared a new secret. She and Miller went to take their place on the wheel. They soared up over Rose's head into the dark.

While Rose was standing there deep in thought over what she had just done, a man came up behind her and whispered, "Space captain to space cadet, come in, please."

She wheeled around. "Coyote. I haven't seen you all week."

Jim Wylie drew himself up straight, pulling on his belt, a broad grin on his face. He had a paper cup of beer in his hand, and behind him Sam from River Ranch, his hair down loose over his shoulders, was wiping the foam from his coarse blond mustache.

"I been up at Gasquet all week, working," Coyote said. "Now I get a chance to come down here and party, and everybody here's all partied out. Wanna smoke some good bush?"

Rose looked around them, a reflex paranoia. "Sure." Miller would miss this, a small price for riding the big wheel with his one true love. She followed Coyote past the game booths that formed a back wall to the carnival. Sam, walking beside her, offered her his beer, and she took a sip to wet her throat.

"You, unh, see Patty?" Sam asked.

"Not since the other night."

He played with his mustache a little. He was shorter than Rose, but stocky and rakishly good-looking. They gathered together behind the basketball toss, in the deep shadow of a redwood.

Rose leaned against the rough bole of the tree. She had just remembered her half-formed resolve to give up smoking dope. Coyote was straightening a crumpled joint carefully in his fingers.

"This is the best bush in Humboldt County."

"Where'd you get it?" She moved a little closer.

"Down behind Garberville. It's just shake, but it's dynamite."

The flame jumped up out of the lighter. The red cherry glowed in the darkness. Rose sniffed, the pungent odor awakening in her the memory of the thousands of other joints, the fun of being stoned, and the comfort of sharing it. When Coyote held out the joint to her, she took it and hit deep on it. A little compromise with the Mystery Tramp. She passed the reefer to Sam.

"A hundred fifty the ounce," Coyote said, exhaling. "And worth every flat fucking dime."

The sweet smoke relaxed her and made her voluble. "Whatever happened to the sixty-dollar key? For that matter, how long's it been since you saw a brick?" She had learned the metric system back when dope sold by the kilo; now, perversely, the trade had gone back to the old measures.

"Somebody's coming," Sam said.

They all swung around. The jangling bells and the neon rainbow of the carnival seemed like another world from this darkness, but now somebody was walking straight toward them. The joint disappeared.

"Fee, fie, fo, fum," said Johan, coming into their midst.

"I smell marijuana. Sister Rose, Peter is down at the City Bar, and he's getting himself in trouble."

"What kind of trouble?" The joint had returned, after making its rounds.

"Somebody's gonna put his lights out."

"Shit," Coyote said. "Everybody knows Peter. He's got more friends than there are sheep in Humboldt County. Nobody's gonna hit him."

"I think perhaps in these circumstances they might," disagreed Johan. "You'd better come."

"Come on," Rose said. She started through the deserted playground to the footbridge.

The City Bar was on Main Street, within a block of every other bar in Springville; a steady flow of people moved down the street from door to open door. Groggy drunks sat on the benches in front of the bars, and the campers and pickups that lined the curbs were loud with party noises and music. Just as Rose reached the City, its door flew wide open and her brother backpedaled into the street, his arms wheeling, and fell on his ass.

"Peter! What the hell—"

Peter was struggling to get up. His eyes were bleary, and the front of his shirt was soaked with beer. He pushed himself up onto his feet. "Watch out," he mumbled. "I was on the wrestling team in college—" His legs went out from under him and he fell again.

Rose bent over him. Somebody bumped into her from behind and nearly knocked her down.

"Get outta my way—I'll kill the little creep!"

Rose put her arms around her brother. He was still fighting for balance, trying to get up, his breath a stench in her face. Her stomach heaved.

"Don't hurt him—" She looked up at the enormous man in the doorway. "He's just drunk," she said. "He's harmless."

"That little creep," said the giant, "insulted every woman in this bar, including my wife, and I'm gonna bust him up."

Peter was pushing at her with both hands; she threw her arms around him, holding him down. "I was on the wrestling team in college," he told her. "I gonna kill y'."

Coyote said, "Hey, Bill, long time no see."

He went up to the big man, his hand out; with him for comparison Rose saw, relieved, that the giant wasn't really very big at all.

"Jim Wylie," he said. "Wily Jim. Where you been keeping yourself?" He reached for Coyote's hand to shake. Rose got up and with Johan's help dragged Peter out of range.

"What was he doing?" Rose opened the door of Peter's old truck and groped along the steering column. The keys were in the ignition.

"He was pairing everybody up," Johan said. "He told everybody there to fuck everybody else."

"Poor Peter." Turning, she looked over the rail of the truck into the back, where they had laid Peter down on a pile of old fertilizer bags.

"Has he got something on his mind, Sister Rose?"

"Yeah," she said. "Haven't we all? Thanks, Jo."

"Mister Peter's done a lot for me," Johan said. It was cold, and the wind turned the damp air bitter, but he wore only his bib overalls, no shirt, his skin glossy in the light of the parking lot lamps.

"Aren't you cold?" she said.

He put his hand to his chest. "I got warmth in here, Sister Rose, that keeps me warm all over."

Rose looked away from his eyes. His saintliness turned her off. "Well, I better get back to my camp. Thanks very much." She reached into the cab, grabbed the steering wheel, and pulled herself up onto the seat. "Can I give you a lift somewhere?"

"I'll get there by myself, Sister Rose. Have a good night."

"Good night." She swung the door shut, started the car, and went looking for Miller and Reina.

.   .   .

"I know, I know," Peter said. "I drink too much. But there's nothing else to do up here." He slid down into the seat, his head supported against its back and his knees tucked under the dashboard in front of him. "I'm an alcoholic. I know that."

"For Christ's sake, why don't you do something about it?"

Peter folded his arms over his stomach and glared at her. Rose could see him through the corner of her eye. She was nearly to their exit off the freeway; she put the turn signal on.

" 'Do something,' " Peter said. " 'Do something.' That's all you ever say. I'll do what I damn well please."

"Good for you."

This was Miller's car. Miller was driving the pickup, by now nearly a quarter of a mile behind them. Rose turned onto the county road. She drove slower than usual, watching for the truck in the rearview mirror.

"Everybody's an alky up here," Peter said. "It's the weather. You know what they say about Humboldters. We don't tan; we rust."

"Sure, Peter."

"Anyhow I don't get that rowdy. I just party a little."

"Sure, Peter."

The pickup was in view now, following her, the horse's head sticking up over the top of the cab. She turned onto the dirt road to the ranch.

Peter was right; she was always trying to push him into things. She resolved to be kinder in the future. He needed kindness, kindness and security. The only son of an ambitious, hard-driving father. Therefore every public failure was a personal success.

The road was dusty, and the winter runoff down the hill had scoured out a deep rut down the side. She kept the car close to the edge of the road, dropped it into second gear, and put her foot into it. The engine howled; a rock flew up and struck the windshield with a thunk. Fishtailing through the curve, the little car bounced up the hill.

The gate was shut. Peter got out and opened it and waved her through. When she stopped to pick him up again, he called, "I'll walk up. Go on."

She realized then how much she had upset him. Peter hated walking.

When she pulled up beside the ranch house, there was smoke floating up from the chimney. The back door hung open. Cautious, she peered into the kitchen before she went in, searching the dim room with her eyes. Seeing nothing, she walked across the room to the light switch. A movement behind her caught her eye, and she wheeled around with a yell.

A big black goat was standing on the counter, eating apples off the window sill. Rose let out a second yell, outraged; grabbing the broom out of the corner, she rushed at the goat, swinging the straw end.

The goat stood its ground. She recognized it now, Hallie's Maggie, her distended udder hanging between her hocks and her eyes yellow with mean temper. Rose swung at her with the broom, and the goat lowered her head and drove her horns at Rose's chest.

Rose screamed; she flailed the broom over the goat's head, dancing backwards, as Maggie sprang down from the counter, stood up on her hindlegs, and aimed her horns again at Rose's midsection. Furious, Rose screamed again. She reversed the broom and brought the green pole down across the goat's head with a force that broke the broom.

That stopped the goat, for a moment anyway; she stood blinking and dazed in the middle of the kitchen. Rose grabbed her collar in one hand and, walloping the goat across the rump with the broken handle end, slung the animal out onto the back porch and from there to the ground. She slammed the door shut behind her.

"Hallie," she shouted. "Hallie!"

No answer. The goat was eating the grass. Rose went back inside the house.

The fire was burning in the hearth in the living room. Through the front window Rose could see Miller and Peter struggling to get the horse out of the back of the pickup. She went through the house, looking for Hallie, but the other rooms were empty, too. On the floor of the bunkroom there was a scattering of small black pellets that looked like raisins. Rose muttered an angry oath. Going back to the kitchen for the broken broom, she swept the goat shit into a little pile and scooped it off the floor with a sheet of sketch paper.

"Hallie!" she screamed once more, but got no answer.

She went outside to help with the horse, but just as she reached the front porch, the horse bounded out of the pickup, snorting, and trotted away across the dirt road to the grass by the rhinoceros. Reina followed him, calling. Peter put the tailgate up.

On the far side of the truck was Hallie, talking to Miller. "We had a lovely time while you were gone. It was so quiet. The goats and I just wandered thither and yon—" She sighed. Miller saw Rose; he started toward her with the haste of one escaping.

Rose stopped behind the truck, ten feet from Hallie, and said, "Damn it, Hallie, you didn't wander far enough. One of your goats was just up on the counter in the kitchen."

Miller's head snapped up. "What? In the house?"

Peter was climbing up into the truck, intending to park it. He said, "Worse things 'n that have eaten in my house." The door slammed behind him.

Rose was staring at Hallie, who seemed blithe and unconcerned about the whole topic. "I found goat shit in my room, too."

Hallie was arranging the sleeves of her dress. Today she was not wearing burlap; what she had on now more resembled a bedspread. She said, "Goats are very tidy. Their droppings are very easy to remove. I'm sure—"

"Hallie," Rose cried, "how many goats did you keep in the house?"

"It's perfectly natural. In olden times people often slept with their animals, for the warmth and the comfort of having another being close by."

"Keep the fucking goats out of the house, or I'll do worse than break the broom over them."

Peter drove the truck away. Miller was standing to one side, watching Rose and Hallie. Hallie clasped her hands in front of her, staring at Rose, the way that Rose had stared at the droppings in her room.

"It's perfectly natural," she said in a lofty tone. "It's part of the modern malaise that we've separated ourselves from nature."

"Oh, Christ." Rose gave up, turning away, back to the house. Miller followed her.

"Goat shit in your room?"

Rose nodded. They climbed the steps to the porch. Under her breath, she asked, "You want to go check up on the garden, or shall I?"

"I'll go," he said and entered the house ahead of her, going toward the back door.

She and Peter unpacked the camping gear and put it all away. Reina came in.

"Can I go to Morrisons'?"

"Are they home?"

"I'll call them." The girl leaped toward the telephone. Rose was washing dishes; through the corner of her eye she watched Reina as she dialed the Morrisons' number. Reina had gathered her thick, unruly hair up into pigtails. As she waited for someone to answer the phone, she bounced in place.

Peter said, "You shouldn't be so hard on Hallie." On the counter he set a box full of dirty pots and pans and packages of food. "She's a city kid. People like that tend to go a little overboard the first time they're in the tules."

Rose made a sound in her chest. She scrubbed vigorously at a plate. "That goat is a royal pain in the ass."

"They're home," Reina cried, already moving toward the

door. "I'll be back for dinner." She sailed away out of sight. Rose reached for the stack of dirty pots and dumped them into the soapy water.

A few mornings later while Rose was drinking her coffee on the front porch, Hallie appeared, her arms laden with wild-flowers. She favored Rose with the sunniest of smiles.

"Here," she said. "A peace offering." She put her face down into the mass of color. "Aren't they glorious?"

Rose reached for the armful. She recognized the pinks, the little blue forget-me-nots, and the extravagant orange of California poppy; other flowers, white and yellow and lavender, she did not know. "They're beautiful," she said. "Thanks, Hallie. Let's go put them in water."

They went into the kitchen and Rose filled an old mayonnaise jar with water. Untimely ripped from their home earth, the wildflowers were already dying. She tried to seem enthusiastic about them to save Hallie's feelings; she made a smile for her.

"Do you know what these are? I don't know much about wildflowers."

"This is Solomon's seal. That's very good for headaches and pains in the stomach." Hallie sat down on the couch, her hands in her lap. "The yellow ones are wild mustard." She quivered with delight. "I love the names of flowers."

Rose was fitting them one stem at a time into the mayonnaise jar of water. There were lots of the little white and purple flowers that she had called quarter-foil as a child in New England, and she arranged their long sprigs like antennae reaching up above the clump of blossoms.

"Did you have fun at the rodeo?" Hallie asked.

"Sure." Rose glanced out the kitchen window. On the grass behind the house, cocooned in his blankets and sleeping bag, Miller slept deep into the morning. While she watched, the long bundle thrashed a moment and was still again.

"Did Petey have fun?" Hallie asked.

"Petey got his ass thrown out of a bar."

"He's an artist," Hal said, as if she were calling him a king. "Artists are very emotional. They need relief from the tensions of their feelings."

Rose scratched her upper lip, doubtful of that in all its parts. She glanced at Miller again, out on the grass, wishing he would get up. Reina wandered into the kitchen, her eyes still dreamy with sleep.

"Hi," she said, in a breathy voice and dropped down on the couch beside Hallie. Her nose wrinkled; with a suspicious frown at Hallie she moved to the far end of the couch.

Rose laughed. She took the jar of flowers out to the front room and put it on the sideboard by the pool table.

With her notebook she sat out on the porch, trying to work. The mountain behind the house still sheltered the sun, and the wide stretch of grass in front of the house was in the shade, but when Rose sat down, the first rays of the sun cleared the peak and flooded the grass with brilliant light. While she was still doodling, Reina came out onto the porch.

"Can I wash Windfire?"

"Sure," Rose said, without lifting her gaze from the page. "Just wash out the bathtub after you're done."

"Oh, Rose."

"Oh, Reina."

Rose drew a bathtub on the top of the page. The warm sun relaxed her. She watched a pea-green truck climbing the road from the flat. In the back was something that looked like an old outhouse. Reina led the horse around to the side of the house; Rose heard her turn on the water faucet there. Rose drew flowers in the bathtub, watching the truck curiously. It passed her; Coyote stood in the back, bracing the outhouse, and waved cheerfully to her. She threw down the notebook and followed.

The truck was pulling up behind the shed. Reina stood, the hose curving down through her hand, to watch Coyote and Sam drag the outhouse down over the tailgate. Rose turned the water off.

Reina swung toward her, urgent. "I haven't rinsed him yet."

The horse was grazing between two cars by the shed. His mane was soapy.

"I don't think that's too cool," Rose said. Going up to Windfire, she passed her hand over his shoulder. Soap bubbled up where her fingers pressed the waterlogged hair. "What kind of soap did you use?"

"Dishwashing stuff." Reina's mottled eyes gleamed with indignation. "I got to get him clean. I was so embarrassed at the parade—he gets so dirty!"

"He's a white horse," Rose said. "The only clean white horses are in the movies."

"Well, Windfire's gonna be the first." She marched over to the water faucet, turned it on, and went back to rinsing the soap off the horse.

Windfire was unenthusiastic. She had a rope around his neck, which she held with her left hand, while her right aimed the trickling hose at him. The horse sidestepped away, his head extended to keep his body out of her reach. They performed a swift circle, with Reina at the center.

"Goddamnit!" Reina dropped the hose and struck the wet soapy shoulder as hard as she could. "Hold still!"

"I'll help you," Rose offered, walking over to the horse's head. She patted him a moment, took the rope from Reina's hands, and looped it over Windfire's muzzle to make a kind of halter. "Come on, you old turkey. Move over." She led him to the nearest car, Peter's pickup, and lined him up alongside it.

"Go," she said, and Reina turned the hose on him. The horse moved once, grazed the truck, and was still. As the water drenched him, his coat darkened to a steel-dust gray.

Rose looked around behind her, where Coyote and Sam had unloaded the outhouse. They were walking around in the field behind the house, kicking at the ground. The back door opened and Peter came out onto the back porch. "Hey, you got to tramp around so loud?"

The men laughed at him. Coyote walked halfway to the porch.

"Lookin' for a place to put the sauna, man."

"What sauna?" Peter walked out to join them. They stood in a knot, talking, and moved off together, up and down the field, kicking at the ground.

Reina said, "I think he's clean on this side."

Rose turned the horse around. Now she had a good view of the little shack they had brought. Taller than it was wide, it stood at a slant, a wooden tower of Pisa; there was a hole in the side, with hinges for a door, but no door. The sun shone in through the gaps in the redwood planks of the walls.

"Here," she said to Reina, tossing the rope to her. "He's clean." She walked over to the men, who were standing in a circle and staring at the ground.

Spiny bear grass and clover covered the field. Under the green carpet the surface was uneven and rocky. That was what they were looking for, a flat place to stand the sauna on. One of Hallie's goats was browsing on a patch of poison oak near the edge of the woods.

Something moved beyond the goat, in the trees. Her gaze sharpened. It was Miller, walking through the woods. He sauntered out onto the sunlit grass, saw Rose, and veered toward her. A few steps later he came into view of Reina, and his course changed again. Rose went over to her brother and his friends.

"Where are you going to put it?"

"Right here." Coyote banged the ground with his foot. "Now we gotta get rocks."

"The river," Peter said.

"River rocks explode." Coyote put his hands on his hips. "Grab your sledge. We may have to bust up some boulders." He swatted Sam on the chest with the back of his hand. "The county just dumped a couple loads of rocks into the river, over where it's undercutting the road."

Miller came up behind Rose, his hands in his pockets. He

wore a ripped T-shirt; his arms were rough with red patches of poison oak. "What's going on?"

"They're gonna make that thing over there into a sauna."

"Oh, yeah?" He twisted to look over his shoulder at the shack.

"Come on," Coyote said, raising his voice to include Rose and Miller. "First we're going to get wasted. Then we're going to get rocks."

"Sounds good to me." Miller went to join them. Rose hung back, thinking of her notebook. Reina was walking the horse up and down, drying him in the sun. Rose cut through the kitchen, to get a cup of coffee, and went back to the porch to work.

The story she had been fussing over with so little success had gone stale. She decided to do something else entirely. Turning to a blank page, she drew circles on the top, waiting for an idea to pop into her mind.

Reina came out of the house. "Do you know where there's an extension cord?"

"In the pantry. In the big drawer. Lots of 'em." Rose did not look up from the page. The shadowy forms in her mind drifted just out of reach. She could name them. Sometimes that brought them into focus. She wrote half a dozen exotic names down the side of the page.

Abruptly the story began to pour out, so fast she could barely keep up with it, the process as exciting, as satisfying as sex.

While she was writing, the pea-green truck struggled up the hill, its engine whining. She lifted her eyes as it roared past. There might have been rocks in the back, but all she could see were the people crowding it; more than twice as many as before. When they had passed, she lost herself again in the story.

A few minutes later Reina screamed.

Rose jerked upright, startled out of herself. She threw down the notebook and dashed into the house.

Another glass-shattering shriek. It seemed to be coming from the bathroom. Rose yanked open the bathroom door.

There in between the sink and the shower, Reina was fighting with Miller, banging him with her fists, the way girls hit, with the butt of her fists, like hammers on his shoulders and chest and face. Miller was not fighting back. He grabbed for her wrists and, missing them both, lunged past her, his hand outstretched toward the electrical extension cord plugged into the wall.

"Miller!" Rose jumped at them, trying to get between them. Miller pulled the cord hard, his right hand out flat to fend away Reina's attack. Before Rose could stop her, the girl kicked him hard in the shins and aimed a second kick at his crotch.

Miller yelled. He twisted his body left, away from her, and struck her across the face with his right hand.

Reina fell into the shower. Rose gripped Miller by the upper arms; she looked at him a moment, amazed, and he turned away from her. She stepped over to the shower. Reina was getting up. A blotch of red covered her cheek where he had hit her. Tears stood high in her brilliant eyes.

"She was blow-drying the horse," Miller said. He wagged the plug of the extension cord at them, his expression inscrutable. His eyes were on Reina, not Rose. "There's an energy crisis, and she's out there blow-drying the horse."

Reina shot up off the floor and pushed through the narrow space between him and the wall. In the doorway she turned and shouted at his back, "You creep—I hate you! Creep!" She burst into tears and plunged out the door.

The window over the toilet was open. The extension cord led out through it. Rose stepped onto the toilet seat to look out. Just outside, half in the shadow of the house and half in the sun, the horse was placidly eating the clover. His white coat gleamed. A gun-shaped blow-dryer lay in the rhododendron under the window.

"I think I oughta go," Miller said, behind her.

Rose nodded. "If you can't handle yourself any better than that—"

"She was trying to kick me in the balls! I'm not letting anybody kick me in the balls." He turned away, his shoulders slumping; he threw down the plug of the electric cord in a gesture that threw away the world. "I'm leaving, Rosie." He walked out of the room.

Rose reeled in the blow-dryer. She wondered where Reina had found it. Maybe it was Patty's. She stuffed it into the shelf over the sink and went out looking for Reina.

The house was empty. Rose stood on the little back porch, her hands shoved into her hip pockets. Most of the population of River Ranch stood or sat in the grass near the sauna. Coyote and Sam were tearing into the ground with picks, while Peter strolled up and down giving them advice. Most of the women sat together on the ground; she recognized Glory Vigg's broad back, deeply indented by the string of her halter top. Next to her was Sunshine Margaret. Reina was nowhere in view.

Behind Margaret, Patty sat with her knees drawn up and her arms around them. She saw Rose and got to her feet and walked toward her.

"Anybody want a beer?" She came briskly up the steps and past Rose into the kitchen. As she went by, she muttered out of the corner of her mouth, "Gotta talk to you."

Alert, Rose went into the kitchen. "What's up?"

Patty wheeled around in the center of the kitchen. "Are you stealing our pot?"

"What? What pot?"

"The field."

"No," Rose said curtly; her temper quickened.

"That's what I thought." Patty opened the refrigerator door. She wore Levi's and a short sleeveless leather vest laced up the front. She tore the cardboard wrapper off a six-pack of Coors, took a can of that and a can of Rainier from the shelf above, and shoved the door shut with her hip.

"Somebody's been taking our plants," she said. "They're having a meeting tonight to talk about it. Press-butt says it's you."

"Why would I steal plants that size? Have you seen Reina?"

"Nope. Haven't. I just thought I'd warn y'."

"Thanks."

Patty walked past her to the back door; on the threshold she stopped. "Oh. Sam says I can live there if I keep house."

"Oh," Rose said.

"So I'm not leaving." Patty banged out through the screen door.

Rose followed her a few steps. Uneasily she wondered about this meeting and Dave Preston's paranoias. Through the rusty mesh of the screen door she looked over the people by the shack. Preston was there; he and his brother were helping the other men unload two-by-fours from the back of the pea green truck.

The horse was far across the field now, nearly to the trees. His black and white tail swept over his flank.

"Have you found her?" Miller asked, behind Rose.

She nodded, her eyes struggling to see details of the dark shape in the grass beside the horse. "She's sitting over there in the meadow." She moved aside so that he could see.

He did not go to look. He had his sleeping bag rolled up under his arm. "Will you take a walk with me?"

"Okay."

They went out the front door. His VW was sitting there in the sun. Opening the door, he tossed the sleeping bag in on top of his other gear. A cold thread of alarm in her gut, Rose saw that he was leaving River Ranch. She had thought, when he said he was going, that he was only leaving the room.

"Come on," he said and started away on foot down the road.

Rose fell into step with him. She fought down the uneasy mood that his going had brought on her. They passed the noisy scene around the sauna; the sweet smell of marijuana drifted down the air. Somebody was hammering. Peter was saying loudly, "Well, you know what *I'd* do—"

Rose stared at the ground. The sound of the hammer echoed off the mountain behind the house. She followed Miller along the side of the road, where the grass was gray with the powdery dust. A little snake wiggled away ahead of them into the high brush.

"I must be crazy," Miller said. "I must be out of my mind."

Rose shook her head. There was nothing she could say. Yet it hurt to see him hurt. She kicked a rock into the grass beside the road.

"Where are you going?" she asked at last, when he said nothing more.

"I don't know. Maybe I'll go over to Tahoe or Reno and gamble."

"You going back to L.A. ever?"

"Oh, sure."

"Say hi to Angie and Felice for me." She glanced at him. His head was down, his shoulders round with unhappiness. Above the T-shirt the nape of his neck was exposed, tender and vulnerable. She clasped her hands together behind her. And now he was going; she might never see him again.

She said, "She doesn't deserve you, Mil. You treat her so well, and she treats you like shit."

The right thing to say. His head lifted, his shoulders squaring.

They walked down past the grove of eucalyptus, the long leaves like gray-green flames rippling in the wind, the pale columns of the trunks like candles. Ahead of them, in the high meadow, Coyote's teepee came in view.

"Take care of the pot," he said.

"Sure."

"When they start to blossom—"

He stopped in midsentence. They walked on a little farther.

"They'll start to blossom in a month or six weeks," he said. "I'll be back by then."

Her mind eased; she drew what seemed her first deep breath in long moments. "What about fertilizer?"

"You know that Rapid-Gro? It's up on the shelf in the closet of that room where you and Reina sleep. Read the directions and give them another dose in three weeks."

"I will."

"Pick off the sucker leaves."

"I will."

"And don't tell anybody it's there."

"I won't."

They were coming to the gate. Beside it the tall, coarse stalks of cow parsnip were drying to brown husks. Yarrow grew up among them like stepchildren. Miller put out his hand, touched the gate, and turned. Rose followed.

"I'll miss you," she said.

"Really?" His blue eyes stabbed her with a quick, shy glance. "Silly Rosie."

The road steepened. On the power pole just ahead of them a woodpecker was drilling for insects, rat-a-tat-tat through the bright morning. The road dust, like brown flour, turned everything along the road the same color, the rocks, the grass, the leaves and flowers of the blackberry vines.

"When is he going to move those logs?" Miller pointed across the meadow to the redwoods, where the felled trees lay half-buried in ferns.

"I don't know. He's been working hard lately; that takes a lot of time, I guess. It takes them hours and hours just to get to the trees."

"You like him, don't you?"

"Sure."

"I mean—you'd like to fuck him."

"Sure," she replied. "That doesn't mean I will."

"Why not?"

She shrugged. The woodpecker's jackhammer stopped a moment and began again. "It's more important than that— I need more than just liking somebody." She studied him for a moment, through the corner of her eye, pretending to look straight ahead. "I'd like to fuck you, too. I bet you didn't know that."

"You would?" He sounded amazed and pleased, his voice buoyant.

"But I won't," she said. "Same reason."

"What more do you need?"

She shook her head. "It would take too long to explain."

They were nearly to his car now. She looked curiously toward the crowd around the new sauna. The hammers were banging again, two of them, out of rhythm, their mixed beats colliding with the echoes off the mountain. She and Miller passed the pea-green truck. On the other side, Billy Vigg, one hand on his back, twisted his body in obvious pain.

"It's m' back again—Jeez—I threw it out, t'other day, working in the field—"

He winced dramatically. Glory Vigg was pulling on his arm, crying, "Let me see, will y'? Let me see!" Patty looked on from a little distance, her head cocked to one side.

"Well," Miller said, "I hate good-bys, so good-by."

"Good-by," Rose said.

He walked to his car and got in. Rose climbed two steps to the porch. The white VW rolled away down the hill. She waved, but he was already gone, in his heart; he never looked back. Through the rear window of the VW she saw him take a joint from behind his ear. The car disappeared over the brow of the hill, and its engine noise faded away, into the chatter of the woodpecker, the singing of the wind in the grass. Rose stood there a moment, her ears straining to hear. From the crowd around the sauna came a braying cheer. She went into the house.

Jim Wylie's red hair covered his head in a mass of springy curls; his curly beard was lighter, strawberry blond. He reminded Rose, as he always did, of the statues of the gods she had seen in the museums in Athens.

"How do you get your hair like that, Coyote?" She was sitting to one side of him, in the big leather chair by the hearth.

"Just does itself," said Coyote, who was eating.

"Aw, I don't believe it." She reached out and fingered the tight, perfect curls. "It's a Toni."

Reina came by her to the hearth, where the cooks of River Ranch had set their casseroles and salads, breads and pies and cookies. Taking a paper plate from the end of the brick apron, she went from dish to dish.

Rose was too nervous to eat. She slumped down in the deep, soft chair, her back curved into a bow. The room behind her was full of people she hardly knew, people whom Preston had convinced that she was stealing their marijuana. She wanted to leave, but she could not. She admired Wylie's hair again.

"If I had hair like that, I'd go on the tour, man."

Wylie grinned, looking stoned; he ate a forkful of cole slaw. "Don't think I ain't had offers."

Reina came around Rose's chair and sat down on the floor beside her. "There's nothing here to eat," she said. She had served herself a salad, a wedge of blueberry pie, a handful of cookies. "Where's the meat?" She popped a chocolate-chip cookie into her mouth and, chewing, scanned the room. "Speaking of the meat," she said, "where's Miller?"

"My God," Rose said, "the child's made a pun. He left. He's going back to L.A."

"Good." The word seemed to explode out of Reina's mouth; she relaxed visibly. "Good." She pushed at her salad with her fork.

"I tend to agree with you," Rose said. "For his sake."

"Seen my sauna yet?" Coyote asked.

"Not yet."

"Come on out after the meeting. I'll fire it up."

Billy Vigg was serving himself huge portions from every dish on the hearth, balancing two paper plates in one hand while the other spooned up the food. Passing Rose and Coyote, he favored them with a broad grin. "Gotta put in the fuel," he said and went on.

"What y' been doin', man?" Wylie said.

"Lookin' for a job," said Billy, his back to them.

"Jesus Christ, the world must be coming to an end."

"Naw, just my unemployment checks." Billy guffawed with delighted laughter at his own joke. He brought his overloaded plates back toward them and sat down with them to eat. "You got any work on your crew, man?"

"Not for you, man, not after the shit you pulled on me last time."

Billy laughed again, but with less delight. Rose leaned her head back against the chair. Out the big corner window she could see the ranch children, playing on the rhinoceros. Peter had worked on it again, adding another cube to the stack of cubes and stringing a long, thin rectangle down the side, but it was still a rhinoceros to Rose.

"Tell you what," Wylie said to Vigg. "I'm gonna haul the logs off my land there in a couple weeks. I only got a week off from work and I got a lotta logs to haul. You can help me with that."

"You got the trucks?"

"I got J.J.'s truck and J.J. driving. Also my boss is loaning me a loglifter, and I'm gonna rent a bulldozer for a couple days."

"I'll help you," Rose said.

Coyote laughed, as if she were joking, and tossed his paper plate into the fire.

"I'm serious," Rose insisted.

He shook his head. "It's hard work, lady. You'd bust your butt and still not get enough done to be much help."

"Goddamnit," she said, "I can do it. I'll work a lot harder than he will." With her chin she indicated Billy Vigg.

"Hey," Billy said, sounding offended.

Coyote was shaking his head. "Naw. There's women in the woods, but they're a lot younger than you are. If you want to help me out, you can cook meals for me. Me and my crew. I'll give you ten bucks a head per day for three meals a day. Bring the lunch down where we're working."

Rose's cheeks were burning; she wished she could have picked up the chair he was in, complete with his ass in it, and shown him how strong she was. Unfortunately he was right, she knew he was right, and she needed money more than pride.

"Ten bucks including the cost of the food?"

He shook his head. "I'll pay for the food. But you gotta make lots. It's hungry work."

"I will."

"Good." He leaned out of his chair and lifted the last of Reina's cookies.

Reina yelled; she snatched for the cookie, but Coyote had already stuffed it into his mouth. He laughed at her. Furious, the girl glared at him and got up and went back to the dish of cookies for another helping.

Behind them, suddenly, Dave Preston's voice cut through the chatter of conversation.

"Everybody, let's get this together. Come on down around the fireplace."

The others drifted down around Rose and Reina and Coyote. Rose folded her legs under her on the leather chair. Her stomach rolled over. Hallie passed her, going to the chair in the corner. She gave Rose a meaningful look. Johan and his old lady sat down beside Reina. The others crowded up close to the hearth.

Dave Preston stood up on the brick apron, in among the dirty dishes.

"Now, you all know what we're doing here. Somebody has been coming in at night and raiding our pot field."

Apparently some of them had not known. A mutter of surprise passed through the people sitting together on the floor.

"Now, we haven't got any evidence," Preston said, shooting a dagger look at Rose. "But it really ain't too hard to see what's been happening."

"For Christ's sake," she said irritably. "If you haven't got any evidence, maybe the way to start is to find some."

"You won't work in the field," he snapped back. "Why should you work when you can get it another way?"

Several people growled in agreement. Rose glanced at

Coyote, who was ignoring all this. She wished he would help her, or Peter or Johan, but all these people were silent.

Preston said, "Now, there's only one way to keep thieves out of the field." His gaze broadened to include the whole crowd. "We gotta patrol the field, day and night, and we gotta carry guns."

Johan's head snapped up. "No guns."

"Hear," someone else called, and a murmur of agreement ran through the massed people. Near the far wall, Peter stood drinking a can of ale, and he lowered it and went forward a little.

"I don't see we need any guns. You know, my sister's right. We—"

Preston shouted, "Your sister's the one's been taking our plants!"

"No guns!" Johan called, cupping his hands around his mouth, and around him others picked up the chant.

"No guns! No guns!"

Preston and Peter were glaring at one another in a face-off. Rose stood up.

"Why don't you tell us more about these thefts, and then maybe we can piece together what's really happening?"

The chanters' voice wavered and died. Peter shouted into the fresh silence, "Yeah! Let's start with when it happened. That'd help."

Preston looked from him to Rose; under this wide-angle, two-pronged attack he lost his single-mindedness. If Peter went forward now, Rose thought, he would take back control of the meeting from Preston, but obviously Peter was not ready for that.

Rose said, "When did you notice the pot was gone?"

"T'other morning," Glory Vigg said from the crowd, "when I went out to work. You know I work in the field Thursdays in the morning. There was a whole row of plants gone, just pulled up. Poor little things."

Rose sat down again, as the others joined in the talk.

"Where was they? What part of the field?" Peter nodded.

"Maybe it was a hiker. You know there's two camper loads of city people down on the river bar now. Maybe—"

Rose grunted. To Coyote she said, "I can't see city people hiking up nearly half a mile from the river and then pulling up plants."

"It's probably one of the kids," Johan was saying. "And if we start carrying guns, somebody's gonna be hurt."

"I was in Vietnam," Preston said. "I know how to handle a weapon."

Billy Vigg was still eating. With his mouth full of cole slaw, he said, "I don't see why we can't sell some of the dope now, man. Like, man, I really need the bread, you know?"

Preston wiped his face on his sleeve. "Jesus, Bill, those plants are only about four feet tall. You wouldn't get ten cents for 'em now."

Rose was watching Billy Vigg; the strong suspicion entered her mind that it was Billy stealing the pot. He went on feeding his face. Catching her gaze on him, he winked broadly.

"And anyhow," Glory called, "it's hard enough getting people out there to weed and water the fucking plants. How the hell you gonna get 'em out there for even more time, walking around and around all day and all night?"

"Hear, hear," a couple of voices chorused.

"Either that, or it's a kid stealing the dope," Johan said. "You wanna shoot a kid?"

"All the time we was at the rodeo there wasn't nobody there at all!" Patty said. "No wonder we can't get anything done and somebody's ripping off the plants—maybe they think the plants are better off dead than being neglected."

Preston waved his arms over his head. "Now, shut up. This is getting confusing. We gotta talk about one thing at a time."

Peter said, "What we oughta do is go by shares."

"I thought that's what we were doing," Patty said to him. They were standing side by side. Peter edged away from her.

He said, "What I mean is, we split up the field now. Everybody gets his own part. Then you work your part and patrol it and then if it dies or gets ripped off, it's your fault. Right?"

There was a moment of quiet, while people ruminated. Preston made a thoughtful face. He raised his hands over his head.

"Okay. Peter has the right idea. We'll divide the field up by the number of people in on the deal."

They did that, over the next twenty minutes, thrashing out the objections one by one. Rose sat watching them argue. She felt removed from this. She missed Miller, whose hard friendship had given her shelter.

Patty stepped forward. "What about if somebody wants a share but like he can't work or something?" She smiled at Billy Vigg. "I mean, we all know Billy's got a bad back. Right, Billy?"

"Yeah, you know—" He assumed the posture of a man with an aching back, his hand pressed to the middle of his spine. "It's down in there, man, down in the lumbar region."

There was general laughter. Patty's smile was sweet with malice. "I mean, anybody who wanted a share but didn't want to work, he could pay somebody else to do his work, right?"

Rose lifted her head, surprised at Patty's ingenuity.

"Well, sure," Preston said slowly. "I don't see nothing wrong with that."

"It's a good idea," Johan called. "That's righteous."

"How much?" Billy asked.

"Oh," Patty said, "I'll work that out. Anybody wants a field hand, I'm right here."

They went to work on that, refining the idea and arguing about how much the work was worth. Rose watched them, an outsider among them. Sam had gone over to Patty and stood talking to her; she leaned against the wall, one foot cocked up against it, her hands behind her, the hustler's stance. Peter was staring in the other direction, his expression so intense that Rose knew he was listening to them. She leaned deeper into the chair, thinking of leaving.

"I don't see that they settled much," Rose said of the meeting. "They just argued and argued."

"I got what I wanted," Patty said.

In the darkness Rose could see only dim shapes, crouched around the sides of the sauna. The joint came at her, a hot red dot, and she reached behind the coal for the cool end. Her fingertips grazed Coyote's. She sat back on the redwood bench, toking on the joint, struggling with pangs of lust.

On her other side, Peter said, "Throw some more water on, Jim. Let's heat it up in here."

Rose passed him the joint. Jim reached down under the bench and brought out an old gallon milk jug of water. The only light in the little room came from the fire in the woodstove. When Coyote leaned over the metal shield that held the rocks in, the room dimmed. The water hissed on the rocks and clouds of steam rolled up into the room, which suddenly became unbearably hot.

"Jesus," Peter cried. He bounced up and down on the shelf. Rose slid away from him. All over her body the sweat poured forth. It hurt to breathe the moist and searing air.

There was a knock on the door. Hallie called, "Can I come in?"

"Take your clothes off," Coyote shouted.

The door cracked open an inch. Rose gasped. The cool air flowed over her legs. Through the slot Hallie whispered, "Can I wear my undies?"

"Hallie," Rose said, "we're all naked. Anything you wear will get soaked. Just peel and get in here."

The door shut again. A moment later it opened wide, and Hallie rushed into the tiny room. She screamed at the heat and steam. Shutting the door, she turned to latch it, silhouetted against the cloudy glow of the stove, a life-size Venus of Willendorf. She turned, uncertainly, and Coyote got her by the arm and helped her up on the shelf beside him.

"What we need is a hot tub," Peter said.

"Hell," Coyote said. "All these naked ladies in here, what we need is a waterbed." His arm fell across Rose's back, hugging her against his side. His skin was slick under her hand. They laughed. They slid together a moment, warm and slippery, chest over chest. Rose put out her hand, to hug him back, and her fingers grazed flesh where he couldn't possibly be. Hallie. He was hugging both of them at once. She slid apart from him. Her body tingled; her groin ached pleasantly, wanting, wanting.

"More water," Coyote said. "Let's catch up on the steam."

In the sudden, swollen glow of the stove she saw that he still had his arm around Hallie. Rose moved back. He just wanted somebody to paw and possibly fuck later on. Wounded in her pride, she heard Hallie's giggle and turned her head away. He treated her the same as Hallie, fat and foolish lady of the goats.

She went back to the safe subject of the meeting. "If we decided anything about the gun, I missed it. Is he going to stalk the pot field with a gun or not?"

"Depends pretty much on Dave," Peter said. "Hell, let him do it a couple nights. He'll get sick of it and give up."

He drew in on the joint. The flush of red light shone on his face a moment. Hallie giggled again, and Rose looked toward them. She took the joint from Peter and leaned back against the wall, taking her hit. The joint was less than an inch long now. She felt along the bench between her and her brother for the roach clip, attached it, and held it out toward Coyote.

"You got a free hand, there?"

Hal moved, a mass shifting through the dark, barely seen. Jim took the roach clip from Rose's fingers. "What'sa matter with you?" he said, sounding amused.

She said nothing more, waiting for the joint to come back.

Wondering what he would be like to sleep with. That hard muscular body. She remembered the first time she had seen him, as naked as he was now, beautiful in the rain. But if he would take anybody, then he would not care very much beyond his own delight.

She put her foot down toward the floor. She wanted to leave but she had to wait a while longer, so that he would not connect her leaving with him, with him and Hallie.

Peter said, "Well, I've had enough. I'm getting out."

"I'll go with you," Patty said. "Don't open the door until I get down—it's cold out there."

Rose slid across the bench into the corner her brother had occupied. The door opened, and a flood of chilly air rushed in. The two left. Rose shut the door and pulled the latch home.

"Get some water, will y'?" Coyote said.

She reached down under the bench where the water jugs were and found a full one.

"Don't," Hallie said, and giggled.

Rose upended the jug over the rocks. Steam billowed up from the hissing rocks, and one cracked, with a sharp pop like a b.b. gun.

"Come on," Hallie said. "Don't!"

"I think I better split," Rose said.

"Either that," said Coyote, "or get over here and join in."

Rose opened the door and went out into the clammy, empty night.

A few days later, while she was folding the laundry, she turned up one of Miller's T-shirts, the torn one, a faded blue. She buried her face in it. The smell of the sun-dried cotton was delicious. She rubbed the shirt over her cheek, wondering where he was, and if he ever thought of her.

She went down to her garden to water the marijuana plants. When she came back, Reina was galloping up the road from the flat, holding the reins high with one hand and the saddle horn with the other. As soon as she saw Rose, she began to scream.

"Sunshine's having the baby! Sunshine's having the baby!"

"Where?" Rose leaned over the porch railing.

Reina brought the white horse to a stop directly in front of her. "She's down in their house. She's gonna have it any time they say. There's a guy there who takes 'em out—"

"Takes what out? The baby? A doctor?"

Peter came out onto the porch, blinking in the bright light; he had obviously just gotten out of bed, his fly unzipped, his shirt rumpled. "What's the racket about?"

"Sunshine Margaret is having her baby," Rose said. She turned to Reina again. "She has a doctor?"

"No, he isn't a doctor. It's something else, I don't remember the name—"

"Midwife," Peter said. He rubbed his hands together. "This'll be the first human baby born on River Ranch." He sounded as proud as if he were the father. Shoving the tails of his shirt down into his pants, he started toward his pickup truck.

"Wait for me," Rose called and ran after him.

Johan's house was full of people. The Vigg children were eating apples off the trees in the front yard; Glory Vigg herself, dressed in a bathrobe, was heating water on the stove. Sam and Patty and Billy Vigg and some other people were crowded together into the room where Sunshine lay, her back supported by pillows, on the very foot of her bed.

She was naked, the enormous taut mound of her belly streaked with red stretch marks. Her legs were bent. Between them Johan knelt, massaging her vulva with the flat of his hand.

The midwife was spreading a clean white sheet on the bed behind her. There was a big canister of oxygen in the corner and an array of little tools on a white tray on the window sill, gleaming in the sun. With the sheet smooth and spotless behind her they helped Margaret move backwards onto it.

"Here comes one," Margaret said.

Everyone in the crowd watching her simultaneously drew in a deep breath. Margaret closed her eyes, her hand on her distended body. Rose murmured under her breath. She could see the huge mass shift under the force of the contraction.

Margaret whined, her teeth clenched. Rose glanced at the midwife. She wondered if Margaret would get anything for the pain; probably not, since they seemed committed to doing this naturally. Margaret was unready for it. If she tensed under the contraction now, she would be screaming long before the baby came.

"Relax," Rose called to her. "It'll hurt less."

Margaret did not seem to hear her. The contraction had passed; she lay slack on the pillows, her eyes half-closed.

"Five minutes apart now," the midwife said. He was putting on a pair of surgical gloves. "Let me see if she's dilating yet."

Johan moved away. The midwife stooped and slid his index finger into Margaret's vagina.

In front of Rose, Patty gave a low cry and turned. She forced her way out through the crowd, away from the laboring woman; her face was wild.

"Not dilated at all, so far," the midwife said.

Everybody sighed, let down.

Rose went back into the kitchen. This was going to take time. Glory was still boiling water. There were dishes to be washed, and Rose and Glory silently went about washing them and cleaning up the kitchen. When that was done, Rose went back to the crowd. As she passed the door to the other bedroom, a sound inside stopped her, and she pushed the door open to see.

Inside the little room Patty was walking up and down, a pillow clutched with both arms against her body, her face seamed with thought.

"Come on," Peter said, behind Rose.

"Come on where?" Rose shut the door on Patty.

"Back up to my house. This baby ain't gonna be born for hours."

"I'll walk up," Rose said. "I need the exercise."

She did not walk home by the road; she cut across the swampy meadow by the creek, nearly dry beneath its curtains of willow, to where the common pot field grew behind a fence of withies. The plants were nearly as tall as she was. She had never seen marijuana plants as big as these, and they aroused in her a sense of them as animate beings, the way that Mescalito personified peyote. The marijuana stirred in the wind; the rustling of their notched, five-fingered leaves was like an alien music.

They needed weeding. Some of them were wilting from lack of water, and most still carried their full canopy of sucker leaves. She turned away, thinking of her own garden, and went up the hill to Peter's house.

On the mountainside behind the house was an old apple orchard. She picked a dozen apples and took them back to the house to make a pie.

While she was cleaning up the kitchen, Reina galloped up to the back door and shouted, "I got the mail. There's a card from Miller."

"Oh, yeah? What's it say?" Rose wiped her hands on her jeans. She opened the door and took the stack of letters from Reina.

"I didn't read it," Reina said. "It's for you."

"So it is."

The front showed downtown Reno, with an arch over the street, the biggest little city in the world. The card was addressed simply to "Rose, River Ranch," with the box and route number. The handwriting was clear but cramped and childish, a masculine hand.

Hi. Very hot and sunny here. I just won 300 and now I am waiting for the results of the Wash.-Dallas game to see if I win any more. Give my love to Reina. Mil.

"What Washington-Dallas game?" She read the postcard through again, absorbing the minutest details. Did he mean baseball or football? She read over the last line of the message, its real point. "He says to give you his love."

Reina shrugged. "I'm goin' down to see the baby get born." She curved the horse away from the porch and clicked her tongue, and he broke smoothly into a canter and galloped away.

Rose put the postcard on the wall above the kitchen sink, where she could see it while she washed dishes. The pie was nearly done; she turned off the oven.

She had finished the new story, and she went into her brother's room to type it. Under the window a big old black Underwood manual sat on a trunk, and she pushed the stool over and went to work. As she typed, she pruned the story and filled it out.

While she was proofreading it, another story occurred to her, a conceit more than real story, about the end of the universe, and she turned to the typewriter and banged it out, straight from her head, without changing more than a few words. Sitting back, she read it through, pleased. Maybe the long weeks of useless work had been a training exercise, to get her writing mind into shape. She typed another copy of that one and went to find envelopes.

The phone rang. She answered it.

"You better get your ass down here, if you want to see this baby born," Billy Vigg said.

Behind him lots of people were talking, even laughing. She said, "Is it B.Y.O.?"

Billy laughed, not understanding, and said, "Come on down. Tell Pete."

Peter was out in his garden behind the house, picking peas. She leaned over the fence and said, "Your newest citizen is arriving by express."

"What?"

"Sunshine Margaret is putting forth."

He turned to the gate, brisk. "Come on."

"I'm not going," Rose replied.

"What? Why not? Everybody else will be there."

"That's why I'm not going. It's a mob scene down there. You should leave her alone and let her calve in peace."

Peter shut the gate shut. "The world curves, but Rosie goes straight on." He took a can of Rainier from a fence post, drained it, and strode off toward the back door. A few moments later, he came out with a six-pack under his arm and got into his truck.

Rose took the stories into Springville to mail them; she was sending them both to an editor at *Future* who had bought several other stories from her. On the way back, she circled around the ranch to come in through the back gate.

Johan's house was crowded to overflowing. People stood in the little orchard, talking through the windows to the people inside, and the door was packed. She forced a way in, saying, "Excuse me, excuse me," every few steps. Someone held out a beer to her, and she took a sip. "Thanks." In the hallway the people thinned out; Patty was sitting in the corner, under a basket of wandering Jew. Rose bent down to speak to her.

Patty glared at her. "Get away from me!"

She was drunk. Rose straightened up, irritated. Patty folded her arms over her stomach and rocked back and forth, staring at nothing. Rose looked into the bedroom where Margaret had been laboring.

She was sitting up, dressed now, drinking a cup of tea. Her belly seemed just as huge. Glory Vigg sat beside her. She had changed from her bathrobe into a tent dress. When Rose came in, she beamed at her.

"You missed it!"

"I'm glad I did," Rose said. "How are you, Margaret?"

"I'm fine," said Margaret. "Tired, but happy."

"You should chase all these people out of here so you can sleep. How's the baby?"

"She's beautiful," Margaret answered and smiled, her face

luminous, her eyes wide and clear. Rose impulsively put out her hand and took hold of Margaret's.

"What's her name? Can I see her?"

"She's in the next room, with Johan," Margaret said. "I want to call her Gabrielle."

"That's very pretty. Congratulations." Rose kissed Margaret's cheek and went out.

In the hall Peter stumbled into her; he stepped hard on her foot. "Rosie! Wanna see the baby?" He dragged her into the next room.

There Johan sat, in the day's last sunlight coming through the west window, the baby on his knees. He was stroking her, as if he were molding her into shape. The room was small; in niches and shelves on the redwood planking of the walls, leafy green plants overflowed their pots.

Johan lifted his face toward her. She was startled at his looks; she had never seen him so excited.

"Can I see her?" Rose asked.

He drew his hand down to the baby's feet. Lying on his thighs, the little thing jerked her arms and legs, opened the tiny petal of her mouth, and bleated.

"Gabrielle," Rose said. "I like the name."

"That's not her name," Johan said. His hands closed over the baby, hiding her, or protecting her. "I'm calling her Redwood."

"Redwood," Rose said. "But white wouldn't? Why not name her Sequoia?"

"Redwood," repeated Johan fiercely. "I love the trees. Besides, your name is a plant."

"My name has been a pain in the ass to me all my life," Rose said. "Margaret told me she wants to call her Gabrielle."

"Sunshine—" he paused, to emphasize that name, "—is from a Christian culture. I am from a tribal culture."

Puzzled, she wondered what he meant by that. "I thought you grew up in Watts, or Compton, or someplace like that."

"Compton," he said. "I'm black, Rose."

He had told her once he did not believe in history. This was none of her business, anyway. She said, "Congratulations, Johan. I hope she'll be happy," and backed away out the door.

Her marijuana plants were growing fast, raising their leaves flat to the sun. She watered them and pulled up the weeds. Afterward she sat on the grassy cliff top, smoking a joint.

A line of snags stood like spines along the very top of the next ridge: tall trees, their tops blasted away by lightning, their branches broken off only a few feet from the trunk. Hawks nested in the top of the tallest one, whose foliage grew all down one side, where the trunk sheltered the needles from the unceasing wind. It looked like an Indian coup stick, except for one maverick branch near the top that stuck out in another direction entirely. She sat admiring it, her mind slack from the joint.

A small private plane flew up over the ridge, behind the coup-stick tree. She watched it idly. Its egg-beater engine noise came down the wind to her. It mounted in the sky until it was nearly overhead.

She wondered if the man inside could see her. He wasn't that far away. Suddenly the implications of that jarred her into a panic.

Of course he could. See anything he wanted to. See the marijuana plants.

She leaped up. There was nothing she could do. He was wheeling away, put-puttering across the sky. His busy racket died to a hum.

Rose let her arms fall to her sides. Her panic subsided. She looked around her, wondering if there were any way to disguise the field, but of course it was impossible. If she hid them, she would block the sun, which made them grow.

Thoughtfully she went down the side of the cliff. After dozens of climbs she knew all the ledges and cracks and small bushes that could hold a hand or foot. Around the base of the crag the blackberry vines swarmed over the rocks and bushes, smothering any support they could arch their vines over. She had beaten a way through the vines in her daily coming and going.

No more of that. The plants would do well enough now if she watered them once a week. She rubbed her hands together, her gaze on the thorny vines, wishing she had gloves. There was no surface without its stabbing prickers. She dragged a long branch out of the dry creek bed and braced it against the rock, across the beaten trail; and taking one vine at a time, she draped it with a thicket of berry bushes.

The thorns jabbed her; worse, their tiny hooks clung to her skin and, when she moved, ripped deep, bloody scratches several inches long across her arms and hands and even her face. When she was done, she went down to the river, to the pool where she had taught Reina to swim, and took off her clothes and dove into the cold water, numbing her hurts.

She walked back up to her brother's house. When she came into the kitchen, he and Billy Vigg were sitting by the woodstove. At the sight of her Peter let out a surprised obscenity.

"What happened to you?"

"I fell into a blackberry thicket," she said.

The scratches stung painfully. She went into the pantry, looking for something to put on them.

"That woman knows nothing about the woods," Peter said in the kitchen.

She grimaced to herself. There was a little box of Corona on the shelf over the canned goods; she dabbed some of that on the worst of her wounds.

"You ask me," Peter said, reverting to the conversation with Billy that she had disturbed, "you should go into business for yourself. That's where the bucks are."

Rose snapped the top onto the little square can of salve and put it back on the shelf. Going out to the kitchen again, she opened the refrigerator.

"You're a fair logger," Peter was saying. "You could get some guys together and bid on some of these contracts, just like Coyote does."

"That's what I'm doing, more'r less," said Billy Vigg.

Actually what he was doing was sitting in a chair from the front room, his feet on the firewood stacked by the woodstove, drinking Peter's beer and letting Peter exercise his droit de seigneur. "I'm trying to get him to hire me on when he trucks out that timber he's got."

"Where's the pie?" Rose asked, searching the inside of the refrigerator. She took out a six-pack of beer to look behind it.

"What pie?" Peter said.

"The apple pie I made yesterday. You know damn well—" She straightened, turning to frown at him. "You ate it all?"

"You just too good a cook, sissy." Peter tipped his chair back on its hindlegs and grinned at her. "Stop looking like a schoolteacher and sit down and smoke a reefer with us."

"Sure, I never turn down a joint." She pulled over the stool and sat. "And I'm glad you liked the pie. Still, you could have left a piece for me. Have you seen Reina?"

"Out riding," Peter said. He took a joint from his pocket and stuck it in his mouth and groped for matches.

"I wouldn't mind going riding with Reina," Billy Vigg said and guffawed. "Long's she's the horse." He slapped his own leering face. "Jeez, I'm bad."

"She went with Bonnie Morrison," Peter continued. The unlit joint between his lips waggled when he talked.

"She's a nice girl," Rose said.

"A little chubby for my tastes," Billy Vigg said.

Rose glanced at him, liking him very little. "De gustibus non disputandem est."

Nobody had anything to say to that. She sat down on the couch, shoving back a heap of *National Geographics* to make space on the threadbare upholstery. Peter was still looking for a match, and now Billy seemed all at once to notice that; he reached into his shirt pocket, saying, "Lemme get that." Taking out a wooden stick match, he struck it on the zipper of his fly.

Rose yelped. "My God. What total couth. The Prince of Wales couldn't get away with that one."

"Oh, sure," Billy said, passing the match to Peter. "You can strike 'em anywhere. Strike 'em on my whiskers, I do, when I ain't got a beard."

"I'll bet you do," Rose said. "I used to know a kid who went around setting fire to his farts. This was before the energy crisis."

"Bet it kinda smarts, now and then."

"Oh, he singed his ass a couple times." Peter was holding the joint out to her, and she took it.

It seemed so long ago, that life, that house she had shared with Georgie Armstrong the Human Torch and his brother, his brother's old lady, a couple of guys from his brother's rock and roll band. A life lightly entered into, lightly put aside. She had left it in favor of her morganatic marriage. With no planning, no idea of the future. She had taken for granted she would always be twenty-five. She had not thought of Georgie and that house in years. The only link between then and now, the clown appearing in both worlds. She wondered if the role were in her mind or in the cosmos.

The phone rang.

Rose looked at Peter, who was looking expectantly back at her. Stoned as she was, she had no interest in trying to deal with the telephone. Obviously Peter was in the same position. The phone rang again, and again, and again. Billy put his lips to the roach.

"Somebody gonna get that?"

"Yeah," Rose said. "I suppose so." She pushed herself to her feet and reached for the receiver.

"Hello?"

"Hello," replied a husky, womanly voice. "Is there somebody up there named Rose? I ain't heard from her in a long time, and I—"

"Okay, Angie," Rose said. "I get the point. I'm sorry. I been deep into it here. What's up?"

"Well, not me, that's for sure." Angie laughed as if it were hard for her to laugh.

"What's the matter? You miss Reina?"

"Yeah, sure. It ain't just that; it's everything. My landlord just raised the rent thirty-five bucks. So I said, 'Well, you gonna do anything about the window that's broken, and the stove that don't work?' and he said, 'If you don't like it, move out.'"

"Hunh," Rose said. "Take him to court. Hold up on the rent. Get it all fixed and deduct it from the rent."

"I got a better idea," Angie said. "I'm moving out."

"Oh, yeah? Where to?"

"Florida."

"Florida," Rose said blankly. "You mean the state of Florida? You're leaving California?"

"Well, I got this friend at work, she's going down to Cocoa Beach, there, and we could go together. She knows people there. She says there's lots of factory work." Angie worked on the assembly line in a toy factory.

"Jesus," Rose said and whistled.

"Well, anyway," Angie went on, "you gotta tell Reina."

"*I* gotta tell Reina!"

"Tell her I'll pack everything up, her horses and everything, you know, her model horses. She can stay up there until the day before we leave. I got some money saved up. I'll send her money for the plane."

"Wow," Rose said. "This is amazing."

"Is she having a good time?"

"Yeah, she's great, Ange—if you could see her, she rides twelve hours a day, and she's tan as a beach bum."

"She's a good kid," Angie said. "A good kid. You tell her I gotta do this, you know?"

"Angie, come on. You're going off the deep end."

"Honey," replied the familiar, throaty voice, "I been off that end of it for years. You tell her."

"Ange—" She stopped, unable to say what she felt.

Finally Angie prompted her. "Yeah?"

"Nothing. I'll tell her."

"Okay," Angie said. "That's a load off my mind, you know? I mean, you're there with her. You can tell her face-to-face."

Reina did have a tendency to explode. Rose nodded. She understood well enough why Angie had no heart for it herself. "Okay. She and I get along pretty well."

"Yeah. Good. So, what's new?"

They talked a little; Rose told her about Mike Morgan's theft of the profit from the house, and Angie cursed him roundly. That made her feel better.

"How's Miller?" Angie asked. "How's my boy?"

"He isn't here. I got a card from him the other day. He was in Nevada then. That was Wednesday."

"Maybe he'll turn up here," Angie said. "Maybe I'll talk him into going to Florida with me." She laughed again, the same unhappy, barroom laugh.

"Maybe," Rose said. "If you see him, tell him I said hi, okay?"

"Okay."

"I'll call you in a couple days," Rose promised. "Although Reina may make it sooner than that."

"Tell her to reverse the charges," Angie said.

"No, I'll pay for it."

"No, you won't, and I won't, either, if they're taking the phone out anyway. Good-by, Rose."

"Good-by," Rose said.

She sat on the porch reading a book by Lévi-Strauss. She did not see Patty coming until the woman stamped loudly up the steps.

"Oh. Hi," Rose said, putting the book down on her lap. "How's things on the flats?"

"Fuckin' Sam," Patty said, slumping down into the next chair, her shoulders hunched, her hands between her knees. "He thinks just 'cause I'm livin' there I'm gonna—"

Her voice ended. She stared away into the sunlight, her eyes puffy and her nose running. Rose wondered how far she was into her pregnancy. She seemed no different than the slim, young woman Rose had met a month before.

"I'm not gonna sleep with him, if he won't marry me," she said, a whine edging into her voice.

"You wanna live up here?" Rose said.

"Could I?" Patty swung eagerly toward her. "Jesus God, what happened to you?"

Rose put her fingertips to the stripes across her cheek. "I fell into a briar patch."

"You look like it." Patty managed a laugh. "You put anything on it?"

"Corona. I figure it works for horses. What y' been up to?"

"Workin'," Patty said listlessly. "Sam's payin' me seventy-five bucks a month to keep his marijuana for him."

"Good."

"Johan wants me to do it for him, too, but he ain't got any money. You know that baby's sick?"

"What? No, I didn't."

"Got jaundice," Patty said. "They took it up to the hospital in Eureka, and they wouldn't even admit it, because it was a home birth."

"Most babies get a touch of jaundice," Rose said.

"Poor little baby." Patty sniffed. Tears stood in her fine, large eyes. Rose saw how close to the surface her feelings lay; any little pressure set them off.

"You been okay?"

"Sicker'n hell," Patty answered. "And I'm so tired of weeding plants." Her hands covered her face. She lowered them, wiping her cheeks with her fingers. "Why did this have to happen to me?"

"What are they doing about Gabrielle?"

"Redwood," Patty said, with a grunt of laughter. "They fight about that all the time. You can hear 'em screaming all the way down the road. They took it up to Mad River. Doctor there tol' 'em to lay it out in the sun a lot."

The phone was ringing. Rose put her book down and went in to answer.

It was Reina, who said, "Can I spend the night over here? I'm at Morrisons'."

"Okay, sure," Rose agreed. "What've you been doin'?"

"Nothing much. Riding and riding and riding. You should see Windfire! I put him on the pasture, you know, with the other horses, and he took off! He's faster than any of the others."

"He's a damn good horse," Rose said.

"Morrisons have a horseshoer coming in a couple days. Should I get his feet fixed?"

"You been picking them up?" Rose lifted her eyes, hearing the back door open. Peter came in with an armload of wood; he dumped it into the corner with such a clatter that Rose heard nothing of what Reina said.

"Can I?" Reina asked, in the fresh silence.

"Get the shoer to look at his feet," Rose said. "If he thinks they're long, get him to trim them. No shoes. Got that? Do you have any money?"

"No. Why can't he get shoes?"

"He shouldn't need them, if you don't ride him on the road. He's better off barefoot, if he stays sound. You come by tomorrow and get some bread to pay him."

"Okay. Thanks, Rose."

"Good-by, Reina."

Peter was stooped before the refrigerator, getting out a green Rainier. Rose hung the phone up. She was dreading the talk with Reina about moving to Florida. "Patty wants to come up here for a while. She's on the outs with Sam."

"Fine with me," Peter said. "Where is she now?"

"On the porch."

He left. Rose put on a pot of water for coffee; she felt restless, cramped, wanting some hard exercise. If Miller had been here, she could have played tennis. She found an old envelope in the trash and sat down to write a shopping list.

The front door slammed. "Oh, no!" Patty rushed into the kitchen. "I'm gonna sleep in your room, okay?" She nodded vigorously at Rose.

Her brother followed Patty into the room, his ale in his

hand. "Come on, Patty. Be real. You gotta pay some rent, don't y'?" He lifted the can to his lips.

Patty wheeled on him, her fists clenched. "I'll sleep in the barn if I have to! Why doesn't anybody leave me alone?" Her voice broke. She began to cry in loud, gulping sobs.

Rose put out her hand. "You can sleep in the bunkroom, with me and Reina."

"Oh no," Peter said. He flicked his long black hair back off his face. "If she stays up here, she's sleeping with me."

Rose said, "Oh no, she isn't."

She faced him, fixing his eyes with her stare. She had bullied him constantly in their childhood, beating him black and blue, making him cry. He glared back at her, but the old rules still shaped his will, and his gaze wavered. He lifted his beer can in an elaborate gesture.

"Sure," he said, "whatever you want. Just name it after me." He pulled his chair around to face the woodstove and sat down in it, his feet out to the fire.

Patty said, "I'll go get my stuff." She went out toward the front door.

Rose glanced at her brother's back, regretting what she had done. Preying on the weak and defenseless. Her mind overstuffed with thoughts, she went back out to the porch to read, sat staring at the book without reading, desperate for a sense of order.

Peter drank steadily the rest of the day. By nighttime he was plastered. He ate no dinner. Rose and Patty sat before the television with him, watching the news, plates of spaghetti on their laps.

"I oughta quit drinking, shouldn't I," Patty said.

"Why?" Peter raised his beer. His hand wobbled. His eyes looked crossed. "If he's half me, he's already part drunk."

Rose looked away. The wind was coming up; it boomed around the corners of the house, and the draft under the

door lifted a piece of paper off the floor and sailed it away
into the corner.

"Better make a fire," Peter said. He stood up, gained his
balance, and made his slow way toward the woodpile against
the wall.

"I oughta quit drinking." Patty sipped her beer, her eyes
turning to the television screen.

Rose scuffed her foot across the floor. "I wish we had
some weed."

"We do," Patty said. "We got tons of it. We're gonna be
rich, and it's all tax-free."

"Marijuana everywhere," Rose said, glancing at her
brother. "And not a shred to smoke. You need help, there,
Bub?"

Peter heaped the wood into the fireplace. He ignored her,
his back to her.

"He's really swacked," Patty said. "He drinks too much."

"Like he says, he comes by it from way back. My parents
are both alcoholics." For years it had seemed to her a natural
and necessary condition of adulthood to drink yourself
insensible night after night.

Peter was trying to strike a match, having no success.
Patty got up suddenly and went over to help him. Rose
watched him, remembering the adored aunt, her favorite
relative, who had encouraged her early writing and who had
died of drink.

That was her mother's side of the family. Intensely loyal,
close-knit, but not from love: from pride. Each one of them
etched by the bitter hatreds, the mortal feuds that never
ended. One after the other, they blunted the ironies of their
cross-grained Irish souls in the only reliable anesthesia, the
water of life.

Now Peter, who had put three thousand miles between
him and his parents, but who had never really left home.

Lord, make me continent, but not yet. She saw that in
herself, in her passion for marijuana, her weakness. Maybe
that was why she saw it in everybody else.

They were sitting by the fire, the other two, side by side, not talking. While she watched, Patty lifted her arm and hung it around Peter's shoulders and hugged him. Rose pulled her gaze away, as if she were looking at something that ought to be invisible.

Reina said, "We're going down to the river. You wanna come? The Morrisons say you can borrow one of their horses."

"I'd like that," Rose said. "Tomorrow, maybe." She unrolled the wad of money she had just taken from her pocket and found a ten-dollar bill. It was the last money she had: thirty-six dollars. "Here. This is for the blacksmith. Don't let him charge you more'n two-fifty a hoof. And make sure he does a good job."

"Okay." Reina bent down from the horse, reaching for the money.

"Wait." Rose drew a deep breath. "I gotta talk to you. Come down here."

While Reina dismounted, Rose paced a few steps up and down the porch, trying to brace herself. She stopped and took hold of Reina's hand.

"Your mom called yesterday. She says to tell you she's moving out." She stopped, looking into the girl's variegated eyes. "She says she's moving to Florida."

"To Florida!" Reina's eyes popped; her mouth fell open. "No!"

Rose still had her by the hand; she squeezed her fingers. Reina yanked her hand free. With a single, stabbing glance at Rose, she flung the reins over Windfire's head, leaped onto his back, and galloped away.

A fine spray of dust slapped the porch railing. Rose leaned against an upright. It was only ten in the morning; she brought her mind to bear on the day ahead, making plans, boxing up the empty time.

The horse was coming back. She looked up. Reina drew him to a stop in front of her.

"I'm sorry," she said. She dismounted and came up onto the porch. Rose reached out for her, and the girl stepped into her arms.

"I'm sorry too, sweetie."

"Florida, hunh?" Reina sank onto the bench against the wall of the house. "Well, you know my mom. She won't get it together for a long time yet."

She sniffed, rubbed her nose, and sat staring down at the floor. The door opened; Patty trudged out, her hair hanging over her face.

"I'm gonna throw up any minute." Patty hugged her arms across her midriff.

Rose sank down on her heels in front of Reina and took her by the hand. "Your mom says you can stay here right up until she leaves. And you're right. Angie isn't organized enough to pull off any sudden moves."

Reina sighed. "Florida," she said. "There's nothin' there but old people."

"There'll be horses in Florida."

The girl's eyes filled with outrage. "But none like Wind-fire." She bolted away across the porch again to the horse and spread her arms around him. "Not like Windfire."

The horse lowered his head to the grass to eat. When he shifted his weight forward, Reina moved with him, her face pressed to his neck. Finally she mounted him and rode away.

Rose scuffed her shoes over the porch; she glanced at Patty. "You wanna go to Springville with me?"

Patty was leaning forward over her arms, doubled over her stomach. "I got to go down to the field and work."

"I thought you were sick."

Patty shook her head.

"Can I make you some tea or something?"

"Leave me alone," Patty said. "You're not my mother."

That rubbed. Rose went back into the house, feeling her-self unappreciated. A few minutes later, while her coffee was percolating, she glanced out the window. Patty was gone off the porch. Looking through another window, Rose saw her walking down the road to the flat. Rose went back to her coffee.

Reina called; she wanted to spend the night at Morrisons' again, and Rose let her stay, although she missed her. Patty went to bed early. Peter and Rose shot pool for a while, until he stopped to watch a rerun of "Hogan's Heroes." Rose went for a walk.

There was a storm blowing up. The night was noisy with a rambunctious wind that seethed through the tall grass and bent the trees on the mountain behind the house. She stuffed her hands into her jacket pockets and strode along at top speed, thinking of Miller.

Lights gleamed in the Viggs' hovel; the wind shrieked through the metal angles of the car rusting away in the front yard. Johan's house was dark. The apple trees rolled in the wind. She could hear apples falling, some striking the house, some bouncing on the ground.

She passed the meadow where one of the settlers grazed his sheep. No light showed in Sam's house, and his truck was gone, but when she walked past, a voice from the shelter of the willow tree said, "Stop right there."

It was Dave Preston. She made a precise half-turn. "What the hell do you think you're doing?"

"I might ask you the same thing." Preston came up to the edge of the road.

He had his gun, a rifle, slung carelessly through his crooked elbow. Rose chewed on the inside of her cheek.

"Well," she said, "I'm nowhere near the field, am I."

"The way I figure," he said, "I can watch the pot, or I can watch you; one's the same as the other."

"God. What an asshole. If that's what it takes to convince you I'm innocent, I'll be glad to come roost in your living room a couple nights."

"You're a mean woman, you know that?"

"Yeah? You're right out of a Roger Corman movie. What'll it be? You want some company? I hope you got some weed because I don't. I might even drink a beer with you."

The dark form in front of her was silent. The wind hooted in the chimney of Sam's house.

"I don't think I could stand it very long," Preston said finally, his voice sullen. "Go on, get outta here."

"Fine. You will note I am proceeding on in the direction I was heading when you stopped me, which is almost directly away from the fucking pot field." She walked away down the road.

Reaching the gate, she turned and walked back up the middle of the road again. When she passed Sam's willow, Dave Preston was gone. She wondered why he disliked her so much. Maybe he just liked to fight. That was why she disliked him, she thought; he was easily fought with. It was all history anyway. She walked with her face into the wind. The first rain struck her cheeks like drops of iron. Up on the mountain the redwoods roared, the bass string of the great wind harp.

Peter was asleep in front of the television. She turned it off. Going into the darkened kitchen, she walked up and down a few times, too jumpy to sit down or even stand still. The storm had gotten inside her head. Different parts of her were all yelling at once, wanting to call Miller, wanting a joint, afraid of calling Miller, disgusted that she couldn't go a few days without getting stoned, trying to remember Miller's real name, which he had told her once. She opened the refrigerator, found nothing tempting, and shut the door again. She put some wood into the stove.

Peter came in, yawning. "God," he said. "This incredibly dull picture came on with Loretta Young in it." Another yawn spread his jaws until they cracked. His hair was rumpled. "Where's Patty?"

"In bed," Rose said.

"My bed or the goddamn fucking bunk?"

"The goddamn fucking bunk, I suppose," Rose answered. "Why don't you just treat her like she means something to you other than a lay? Maybe then she'd like you better."

"God's balls, it's Emily Post." He got another ale out of

the refrigerator. "Oh, by the way, that guy called you. Miller. His number's there on the wall by the phone."

He went out. Rose turned on the ceiling light, read the number off the wall, and dialed. A strange exuberance galloped in her veins.

"Hello?"

"Is Miller there?"

"Just a second."

There was a click. "Hello?"

"Hi," she said. "It's Rose."

"Hi," he said. "It's Miller."

"Yes, I know that."

"Thanks for calling me back."

"Think nothing of it," she replied. "I was thinking about calling you anyway."

"Were you really? How come?"

"Oh—" That held her up a moment; she had not thought much why. "I need some dope," she said. Which was not why.

"Okay," he said. "You talk to Angie yet?"

"Yes," she said.

Her ardor cooled. He was calling for Reina's sake. She was glad she had extemporized about the dope.

"Listen," he said. "Would you mind if I came up again?"

"Until she goes," Rose said.

"Yes," he said. "I'll keep out of trouble."

"Sure," she said. "It's fine with me. I could use some help with the pot field anyway."

"Where are you?"

"In the kitchen."

"Then shut up about the pot field."

"Yes," she said. "I'm sorry."

"So am I. Okay. I'll be up in a couple days. I'll bring some marijuana. Is there anything else you need?"

"No, not really."

There was a little silence. She felt cool and in control, one step removed from this, a spectator at her own life. She said, "Okay, Mil. I'll see you in a couple of days."

"Right," he said. "Thanks, Rose."

"Good-by," she said.

She hung the receiver up on the hook. Tarananovitch, that was his name. She put out her hand and flicked off the light.

"This world is dying," Johan said. He was stooped over the chessboard, but Peter had gone for a beer, and Johan was pressing his favorite argument with Rose. She sat up on the porch railing and smiled at him.

"The world's always coming to an end, one way or another. So what's new about that?"

He shook that off. "This world, this country, all countries, all that bullshit life, that's all going, Sister Rose. And unless we act now, to separate ourselves from it, we'll go down the tubes with it."

As usual when he was proselytizing, his voice swelled round and full and loud. She folded her arms over her chest. A glance up the road gave her no sign of Reina and Bonnie Morrison and the borrowed horse she was to ride.

She said, "Well, that I kind of agree with. It'd be nice to cut out of the power grid before everything goes dark. But that's a little hard, especially in the United States."

He was shaking his head. "It's easy, Sister Rose. You just decide, and that's enough."

"Oh, really?"

"It is, Sister Rose." He put out his small, thin hand to the chess board, moving his pieces neatly into the center of each square. "As soon as I sell my share of the pot, I'm going independent. Self-sufficient. We will grow our own food, generate our own power, and mind our own business."

Rose studied his earnest, wide-eyed face. "The revolution will not be televised," she said. "I have the feeling anything you plan like that can only be a repeat of the past. When there's a real need, things change to fit. We change. Then we spend a couple hundred years wondering what the hell happened."

"I know what is happening, Sister Rose."

"Congratulations."

Peter came out onto the porch, bringing along an open beer and a spare. He sat down, pulling the stool up between his legs.

"Here comes Reina." Rose swung around on the railing, glad to get away from Johan before she picked a fight with him. The girls were galloping up the road. Between them, saddled and bridled, was a riderless, chestnut horse.

"I'll be back," Rose said and jumped down from the porch.

She mounted the little chestnut horse and with the girls rode off across the hillside.

"We got something to show you," Reina said, and Bonnie giggled, covering her mouth with her hand.

"What?" Rose drew her horse up and dismounted to put the stirrups higher.

Now they both giggled. "You'll see."

"Come on, I'm dying of curiosity." She fought with the stiff leathers of the western saddle. "By the way, I've got a surprise for you, too. Miller's coming back."

Still fussing with the stirrup leather, she cast a swift look across the saddle at Reina. The girl's face smoothed out, but she showed no concern; she only shrugged.

"Okay," she said.

"And I want you to be friendly to him. Don't fight with him."

"Oh, Rose."

"Don't call him a creep."

"I won't. Why's he coming back? Because I'm going to Florida?"

"Yes," Rose said.

At that, Reina smiled a little; she looked away, the sleek, catlike smile curving her lips. "Okay."

Rose swung into the saddle and gathered up the horse. "Now show me what you've got."

They cantered away down the slope, cutting through the meadow where Coyote's teepee stood. Rose relaxed, enjoying the pace and the feel of the horse under her. By the natural order of things, their loose gallop turned into a race. The girls charged ahead of her, yelling and laughing and flogging their horses.

They broke into the stand of redwoods, where Coyote's trees still lay here and there on the ground. The hill trail turned steeply upward. Rose followed behind Reina and Bonnie, letting them show her the way. Branches whipped the air over her head. She flattened herself to the chestnut's neck. Digging hard, he raced through clumps of ferns like green fountains, through brilliant green swamp grass, into the sunlight again.

The girls yelled, "Over here!"

At a trot she rode over toward them, where they had drawn up their horses at the edge of a high meadow, cupped in the shoulder of the hill.

"Holy cow," she said, amazed.

There in front of her was a stand of marijuana.

"Are you glad?" Reina clapped her hands, bouncing in the saddle. "Do you want it? Shall we take it back with us?"

Rose let the reins slide through her fingers. She looped one leg up around the saddle horn. "No."

"Oh." All Reina's lively delight faded away.

"It's somebody else's," Rose said. The plants were ten and twelve feet tall, well tended, plucked of their sucker leaves; a grassy mulch covered the ground around their scaly trunks. She said, "I'll lay you any odds it's Coyote's."

"Oh," Reina said, again. Bonnie jogged her horse over to Rose's.

"Well, anyway, it's a surprise, isn't it?"

"It sure is," Rose said. "I'm glad you brought me here."

Reassured, Bonnie smiled broadly. "Come on. You wanta go swimming?"

"Sure."

They rode off, cutting back through the redwoods toward the river. Rose lagged a little behind. She liked seeing the girls together.

"Come on, Bonnie Big Butt," Reina cried.

"Raunchy Reina," Bonnie said. "Reina Raunch Rat."

"Bonnie Broadbeam!"

Bonnie rode like a centaur, trotting her horse in circles and short dashes, all her attention on the bantering with Reina. Rose thought about the pot field again; she wondered if everybody on River Ranch had a secret garden somewhere, an ace in the hole. Bonnie and Reina were trying to pull each other off their horses; their screams of laughter rang off the trees around them. They reached the meadow and broke at once into a run. From the tall grass ahead of them a dozen quail exploded up into the air, zoomed twenty feet, and dropped out of sight into an island of chamise and poison oak in the midst of the field. Reina screamed.

"Look! Quail! See?" She steered the old white horse around toward Rose, her face glowing. "Did y' see that?"

"Just wonderful," Rose said.

"I love it here," Reina said passionately.

At that, her face settled a little, her smile drooping. Rose rode up beside her and leaned out to give her a quick caress.

"Let's go down to the river and swim with the horses."

"Okay! Race! Race!" She clapped her heels to the white horse's sides, and they charged away over the meadow.

"I figure you are the best witness I could get," Preston said. "Everybody knows we hate each other."

Rose put out her foot and nudged the dead goat. It was Maggie, the black nanny from Hallie's flock. There was a little hole behind her ear; it looked too small to kill anything. There was almost no blood. The goat had been eating the marijuana plants; three or four of the plants around the carcass were stripped entirely of leaves.

"Well," Rose said. "She went off in high style."

She pushed the goat again with her foot; the coarse black hair stood up in a fringe over the knob of its hip. "I can't say I'll miss her."

Preston cleared his throat. "Gimme a hand with this critter."

He leaned his rifle against the nearest pot plant, a robust giant standing twice as tall as Rose. The leaves at the tip of each branch and twig looked odd to Rose. Instead of opening into leaves, the new growth was forming a tight bud. With a start she realized these plants—this plant, anyway— was beginning to bloom. Preston was staring impatiently at her. She gripped Maggie by a stiffening hindleg; Preston got it by the one remaining horn. They hauled the carcass out to the fence and heaved her over.

"Take her out a little ways," Preston said. "Let the turkey vultures get her."

"Hallie's gonna have kittens. Still, I can't imagine she'll get much sympathy."

"From Johan she will," Preston said. "They're both the same. They're both flakes."

Rose looked him over, his baggy jeans, his wild black beard, the manic intensity of his pale eyes. "I think we're all bozos on this bus, don't you?"

"Hunh?"

"Forget it. Come on, let's go up and tell my brother."

Peter was sitting on the front porch, a sketch pad on his knees. Before him, Patty was sprawled comfortably in one of the sling chairs from the front room, her feet up. Climbing up the steps to the porch, Rose saw that she was dozing.

"Jeez, Peter, you really put people to sleep sometimes." Preston laughed, an unexpected, high-pitched horselaugh.

"Sssh," Peter said. He used the side of a charcoal stick to brush in the curve of Patty's jawbone over her throat. He glanced quickly up at Rose and turned back to his work. "Your cub called. She wants to spend the night at Morrisons' again."

Rose looked down at the sketch pad. He had always had a gift for catching a likeness in a minimum of strokes. The Patty on the nubbly white paper was prettier than the real Patty. Softer. Kinder.

"Pretty good, there, blubber." She clapped his shoulder and went in to call the Morrison house.

Reina had gone out. Rose left a message for her to call River Ranch and returned to the front porch again.

Preston was half-sitting on the rail of the porch, lighting a joint. Rose glanced at Peter. "He tell you?"

"Goddamnit," Peter said. "I'm sick of trouble. Whyn't we just shine it on? Maybe if we pretend we don't see it, it won't be there."

Patty's eyes opened. She blinked at Peter and sat upright. "What are you doing?"

"I'm drawing your picture," Peter said.

"Oh, yeah? Let me see." She got up from the chair and came to bend over his shoulder, her cheek close to Peter's, frowning at the girl on the page.

"That doesn't look like me." She stood back, turning to Rose and Preston. "What's going on?"

Preston held the joint out to Rose. "I just shot that goddamn black nanny goat of Hallie's. Eating our pot. They were all gonna be females, too."

"Shot it," Patty said. "You couldn't 've just, you know, chased it off? Hallie's gonna flip."

"You ever had any dealings with that goat?" Rose said, exhaling a haze of smoke.

Patty shook her head. "Which plants?" she asked.

"In Glory's share," Preston said.

"Then it ain't jack-shit to me," Patty said, airily, and walked away into the house.

Peter took a hit of the joint.

"Not bad," he said. "Whose reefer is this?"

"Mine," Preston answered.

"Where'd you get this? Got a nice flavor."

"Just some lumbo," Preston said. "It's okay with me, you know; I'd just as soon forget the whole thing. But you know that lady is going to bust a gut, and the way things been around here—"

Peter was sampling another toke of the joint. He looked it over, elaborately disinterested in the matter of Hallie's goat. "Got a nice taste, for Columbian," he said, then held out the joint to Preston.

"Who's gonna tell her?" he said in a genial voice.

For a moment nobody said anything. Preston sucked his cheeks hollow. Then words burst out of him.

"Don't tell her. Let it lie. The birds and ants and the night critters will pick it clean in a while. She'll never know."

Rose folded her arms over her chest. She looked Preston up and down. "God, you are dishonest."

"So what d'you want to do?" Preston shot at her, his eyes burning.

"Tell her," Rose said. "She loved the goat, man. She'll go all over the ranch until she finds it, and it don't exactly look as if it died of natural causes. Better yet," she went on, swiveling her head toward Peter, "let Peter tell her. She loves Peter."

Her brother grunted angrily at her. "All right," he said. "All right. I'll tell her."

"What if she wants to call a meeting and discuss the whole issue at length and in detail?" Rose asked.

Peter's eyes narrowed. He looked more intent than she had seen him in a long time. With a new interest, she looked around him; there wasn't a beer can in sight.

He said, "No meeting. I'm sick of that." His head snapped around toward Dave Preston. "But you put that rifle up on top of the cabinet and keep your fucking hands off it."

"Hunh," Preston said. "Shit, man, that goat ate—"

"I know. I'm just telling you, put the gun away."

"For Chrissake! That ain't the only goat on—"

"Put it away!"

Preston faced him a moment, his jaw thrust out, finally he pulled it in again, looking grim. "Okay. If that's the way you want it."

"Right," Peter said. "I'll take care of Hallie."

"Okay," Preston said.

The three of them stood looking at one another, unsmiling, and saying nothing. Finally Preston said, "Well, catch you later," and walked down the steps into the sunlight.

Rose sighed. She turned toward her brother. "What's with you?"

He wiped his sleeve over his face. "I'm dying," he muttered, rubbing and twisting his hands together. Startled, she saw he was trembling. He sat down. "What time is it?"

"I don't know. Maybe four-thirty."

"Go see," he said.

With another searching look at him, she went into the house. The clock on the kitchen wall said ten minutes to four. She took that news out to him.

"Okay," he said. "Let's go tell Hallie the old gray mare—"

"She ain't what she used to be," Rose finished. "What's the matter?"

"I feel like homemade shit."

"I can see that."

They walked across the sloping meadow, past the sauna, down toward the trail into the woods. Rose said, "You got the flu or something?"

"Shut up about it."

"Okay."

A few steps on, he said, "You think Preston's telling the truth? I mean, you didn't actually see him shoot the goat, did y'?"

"No. He called me on the phone." She tried to imagine another explanation for the evidence and shook her head. "On the basis of Occam's razor, I say it's 99 to 1 he's telling the truth."

Peter said, "I wonder where he got that weed."

"Ask him. I'll go in with you on some."

"It's a deal."

"On the other hand, Miller's bringing some up, too."

"Miller?" Peter glanced over at her. "He's coming back?"

"Yes."

"Oh ho," he said. "Oh ho, ho, ho, ho."

"What the hell does that mean?"

"You invited him back up."

"No, damnit, he's coming up because of Reina. Her mom's moving to Florida. If she goes to Florida, he'll never see her again."

They reached the woods. He walked ahead of her along the narrow trail.

"That's pretty weird, if you ask me," he said. "Him and Reina."

"Maybe," Rose replied. "She's a good kid, Reina. It's hard not to love her."

"Yeah, but like that? That is weird."

"Maybe."

Ahead of him the trail curved along the edge of the marsh. Redwood sorrel like gigantic clover grew thick in the damp shade of the trees. Coming toward them on the trail was Hallie.

"Hi, there," she called, waving. "I was just coming up there. Have you seen Maggie?"

Rose stopped where she was. She clasped her hands behind her back, wondering nervously what Peter would say to her. Peter took a few more steps.

"Hallie," he said. "Dave Preston shot her in the pot field. She was eating our plants."

Hallie's mouth fell open. She blinked at him. "Shot her? Is she badly hurt?" She broke into a lumbering run up the path. "Where is she?"

"She's dead, Hallie."

She had passed Peter. When she stopped, her face pale as a cheese, she was facing Rose. She said, "My poor dear goat," and began to cry.

"Hallie," Rose said. "The goat was a pain in the ass."

"He didn't have to shoot her, did he?"

"If you'd kept her tied up—"

Hallie glared at her. "He didn't have to kill her!"

"It was your fault, Hallie!"

Hallie gasped. Clumsily she struck out at her. Rose jerked her head back out of the way. The blow barely tapped her chin. Behind Hallie, Peter was standing with his shoulders hunched, his face sour. He walked in between them, pushing Rose roughly ahead of him.

"No cat fights." He glanced at Hallie and lowered his eyes quickly to the ground. He kicked at a root that lay exposed across the path. "She's right, Hallie."

"How can you say that?" Hallie cried. "Poor Maggie— she only obeyed her nature. Goats are—"

"I said she's right, Hallie." He raised his head sharply to stare at her.

Hallie stopped. Her face was regaining its color. She wet her lips with a quick dab of her tongue.

"I thought," she said, "when I came up here, I'd find people with values like mine, people with love and respect for nature, but I was wrong. You're just as corrupt as the capitalists in Oakland."

She turned and walked away down the path. Rose let out her breath, relieved. She leaned against the tree whose root Peter was kicking again, beating his heel against it in a furious, hard rhythm. Finally the root broke. Under his breath he said, "It's about time," and walked away up the trail. Rose followed him.

When they reached the house again, the clock in the kitchen read five after five. Peter let out a gusty sigh, more than half a cheer, and going to the refrigerator, he took out a can of Rainier ale. The phone rang.

Rose went to answer it. "Hello?"

"Hi, Rose," Reina said. "I wanna spend the night over here again, okay?"

"You've been over there four nights in a row."

"It's okay with them."

"It's not okay with me. Come on home."

"But, Rose—"

"Reina," she said, she fumbled a little, trying to sort out her feelings. She turned toward the wall, to shield the phone from Peter, and lowered her voice.

"Reina, when you leave here—" Wrong. She began again. "I love you," she said. "I like being with you. When you go,

I won't—" She licked her lips. "It's a long way to Florida, Reina."

She paused. Reina said nothing.

"I want to be with you," Rose said. "I love you. There isn't much time left. That's all. It's up to you, but I want you to come home."

There was a little silence. Then Reina said, softer, "Okay. I'll be right there."

"Thanks," Rose said.

"Can we make something?"

"What?"

"I don't know. A pie, like that other one you made."

"I don't know if I have the apples."

"Anything. Cornbread."

"Sure. I can get some apples from Johan." Her mind flew to the pantry, checking ingredients: flour, Crisco, brown sugar, cinnamon, and lemon. "Sure."

"Rose," the girl said, "I love you, too."

"Good," Rose said.

"Good-by."

Rose hung up; she stood a moment looking at the phone numbers on the wall, struggling with her feelings. When she turned, her brother was going toward the door, the green Rainier can in his hand. She turned back to the phone to call Johan, to ask him for some apples.

"Ouch."

"I'm sorry," Reina said. "God, your hair is so long."

"I haven't had it cut in ten years," Rose said. Her head moved back under the pull of the brush. Reina's hand smoothed over her crown. Rose shut her eyes. She loved having her hair brushed.

"What if I put it up like this?" Reina gathered the thick mass of hair up onto Rose's head. The ends fell over her eyes.

"The old English look?" Rose parted the hair with her hands and peered through. Reina laughed; their eyes met in the mirror propped in front of them on the hearth, and Reina's arms slipped around Rose's neck and hugged her chokingly hard.

"I know," she cried, exuberant. "Braids!"

"No!"

Already Reina was plaiting the hair. She got a strand too short, plucking at Rose's scalp, and Rose yelped.

"Sorry," Reina said cheerfully. She wound the great, shining loop of hair around Rose's neck. "How's that?"

"Somebody's at the door," Rose said and stood up.

It was Miller. He came a few steps into the room and said, "I walked up from the gate. Can I get the key?" His eyes slid from Rose to Reina, fidgeting behind her.

"Hi," Reina said to him.

"Hi."

Rose moved out from between them. Miller looked tired; there was a long scratch on his face just below the eye. A joint poked out of his wiry hair over one ear. He and Reina stared at each other a moment, awkwardly silent, and then the girl lifted her arms and slapped her sides.

"Want some pie?"

"What kind of pie?" He went a step closer to her.

"Apple." Reina flew toward the kitchen. "Rose and I made it. It's super."

With Reina out of sight, Miller moved his attention to Rose. "She looks beautiful."

"She is beautiful," Rose said. She was glad to see him, but there was no telling him so. No telling anything but worthless things. "They all went into a movie, in Springville. Peter has the key with him. I guess you'll have to wait until they get back."

His gaze dropped. Reaching into his hair, he took down the joint, lit it, and handed it to her.

"Thanks. I haven't had much smoke since you left."

"You look okay, too."

"Fresh air and clean living. What happened to your face?"

"I was fouled, playing basketball."

Reina marched into the room, holding out a piece of the apple pie. She had enthroned it on a china plate and laid a fork down its side.

"Looks pretty good," Miller said. He sat down and began to eat. After the first bite he raised his eyes to Reina. "It is good." He sounded surprised.

"Rose showed me how to make crust."

"Rose knows all about crust." He chewed steadily through the bite of pie. "How's the horse?"

"He's super," Reina said.

"You have a good trip up?" Rose held out the joint to him.

"I got two speeding tickets." He shook his head at the pot. "Not while I'm eating."

"Well." Reina lifted her arms and slapped her sides again. "I'll make y' a cup of coffee," she said to Rose and dashed off to the kitchen again.

"How fast were you going?" Rose asked. She sat down on the couch facing Miller and propped her feet up on the hearth.

"Eighty, eighty-five." He put the plate down, next to the mirror lying on the hearth; he tapped it with his finger. "What have you been doing with this?"

"Looking into it," Rose said.

"I got something down in my car we could use it with. You wanna walk down with me to get it?"

"Let me see if Reina wants to go."

Reina did not want to go, but she was afraid of staying in the house alone, and went with them anyway. Miller walked along between them, his hands in his pockets.

"Scared of the dark, hunh?" he said to Reina. "I guess you think there's a bogeyman behind the stove."

"I don't care who it is," Reina replied. "I just don't like, you know—"

"You're so silly, Reina. God, girls are so silly. Such feeble creatures—"

"Oh, shut up," Reina cried.

"Such a silly, little—

Reina flounced angrily away, running down the road ahead of them, her arms high.

"She runs like a girl," Miller said fondly.

"Well, what do you expect?" Rose said.

"I'm just teasing, Rose. God, can't you take a little ribbing?"

Rose made a face into the darkness. "It's very hostile ribbing."

"Jeez, how can you say that? I'm just kidding. Can't you take a little teasing?"

She rubbed her hand over her mouth. "You see Felice at all?"

"Unh-unh. I heard they got married."

"Married! You mean, like, an official wedding?"

"In church, I heard."

"Aw, Jesus."

"It could all be buzz. Angie told me most of it."

"How's she doing?"

"Like always. She'll never move. She can't get it together to go down the street sometimes."

Rose shook her head. "No, she tries to do too much at one time, that's all. Is she getting ready to go?"

"No."

Rose searched the night ahead of them for Reina. "Well, maybe she won't go." But she knew Angie; Angie would put everything off, talking and talking, until the pressure of time separated the superfluous from the necessary. Then in a space of days she would pack, sell everything she could, throw the kids and the bags in the car, and drive off to Florida.

Miller's car stood squarely in the road just behind the locked gate. Reina was waiting for them, sitting on the top rail. Miller leaned into his car, tossed a sleeping bag and a pillowcase full of clothes onto the bank behind him, and backed out clutching a half-empty quart bottle of Coke, a little plastic flask of Sinex, and a leather case. He paused to chug the Coke and squirt a charge of Sinex up each nostril. Rose watched him curiously. Sometimes he seemed to do things simply to have things to do. He gave her the leather case and the empty bottle. Reaching in through the window of the car, he cranked the wheel over, shoving the car forward, and rolled it off to the side.

When they reached the house again, he opened up his sleeping bag across the floor. In the middle there were a big plastic bag of weed and a vial of cocaine. While he was chopping some of that on the mirror, Reina came in from the kitchen with Rose's coffee.

"What's that?"

"Cocaine," Rose said. "Thanks." The smell of the steaming coffee reached her nose, and she took the cup. Reina was watching her expectantly. Rose sipped the hot, strong coffee.

"Just right," she said. "Thanks."

Reina grinned at her. She looked at Miller and down to the white powder on the mirror; with a single-edged razor he was pushing the coke into lines. The razor screeched on the mirror.

Rose shivered in a violent spasm. "Oh, don't do that."

"Sorry."

"What does it do to y'?" Reina asked. "That stuff?"

"Makes you broke," Rose said.

"I won it playing chess." From his shirt pocket Miller took a straw, still in its McDonald's wrapper, and cut it in half with the razor. "Here."

Rose snorted up one line, holding the other nostril closed. "Oh, that smarts."

"This is reasonably good blow," he said, taking the straw back.

"How does it feel?" Reina said.

"It just makes you feel good."

Rose's front teeth were turning numb. A bitter taste crept down the back of her throat. She leaned back on the couch, her arms stretched across the top.

"Can I try it?" Reina said.

"No," Rose and Miller answered together.

"Okay. I was just asking." Reina shrugged. "I'm gonna go to bed. Good night."

"Good night, kid," Rose said.

Miller said nothing. When she reached the door, Reina turned and said, "I'm glad you're back, Mil." She disappeared into the hall.

"She never said that before," Miller said. He stuck one end of the straw into his nose and the other end over the cocaine. With great honks he drew the powder up into his face.

"She's growing up," Rose said. "You should see her ride. She's gotten pretty good."

"She could do anything," he said. "She's really athletic. If she wanted to, she could play really good tennis. But she won't try."

"She might try now," Rose said. The cocaine was lifting her mood; suddenly she was supremely happy for no reason at all.

"How's the garden?" Miller asked.

"Okay. I think they're starting to get flowers."

"Oh, yeah?"

"The ends of the branches are getting buds on them."

"Yeah. I got back just in time."

Rose rubbed her hands together, studying him; she wanted to talk, to hold his interest. She said, "I've found—or the girls found it, really—another garden. Up on Coyote's place."

"Oh, yeah?"

"There must be secret patches all over the place."

"Probably are." He was rolling another joint. She watched his hands. He had long, elegant hands, which he kept very well. Vain of them, maybe.

"How was your trip to Nevada?"

"Okay. I won fourteen hundred dollars in Reno, betting on football games."

"Oh, yeah?"

"Then I lost it all in Las Vegas."

"Shit."

He shrugged. "It's only money." Lifting the joint, he licked the gummed edge. "I talked to some people down south. We can sell them sinsemilla for two thousand a pound." His eyes slid toward her. "We're gonna be rich, Rose."

"Maybe," she said. "I don't know. It makes me nervous, finding that other garden."

"Why?"

"I don't know. Just—if I found it, I mean, somebody else can find it; and if somebody can find Coyote's, somebody can find ours. I guess I'm just paranoid."

"If anybody's found it, they'll wait to rip it off until the females bloom." He lit the joint. "Don't get paranoid yet."

"Somebody who wants to smoke it will wait," she said. "The Man won't wait."

"You seen any cops around here?"

"No."

"Then don't worry about it." He passed her the joint. "Just be quiet and be careful, that's all. And then take your chances."

She took the joint from him; their fingertips brushed together. She seemed to feel his light touch all the way up her arm. Pleased, already rushing, she hit deeply on the joint.

"Yeah," Miller said. "This one's gonna be a male."

He bent the supple tip of the plant down so that she could see it. The green bud was opening a little. Along the bottom, tiny pods were forming, hard to the touch; between her thumb and forefinger the whole bud felt lumpy.

"This one's a female. Come here and look."

On this plant, in between the unfolding layers of the terminal bud, pale tendrils uncurled to the light, so fine she could barely see them.

Miller bent and pulled up the male beside her. He said, "Are they blossoming down in that big field?"

"I don't know. I think so. I don't go there too much."

"Are those people pulling up plants yet?"

"I don't know."

"They better start. One male plant will ruin their whole crop." He tossed the uprooted plant onto the grass by the side of the garden. "You can't get gas money for homegrown with seeds."

"What if they don't get them all? Can they pollinate ours?"

"No, we're too far away. I hope." He was walking down the next row, pulling the limber branch tips down to inspect the buds.

They pulled up a dozen plants that were obviously males. Miller had brought a couple of sheets of twist-ties from a box of plastic bags; he went up and down the rows, tagging the plants he was unsure of. Rose stuffed the male plants into one of the big green trash bags. The root ends stuck out. She beat them on the rock lip of the crag to knock off most of the dirt.

Miller was uprooting another plant. The roots tore out of the soil with a sound like cloth ripping.

They climbed down to the foot of the crag; Rose took the work gloves out of her pocket and draped the berry vines over the trail again. Miller carried the bag of plants. The brush around the crag was so thick in places that they had to beat it down to pass. It grew up above Rose's head, especially near the creek. With her gloved hands she pushed down the poison oak to let Miller get by.

"God," he said. "I'll have poison oak all over me by tomorrow morning."

She looked behind them. The path they had forced was already disappearing into the robust, resilient wild growth. Miller was turning toward the river.

"I'm going swimming. Wash off the oak."

She followed him into the sunlight.

. . .

"Next spring I'd like to raise turkeys," said Glory. "We could sell 'em to cover our expenses and still have enough left over to feed everybody on the ranch."

"Why not rabbits?" said Rose.

She was hovering over the woodstove, waiting for her coffee water to boil. The three women sitting on the couch were engrossed in their work; Glory was letting down the hem of her girl's dress, and Patty and Margaret were knitting.

Suddenly Patty threw down her work. "I can't do this." Her hair straggled over her face. "Margaret, help me."

Margaret leaned forward and took the piece of knitting from her. "See? You've done it okay. You just dropped a stitch here and purled over here where you should have knitted."

"I'll never get it done."

"You will. Keep trying." Margaret showed her how to pick up the stitch she had dropped three rows before and carry it up to the current row. "There." Smiling, she went back to her own knitting, which was perfect. The baby slept in a basket at her feet, a tiny bonnet on her head, mittens on her hands.

"Why not rabbits?" Rose asked again. "That's good meat."

Glory shook her head. "I couldn't kill a bunny." She shook out the dress and folded it neatly on her lap.

"Rose, will you please get me a glass of water?" Margaret asked, lifting her serene and smiling face toward Rose.

She brought her a glass of water, and Margaret thanked her. Rose made the coffee.

"What does it take to raise turkeys?'

"Not too much," said Glory. She was working on a pair of pants now, patching a hole in the knee. "The climate's mild enough here."

"Then let's do it. The less I have to pay for food, the less money I have to make."

"Are you writing something now?" Margaret asked.

"I'm thinking about doing a novel."

Patty was hunched over her knitting, her teeth clenched, struggling with every stitch. Glory said, "I've always thought I'd like to write a book."

"Practically everybody in the world thinks he'd like to write a book," Rose said. "Maybe everybody in the world has a book in him."

"Not me," Margaret said. "All I ever wanted to be was a mother." She bent down over the basket to admire her baby.

Rose sat down in Peter's rocker, watching them, her coffee in her hand; it was good to have the company of women again, like old times, when she and Felice and Angie had sat for hours talking. She watched Glory taking tiny blanket stitches around the edge of the knee patch. Vast and unlovely, Glory still gave off an aura of power, the ultimate power, the only power, what Margaret had hinted at, being a mother. Billy Vigg thieved and cheated and never worked, but behind him there was always Glory, weeding plants, keeping house, sewing, holding her family together, making and remaking her world.

Patty held up her knitting. "Oh, God," she said, and jamming the crooked mass of yarn down into her lap screwed up her face in frustration. "I'll never do it."

"Here." Margaret took the work and looked it over. "Oh, you're doing fine. It's just a little loose, that's all."

Rose sipped her coffee. Being with women was different from being with men. She had grown up with a gang of boys; only in her adulthood had she come to love other women, their honesty and their sympathy.

"Are we gonna raise the turkeys?"

"Sure," said Glory. "I know somebody with chicks."

"There's an old coop in Sam's backyard." Patty pushed her long hair back off her face with her wrist. "We could drag it up here, or over to your house, or something."

Someone came in the front door, banging and stamping feet in the front room. Rose moved to look out through the kitchen door, to see who it was.

Reina and Miller and Bonnie Morrison were shedding their jackets and prying off their boots in the warmth before the fire. Reina wheeled, her arms outspread. "Oh, let's play pool! Come on!" With Bonnie at her heels she made for the pool table, out of Rose's range of vision.

Miller came into the kitchen, passing her, and opened the refrigerator door. "I'm starving," he said to Rose. "What's there to eat?"

"I'll make you a sandwich," she said.

"Are we out of Coke?"

"In the back."

He took a can of Coke from the back of the refrigerator and went out to the front room again. A moment later the record player came on, loud.

"There!" Triumphant, Patty held up her knitting. "I finally did one whole row without a mistake."

The other women applauded her, and she took a bow, not standing up, her cheeks bright with pleasure. Rose moved around the kitchen collecting the meat for the sandwich, lettuce, a ripe tomato, bread, mayonnaise, and the mustard he liked. In the next room the rattle of billiard balls broke in on the music.

"I thought you had to keep turkeys really warm," she said over her shoulder. "And don't they get diseases? Maybe we should start with something small, like a chicken."

Glory laughed. "One chicken?"

"I have a book on raising poultry," Margaret said.

"Bring it up," Rose said. "I'll be the librarian. I'm good at that."

She took the sandwich out to the front room, where Bonnie and Reina were shooting pool. Miller sat up on the sideboard, his legs hanging, the Coke beside him, his hands rolling a joint. Rose put the plate down next to the Coke.

"Have a good ride?"

"Great," he said; his eyes followed Reina around the table. "I'm next," he called to the girls. "I play winner."

Rose leaned against the sideboard; she liked the Steve Miller album that was coming through on the box.

> *Fly like an eagle, 'til I'm free*
> *Right on through the revolution*

Bonnie knocked in the eight ball out of turn and groaned and flung her arms out, her hair butter-yellow in the humid air. Miller took a bite from the sandwich. Putting it down, he slipped off the sideboard and went to take a cue out of the corner where the sticks all leaned. Rose laid her hand on the wood where he had been sitting. Her gaze clung to the back of his neck, bare and tender above the collar of his T-shirt.

Reina had the balls racked up and was centering them. "I'll break." Angular as a stork, with her long arms and legs, she raced around to the other end of the table to open the game. Rose went back into the kitchen; she put away the mayonnaise.

"We'll all go in together, right?" Patty said. "The four of us. All together."

"Fine," said Glory. "It'll give me something to do when the pot's harvested."

Rose leaned on the sink, her gaze turned out through the dark window. The overhead light made the glass opaque, reflecting back the scene behind her, the three women, their hands moving.

> *Fly like an eagle, 'til I'm free*

If she loved Miller, who loved Reina, who loved the horse, then by extending the pattern she came to the conclusion that somebody somewhere loved Rose as well. *And you know that can't be wrong.* She watched the tiny movements of the women's hands in the glass, all the world in one image.

The baby peeped. Margaret lifted her up and gave her the breast.

Reina burst into the room, her head back. "He beat me Baretta-style!" she cried, exuberant. Behind her came Miller, his face shining with his love. Rose turned around toward them and laughed.

" 'So foul and fair a day I have not seen,' " Rose said; it was raining again, although directly overhead the sky was a blazing blue, and the midmorning sun shone.

"Why do you say things like that?" Miller glared up at her. He was walking; she was riding the old white horse. "That's not English."

"It's English. Maybe it isn't American."

"Why do you talk like that, then?"

"I don't know. It's fun."

"It's stupid."

"My father was a compulsive punster. We used to spend dinner throwing bad puns at each other."

"That's not a pun—what you said. There's no joke in it at all, just bad English."

"Well, she said, "I don't think Macbeth was talking entirely about the weather. I don't know why I do it. It's fun. It's a game, like checkers, or jacks. Sometimes it's comforting to know somebody else once felt the way you do. It's—"

"You don't," he said. "You can't know for sure that it means what you think it means. Words are just approximate. It could mean lots of things. It could mean nothing at all."

Rose watched the flare of anger spread across his face; uncertain things always made him impatient. She shrugged, looked ahead toward the road, and closed her legs on the horse, urging him into a long-striding walk. "I thought you were going to run."

"That horse can't—"

"All the way to Morrisons', you said."

"That horse can't outwalk a baby." He broke into a jog to keep up.

They were on the county road, a tarmac pathway through the broken woods and old fields of River Ranch, on the inside of the curve, and through an arm of the National Forest, on the outside. The rain had stopped, scarcely dampening the road, but now a vast, dark cloud crossed the sun, and the raw air made her shiver. She took her jacket from the back of the saddle and put it on.

Miller ran easily down the middle of the road. He was beginning to draw away from her, and she pushed the horse sideways with her leg, to the soft berm of the road, where he could trot.

The Morrisons loaned them the little red horse that Rose had ridden before. Miller swung into the saddle, and they rode down to the river where it swept under a concrete bridge. Miller rode ahead of her across the gravel river bar to the edge of the water.

"Which way d'y' want to go?"

"Go back to River Ranch. We can stop and check our garden."

He swung the horse around to head downstream and trotted it into a plunging, hard gallop. Rose let the white horse follow. The loose pebbles of the beach slid rattling away from the horses' hooves. The ground changed to fine gray sand, studded with brushy plants. The red horse swerved to follow a trail worn into the riverbed. They passed a tire half-buried in the sand. Beer cans glittered in the mats of scrub grass. Sand and small rocks pelted her. She moved the horse out a little, to one side of Miller.

The sun came out. Ahead there was a camper parked, where the river curved, the higher edge of the curve deep with sand. A woman in an orange sunhat was trying to set up a lounge chair in the camper's lee. Down in the river, a man stood in the hip-deep water, casting for trout in a pool behind a massive redwood stump.

Rose slowed her horse to pass them and waved. The woman waggled her hand in a cheerful answer.

Miller was far ahead of her now. Standing up in the stirrups, she kicked the white horse into a long, hard run. Where the river cut across his path, he stopped, and she galloped up to him.

He was looking up and down the river, which curved around here into the sheer eight-foot riverbank, so that they had to cross it to keep going on. He pointed his hand up-stream again.

"We oughta go back up there, where it's shallower."

"Oh, for Christ's sake." Rose booted her horse toward the water. "We can get across here."

The white horse strode willingly enough into the river. She lifted her feet up to keep from getting her shoes wet. Miller was following her, his horse's hooves splashing her back. The water climbed to the horse's belly, higher, up to his shoulder, and with a lurch the big animal began to swim.

Off-balance, Rose yelled. With her legs nearly doubled up in front of her, she could not keep her seat, and she fell sideways into the river, dropping the reins.

The horse swam away from her. "Whoa," she shouted, grabbing for his floating tail, but he was already by her. He was turning, swimming in a broad arc back the way he had come. She struggled to swim, her shoes heavy on her feet, her clothes cumbersome.

The red horse snorted. Spinning around in the river cur-rent, he dumped Miller into the dark water and hurried af-ter Windfire back to land.

Rose yelled again, thinking this funny. She flailed away at the water with her sleeve-laden arms. Miller was going on to the far bank, which was closer. A glance at his face warned her that he took this much more seriously than she did. She concentrated on getting back to the shore after the horses.

The white horse was already out; he stopped long enough to shake all over, showering water over the pebbly beach, and at a brisk walk started away in the direction they had come. Halfway up the beach, the woman in the orange sunhat was sitting up on her lounge chair to watch. The Morrisons' chestnut horse followed Windfire at a trot, reins trailing.

Rose walked onto the shore, her soaked Levi's clinging heavily to her legs. "Whoa," she called, "whoa now."

She glanced back across the river, where Miller was standing, staring at her. He put his hands on his hips. Hastily she looked away from him. He would never let her forget it if they had to walk all the way home.

But the white horse had stopped, halfway to the camper, and he turned his head to watch her, trudging after him in her squelching clothes. Raising his head, he looked out over the river, his ears pricked, his nostrils flaring out like cups. She guessed he was confused, knowing they had come down by way of the road, but sensing the familiar country back across the river. The red horse went up beside him, and the two snuffled at each other.

Rose came up quietly beside Windfire and got the reins. "You devil," she said to him. "You get me in a lot of trouble sometimes, you know that?" She scratched him under the jaw. The red horse was standing a few feet away, watching her. She mounted her horse and grabbed the Morrisons' horse's dangling reins.

The woman in the orange sunhat waved, gay and smiling. Opposite her, just downstream from the fisherman, the river ran broad and shallow over a bed of stones, its ripples gleaming in the sun. Rose put Windfire at a short trot through the shallows, leading the red horse after, and loped down the far bank toward Miller.

His face was rigid with bad temper. He shot one short, hard look at her and swung up onto the red horse. Before he had both feet in the stirrups, he was kicking it into a hard run. "Yaah! Yaah!" They sprinted away across the sandy shore.

Ahead of them the dry bed of the Eel ended against a steep little cliff. Miller swerved toward it. He slapped the red horse with his bare hand. "Yaah!" The horse gathered itself; in two leaps it went up the bank. Rose got up out of the saddle, giving her horse a slack rein, and the big horse launched himself onto the top of the bank in a single athletic leap.

The meadow rippled away from her in tall grass, sunburned to straw. The sun was rolling behind a cloud, and the shadow rushed toward her over the windblown grass. A few raindrops struck her face and shoulders.

The red horse was far ahead of her. She collected Windfire a little and lined him out after Miller. The horse stretched into a driving run. Before he reached his top stride, he tried to drop behind the bit, but she whacked him with the reins and he took off again.

Miller's horse was slowing down. Hearing the white horse behind him, he put on a burst of speed. Rose bent over the horse's neck to stay out of the wind. She yelled to him and kicked him hard, and he swept up on the heels of the red horse, who was tiring rapidly under Miller's weight.

The red horse strained for more speed. The reins shaved the lathery sweat from his neck. Windfire drew even with him, head to head, and Rose drove him on with her legs and her hands. He burst into the lead, on into the forest, crashing through brush and vines, until Rose jerked him to a stop.

She turned to look behind her. Miller's horse had stopped at the margin of the forest. She wheeled Windfire around to go back.

He still looked sour. "What's wrong?" she said. "Why are you so depressed all the time?"

"There's nothing wrong!"

They rode along the edge of the forest, back to the river, saying nothing for a while. The red horse was soaked with sweat, but Windfire was only warm. Rose had to nudge him every few strides with her legs or he would lag, but he was fit as a champion.

"God," she said. "This horse was filthy when I found him. Two months ago! He was bony as old Ichabod. Now look at him." She slapped the sleek neck. "She's turned him into Secretariat."

"Has she been blow-drying him lately?"

"What is the matter with you?"

"There's nothing the matter with me!"

"Are you mad at me?"

He wheeled toward her, his face red. "That was your fault—getting me dunked in the river."

"I'm sorry," she said.

He said nothing. They walked the horses along the stony river bar. A hawk came up the river in a long glide, passed them, and circled around to land on top of a snag on the riverbank. Rose fumbled for words, afraid of saying too much, to him and to herself.

"I like you a lot," she said. "I'm very fond of you. It makes me feel bad to see you feeling bad."

"I can't help it. Now she's being so nice to me, she's so beautiful, and she's going away."

There was nothing to say about that. Rose let the leathers slide through her fingers. Twisting, she looked back at the snag, where the hawk was eating something clutched in its talons.

"I like you, too," Miller said. "You're a good friend, Rose."

"Thanks," she replied.

Ahead of them the river gurgled over stones, the sound magnified in the arch of a bridge. The sun shone down on the water just beyond it, and the reflection played in ripples over the concrete arch.

Miller said, "I guess I even love you, in a way."

A surge of excitement went through her. "I love you, too," she said.

"Like a friend," he said.

She wondered if he were asking her or commenting on his own love. They had come to the little creek, dry now, its sandy bed full of grass and nettles. They drew rein.

Miller said, "I'll go take care of the plants. If we take the horses in there, they'll beat down a path like a freeway straight to the garden."

"Right."

"You wait here, okay?"

"Sure."

He swung down from the saddle and threw her the reins.

Rose looped them onto her saddle horn. Miller's eyes met hers once, and he smiled at her. He walked away up the creek bed, knocking down the brush in his way. She watched him until he was gone from sight into the forest.

Something had changed between them, in that parley. Some new trust had formed, like a shell around the two of them.

She watched the river. A dragonfly hummed over the red horse's ears a moment and zipped away. The water racketed under the bridge. The sun was bright and strong again, and Rose took off her denim jacket and lashed it to the cantle of her saddle. Clouds like great airships traveled overhead. Up on the mountain a thunderhead shadowed the trees; it seemed to be raining there. She looked around for a rainbow, but the sun was too high in the sky.

She saw it was all different now, somehow, all changed, because of what she had said to Miller and what he had said to her.

After a long while he came back, still gloomy, his wet jeans flecked with cockleburs. He climbed onto his horse, and they rode through the forest toward the house.

Peter was behind the house splitting wood with a sledge-hammer and a wedge, to bundle time away, Rose thought, until he could start drinking. Miller and Reina went off to ride. Rose wiped off a roast and put it in a pan to brown. Through the kitchen window she could see Peter only on the up stroke. When he disappeared behind the corner, the hammer rang like a bell.

She sliced a couple of yellow onions and put them in with the meat. The phone rang.

"Hello?"

"Hello," Margaret Sunshine said breathlessly. "You better get Peter down here. Patty and Glory are going at it in the pot field."

"Going at it. Arguing?"

"No," Margaret said. "They're tearing out clumps of each other's hair."

"We'll be right down."

When she dashed out to the woodpile, Peter straightened up, leaning on the sledge, and wiped his face. He had taken off his shirt; his chest was white as a baby's. "Come on," Rose said. "There's a fight down on the flat."

"Let 'em fight. Who cares?"

"They're fighting in the pot field," she said, and when that seemed not to move him, she added, "It's Patty. She might hurt herself."

At that he dropped the hammer and strode to his truck. Rose jumped into the cab with him.

When they reached the pot field, Patty was sitting on the ground holding her stomach and Glory was walking up and down, shouting, "I don't care! I don't give a damn!" Margaret hung on her arm like an anchor.

Johan came out of the field, three or four marijuana plants under his arm. "These are all the ones she uprooted. Maybe we can replant them."

Peter walked into their midst, his face dark with bad temper. "What's going on?"

"I came out here and caught her pulling up my plants!" Glory pointed a shaking finger at Patty.

"They're males," Patty cried. She jumped up onto her feet again. Her glasses were gone. "You'll ruin my whole crop."

"I don't care," Glory shouted. Her shapeless body was stuffed into a pair of jeans and one of her endless supply of halter tops. The dark roots showed at the part in her yellow hair.

Patty yelled, "I'm not letting them ruin my crop just 'cause they're too damn dumb—"

"Bitch," Glory shouted. "Garbage mouth."

"Fucking stupid broad!"

Other people were gathering around them. Johan raised his arms.

"Come on, everybody quiet down. Let's remember what's important here, and try to love each other."

"Bitch," Glory said smugly.

Patty launched herself across the short space between them and knocked Glory down. Like a kid in a street fight she landed on Glory's chest and flailed away at her face with both fists.

The crowd yelled. In the back somebody called, "Five says Patty creams her."

Peter muttered an oath. He strode up to Patty and, grabbing one arm, yanked her back away from Glory, who was yelling and crying and holding her belly, now that Patty was off. Peter hauled Patty back several steps; she struggled a moment, whining, and finally burst into tears.

"My crop," she said, sobbing. "My crop. You don't understand. It's all I have for my baby."

Peter's arm slid around her, and he hugged her close to his side.

Rose went over to the uprooted plants. "These are definitely males." She had never seen male marijuana as mature as these; the whole bud had developed into a potent cluster of hard pods.

"You people got to stop fighting," Johan said solemnly. His voice swelled to reach the other people around them. "That's worse for the plants than anything else, all these bad vibes."

"One male plant can ruin the whole field," Rose said.

"Sister Rose, we got to have order. Nobody can—"

Preston elbowed his way up through the crowd. "What's going on?" His rifle hung in the crook of his arm.

"We got to respect each other's property, Sister Rose."

"Your idiot brother left three male plants standing," Rose said to Dave Preston, "until the goddamned pods were practically ready to open." She kicked at the plants on the ground. Their saw-toothed leaves were already wilting.

"There's a higher matter than that here," Johan said. "The plants are alive. You can't just kill something—"

"Johan," Peter said, "shut up." He stood with his arm around Patty, who was staying as far from him as his grasp allowed. "The plants are males, they have to go." He stuck his finger out accusingly at Glory. "You go through your plants and pull up every male. You got it?"

Glory pressed her lips together. Waves of color beat into

her fat, fair face. She blurted, "I can't remember which is which."

One by one, the others laughed. Glory scowled around her. Deep scratches creased her arms, her shoulder, the roll of flesh between the tight band of the halter top and the waist of her jeans. Patty was bleeding from a gash near the eye. She moved away from Peter, who let his arm fall to his side. Going into the grass, she picked up her glasses from the ground and wiped the lenses clean on the tail of her shirt.

"Who knows how to sex pot plants?" Peter asked.

No one spoke for a moment. At last Dave Preston said, "I can."

"Okay. Then you go through the whole field, every day, and pull up the boys." Peter frowned at him. "And put that gun away."

"I'm just hunting rabbits."

"Put it away. The next time I see you with it, I'll run you off River Ranch."

Preston lifted his head. "You ain't telling me what to do, mister."

Peter's hands curled into fists. Rose touched her lips with her tongue, her eyes darting from her brother to Preston, facing each other in this circle of their friends. Preston lowered the gun slowly to his side.

"You wanna fight?"

"You keep that gun locked up."

"I can do what I want on my own propitty."

"You'll destroy everything if you fight here," Johan called. He was frowning at Peter and Dave Preston. A low noise, far in the distance, broke the threshold of her hearing. She looked up.

A little private plane was flying slowly toward them across the forest. As its engine noise swelled, more and more of the people around Rose were looking up to see it. Preston and Peter ignored that; they were staring each other down.

Abruptly someone said, "That's the Man, man."

Peter's head jerked up toward the plane, and he shaded

his eyes with his hand; a low exclamation escaped him. The plane circled around over the field. The black numbers on the undersides of its wings were clearly visible from the ground. If it were a police plane, Rose saw no sign of it. But suddenly Preston wheeled his gun up and took aim at the plane as it soared overhead.

With a yell Rose leaped on him and grappled with him; another body struck them and carried them both to the ground. Rose gripped the rifle with both hands, not minding about anything else. The dust got into her eyes and up her nose, and she began to cough. Someone was on top of her, shouting. She wrenched the rifle free and lay down on it.

"It's okay," Peter roared. "Come on, everybody up." He tapped Rose briskly on the shoulder. "Come on, Mean Joe, get up."

She got up, leaving the gun in the dirt. Her throat was lined with grit. The plane was gone. Coughing, she swiped at the dust that coated her arms and legs. Everybody seemed to be staring at her.

Peter said, "I mean it, Dave. If I see you with that gun again, you gotta get off my place." He marched away toward his truck, parked on the edge of the meadow. Rose followed him, still coughing.

"You were a trip." Patty thrust her sleeves above her elbows, pushing Rose away from the sink. "I'll wash 'em. You bring 'em in and scrape 'em. God, I thought I'd bust a gut when you jumped on ol' Dave. Then Peter jumping on both of you—"

Rose muttered something. Everybody said she had looked funny leaping for the rifle. She pushed pork chop bones off a plate with a fork. Her shoulder hurt whenever she used her right arm.

"Your eyes bugged out like a frog's," Patty said. "I never seen you move so fast. You moved so fast I think parts of you got left behind."

"I feel like parts of me got knocked off."

"I suppose you were right, though. It might not even have been a cop at all." Happily Patty churned and scrubbed in the froth of soapy water, clashing dishes together.

"You feeling better? She didn't hurt you, did she?" Rose asked.

"Who, Glory? Naw." Patty laid a stack of soapy dishes in the other well of the sink and Rose went to rinse them. "I don't get sick in the morning any more. I feel like I could bust rocks; I feel that good."

"You look good," Rose said.

Patty's hair was streaked with paler shades of blond, and she was as tan as Reina. A constant little smile played over her lips. She said, "I can feel it now, I think. I can feel it moving."

"Right now?" Rose looked startled at her belly, beginning to swell against her jeans; she had the top button unbuttoned.

"No. Just sometimes. At night sometimes."

"When is it supposed to be born?"

"In January." Patty smiled. "An Aquarius."

"Are you scared?"

"No."

"What's it feel like, when it moves?"

"Like somebody running a finger down the inside of me." Patty was still smiling. She had the look Rose had seen before on pregnant women, the look of knowing a good deal more than anybody else ever could, like the Mona Lisa. She said, "Have you ever had a baby, Rose?"

"No," Rose said.

"Do you want to?"

"No, not really. What sign are you?"

"A Gemini. At least that's what they told me, the people I grew up with. Who knows? I could be anything. I feel more like a Leo."

There was a knock on the back door. Rose turned off the water, stretching her neck to see who it was; the ceiling light made mirrors of the windowpanes. "Come on in!"

The door opened, and Hallie came in.

"Oh," Rose said and stood up. "Hi, Hallie." She could not help staring at Hallie, who wore a skirt and blazer and vest all of the same gray flannel. She had stockings on and makeup. She looked like a woman out of a television commercial.

She said, "I'm leaving. I sold my goats to Johan. I hope they eat every plant in your pot field." She turned and marched out the door.

The door hung open, as if maybe Hallie wanted to be called back. Rose went over and shut it. "Well," she said, "if wishes were horses."

"Good riddance," Patty said, smiling.

"Well," Coyote said. "You ready to start cookin' for me?"

Rose chalked her cue. "Wha'd'you mean? You're gonna haul those logs out?"

"Starting Monday."

Miller was ambling up to them, his hands in the pockets of his shorts. "Who's playing?"

"Her and me." Coyote picked up his cue and went around to the end of the table to break. Rose glanced up at Miller, standing beside her.

"Have a good ride?"

"Pretty good."

Coyote punched the cue ball down into the setup, and colored balls rolled off in every direction, bouncing off the cushions, off each other; one dropped into the pocket by Rose's hand. She looked in.

"Stripes."

Coyote punched the cue ball down into the setup, and the balls. As he passed them, Rose and Miller backed away to give him space. Peter was watching television at the other side of the room, and Reina was outside with the horse, although it was dark and she could not ride.

"I have to feed you and who else?" Rose asked Coyote. She took the joint from Miller and toked on it.

Coyote bent over the cue stick, sliding it back and forth in his hands. "Billy Vigg and me." He stroked the ball into whirling flight across the green felt bed. The fourteen dropped into the side pocket.

"Good shot. Billy Vigg? I thought you weren't gonna hire him."

"Nobody else around here will do it." Coyote was moving again, his eyes on the balls. "Peter don't work. Johan says he won't destroy things, only build things—" With a crack the cue ball sent the orange-and-white nine ball into flight across the table. "Dave and Sam and the others all got jobs already."

"How much you paying?" Miller asked.

"Four hundred a week."

Miller's eyes widened; the blue intensity of his gaze fixed itself on Coyote. "I'll help you."

"You know anything about logging?"

"I can learn."

"Sorry. I already got Billy. There's only work for two of us."

Miller said nothing. He drew his head down between his shoulders.

Coyote strolled around the table and from the far corner tapped the eleven ball neatly from between two of Rose's; it rolled in a slow curve across the table into the corner pocket.

"Hey, man," she said, "gimme a chance."

He laughed. "You gotta know this table, that's all."

At that she watched him more keenly; she saw that he was aiming most of his shots toward one corner pocket. The table dipped slightly in favor of this pocket. She breathed a soundless whistle.

He had cleaned house on her. The only balls left on the table were solids. Saying, "Eight ball in the corner pocket," he poked the black devil into a slow ramble. When it came down near the pocket, its path veered a little and it fell into the hole.

"Wanna play?" Miller said.

"Sure," Coyote said.

"What about a little bet on it to keep things interesting?"

Rose backed away to the wall, her hands behind her. Glumly she wished she had paid more attention to the game; maybe then she would have understood the table.

"Sure," Coyote said. "How much?"

Miller held out the joint. "Twenty?"

"Sure."

Coyote took the joint from him. It was a windy night, the windows behind her rattling in their frames, and the room was cold, so far from the fireplace. Coyote held out the roach to her, and she took it and looked for a roach clip. Miller gave her his hemostat.

Coyote broke the balls and got the stripes again. Methodically he worked around the table, knocking in the balls closest to the pockets. Rose thought, He'll do the same to Miller, and her mood slipped even more.

Miller did not seem to mind. He stood watching Coyote, his hands folded over his stick.

At last Coyote missed a shot; he had knocked in four balls. While Miller prowled the table, he came over to Rose's side.

"Remember. Breakfast up here, lunch down there, dinner up here."

"Gimme some bucks, man, so I can buy the food."

He pulled a roll of bills out of his pocket and peeled off five twenties. Miller had knocked in one ball and missed his next shot. Rose frowned. She had never seen him play pool; everybody said he was good, but he did not look good at it to her. She stuffed the money into her pocket. Coyote went around the table to find a shot.

He cleaned out his balls, shot for the eight ball, and missed. "Yours," he said to Miller and went back over to Rose.

"I like lots of breakfast. Pancakes, waffles, bacon, eggs— all you got."

"Okay. What time?"

"Seven."

"Jesus."

"Hell, lady, when you're working for yourself, you put in long hours."

"That's true."

Miller had lowered another of his balls and missed the shot after. Coyote walked smartly around the table, trying to line up the cue ball, the eight ball, and a pocket. He swore.

"You don't give me nothin' to shoot at here."

Miller shrugged. "That's the way the game is played."

"You don't have to tell me—" Coyote flattened himself over the cue stick—"how the game is played." He drilled one straight for the high corner pocket. The black ball ticked off the side and rolled away into the center of the felt.

"Wanna raise the bet?" Miller said.

Coyote snorted. "Boy, you are a sucker for punishment."

"Forty?"

"Let 'er rip. I got ya this time, by God."

Miller drifted slowly around the table. Rose sorted through her memory of their kitchen stores; she would give him bacon, eggs, and pancakes in the morning, orange juice, milk, coffee. Biscuits if she had baking soda. Miller knocked in one of his balls.

"You got any preferences for lunch?" Rose asked Jim Wylie beside her.

"Meat. Bread. Lettuce. Tomato."

Miller hit another of his balls in. He picked up the chalk and touched it to the cue tip.

"Make me a pie for dinner," Coyote said.

"Sure."

"One pie for me. One for everybody else."

"God, what a braggart. Is Billy eating dinner here, too?"

"I think so."

Miller sank another ball in a difficult angle shot into the side pocket. Coyote pursed his lips.

"I never oughta trust that boy."

She said nothing. Miller sauntered around the far end

of the table and came toward them, pausing halfway to knock in two more balls. Now there was none left but the eight ball, in the center of the table. He reached for the little cube of blue chalk again. He had blue chalk on his cheek.

"Side pocket," he said and lightly, neatly stroked the cue ball past the eight, just grazing it. The black ball rolled over to the side pocket, hung on the lip a moment, and dropped in under the force of gravity.

"You done it to me again," Coyote said.

Miller took another joint from behind his ear. He accepted Coyote's money. "You did it to you again." He put the money into his pocket.

Halfway through the next morning, while she was making sandwiches, Miller tramped into the kitchen. "God, you make a lot of noise." His hair was matted like wool. His fretful, bitchy humor dragged the corners of his mouth down. "Can't you let me sleep? I didn't get any sleep at all last night."

"For Christ's sake. You're fifty feet from the house." She glanced out the kitchen window toward the meadow, where he was accustomed to sleeping. "How could I wake you up?"

"You make so much noise! Banging dishes around at dawn—"

"Miller, maybe the reason you can't sleep is from drinking all that Coke. I—"

"It is not! I'm a very light sleeper. When you come in here and throw pots and pans around, it wakes me up!"

She looked him full in the face, wondering if this were another game he was playing, but the fitful discontent in his expression was real. Angry, she went back to making sandwiches.

He dropped down onto the couch and put his shoes on, yapping at her still. "Can't you shut the cupboards quietly? Why d'you have to bang everything around?"

"Goddamnit, Miller, you can't expect the whole world to shut itself off so you can sleep."

"Why not?" He pulled on a white tube sock. "What's wrong with asking for a little courtesy—"

"You're unreasonable."

Her back was to him. She wrapped a sandwich in waxed paper, her senses tuned behind her, but he said nothing. She dropped the sandwich into a bag on the counter.

"Now where are you going?"

"I'm taking Coyote's lunch down to him."

"Sure," he said. "You'll feed him with a spoon, but you won't make me any breakfast."

"I'm gonna punch you in the mouth pretty soon if you don't get off my back."

"Where's Reina?"

"She went riding. Why, didn't she wake you up, saddling the horse?"

"Where are you going?"

"I told you, I'm taking Coyote's lunch to him!"

"What about me? I'm hungry. Don't I get to eat?"

She strode out through the front room, swinging the brown bag of sandwiches. Her temper was sawing through its restraints of logic. He wanted her to get mad; he liked to fight. She hid herself away in a sullen silence. Walking across the front porch, she jumped down to the grass and made for her car.

Miller was right behind her. "You gonna drive down there? Why can't you walk? It's under half a mile."

"It's a little farther than that to Springville." She yanked open the door of her car, facing Miller over the roof, her face and neck prickly with anger. "If you don't mind, I've got things to do."

"You're going to Springville?" His eyes glittered. "Wanna play tennis?"

She stared at him, sorting out her feelings. She decided she wanted to be with him, even if he was grumpy. And she did want to play tennis. "Okay."

"I'll get the rackets and roll a couple joints."

"Okay."

"You go down to Coyote's with the lunch, and I'll meet you at the gate."

"Okay."

"Take my car, so we can listen to tapes."

"Okay."

He went back into the house. She took his car to Coyote's place.

In the green meadow where his teepee stood, two huge engines were waiting in the tall grass, daisies and yarrow dancing in the wind by the huge mud-clogged wheels. One was the back wheels and fork for a log truck and the other looked like a big yellow lobster with two pincers. From local television she recognized this for a log-loader. She walked between them and the teepee toward the woods, where the men were working. Already the grass was beaten down into ruts, although only three logs were visible, piled neatly in the grass at the edge of the trees. The bellow of a motor drew her into the woods.

They were snaking the logs down into the meadow with a bulldozer; she saw the yellow bulldozer first, bright among the trees, the high whine of its engine coughing in the gear changes. Coyote was driving it. She stopped, waiting until he noticed her. They were higher on the hill than she was. The bulldozer's treads had ground the dirt and ferns into dusty pulp along a path four feet wide, winding in through the trees.

The bulldozer was coming toward her. She moved behind a tree. Unfamiliar machines spooked her. They seemed alive to her, malevolent, ready to leap at any minute and grind her up in their gears. This one rocked and bumped down the slope with a racket that hurt her ears. In the cage Coyote sat twisted to watch behind him.

The bulldozer was dragging a log through the standing trees, pulling it by a heavy wire cable. Billy Vigg walked after it. Coyote steered carefully between two redwoods toward the meadow; the log slipped a little, leaping forward as if it were alive, and he speeded up the bulldozer to keep the cable taut. The engine screamed. With a clash of gears he drove out onto the open meadow.

The log bumped into a tree trunk, caught an instant, and jerked free. The line slackened. Curious, Rose went up closer. Behind the log, Billy waved happily at her.

"Got our eats?"

She waved her arm over her head.

The log rolled. Billy yelled, coming down after it, and Coyote rushed the bulldozer forward to take up the slack in the line. The log, still rolling sideways, hit a stump. Rose stood where she was, watching the line strain and the log, answering, nosed forward, jamming itself against the stump.

"Pull it out," Billy roared. "It'll pull."

On the tag end of his words the cable snapped with a crack like a huge twig popping.

"Heads up!" Billy dropped flat to the ground. Rose crouched, her hands flying up to protect her head. Something sailed by, three inches above her hands. She blinked. Ten feet in front of her the log had broken free and was sliding down toward her, banging and slithering over the ground.

She dashed for the shelter of the nearest redwood. The log mashed the ferns and flowers in its path. Gaining momentum, it careened past her, dove down the steeper slope at the foot of the hill, buried its nose in the soft earth of a little landslide, and flipped over with a crash that rocked the forest.

Rose stood up, shaking, impressed by all these big moves. Coyote was bounding across the battered hillside toward her. "Are you all right?" His arm closed around her shoulders. "Did it hit you?"

"I'm fine," she said, surprised; she had not felt herself to be in any real danger.

"Look." He turned her around and pointed.

Just over her head, on the trunk of the tree where she had sheltered, a slash nearly two feet long cut the bark.

Tendrils of the furry bark hung down from the lip of the wound.

"That was the end of the cable," Coyote said. "If it'd hit you, it would've taken your head off." He wheeled around.

Watching them from the hillside above was Billy Vigg, his arms hanging loose and his mouth open. When he saw Coyote looking for him, he straightened up, and a yell filled his throat.

"It wasn't my fault! I didn't—"

Coyote charged up the hillside toward him. Billy's yell dissolved into pure noise. He raced away through the trees. Coyote shouted, "I'm gonna get you!" His legs driving him up across the slope, he raced into the woods after Billy.

Rose went down to the meadow again. She left the sacks of lunch on the seat of the bulldozer. There was no sign of Coyote's coming back. She walked thoughtfully away toward the gate.

Miller was waiting there, in his car, smoking a reefer. She got in beside him.

"What took you so long?"

"I was watching them work." She shut the door.

They drove down through the woods toward the county road. Miller handed her the joint. "How are they doing?"

"They is about to be reduced to he. Perhaps he and several small pieces of Billy Vigg. You want that job, I think there's a new opening. Hold up."

He stopped the car; they had reached the county road, and Rose got out and went over to the edge of the road where the ranch's big wooden mailbox stood on a pole. She sorted through the collection of junk mail and magazines, found nothing for her, and dropped it all back into the box. She turned back to the car and Miller.

They went up the freeway to Springville. Miller pushed the cassette tape into the deck under his car's dashboard. A guitar hammered out a thundering beat, and a reedy, male voice came in at half-speed.

I see your red door and I want to paint it black—

Her mind snapped backwards, back into the time when she had first heard this song, back in college, a time when she still wore makeup, tinted her hair, wanted to be rich. Believed in God; supported the war in Vietnam. God, she thought. What a long, strange trip it's been.

Miller was lighting a joint. The freeway carried them past the enormous buildings of the Scotia mill; ahead lay the Eel's green delta. She reached for the joint, her mind still working on the war in Vietnam, lying in her memory like a great undigestible lump that broke and whirled the rushing currents of her life.

"Here comes a cop," Miller said, his voice taut.

She was holding the joint. She jerked upright, her eyes searching the road for the badge, the car, the flashing lights. There was no cop. Miller smiled broadly at her.

"Why'd you do that?" she said, sinking back into the seat of the car. She put the joint to her lips again. It had gone out.

"I just wanted to bring you out of your zone. You think too much. You miss what's going on around you."

"Not really." She lit the joint, careful not to singe her nose.

"Really. What happened with Coyote and Billy?"

"The last I saw of them they were doing the four-minute mile in tandem over the hill."

"What the hell does that mean?"

She told him what had happened in the woods by Coyote's teepee.

"Jesus," he exclaimed.

"It's dangerous, you see," she said. "Maybe you better not try it." She held out the joint in front of him so that he could take it without moving his gaze from the road.

"Anything's dangerous if you don't concentrate on what you're doing."

"Yeah, well, it's real hard work, too. Maybe you oughta give up the idea."

"What's the matter with you?"

"Why do you want to work for him, anyway?"

"For the money." He fastened a roach clip to the joint, the steering wheel braced against his knee and his forearms.

"What d'you need the money for?"

"God, what a snoop. Is that why you got such a funny nose? From sticking it in where it shouldn't be?" He grabbed her nose between his thumb and forefinger. She knocked his hand down.

"What a turkey."

"You calling me a turkey? I thought you liked me."

"I do," she said. "Otherwise I wouldn't put up with you."

He glanced at her and addressed himself to the joint again. They were crossing the flat farmlands south of Springville; the railroad ran parallel with the freeway, a few hundred yards away, and a row of cypress and Monterey pine stood behind that. These trees broke easily, the shattered stumps of branches supporting a scarf of foliage. She never saw a stand of them without half their branches broken off.

Miller said, "Are you zoning out on me again?"

"No." She faced him, reaching for the joint.

"Reina's being so nice to me, and she's going away. I don't see why I'm so unlucky."

Rose tapped the ash off the roach, now down to its last hit.

"Maybe that's why she's being so nice—because she's leaving. She knows it won't have any consequences."

"Maybe she knows what she's losing."

"Maybe. Don't you have any other girlfriends?"

"Reina's not my girlfriend."

"What is she, then?"

He did not answer for a few moments; they were coming into Springville, and he put on his turn signal, glanced behind him, and sidled his car into the right-hand lane. He said, "Someday she's going to be my lover."

"Don't you have any lovers now?"

"Not lovers. I have people I sleep with."

"A very good distinction."

"I slept with three girls at once, one night when I was back home last time."

Rose turned her gaze out the window; the talk was leading into dangerous places. They passed the sawmill and crossed the railroad tracks; on the left was a little store selling apples and cider, and she said. "They make great cider there. Let's stop on the way back and get some."

"What'sa matter?" he asked. "You don't like talking about sex with me?"

"No," she said, "as a matter of fact, I don't."

"Why? We talk about everything else."

"Why do you want to talk about it, anyway? You think there's something remarkable about making it with three girls at once?" She glanced at him, her curiosity caught. "Simultaneously or in sequence?"

"One after the other. Yeah, I think it's remarkable, don't you?"

He pulled the car into the parking lot beside the high school, where the tennis courts were. Two boys were driving a little remote car around and around on the black top; it buzzed like an enormous wasp. Miller turned off his engine and let the car coast to a stop beside the gate to the tennis courts. Neither of them moved to get out of the car.

"Did you enjoy it?" Rose asked.

"Not really. Not as much as they did, anyway."

"Were they girls you knew?"

"No—I was going home late, after playing basketball, you know, smoking a joint, and they pulled up next to me at a stop sign. They wanted to smoke some, so I took 'em to my place."

Rose was staring straight ahead, into the broad field behind the high school, where half a dozen horses grazed. The yellow grass reached to their bellies. "Did you ever see any of them again?"

"One of them came back again the next day. She already had a boyfriend, but she liked my cock."

L.A. was like that. No yesterday, no tomorrow, nothing lost and nothing gained; the people rebounded from their accidental collisions with each other with the elasticity of billiard balls. In so featureless a place, what landmarks could he find to guide him? Winning at games. Smoking dope. And loving Reina.

That was why it didn't matter that Reina gave him nothing for his love. What he got back from it was himself.

She turned her eyes on him again, intrigued by that. He smiled at her. "When are we going to have sex together, Rosie?"

"Jesus. What an ambush." She reached back into the rear seat for her tennis racket. "Talk to me after Reina leaves."

She got out of the car; he got out of the car. He said, "Why can't I talk to you now?"

"Wait until Reina leaves." She walked past him toward the courts, where several people were already playing.

"Why?"

"What side do you want?"

He glanced at the sky. The sun was bright enough to make him squint. "I'll take the sun side."

"We could change sides every other game."

"It'll even out my advantage over you somewhat. Why can't I ask you to have sex with me?"

"Wait until Reina leaves," she said patiently.

He stared at her a moment; he had on a blue T-shirt, and his eyes blazed like blue neon. Finally he shook the balls out of the can, scooped up two of them, and trotted down to the far side of the court.

"I'm gonna clobber you today," he called.

"You always do."

"Yeah, but today it's gonna be an annihilation. I'm not going to let you win a single point."

She tossed up a ball and hit it over the net to him.

When they got back to River Ranch, Reina was in the front room. Rose was carrying two paper sacks of groceries; she stopped and said, "What's the matter?"

"My mom called." Reina slumped on the couch, her

shoulders hunched over and her head sunk down in between them. The green and white bows hung drooping from her pigtails. "I gotta go home in four days." She gave a little sob, half-choked. "I don't wanna move to Florida!"

"Come talk to me in the kitchen so I can put this stuff down."

Reina followed her into the kitchen. Rose set the bags on the counter and began taking out loaves of bread. "Here. Stick this in the freezer for me."

They passed the food from hand to hand into the refrigerator. Reina said, "Can't I live here with you? Bonnie and me was going up to Cutter's next week and camp out. I'll work. Let me stay here. I'll help you. I like helping you. I won't even ask for money."

Miller came in with more sacks of food. "What's the matter with her?" He set the bags down beside the others on the counter. Rose handed Reina a bunch of celery.

"Her mother called. She has to go back in a couple of days."

"Angie's leaving for Florida?"

"Sounds like it."

He wheeled around to the telephone and began to dial numbers. Rose put the few canned things away on the shelf over her head. Reina leaned against the counter, picking at a break in the Formica countertop with her forefinger.

"I don't wanna move to Florida. All the kids will be gorps. East Coast people. Shit."

Rose said nothing. Reina would love Florida within days of arriving, would find friends at once, would hardly ever think of River Ranch. She grabbed the girl's hand.

"Help me make a couple of pies."

"A couple?" The girl's eyes widened. Although she had looked into Reina's eyes perhaps a thousand times, Rose still was amazed by the mosaic of their color. "What kinds?"

"What about apple?"

"Shut up," Miller said. "I can't hear."

Reina slumped against the counter again, her arms folding over her body. "I hate Florida."

"Hello," Miller said. "Angie?"

Rose looked toward him, wondering what he was doing. Reina lifted her head.

"Yeah, yeah," Miller said. "I heard all about it. Listen, Ange. I think I can get a job up here. Let her stay here until you get to Florida and I'll pay her way there on the plane."

Reina hopped once, her hands clasped together, her eyes glistening.

"Okay," Miller said. "It's a deal."

Reina screamed. She flung herself on Rose and hugged her and carried her in a little circle. Miller was hanging the phone up; as he turned toward them, Reina leaped at him, her arms going around his neck, and pressed herself against him. His arms closed around her. One hand on her hair, he laid his cheek against the side of her head. Rose went into the pantry, her cheeks burning, to give them some privacy.

"You ever catch Billy?" Rose said.

Coyote was spreading butter on a biscuit. "Nup. Got too much to do to run after him all day long." He stuffed the biscuit into his mouth.

Peter said, "What'd that asshole do now?"

"Damn near give your sister there a free trip to Eureka."

"What?"

"He set the choke too loose, and it came off. Also broke up a pretty good log."

They were sitting grouped around the hearth in the front room, the food laid out on the brick apron of the fireplace. Reina and Patty sat on the couch, Miller on the hearth itself, and Rose, Coyote, and Peter on chairs between them. Reina said, "Pass me the salad, please."

Rose took her plate and served her salad. Miller put his fork down, chewing, and fixed his eyes on Coyote.

"You need help now. I'll help you."

"You don't know anything about logging." Coyote served himself three or four more pork chops.

"I can learn."

"It's not exactly easy work. He could've killed her today. 'Course she shouldn't't've been there in the first place." Coyote gave that more emphasis with a hard look at Rose.

"Curiosity," she said. "It's always been my ruin."

"If I don't do it right, you don't have to pay me," Miller offered.

Coyote's fork stabbed into the pork chops. "If you fuck it up, you could wind up costing me a fortune."

"He can do it," Rose said suddenly.

Coyote looked at her. "What d'you mean?"

"He can do it," she repeated. "He can do anything. He's very good at everything he tries."

"Except horses," Reina said.

"Ah, it ain't that hard," Peter said. "I know some real dumb people who're loggers."

"If Billy Vigg can do it, he can," Rose said.

Coyote's head swung toward Miller; they looked one another over for a while. Finally Coyote's head bobbed once. "Sure. Starting tomorrow."

Rose put down her plate, her hunger gone. "Come on," she said to Reina. "We'll get the pies."

Miller started working with Coyote the following morning. Reina went off to Bonnie Morrison's. When she had cleaned up the kitchen, Rose wandered around the house, looking for something to do.

On the front porch she came on Peter, sketching one of his cars, but when she leaned over to see how he was doing, he said, brusque, "You're in my light."

"Jeez, what a grouch." She sat on the rail.

He was feathering the edges of a shadow. The drawing was of the pickup truck, which she had seen thousands of times; but in composing the picture, he had made it somehow different, not a pile of junk now, but a metal creature.

"Where's Patty?" she asked, after a moment.

"Down working." He rubbed out the circular rim of a

headlight and drew it in again, a series of three delicate curves, one inside the other.

"Would you draw me a portrait of Reina sometime?"

"She won't sit still long enough."

"Oh, come on. You could probably do it from your head."

"It's harder than it looks."

"I know, but—"

"I said no!" His head jerked around toward her. Two lines she had never seen before appeared between his eyebrows, bunched down into a scowl. He glared at her. "I said I won't do it, you understand? Now shut up!"

"Peter—"

"Shut up!"

She slid down from the rail and went into the house again. Her neck and cheeks felt prickly with warmth. She had said nothing offensive. He had no right to yell. She almost wished he would go back to drinking during the day, if it would improve his humor.

At noon she took lunch down to Coyote's meadow and sat with him and Miller while they ate. Miller said almost nothing; he ate two sandwiches and all the apples. He looked exhausted already. When he had eaten, he got up and walked away toward the woods a few feet, to a log in the beaten grass, and lay down in the sun on the log and shut his eyes.

Rose glanced at Coyote, who was finishing the leftover pie. "How y' doin'?"

"Okay. Slow, but okay."

"Is—" She waggled her thumb at Miller.

"Yeah, sure. He'll do. He's a lot stronger than Billy, anyway."

"Stop talking about me," Miller said.

"God, everybody's in a bad mood today," Rose said.

Coyote shrugged. He wore no shirt, only his jeans, and his chest and arms were coated with fine sawdust from the trees, pink as salmon flesh. "Go over there, on the dozer; you see my shirt? There's a joint in the pocket."

On the log Miller turned his head. Rose went to the bulldozer and got the joint.

"Couple a weeks now," Coyote said, firing up the reefer and pausing to exhale, "we're gonna have some buds to smoke." He held out the number to Miller. "Want some of this?"

Miller shook his head. "Later."

Rose yelped. "Jesus Christ. I never thought I'd see that."

He gave her the briefest glance and shut his eyes again, his body lying on the log, his hands on his gut.

"Well," Coyote said, "time to get back into the action."

"Wait." Rose lifted her head.

The wind was carrying the sound of horses down the hill to them. Rose stood up, shading her eyes. Over the flank of the hill came Reina on Windfire and Bonnie Morrison on her bay mare. Miller turned his head to watch them. He stood hastily up, brushing the dust from his hands on the thighs of his Levi's.

The girls galloped down toward them. Bonnie's mare shied at the log-loader and again at the bulldozer, but the old white horse went calmly by these monsters without twitching an ear. Reina stopped him near Miller.

"Hi," she said.

The ride and the wind had brought a blaze of color into her cheeks. Her hair was caught up in two pigtails, wound with red ribbon.

"Hi." Miller went up beside her, one hand on the horse.

"I thought we'd come see how you're doin'," Reina said. "So how y' doin'?"

"Okay," he said. "Okay." He smiled at her. "You look great."

Her shoulders moved, putting off that discomfiting adoration. With her fingers she smoothed Windfire's mane down. "You wanna go riding later?" As she spoke, she turned her face again toward him.

"I won't have it in me," he said. "I'm beat already, and it's only noon."

"Oh. Okay." She gathered her reins up.

"After I get done working. Next weekend." The horse moved away from his hand, and he moved, following, his hand still stroking the sleek white shoulder.

"Good," she said. "Well, gotta go. So long."

She whirled the white horse and galloped away, and Bonnie followed. Coyote scratched vigorously in his curly red beard.

"I'm here to say I wouldn't mind being the first one into her pants."

Miller's head swiveled around. For an instant, his blue eyes fierce, he clenched his fists. Coyote laughed.

"Come on, let's get to work. Thanks, Rose." He walked over toward the yellow bulldozer.

Miller lowered his hands. Picking up the front of his T-shirt, he mopped his face with it, although she could not see that he had been sweating particularly much. He mumbled something and went away to work. Rose climbed back up the hill to the house.

It was Reina he loved. Reina. He wanted Rose only because he could not have Reina.

She kicked at the hawkweed in the grass, the yellow heads gone entirely to white puffballs of seeds. Caught in a clump of grass, a shed snakeskin dangled like a Christmas ornament above the ground. The black and red caterpillars that seemed to be everywhere this time of the year were spinning their cocoons on any support available. Coming up to the house, she noticed the white woolly cases stuck in the cracks of the siding.

Reina he wanted. Reina only.

She expanded her lungs with air. Idiotic, to be jealous of a fourteen-year-old. Especially since—with the irony of the times—the fourteen-year-old loved Rose more than she did Miller.

When she walked into the house, Peter was slumped beside the hearth. She went toward him, needing company, and smelled beer.

She stopped. In front of him on the hearth were four tall, green cans of Rainier. Moving forward enough that she could see his face, she realized that he was asleep.

Passed out, really. In a burst of bad temper whose origins she preferred not to consider, she kicked the nearest can into the fire and went down to her room to find a book to read.

Peter dragged himself out of bed at eleven, while Rose was making the loggers' sandwiches for lunch; he staggered into the kitchen and slumped down on the couch by the woodstove. "God. My head is killing me."

"You want some coffee?" Rose washed her hands and dried them on a towel. She lined up the two sacks of lunch on the kitchen counter by the back door.

"I want a beer," Peter said.

"I'll make you some coffee."

"Get me a beer."

She faced him, the width of the kitchen between them. His face was puffy with sleep and pain and disease. In this mask his eyes were glazed and uncaring. When he saw she was not bringing him his remedy, he lurched up onto his feet again.

"Guess I have to get it myself."

She went over to the refrigerator and leaned her back against the door.

"Get out of my way," he said, without moving. Rose said nothing, watching him, curious to see what he would do, and determined to keep him away from the beer.

He moved toward her, shaky on his feet, and she braced herself against the door, her feet thrust forward. Peter stopped. His face still sagged, disorganized, but his eyes narrowed to slits.

"You don't have any right to keep me from doing what I please."

"For God's sake, Peter—" She spread her arms out to him. "Don't give up now. Don't quit. You've—"

"Get out of my way."

"Peter, I'll make you some breakfast. I'll—"

He grabbed her by the shirt front and slung her around into the middle of the room, away from the refrigerator. Rose lost her balance. Half-falling, she gripped her brother's arm to stay on her feet. He pushed her violently away. She sprawled across the floor on her back and conked her head so that for an instant all the sense flew out of her and the room whirled.

"You stay off my case, hear?"

Slowly she sat up. Peter opened the refrigerator door.

"You made me do that."

"Fuck you, Peter." She touched the side of her head, where a tender spot was swelling.

"You don't have any right telling me what I can do with my life."

She got up, not looking at him. Possibly he was right. Anyway he had won. Behind her there was the pop of the pull-top, the fizz of the beer.

"Don't try anything like that again," he said. "I was on the wrestling team in college, remember?"

Rose took the two sacks of lunch and went out the back door.

They were loading the logs onto the truck, which stood in the center of the meadow. Its four-foot tires and the bulldozer's treads had ground the meadow into a wasteland. The dirt was pulverized to a fine dust that blew up into the air like a red mist. She walked across the desert of tire tracks and tread marks, toward the area where the great log-loader roared steadily at its work.

Coyote was sitting up in the cage, working the levers; a blue bandanna hung over his nose and mouth to protect his lungs from the dust. He rolled the monster forward, its raised claws carrying a single log. A shrill whine of the overworked engine ushered it over to the truck. With a clang the pincers of the yellow loader sank slowly down on its telescoping limbs to set the redwood log between the forks of the truck as lightly as a dowager might set her teacup on a china saucer.

"What's happening?" Coyote asked when they had walked into the woods, away from the choking red haze of dust, and were sitting down to eat their lunch.

"Peter fell off the wagon." Rose gave Miller a sandwich and a quart of milk.

"Hell," Coyote said. "You could let the guy have his beer."

That stung her where she was already sore. She withdrew into a sullen silence.

Miller fingered one sandwich and took another out of the bag. There was a welt on his forehead. Over his ears the silky tendrils of his hair were sun-bleached almost colorless.

Rose picked at the grass by her feet. They were sitting next to the stump of Hallie's redwood, and the sun flooded through the hole in the forest into a place little used to the full glare of its light. The tender ferns were dying, the woodland violet and the miner's lettuce had already shriveled away, while on the torn, battered ground the tougher chickweed and scarlet pimpernel were spreading their runners over the soil like Dido seizing Carthage in a round of rope.

After they had eaten, she walked down to the mailbox. Miller went with her. They walked along the steep dirt road that led down the mountainside to the county road. Her mind turned back to Peter.

"God, I can't stand to see him like this." She pressed her fists against her thighs. "Before he tried to quit, it didn't bother me so much, but now—"

"Don't let it take you over."

"He's my brother!"

They walked along the switchback curve. A snake lying in a patch of sun bolted away from them into the grass on the low side of the road. Rose's mood weighed her down like lead feet. She trudged slowly after Miller.

He had already reached the mailbox; he lifted out the mass of envelopes and magazines and dumped it all onto the road. They sat down to paw through it.

"Here," he said. "Can I have this?" He showed her a piece of junk mail from Oxfam, addressed to Ms. P. McKenna.

"Sure," she said, puzzled. She watched him tear open the letter and fish out the folded papers inside. Among them was a return envelope. He put that on the road beside him, took a piece of paper and a money order out of his pocket, and stuffed them into the envelope to Oxfam.

"What are you doing?" she said.

"Paying off my credit card." He took a pen out of his pants pocket, scratched out Oxfam's address, and wrote in the address of the Union Oil Company in San Francisco.

Rose laughed. "God, you're cheap. You're even tighter than Felice." Her eyes returned to the pile of letters, and she put that stack down again and reached for another.

"Uh-oh." A return address had caught her eye. She grabbed the envelope and ripped it open, her heart at the gallop.

A check fell out with the letter. She yelled.

"Money?" Miller snatched the check up. "Somebody's sending you money?"

She opened the letter from *Future,* the magazine to which she had submitted her two stories, and scanned the three close-typed paragraphs. The editor had not thought much of the longer story, which he was returning separately, but the shorter story moved him to some very courtly phrases—"a strong and singular voice," "stunning original-ity," "solidly crafted"—and he hoped the enclosed check would cover it.

"Six hundred dollars," Miller said.

"Who sends you money?"

"It's for a story," she said. "I've sold a story, that's all."

She beamed at him, the morning's gloom gone like a fog before the sun. He grinned back at her, the wonderful wide smile she saw so seldom on his face, and impulsively she tilted forward and kissed him.

His arm wound tight around her neck. His mouth was softer than she expected. In her ears the booming rush of blood quickened, and she pressed herself against him, her hands on his shoulders, her mouth against his, ready to do it all, right there.

A car passed and honked at them. They separated.

"Look what you're doing to me," he said and pulled at the crotch of his Levi's, trying to ease the pressure on his erection.

They walked back up toward the gate. They walked side by side, not touching, although to Rose the air seemed hot between them, where their empty hands swung, inches apart.

When she reached the house again, the back door was hanging wide open. On the corner post of the fence around Peter's garden a blue shirt fluttered. Rose went slowly through the tall grass toward it.

Peter was hoeing up his melons; he claimed he was the only farmer on River Ranch who could grow melons, which needed more heat and light than Humboldt County ordinarily supplied. When he saw her coming, he straightened up and turned to face her.

"I'm sorry," he said.

She stopped, the fence between them, her hands jammed into her pockets. "Well, whatever." Her gaze traveled over him, leaning on the hoe, his back sunburned and his ears red. "You look pretty sober to me."

"Ran outta brew."

"Oh, yeah?"

He waited expectantly for her to say something, but Rose was not playing. She stood where she was, keeping silent, knowing that he would eventually go on, and finally he did. "I'm sorry I knocked you down. Did you get hurt?"

"I'll live. I sold a story."

"Oh, yeah? How much?"

"Six hundred dollars."

"Well, it'll keep you in beans for a while."

"Okay, Peter," she said. "Do you want me to go for beer?"

"No."

"Okay. You're quitting again. For how long this time?"

"Don't argue with me. God, aren't you happy I'm doing it?"

"Yes."

"You gotta help me, that's all."

That stiffened her, like a shot of iron down her spine; her back went rigid, and her head sank down between her shoulders. Bad-tempered, she glowered at him. "Oh, yeah? What does that mean? That you're gonna blame me when you sneak a drink?"

"Rose—" His hands came up between them, palms raised, begging. "You gotta help me! Don't you love me any more?"

"I love you," she said, "but I'm tired of the game."

She turned her back and strolled toward the house.

"Rose! Are you telling me no?"

Her steps dragged. Help him, a voice in her head told her. Help your poor little brother. Behind her, seeing her uncertain, he bellowed her name again.

They played this game over and over, and they had, as far back as she could remember: Peter got in trouble, and Rose rescued him. It made him feel good; it made her feel good. Easy to slip into during times of stress. Comfortable. She wondered, staring into nothing, what else they had between them, if anything.

"Rose! Come on, Rose, give me a chance."

Somewhere back in her mind there was a sympathetic vibration. Someone else had played on this same set of strings. Mike Morgan, in the house in Pasadena, calling her a quitter. The same thing. It was all the same thing, the pattern of her life, laid down in her childhood, in the very growth and connecting of the neurons. Probably it underlay her friendship with Miller, too.

"Rose!"

This time she would break it. She squared her shoulders, careless of what she did, as long as it was not what the pattern required. She walked across the grass toward the house. Her brother's voice followed her, rough with panic. She went into the house to read.

"You're pretty quiet," Coyote said.

"I'm just thinking."

In the darkness a cherry-colored coal glowed bright, then dimmed and moved toward her. She reached just behind it for the cool end. Peter and Miller were supposed to be in the sauna with them, but they had not shown up yet, and she and Coyote were alone together. The little room was still only warm, the stove roaring behind its barricade of rocks sounding hotter than it was.

"What're you thinking about so hard?"

"I don't know. Helping people. Whether it does any good."

"Don't do any good a'tall." He picked the joint neatly from between his fingertips and lifted it to his lips. "Just gives 'em the idea, each time they're in trouble, head for your door." He gasped, filling his lungs again, trying to hold his hit and speak at the same time. "You mean Peter."

"Yeah."

"Hell, Rosie, Peter's a drunk. I mean, he's that kind of guy, that's all. Why get on his case about it? He's not hurting anybody."

"Me," she said. "He hurts me."

"Hurts you? Or scares you?"

She doubled her legs up and wrapped her arms around her knees, brooding on what he had said. The door opened to let her brother into the warmth.

"Shut that door!"

He shut the door and climbed onto the bench beside Rose. "You talking to me yet?"

"I really am sorry I knocked you down, Rosie—that's what made me quit again."

She slid her arm around his shoulders and hugged him.

They sat silent in the darkness, passing the joint. Miller came in and squeezed onto the bench, jamming them all together flesh to flesh. Coyote poured water over the rocks, and the steam flooded the room, searing hot.

"Ooh!" She twisted away from the bodies around her, unbearably close in the heat; everybody else was sliding around, too. The sweat popped from every pore in her skin. She sighed. Her hair dripped. Her body was oiled all over in its own juice. The temperature was subsiding, and she eased herself back onto the shelf, back in among the pack of other people.

"Patty's plants are in full bloom now," Peter said. "I went down there this afternoon. You should see them; the colas must be four inches, six inches long. God, I can't wait for them first buds."

Coyote said, "I had flowers so full of resins your fingers stuck to them."

"You have a garden, man?"

"I did. Somebody ripped it off."

Surprised, Rose sucked the air in between her teeth.

"Your whole garden, man?"

"Every goddamn plant."

"Do you have any idea who did it?" Rose asked.

Coyote leaned out to pour more water onto the rocks. The billows of steam rolled into the room; Rose moaned at the heat in her lungs.

"I got an idea," Coyote said. "I got a pretty good idea at that."

She wondered if somebody had his eye on her field, if one day soon she would go down there and find the crag empty. The slow fear collected in her stomach. She reached for the joint, and her hand bumped into another hand, reaching for the coal; the room was too dark to see whose it was.

"So, who do you think did it?" Peter said.

"Nothing I can do about it," Coyote said. "Might as well leave it lay."

She peered suspiciously through the pitch darkness toward the sound of his voice, knowing he was lying.

Nobody said anything. Pressed together, shoulder and back and side, they crouched in the darkness like apes in a cave, waiting for the sun. That was all they were, actually; she saw that with a sinking heart. There were a few embellishments—cooked food instead of raw, cars instead of feet—but where it mattered, in their doings with each other, they still followed the rules cooked into the genes through thousands of thousands of years. The mind constructed fantasies of rationale but knew nothing of itself, although it saw nothing in the world but itself, no truth but only its way of knowing some of the truth.

While she sat there, stoned and miserable, her arms folded behind her for some comfort against the rough wall, another hand came through the darkness, felt gently along her arm, and clasped her hand.

She had no idea whose hand it was, but she held it anyway. She loved them all, Miller and Coyote and her brother. Fellow apes. Yet the strange hand she was holding made a poor lie out of that image; her spirit rebounded; she felt better right away.

If Reina could have taken the horse in the car to the airport, she would have. She kissed him and hugged him and gave him an apple to eat, and while he ate, she put her face against his shoulder and cried.

The airport was over an hour away to the north; when Reina's plane landed in San Francisco, Miller and Rose would still be on their way back to River Ranch. Miller carried Reina's bags into the waiting room. She checked the two bags she was allowed, and he carried the other for her down to the gate.

The bag set off the metal detectors in the luggage screening device.

"What do you have in there?" Miller asked her. "It feels like rocks." He opened the bag for the inspector.

Inside there were very few clothes. Instead she had sacked up horseshoes, the hoof pick, a tattered saddle blanket, a bit, rocks and driftwood from the river.

"Bonnie gave me that," Reina said, touching the saddle blanket. "Is it okay? I figured you wouldn't need the hoof pick." She faced Rose, her eyes brilliant, direct, and hopeless. Rose hugged her.

"You can have anything you want, baby."

Miller closed the suitcase. The plane was at the gate, and the other passengers were lined up there, waiting to board. Quiet now, Miller, Rose, and Reina stood at the end of the line.

The sky was overcast and the wind was raw, whipping the flags around their poles. Rose could think of nothing to say. Suddenly Reina overflowed with talk.

"I'll write. You write me back. Will you?"

"Yes," they said. "Yes, of course."

"I want a picture of Windfire. Will you take me one?"

"Yes," said Miller.

The gate opened. The first passengers walked out across the pavement toward the yellow DC-9 waiting there. Reina clutched Rose by the coat.

"Say hi to everybody. Tell 'em I said hi."

"I will."

The line was walking away from her. She turned to go, her bag of horseshoes in both hands. "I'll come back." Tears spangled her cheeks. "I'll come back," she called again, fiercely, and walked away toward the plane.

The two who were left behind stood there a moment, separated from each other by their loss. Reina climbed the steps of the ramp into the plane. The door shut; an attendant wheeled the aluminum staircase away to one side.

Rose glanced up at Miller, standing beside her, his face set in an expressionless mask. His vacant stare was still directed toward the plane. Rose looped her arm through his and led him away.

· · ·

All the way down the freeway through Eureka and along the southern edge of Humboldt Bay, Miller and Rose said nothing. As they passed the marshes on the fringe of the bay, Miller said, "Go to the beach."

She put on the turn signal.

They left the freeway for a road that ran beside the marsh, where the land tilted up into a ridge dividing the bay from the valley of the Eel River. Climbing the steep slope, she drove out across the bluff toward the ocean. Beyond a broad, sunburned field was the bay, stretching into the haze; to the west of it a long sandspit sheltered the quiet waters from the ocean. She drove that way, past the old lighthouse on the top of the ocean cliff and down onto the sand.

The wind was coming off the ocean so hard that the car dragged sharply to the right, and she had to use all her strength to keep it straight on the road. A sign beside the road warned of drifting sand. She drove out onto the spit a mile and a half and stopped where the shoulder of the road looked firm enough that she'd be able to turn the car around.

Miller got out and walked away into the dunes. Rose went off in another direction, cutting in between the low dunes, where a high wave had left a mat of driftwood and seaweed. On the sand hills the prostrate vines of morning glory shuddered in the blast of the wind. Rose hunched her shoulders. Sand flying in the wind beat on her cheek and got into her eyes. She walked over the saddle between the dunes, into sight of the ocean.

It was thundering onto the beach with a power that seemed to jar the ground. The water was steel gray under the lowering sky. Now the wind carried a mist of seawater, wetting her nose and her hair. She blinked rapidly to clear her eyes.

The force of the wind awed her. It blew hard at the ranch, too, but there the hills and trees broke it up into gusts. Here nothing had stood against it for nine thousand miles, and it came at her like a moving wall.

Miller was down the beach, running along the hard, wet sand below the tide line. She watched him until he was gone from sight, and then she sat down on the sand, watching the ocean.

She missed Reina. She felt much older, now that the girl was gone. With a little stick she dug in the sand, drifting up now over her shoes and against her body. A seagull flew into the wind over the surf and hung there, its wings motionless. She wiped the salt spray from her face; her lips tasted salt, like tears, or blood.

She had come here to Humboldt to get away, to heal over the wound where she had torn away from Mike. That was done; she felt whole again. But she still needed this place. Something about it reassured her: the enormous frame of nature, perhaps, undetectable in cities, showed her the scale of her own life.

As she thought that, her spirit lifted, turning hopeful, assured of its solid footing in the real.

A long time passed, perhaps half an hour, forty-five minutes; she was a poor judge of time. At last Miller reappeared, coming up the beach at a run. Rose stood, her shirt flapping in the wind. He saw her and swerved toward her up the sand. A few feet from her he dropped to a walk, breathing hard through his open mouth. Rose met him, and he slumped against her, his skin and his shirt sodden with sweat and the spray off the surf. They went back to the car and drove home.

When they reached River Ranch again, the old white horse was grazing on the lawn by the rhinoceros. Rose went over to him and patted his neck where the hair turned dark. His skin was soft and smooth, glossy with health and vigor. Reina had made him like this, giving him the love that Miller pined for. In a few days the old horse would have wandered off into the woods again; he would have forgotten all about her. He had done what no human could have done, perhaps: loving him, Reina had learned the art of being loved.

He bumped Rose's arm with his head, blowing softly, his ears pricked up, looking for treats. She stroked her hand along his body and went away to the house.

He did not say, "Remember what you said we'd do when Reina left?" What he said was "Would you like to go to Reno with me?"

"Okay," she replied.

"Which car do you want to take?"

"What kind of mileage do you get?"

"Thirty-two, thirty-five."

"Let's take my car. It's more comfortable, and the mileage is about the same."

"My car has the tape deck."

"Oh. That's right." It would be a longer trip without music.

"I can put it into your car."

"Oh. Sure. Good idea. My car's even got the holes for speakers from when I had a tape player."

"Okay, then."

He spent the rest of the afternoon transferring the tape deck from his car to hers. Rose was making dinner; she looked out the window once and saw him lying half in and half out of her car. Something in this delighted her, although she could not say what, only that she loved Miller, and everything he did was wonderful to her.

All the way to Reno they talked about geology and gambling, the canals of Mars, the failings of the government, food, buildings, and time. They said nothing about each other, about loving each other. Rose had it back there in the deep of her mind; she would not bring it forward into the light of conscious scrutiny, as if that controlled it somehow.

They got to Reno near midnight. She waited in the car in the parking lot of a motel while Miller checked them into a room. The motel sign read TV—PHONES—BABYSITTERS—CASINO COUPONS—FREE WEDDING INFO. Miller came back with the room key.

The room was on the second floor. She went first, opening the door into the darkness. Two double beds, hung with red plush spreads, nearly filled the room. Miller was coming after her with the suitcase. She turned off the light and undressed. Her hands trembled. An impatient delight hurried her on. Naked, she slid between the smooth, cold sheets. He came through the door, a bulky silhouette against the night glow of Reno. Put the luggage down, shut the door, and got into bed with her.

Now that she was committed to it, her stomach fluttered with panic. It took an act of will to put her arms around him. The warm touch of his body was like the shock of diving into icy water. Skin touching, all the way down, the silky hair over his chest that she had never even noticed before. Their mouths joined. First the little ritual of the kiss. Introibo. Touching the inside of his mouth with her tongue. Their legs wound together. His arms slid around her. The palms of her hands stroked up over his arms and shoulders, solid with muscle. Lying in his arms, she felt his strength around her like a shelter; her body softened, trusting. She turned her face into his shoulder.

What an amazing thing this was. From babyhood on, the constant warnings to hide your body away under clothes—touch not, nor let yourself be touched—and now suddenly to be free of all that, fear and suspicion gone, her body smoothly fitting his, sharing this warm, close witness, making each other real.

"I love you," he was saying. "I love you." Which was one way to put it.

When they were done, she turned on the light and they lay there in the bed, smoking a joint and inspecting each other's bodies with the pleasure and fondness of new owners. She loved even the slack, fat bulge around his middle, connected now with the memory of their sex together. She ran the tip of her finger along his collarbone and laid her palm flat to his chest. He was bigger than she was, eight inches taller and nearly twice as heavy. He had held her down under him with his weight, his arms around her, their legs locked together. Thinking about that made her lusty again. She reached for the joint.

"That wasn't how I meant it to happen," he said. The smoke hung in the still air, and he waved his hand to stir it away. "I thought, you know, I'd have to do it."

"You did it," she said.

"Yeah, sure. Did you like it?"

"Oh, yes."

"Did you come?"

She was holding a hit and did not answer. Once at a party in a spirit of stoned adventure she had seduced another woman; bringing her to the peak had filled Rose with a sense of exultant power, and she could see why he wanted to know.

"Did you?"

"Yes," she answered. "Couldn't you tell?"

"No."

She sighed, thinking of it, her gaze drifting down his body. "It feels so strong to me, I can't believe you didn't notice."

"Sorry."

"Guys are always worrying about that." A man's coming was so obvious she never had to ask. Especially Miller, who shouted, as if the force of his eruption blew all the air out of his lungs. She touched his wilting organ.

"You want to do this some more or go out and gamble?" He wiped his face on the sheet.

"I'm hungry."

"Okay. I'm going to take a shower."

"Sounds good to me. Do you mind some company?"

"Come on."

He started up, and she reached out to draw him down again, where she could kiss him. He sank back into the pillow. Rose rolled onto him and took his mouth. Her passion was fading. A flood of tenderness rushed in behind it, into a space made wider by the power of sex.

"I love you, Miller," she said.

"I know," said Miller.

. . .

She had been to Disneyland, but never before to Nevada. Miller led her into the noisy glow of a casino. They threaded a path through row on row of slot machines, marvels of polished chrome and bright red and white plastic. Nobody played any of them. The carpet underfoot, a soft cushion to her feet, absorbed all sound. She had expected throngs of people mad with an unhealthy excitement, but there seemed to be no one here at all until they left the forest of slot machines and came on a crap table, where an old man in a cowboy hat was silently dancing a jig on the brothel-red carpet.

Three or four other people stood around the long, deep-bedded table. Miller went up among them, taking a roll of bills out of his pocket, and slapped a ten down on the pass line. "Come on," he said to Rose. "You wanna gamble?" He waved another ten-dollar bill at her.

"No—you do it." She looked up and down the table at the strange markings on the felt. The old man in the cowboy hat jingled a stack of chips in his hand. He had a pheasant feather in his hatband.

"Roll 'em."

On Miller's right was a dark woman in an evening dress, a rope of pearls around her neck. She leaned down over the bumper rail, took two of the several red and white dice on the table there, and bounced them away over the green felt.

"Four the hard way." The croupier raked in the dice with his little curved stick. Rose shoved her hands down into her pockets. The stick reminded her somehow of the flail of ancient Egypt. The croupier removed the ten-dollar bill Miller had put on the pass line.

The old man in the cowboy hat, his eyes gleaming, sprang forward to pile chips on a square marking in the center of the table. "Four the hard way!"

Rose's eyes swept the table again, its mystic signs and

patterns. It was a form of magic. She had never realized that before. Cabalistic as hell. She glanced at Miller, who seemed to be waiting for something.

"Did you lose?"

"No," he said.

Simultaneously the croupier looked up, startled, and said, "No, I've got it back here on the bar." He gestured toward the table in front of him, talking mostly to Miller, who nodded at him.

"I'm betting she won't make the point." Miller indicated the woman in the black evening dress, who had recovered the dice.

They all hunched over the table, and the woman rolled the dice down across the felt. Rose watched them intently. After two rolls the woman did make a four, and the old cowboy whooped and did his jig again, and Miller lost.

He put up another ten dollars, the woman rolled the dice again, and again Miller lost.

This time he put forty dollars on the line. The croupier said, "Figure her luck's run out, hunh?"

"She can't do it three times in a row," Miller said.

The woman rattled the dice in her hand. "Wanna bet?" She leaned over the table; the top of her dress slid down almost to the nipples of her breasts, and all the men turned as one to look. She shook her hand with the red dice cubes.

"Come on, lucky sevens!"

The dice turned up a three, and in the next roll she got the seven. She groaned, straightening up, and the men went back to looking at their money.

Miller got his forty back, and the croupier gave him a short stack of red and gold chips. "Come on," Miller said and went off into the depths of the room. "Why don't you want to gamble?"

"I don't like to involve myself in religious activities."

"Religion. What do you mean by that?"

"It's a form of magic. Magic is religion. Q.E.D."

"God, you make everything so intense. Why can't you just

let go and have some fun, hunh? Here." He held out his roll of money, his thumb rippling the edges of the bills. "Take all you want." He veered toward a booth where a woman dealt blackjack, his arm drawing Rose after him. "Come on, try it."

"I'll watch."

He won twenty-five dollars there, while Rose wandered around the casino. It looked like a movie set. If she had never seen a gambling hall she would have imagined it like this, the blood-red carpet, the mirrors on the walls that tricked the vision and made the place look endlessly large, trebled every slot machine, and turned each person there into a crowd. The woman dealing blackjack to Miller wore a ruffled, white chiffon blouse with a high collar. Her cheeks were red with rouge and her hair was piled up in sinuous curls on her head. On her left hand was a wedding ring. Her eyes were expressionless with boredom.

Miller drifted off again. Rose followed.

He never stayed long at any game. If he won the first bet, he played until he lost and moved on. If he lost, he usually moved on right away, but sometimes he doubled the bet and redoubled it, chasing what he'd given up, and that way he sank nearly a hundred dollars playing red and the high third at roulette.

At that, he left the casino completely. Her hands in her pockets, Rose went along at his heels. The street was bright with the lights of the neon signs. A constant stream of people moved up and down the sidewalks, people in loud holiday clothes, in denims, in suits and ties, women in evening gowns and men in tuxedos with lace shirts. The neon flashed its colors over them, red and green and blinding white.

An old song crept into her mind. *What they take, the glow erases*—Miller laid his arm possessively across her shoulders.

"You're my lover, Rose."

"You bet."

"My lover." He hugged her hard.

"Yes, Miller."

"Wha'd'you wanna do now?" He herded her on down the street, weaving through the people moving slower than he wanted to. At the corner a longhair in a raincoat held out his cupped hand.

"Hey, man, got a buck, man, hey, got a rolling paper?" Bellowing now because Miller had passed him without a look, smiling. Rose skipped to keep up with his swinging stride.

> *What they take, the glow erases*
> *What they lose, the glow replaces*
> *The neon rainbow—*

It wasn't real, this place; the people were meaninglessly friendly, like all people away from home, knowing they would never see each other again. The money wasn't real, and so there was a huge amount of it. And Miller was different here. At River Ranch he hoarded everything, prowled the house turning off lights, but here he threw money away. Or perhaps spending money was a kind of chum.

They wandered into a casino with a midway on the mezzanine, a dazzle of hardware and games. Above it all, two women in pink-sequined body suits were riding unicycles on a tightrope to the accompaniment of a drummer and an organist. Rose played a computer space war, shooting down enemy ships with a laser. She got her handwriting analyzed by a computer that told her she was conscientious, anxious, generous, and destined to be famous someday.

At a booth with a computer camera Miller bought her a T-shirt printed with his face, smiling, and underneath it ROSE LOVES MILLER. He bought her a chocolate milkshake and spent nearly thirty dollars trying to win a stuffed lion to send to Reina.

Out on the street he fell into his word game again.

"You're my lover, Rose."

"Yeah, you keep saying that."

He hugged her. He was crowding her nearly off her feet; she felt smothered in his affection.

"I love my lover."

"I thought you loved Reina."

"I do," he said. "I'll always love Reina."

"Hunh."

"But I love you more." He hugged her again. "You're my best friend, Rose."

She put her arm around his waist, mostly to keep her feet when he hugged her.

They had been eating at McDonald'ses all the way from Springville. This time they went to a taco joint. Rose was exhausted, too tired even to eat; and after she had forced half a tostada down her throat, she slumped down in the formed plastic chair watching Miller consume his meal.

She knew she was not ready for this relationship. She had hardly cleaned Mike Morgan out of her mind, and she needed time to recover her own shape again. But Miller was different. Mike had been familiar everywhere, at all times, flamboyant and foolish. Miller was two people, aloof and thorny, even arrogant most of the time, but inside there was a person she had hardly seen before, a sentimental and tender person, throwing out his word games like radar, searching for a love.

She wondered how many other people had even seen this Miller. She could not resist it; she loved secrets.

They went back to the motel and their bed again. This time, unhurried, they made slow love, touching and kissing and offering various caresses. "Do you like this? What do you want me to do?" Dawn was coming. They took another shower together and went to sleep.

"Who do you think I should bet on?"

"I don't know. I don't follow football."

"There's three games on television here." He folded up the green sports section from the *Chronicle* and stared at the point spreads for the day's NFL games while the other hand shoveled food into his mouth. "Oakland at New Orleans and L.A. at San Diego and San Francisco hosting Atlanta."

"Bet on S.F. to lose. They haven't won a game all year."

"How do you know? I thought you just said you don't follow football."

She snorted. They were at McDonald's again; she pushed the insipid scrambled eggs around with her plastic fork. "You watch four or five sportscasts a day. How d'you expect me to avoid it?"

"What a clever person." He smiled at her over the edge of the green sheet. "What a clever person my lover is."

"Then bet on Atlanta against the Forty-niners."

"No. The point spread is six and a half. S.F. loses constantly, but they've been beating the spread all season. Oakland is giving six and a half to the Saints. Maybe I'll bet on them. It's on artificial turf, and the Raiders don't play well on artificial turf."

"Aren't you a Rams fan?"

He nodded, his eyes directed toward the sports page again. "I never bet on L.A. I'm too emotionally involved."

"Good thinking."

He went to Harrah's to bet on the New Orleans Saints against the Oakland Raiders, and Rose went down the street to Woolworth's and browsed through the paperbacks. With a Georgette Heyer novel in her hip pocket, she met Miller again and they went back to the motel room.

The game started at two. The Oakland Raiders wore black and silver; the Saints had the forked lily of the Kings of France on their helmets. By the end of the first half the Raiders were down by three touchdowns. On virtually the last play of the half, the Raiders' quarterback threw a sideline pass, which the Saints' cornerback intercepted for a touchdown. At the same time, the defensive end slammed into the quarterback.

The camera closed on the downed man, stretched full length on the field. Rose saw him lift his eyes, see that his pass had gotten into the wrong hands, and lower his helmeted head to the ground in despair. Her heart leaped in sympathy for him.

"Well," she said. "Looks like a good bet, Mil."

"Yeah," he said. "This is the kind of game I like when I'm betting." He switched the channel to the San Francisco game, still in progress. Rose lay down on the bed to read.

"What are you doing?" he said sharply.

Startled, she lifted her head. "I'm reading."

"You can't read while there's a football game on."

She diverted her attention to the television screen, where a commercial for beer was playing. "I watched half the game. Isn't that enough?"

"I don't want you to read when you're with me."

She sat up straight, her temper catching fire. "For Christ's sake, Miller. It's my work. You think I'm going to give up working for you?"

"That stuff isn't life—" He spread out his arms, his eyes bright with energy. "There's life all over and you want to bury yourself in a dead book."

"I like to read. Is that—"

"If you're gonna be with me, you can't read."

"Okay." She slid off the bed and stood up.

"What're you doing?"

"I'm leaving," she said, sticking the book in her hip pocket.

"You'd rather read a book than be with me?" His voice ended in a squeal of disbelief.

"I want to read." She went out the door onto the motel balcony.

It was sweltering hot. While she stood there wondering where she could go, the door behind her opened again.

"Come inside," Miller said.

"I'll go read in the car." She started off along the balcony toward the stairs.

"The car is locked," he said. "Come in here. The second half of the Oakland game is starting."

She vacillated, wanting to demonstrate her independence, wanting to watch the game. Finally she went back into the room.

With the score at 28 to 7, the announcers were already talking about the decline of the Oakland Raiders from an undefeated Super Bowl champion four years previous to this pitiful assemblage of second-raters, who gave further evidence of their incompetence early in the third quarter, yielding yet another touchdown to the Saints. Rose sighed. The Saints lined up to kick the extra point; the ball sailed off the side of the kicker's foot and passed well left of the goalposts. The Raiders' offensive team jogged out onto the field.

In their pads and helmets they looked less like men than mythological beasts, minotaurs, part human, part beast or god. They were beautiful when they ran, especially in the slow-motion replays. She had never realized before how beautiful men were in their running and leaping. She leaned forward, her elbows on her knees, to stare at the television screen.

The Raiders' quarterback brought his team up over the ball. They ran to the right and gained a few yards, ran to the left and gained a few yards; on the third down, they set up as if to run, and the quarterback pretended to hand the ball off, danced back, wheeled, and almost without looking hooked a little pass off toward the sidelines. The tight end caught it, and they had a first down.

Rose murmured, her interest deepening. There was something new in this; the flow of the action had mysteriously changed direction.

The Raiders pushed and shoved and fought their way down the field, doing nothing spectacular, gaining three yards, four yards at a time. She kept waiting for them to give the ball away, but this time they made no mistakes, and at the end, they scored a touchdown.

"God," she said. "Is that the same quarterback?"

Miller nodded. On television they were showing a replay of the touchdown run: at the snap of the ball, the men on both teams lunged together into the center of the line, and the ball carrier leaped up across the mass of their bodies and fell into the end zone. They kicked the extra point, and the Saints took over the offense.

New Orleans, which had looked unbeatable in the first half, seemed to have relaxed behind their enormous lead. They fumbled the ball away, and again the Raiders in their black shirts took the offense and went down the field, step by step, pounding out the yards. Rose began to get a sense of the thing as a whole, the brutal clash in the middle where the linesmen milled together, the battles on the fringe, where the receivers and the defenders duelled for space in the secondary. In the center stood the quarterback, cool and intelligent, the whole great battle whirling around him. The linesmen formed a U-shaped wall around him, shoving back the onrushing defense, while he cocked his arm with the ball and looked for receivers; the leaps and thrusts and charges of the other men only emphasized his stillness; he ignored the huge bodies crashing together around him until almost in the arms of the Saints' defensive end he reared his arm back and threw the ball up, up in a perfect spiral. It fell softly down into the arms of a running man in a black shirt, who bore it like treasure over the end zone, and then, as if to show the ball itself was nothing, bounced it full force off the ground. He leaped into a teammate's arms and they danced around the field.

"You know," she said, "if a man in street clothes came up to another man in street clothes and patted him on the ass like that, you'd think there was something funny."

Miller grunted at her. Obviously he wasn't into the sociology.

The score was 34 to 21, with the whole fourth quarter to go. "The Saints don't know how to win," the announcer was saying. The camera panned the silent crowd, sprigged with the limp flags of the New Orleans' fans; there was a close-up of the Saints' coach, looking grim; the camera cut to a head shot of the Raiders' quarterback, standing on the sidelines, his expression masked in a wild blond beard. The announcers, who half an hour before had been singing at his wake, now pronounced him one of the premier quarterbacks of the NFL.

The Saints took the ball. They worked it down inside the Oakland ten-yard line, where with first down and goal to go, they ran four plays up the middle. The Oakland defense like a wall of bone and muscle held them to a total gain of three yards.

Rose howled; she bounced up and down on the bed, entranced by the magical coherence of the game. "They're gonna win! They're gonna win!"

"They're still down by two touchdowns," Miller said.

"I bet they win. Bet you ten bucks."

"Even?"

"Yes."

"It's a bet."

Oakland had the ball again. The quarterback lined his men up and bent over the center; his head turned, looking from side to side. She guessed he was reading the defense. His voice came through on the audio, faint and clear, yelling numbers. "Hut! Hut!" He seized the ball and danced backward three long strides, while the offensive line surged up to meet the defenders in their bull-rush after him. Rose sucked in her breath, her heart racing. She wondered how he could stand there so calmly, while huge men struggled to tear him apart. He pumped the ball once to the right and leaned back and hurled it to the left in a rainbow arc. The camera followed the ball; it fell toward a knot of bodies that all seemed to be Saints, until at the last moment a black-shirted man sprang up out of their midst and brought down the ball in his grasp.

"What a catch," Miller cried, and banged his hands on his thighs. "What a catch!" Rose's tension exploded into a triumphant roar of laughter.

"Touchdown!" the announcer was screaming. "Touchdown Oakland!"

The camera held on the receiver, trotting back toward the bench, through his comrades who seized him and grabbed his hand and pounded on his back. Rose stretched her arms and legs. The game had brought up a thousand feelings unused for years, the lust to win, to overcome, even the excitement of fighting and of sharing the fight. On the screen was a replay of the touchdown catch. It seemed impossible the ball had gotten through the mass of defenders: a camel through the eye of a needle. She felt the stretching of her own muscles when the receiver leaped, the impact with the ground when he fell.

Miller rolled a joint. Rose sat canted forward over her knees, her breath stuck in her lungs, while the Saints ran two successful plays on the ground. They lined up for another.

"Illegal motion," Miller said immediately, as they leaped forward, and sure enough the camera swung to show a yellow handkerchief lying on the field. The play stopped and the officials in their black-and-white striped shirts conferred and signaled, took the ball, and walked it backwards. The crowd booed.

"Aren't you afraid for your bet?" Rose asked.

Miller shook his head. Joints stuck out of his woolly hair just over his ear. "The Raiders are still down a touchdown. Even if they win, they won't beat the spread."

"I mean the bet with me."

He smiled at her. "I figure betting with you is like betting with myself."

She made herself laugh at that; she did not like that.

The Saints were setting up to punt the ball away. The skin-tight pants and leggings they wore exaggerated the bulk of their great masked heads and shoulders. She watched a hard beautiful backside walk away across the field—the Saints were making a substitution, the teams milled around—and tried to analyze the appeal of the game. It was intellectual, in the complexity of its workings, but the plays happened too fast for thought: that was the crux. In play they had to work from the heart, from the gut, intuition and emotion, all the things men weren't supposed to have. Sexual and masculine as the game was, yet it freed them from their sex.

Her eyes followed another trim backside encased in tight revealing cloth. It reminded her of hers.

The punter kicked the ball into a high, high floater. The camera swung toward the receiver, waiting in the end zone. As the ball fell toward him he cupped his arms to take it.

"He'll put it down for a touchback," the announcer said. "No! He's gonna run it!"

The ball fell into his arms, and the receiver closed his hands over it and bounded forward. Two incoming Saints flew at him and he dodged between them and wheeled around a third. Others came at him from either side, but he outran one, and a black-shirted Raider charged into the screen and threw himself across two defenders' paths and knocked one down and held up the other enough to let the ball carrier through.

Now he met four of his own men, who made a screen around him and ran with him. The Saints attacked like arrows and one by one the Raiders in the screen flung themselves like shields against their flight.

Like a rabbit the man with the ball dashed on, darting from side to side. "There's nobody left but the punter!" the announcer was shouting, his voice thin with excitement. "Matthews puts a good fake on him!"

The ball carrier dodged around the last Saint in his path and ran down across the white lines. "Ira Matthews all the way! A hundred and four yards! Touchdown Oakland!"

Rose roared; she leaped up off the bed and bounced around the room, clapping. Miller lit a joint.

"I thought you didn't like football."

"I never paid much attention to it before." She sat down again, her hands between her knees, her eyes intent on the television screen. "I love a good plot. This one's one of the best. An oldie but a goodie."

"Well, it's all down to the extra point the Saints missed."

"I guess so."

The Raiders did not miss; they kicked the extra point, and led 35 to 34. The two-minute warning sounded. The Saints took the field again on their own twenty-yard line. The two teams froze over the ball. At the snap the Raider defenders charged forward, but the Saints formed a wall around their quarterback and held off the rush while he danced and searched the field, his arm poised with the football. Finally he threw it, and the camera wheeled to show the other end of the field, the men running, running, one in a light shirt and two in black, while the ball sailed down toward them. The receiver stretched out his hands, and the ball glided past his fingertips. His head and shoulders flopping forward in defeat, the Saint ran on a few loose steps without it.

Twice more the Saints tried for the long bomb, and as each pass hung in the air Rose gnawed her lip and strained her muscles with the little figures on the screen. The first pass fell incomplete. The second arched down toward the goal line, well ahead of the man it was meant for, right into the arms of an Oakland Raider.

"Interception!" Miller shouted. "That's it."

It was; taking the offense, the Raiders lay down on the ball and let the clock run out. Rose flopped back on the bed, exhilarated and drained.

"Wow," she said. "Wow, that was fun."

"What a silly lover I have." Miller stuffed ten dollars into her shirt. "God, you get so excited. Don't have a coronary."

On the television someone was poking a microphone into the face of the Raider quarterback; they talked about the game. The Raider pulled off his silver helmet. He spoke with a southern accent. He was her age, getting old for football. She sighed, longing for that high pitch of excitement, that moment when the pass fell complete, when the bodies collided.

"He was sensational," she said. "I've never seen a game turn around like that before. He was flat on his face, and he got up and turned them right around."

"Stabler's a good quarterback." Miller took out the blue betting slip and smoothed it in his fingers. "Let's go cash this in."

They went to play tennis when the evening cooled the dry desert air to a bearable warmth; Rose thought continually of the football game and the quarterback's courage. She won three of nine games, the best she had ever done against Miller.

"Wha'd'you say we gamble a little bit and then go home?" Miller asked.

"Whatever you say." They were cruising down Virginia Street toward their motel. Rose had played in shorts. As he drove the car, she peeled the shorts off and put on her jeans again; even in the summer the nights here were chilly. The novel she had been reading was in the hip pocket of the jeans, and she pulled it out and put it up on the dashboard while she buttoned her pants.

Miller slowed for a stoplight. He gave the book a frown, reached for it, and threw it out the open window of the car.

"Hey!"

"You don't need that."

He was rolling to a stop for the light. She opened the car door and jumped out.

"Rose!"

Her face flaming with anger, she walked back along the street, looking for the book. The passing cars were bumper to bumper going both ways. Finally she sighted the book, lying on its open face in the gutter across the street. She waited for a lull in the traffic and crossed the street to get it.

Miller was nowhere in sight. She stood on the sidewalk, looking up and down the street, and shoved the book back into her hip pocket. Her heart was pounding. Miller had taken her car and disappeared. She shoved the tails of her shirt down into her jeans, wondering what to do next.

She had the Raiders' ten dollars in her pocket. Also she

had the motel key. She turned up Virginia Street and walked long-striding toward the motel.

The flashing neon signs of the casinos shone through the night sky like ornaments. She passed a group of people in evening clothes and furs and stopped for a traffic light. Miller's attack on the book still burned in her mind. He was trying to take her over. No wonder Reina had feared his love. Blind to the world around her, she glared at him in her mind. A car rolled up in front of her.

It was her car; Miller leaned across the seat to open the door on the passenger side. "Come on, get in."

"You turkey." She slid into the seat beside him. "God, you're always accusing me of waste. That book cost me money."

"You read too much."

"Miller, I like to read. I intend to go on reading as much as I can. Just because you can't see the value of received knowledge—"

"Shut up, I'm not in the mood for one of your harangues."

That brought her temper to the boil. In a silent rage she sat thinking of cutting retorts, until a sideways glance at him showed her he was smiling.

He was just baiting her. She relaxed, her arms sinking to her sides.

"Besides," he said, "you're a woman. If there were any use in books, they'd be reserved for superior creatures like me." He glanced at her. "Superior creatures."

She arched her eyebrows at him. "Whatever you say."

He made a sound in his throat, looked straight and then around over his shoulder down the street, and nosed the car into a parking space. "Come on, let's go gamble."

They left Reno at four in the morning and drove back across northern California to Springville. The road that led them over the Sierra was wide and straight, and they made good time from Reno to Red Bluff, in the high valley, where they stopped to eat breakfast.

Naturally there was nothing open but McDonald's. When she had eaten, Rose went down to the rest room to wash her face and hands; while she was lathering the soap between her palms, she struck up a conversation with a woman who was in the toilet stall, out of sight.

"They sure don't let the hot water get very hot," said Rose, who splashed the tepid water on her face.

"Look," said the unseen woman in the stall. "Be glad they have running water. We were stationed in Turkey for a couple of years and I never once dared use a public rest room."

"You were in Turkey? With the army? D'you go to Istanbul a lot?"

"Oh, yes."

"God," Rose said, envious, "it must be beautiful. I'd love to go just to see that mosque." She was afraid of mispronouncing Hagia Sophia.

"There are hundreds of mosques in Istanbul," the lady said.

"I mean the big one, that Justinian built."

"Oh, yes. Well, it's absolutely marvelous. The colors are like jewels."

"I bet it's something else."

The toilet flushed, and the door opened; the woman who emerged was nothing like what Rose expected, she was a plain, dumpy creature in late middle age. They goggled at each other a moment; obviously Rose's looks surprised the other woman as well. With a mumbled good-by she went out the door.

When they got into the car to drive on, Rose saw the woman eating at a window table. She thought of waving, but the woman was paying attention only to her food. Miller rolled the car out of the parking lot. Rose put her head back. The moment's encounter lingered in her mind. Her life seemed so full to her that it took up all the world. Yet there were millions of other lives, each as full as hers. She watched a pickup truck approaching them in the next lane, two men inside, deer rifles racked across the window of the cab. A black Lab leaned its head out over the back. They passed by and were gone. Miller held out a joint to her, and she toked on it, haunted by the woman she had met. By the two men in the pickup. By the billions of other people whose lives touched hers only on the fly. In each of the houses they passed there were people she would never know. Lonely for them, she watched every house and every car, hoping for some clue to their separate meanings.

"You want to drive?"

"Okay," she said. The concentration of driving would sweep away her bothersome feelings, probably induced by lack of sleep.

She had Miller, anyway. Another life to share and explore. Sliding in behind the wheel, she stopped to kiss him, his mouth soft and sweet. A message sent and received. She turned the key in the ignition to start the car.

Miller watched two hours of news every night. Rose wondered why. The news on television never changed much; only the places changed, Korea, Iran, Cambodia, Rhodesia, Ireland, and the announcers changed. They went on talking and talking as if they were saying something new, but it was nothing new. It was the same story, over and over, as one people after another was whirled out of its safe, traditional fit into the stampede toward the future. The events on the television screen were like the X rays that betrayed the existence of a black hole. As each culture shattered under the pressures of change, it gave forth bursts of violent energy, in pain and rage at the loss.

"A couple of years ago it was the Sahel," she said, while the screen showed them starving people, the wizened faces, the enormous heads of babies whose bodies had wasted to limp bundles of bones. The Cambodians this time. "In a couple years it'll be somebody else. The Iranians. Somebody."

Miller made a noncommittal sound in his throat. He had no use for her harangues. He watched the sports segments of the news, flipping back and forth between the two Eureka channels. He liked the satellite pictures of the weather report, showing the storms that rolled in over the north Pacific, where above the open ocean the clouds formed perfect spirals, a thousand miles from edge to edge.

"Want to go for a walk?" Rose asked him. They were sitting in front of Peter's television, with Coyote in a chair on Miller's right.

"Not right now," he said. He shot a sideways look at Coyote, who was eating pie.

"What's going on?" Rose asked. She slid her hands between her knees, watching them with interest.

"Wha'd'you mean? Nothing's going on." Miller took a little white flask of Sinex from his pocket and without taking his eyes off the screen shot a good squirt up each nostril.

"Come on. Something's up, I can tell."

Laughing, Coyote leaned forward to nudge her in the side. "Maybe your sense of suspicion needs a tune-up."

"Hunh." She looked from one to the other; their smooth, bland expressions excluded her. They passed the joint in silence.

Stoned, she went into the kitchen to wash the dishes. Patty helped her. Peter was outside chopping wood for the fire, and the racket covered the sounds of the television and the two men talking before it.

When she went back out to the front room to pick up Coyote's pie plate, he and Miller were gone.

Peter came in with a load of wood and set about making a fire in the hearth. Darkness was falling, and the room was cold. Rose went over to help him.

"How do you feel?"

"Like two cents," he said, sinking down in the chair. "God, Rosie, I want a drink so bad—"

"When d'you get to have another one?"

"At nine. I'm going half an hour later every day."

"Peter, maybe it would be easier if you just went cold turkey."

He frowned at her. The skin of his face was coarse-grained and leathery, especially around the eyes, from the years of hard drinking. "God, woman, you gotta tell me everything to do?"

"I'm sorry." She turned away quickly, ruffled at that remark. Getting to her feet, she searched the room for paper trash to burn, to get the firewood going.

Patty came in, pulling her jacket on. The smooth bulge of her stomach forced the jacket open wide in front, although she buttoned the top and the bottom.

"Peter, lemme take your car. I want to go down to Jake and Sally's." This was the little country store just on the other side of the freeway.

"Get me something." Peter twisted in his chair, his voice urgent. "Something sweet. A surprise." He leaned over the back of the stuffed chair, his bright gaze on Patty.

"Rose?"

"Nothing for me, thanks," Rose said. "Get me a Hostess lemon pie for Miller. Cherry, if they don't have lemon."

"Okay. I'll be back." Patty wheeled and went through the kitchen to the door.

"That guy's fat enough as it is," Peter said, now watching Rose.

"Yeah, well, everybody to his own jones, right?"

He was looking at her with a hard, unwavering gaze. She moved a little, nervous under this scrutiny. "What's the matter? I got televisions in my eyes?"

"Have fun in Reno?" he said.

"Sure."

"Win anything?"

She shook her head. "I don't like to gamble. Miller won. He paid all our expenses and made forty, fifty dollars."

"Why don't you gamble?"

"Well, you know, I don't like getting something for nothing."

"Bothers you, does it?" His attention was still steady on her. She wondered what he was getting at.

"Yeah," she said, "that's my major axis, man; stay out of debt, close gates after you go through them, be wary of women who wear makeup and men who wear ties. What's on your mind, Bub?"

"What else did you do?"

She understood at last what he meant, and she smiled at him. "Well, I played tennis, I ate at every goddamned McDonald's between here and Nevada—"

"You fucked Miller, didn't you?"

"Oh, yeah. I knew I'd forgotten something. Yes, I went to bed with Miller. You got some objection?"

"You could do better than that."

"Love isn't a talent show, Peter. It's a neurosis."

"You think you love him, do you?"

"I—"

The front door crashed open, and Miller stamped in, his tread heavy, his back bent under the weight he carried on his shoulders. "Help me! Come on, he's hurt."

What he carried on his back was Coyote.

Rose gasped and crossed the room toward him. "Come on, put him down on the bed." Coyote was unconscious. Or dead. She put her hand against his cheek; the skin was warm with life. Miller carried him swiftly away from her, down the hall to the bunkroom.

"What's going on?" Peter called and came after them. "What's that—God! It's blood!"

Rose whirled around toward him. He stood in the hall pointing goggle-eyed at a glistening trail of droplets that led straight down the floor past Rose. She gulped. Squatting, she touched the drop at her feet.

He was right. It was blood. She raced after Miller into the bunkroom.

They laid Coyote down on the bottom bunk, where Rose usually slept. She pulled the rucked covers out from under him, scraping the raw, red mud from his boots as she did. Miller sat on the edge of the bed and picked up Coyote's arm and felt for his pulse.

"Go get me a watch. Something I can time his pulse with."

"What happened?" She twisted toward the door, where Peter stood, his face green with shock, one hand braced on the door frame.

"Give me your watch," she said.

He made no move to do it. She got up and pulled the watch by its leather strap out of his jeans pocket, unclipped it, and took it to Miller.

Coyote lay on his back, his head rolled to one side. The front of his red plaid shirt was soaked through with blood. She unbuttoned his shirt and spread it open, revealing his chest, smeared and splashed red.

"He was shot," Miller said. "We went to steal some pot and somebody shot him."

"My God." Peter's legs folded limply and set him down on the floor. "Oh, my God—"

Rose brushed past him, going down the hall to the kitchen. Her hands were shaking. She turned on the hot water full blast, filled one large kettle, and put it on the woodstove. Filling another pot, she took it back to the bunk room. At the linen closet in the hall she paused to find an old sheet.

"How is he?" she asked Miller.

He put the watch on the chest of drawers beside the bed. "His pulse is pretty good. His color's pretty good. I don't think he's in shock, but we got to keep him warm. Go boil some water."

"I've got it on now."

He took the sheet from her and ripped a piece from it. "Go get me a thermometer. Some tweezers, alcohol—"

"What about a doctor?"

Behind her Peter said, "Oh, my God."

Miller tipped his head back, raising his face toward her, his forehead ridged with tension, his mouth set in a scowl. "If you call a doctor, we'll get the heat up here for sure."

"Miller, for God's sake, what if he's really badly hurt?"

"I don't think he's that bad! Now go do what I said. Boil the tweezers. Go in my car, in the glove compartment. Get my hemostats. Boil them."

"Maybe we ought—"

His eyes blazed at her in a sudden fury. "Damnit, Rose, don't argue with me! Do as I say!"

She went down the hall at a run. Outside, she stepped off the porch into a whirling gusty warm wind; it would rain again soon. Single drops flew now in the bosom of the wind. She ran through the bending grass toward Miller's car. What have we done now? she thought. What have we gotten into now? She fought with the passenger-side door, which stuck, and could not open it; giving up, she raced around to the other side of the car and flopped on her stomach across the front seats. From the glove compartment she got the long, steel surgical tool, most coveted of roach clips, and ran back to the house.

The water on the woodstove was simmering. She dropped the hemostats into it. What else—what else? She went into the bathroom and opened the medicine cabinet.

A treasure. Old bottles of medicine, half a bottle of isopropyl alcohol, a roll of gauze, even a needle and thread. She carried all this back to the kitchen, cradled in her arms against her chest.

Patty came in, a sack of purchases in her arms. "What's happening?" She came over to the woodstove to look into the pot. "Making soup?" she asked uncertainly.

"No," Rose said. "Coyote's been hurt."

With a half-worded exclamation, Patty dumped her sack on the counter and charged down the hall. Rose followed her. The bathroom door was open, and the light was on; she paused, looking in. Miller was there, washing his hands in the sink.

"Miller," she said. "We need a doctor."

"No."

"What if he dies?"

Miller went right on scrubbing his hands with a soapy

washcloth. "He's not going to die. He's doing pretty good now; he's awake." He took a toothbrush from the rack and ground the bristles into the soap. Cocking his hand, he scrubbed his fingernails.

Down the hall, Patty yelled. Rose wheeled around and went down to the bunkroom.

Patty was standing over Coyote, shouting at him. "You rip-off! You fuckin' son of a bitch!" Her voice was shrill as a child's with rage. When Rose came up behind her, she spun around and jumped away from both of them. Her eyes flashed. "You, too, hunh?" she said to Rose. "God, you can't trust—"

"I didn't know about it," Rose replied.

"I'd 've thought you at least I could trust!"

"She had nothin' to do with it, Pat," Coyote said. "Leave her alone."

"You! I hope I never set eyes on you again as long as I live!" Patty took two long strides to the closet and dragged out an antique suitcase. She rushed around the tiny crowded room, collecting her belongings and stuffing them into the bag. "You'd think I'd 've learned by now, hunh? Not to trust anybody. Especially not people I like." She straightened and gave Coyote a stare down her long, patrician nose. "Used to like."

She made for the door. Rose said, "Patty, wait a minute."

Patty ignored her, and Rose trotted after her all the way down the hall and into the front room. Still Patty did not slacken stride. Side by side, the two women burst through the front door onto the porch, Patty walking at top speed and Rose keeping up with her.

It was raining. They tramped across the porch and down the steps, and there, in the steady downpour, Patty turned at last.

"Yeah?"

"Somebody ripped off his garden," Rose said. "I know how you feel, but at least you still have your plants. All his are gone."

Patty's face was still wild with anger. "I hope he dies." She strode off down the road again.

Her shoulders slumping, Rose did not follow her. The rain pelted her, and she was cold in her short-sleeved T-shirt. Slowly she started back into the house.

"Rose!"

At the steps she looked down the road, where Patty was standing, almost invisible in the rain.

"I know it wasn't you," Patty called. "You're honest, at least." She went down the hill.

Rose walked back into the house, shivering with the wet cold, and went down the front room to the fire to warm herself. Peter was sitting in the big chair there. As she came up beside him, he picked up his beer can and took several swallows from it without lowering it once. Rose did not stay. She cut back across the room to the hall door.

Coyote was still awake, lying on his back, his head propped on a couple of pillows. Rose sat down beside him.

"How d'you feel?"

"Not too good." His voice quaked like a crone.

"You want us to get a doctor?"

"No doctor." His head twitched from side to side.

Miller came in, holding his arms crooked before him with the hands raised, a towel across his elbows. To Rose he said, "Go down and bring those hemos. Do you have any kitchen tongs? A flashlight? Any gloves? Get everything down here. Peter!" His voice widened to a bellow.

"Forget about Peter," she said. "He'll be out cold in half an hour."

"Jesus." Miller sounded disgusted. He glanced at Coyote again, turned his eyes back toward Rose, and ordered, "Bring me all that and a glass of warm water with some baking soda and salt in it. Hurry up."

She ran down to the kitchen. The pan of water on the woodstove was boiling so hard that it splashed drops onto the stove that danced and hissed and were gone. She found a pair of kitchen gloves and a tray to carry everything and hurried away down the hall again with the tray, bearing the gloves, the tongs, the pot of steaming water, the instruments, and the glass of bicarbonate of soda. Miller was sitting on the side of the bed, his bare hands in the air, talking to Coyote.

"Anything else?"

"That's all I can remember," Coyote whispered; he was losing strength noticeably by the second. His skin looked gray. "They stuck me in the butt and flew me to the hospital, and they—"

His lips moved a little, but nothing more came out. Miller turned to Rose.

"Put that stuff down and help him drink the soda."

"Are you sure you know—"

"Goddamnit," he said, "do it." His eyes burned blue with the intensity of his will.

She took the glass of smoky water and sat down next to Coyote. Bracing him up, she held the glass to his lips, and he drank it in slow, shallow gulps.

"Good. Good," Miller said. "Now go wash your hands, Rose. Do a good job, a Tarn job, not a McKenna job. I could really use your fucking brother right now."

"Yeah, I know. I hope to God you know what you're doing."

"Go wash your hands."

She went to the bathroom and washed her hands and arms, grinding the soap over her skin, rubbing until her skin hurt.

"Rose!" Miller bawled.

She went down the hall again, her legs quivering and weak as a baby's.

She washed Coyote's chest, while Miller watched and gave orders now and then; Coyote passed out in the middle of it. There was a ragged hole in his chest, high up under the bone of the shoulder, leaking a steady bloody stream. At Miller's direction she opened packages of sterile gauze and jammed a wad of bandage against the wound and taped it down with masking tape, the only kind in the house.

"Now you have to roll him over," Miller said.

"Miller, I can't. He's too heavy."

"Shut up and do it."

She moved uncertainly back to Coyote, wondering how best to turn him without hurting him. Miller yelled at her to hurry. Bending, she got Coyote by the arm and hauled him halfway up, braced him against her shoulder, and grabbed the back of his belt. Crawling onto the bunk herself, she dragged him slowly around; the pain woke him, and he helped her, groaning. She pulled the pillows out from under him so that he could lie flat.

Miller nodded. "Good. Now give me the hemostats."

She crawled back over Coyote and with the tongs removed the hemostats from the water. They waited a moment for the steel to cool. The phone rang.

Rose turned her head toward the sound. "I guess Patty's got to the flats." She lowered her gaze to Miller. "Who shot him?"

"I didn't see. Somebody inside the fence there. We're just lucky it was a tiny little bullet." The phone rang and rang and rang.

"Like a twenty-two," she said. "Then it was Preston."

"Maybe." He took the hemostats from her and pulled the blanket down to Coyote's waist. "Hold the flashlight so I can see what I'm doing."

She leaned forward with the flashlight. The hole on this side was much smaller, lower and more toward the backbone than the other exit hole. "Get a wad of gauze to sop up the blood," Miller said and, bending over the wound, began pulling things out of the hole.

Rose held the flashlight straight above the wound, bracing her arm on the frame of the bunkbed, her eyes following the deft moves of the hemostats. Miller was dropping what he found on the tray: threads, lint, a bit of fleece from the lining of Coyote's jacket.

"Where'd you get your medical degree?"

"Watching 'M*A*S*H,'" he said.

She snorted at that, half-believing. He pressed a great mass of sterile gauze against the wound. "Help me tape this."

"Did you take his temperature?"

Miller slid backwards, down off the bunkbed to sit on the floor; he rubbed his forearm over his eyes. "Yeah. It was a little under a hundred." While she covered the man in the bed with a clean sheet and blankets, he sat watching, making no effort to get out of her way, so that she had to step around him. Done, she sat down beside him.

"What happened?" she said. "When you raided the field."

"We went around the back of the field, didn't see anybody, and he went in through the fence. I stayed outside to keep watch, but whoever it was was inside the field." Miller's hands lay in his lap, the fingers curled, white from the scrubbing, flecked red from the work. "All I heard was a shot and then Jim came running toward me and fell on his face by the fence."

Outside, the wind buffeted the house. A clatter of raindrops hit the window glass. Rose put her hands on Miller's arms, the heavy rounds of muscle. He had carried Coyote on his back all the way up from the flat. She leaned forward and kissed him. The phone rang.

"Go to sleep," she said. "Lie down. Or do you want something to eat?"

"Answer the phone," he said. When she got up to go to the phone, he stood and followed her.

On the phone was Dave Preston. "Patty tol' me Wylie Coyote's up there."

"Yeah," Rose said. She looked at Miller and nodded. He was standing in front of the open refrigerator, more interested in Coca-Cola than anything else.

"I want t' talk to you," said Preston.

"To me," she replied, surprised. "Why me?"

"I'll come up there."

"No," she said. "No." She glanced at Miller again, thought swiftly of Peter, and repeated, "No. I'll meet you down at the eucalyptus trees."

"It's raining!"

"Do you want to talk to me or not?"

A pause. "Okay."

"Good. Then meet me at the eucalyptus as soon as you can." She hung up the phone and turned to face the room and leaned her back against the wall.

"What does he want?" Miller asked, his back to Rose. He was bringing out meat and mayonnaise and lettuce from the refrigerator.

"I don't know, really. He called me when he shot Hallie's goat. Maybe he thinks it'll work twice." She went down the hall to the bunkroom, to get her jacket, and then toward the front door.

Miller intercepted her in the front room. "I don't want you to go down there." In one hand he held a plate with an enormous sandwich.

Rose cast a look over her shoulder toward the fireplace, saw no sign of Peter, noticed a pile of green cans beside the heavy old chair, and circled around to see the front. There Peter slumped, his chin on his chest. She arched her eyebrows at Miller.

"You want him to come in here and see that?"

"I don't know why not."

"Peter told him the next time he saw him with the gun he'd run him off River Ranch," Rose said. "I don't think he looks in any condition to run himself down into bed, do you?"

"Doesn't matter about Peter," Miller said, with force. "When Jim gets better, he'll kill Preston."

"No, he won't," Rose said, going to the door. "Peter will run him off." She stepped onto the porch, snapping up the front of her jacket, and descended the steps into the rain.

She walked straight ahead, past the rhinoceros, down the hill the way she had gone with the men's lunches, day after day, so that she knew the path even in the dark and the rain. The wind struck her, coming up into her face and the wet grass quickly soaked her tennis shoes. She jammed her hands into her jeans pockets to keep them warm.

Halfway down the hill she turned toward the eucalyptus trees. As the wind tossed them, they screamed and sighed, and the big trunks swayed their feathery heads against the sky. She walked into the shelter of the trees and picked her way over the fallen branches and rotting leaves and bark to a place deep inside the grove.

There the oldest trees stood so close that their trunks had grown together into a wall. She sat down out of the wind. Now and then a raindrop fell through the many-leveled canopy of the leaves and struck her face or her hands. At first the spicy odor of the trees bothered her, but her nose swiftly got accustomed to it. She had heard once that the Chinese who came to California for the gold had brought the eucalyptus with them, since they put a high value on its medicinal properties. On the other hand she had heard that the people who built the Union Pacific had brought the trees over for railroad ties.

She had named this place for the meeting because she had wanted to hear Preston before he reached her. The rattle of the rain and the branches made enough noise to drown a symphony orchestra; but she saw a light in between the trees bobbing as it moved, a flashlight carried by a walking man, and she stood up and called.

Preston tramped into the grove. A branch hanging down from a tree swung in the wind and caught him across the head, and he swore. He waved the flashlight back and forth, surveying the ground in front of him, like a knife blade cutting through the dark. Rose sat down again.

He walked up to her and stood over her. "What the hell did you have in mind, dragging us out here in the woods?"

"What did you have in mind shooting people?"

"He was raiding the pot! He—"

"He's a human being, Dave, for God's sake. What if it had been your brother? Or one of the kids?" She could no longer keep still, and leaping up, she paced along the line of the trees, a few strides up, a few strides down. "Didn't you get plenty of warning? First the goat, then the airplane—"

"What does Peter have to say?"

She faced him. The flashlight hung between them, lighting up their feet. She could just make out the glitter of his eyes, the arch of his nose above the black mask of beard.

"He wants you off."

"Look here, lady. I like it here. I want to stay. I'll settle it with him, somehow—I gotta talk to him."

"Why'd you want to talk to me, then?"

"Because—" He raised his hands, the flashlight's beam slicing over her body and across her shoulder. "I want you to explain to him why—"

"Forget it! Christ almighty, you shot somebody! You may have killed somebody!" She paced off a few feet, turned, and marched up into his face again. "What about the rest of us? What's gonna happen to us if he dies? The Man will wipe us off the map."

His eyes widened; she saw he had not thought of that.

"We can't call a doctor," she said. "Doctors have to report gunshot wounds to the police. You just better hope to God that Miller Tarn knows what he's doing."

Preston's head lifted an inch. "Oh," he said, under his breath, "so it was the fat man who got him out."

Rose said nothing for a moment, annoyed with herself for giving up that piece of information. She watched Preston's face, caught in the edge of the light of the flash, as he chewed over what she had said.

In a softer voice she went on. "Look, Dave, for the good of everybody, you've got to split."

"Goddamnit," he said. "I like it here. And what about my share of the dope? I've worked my ass off for that dope—"

"You know Coyote. If he gets well, you know what he'll do to you?"

"He don't scare me."

"Then you're an asshole." She pushed her face up into his, always effective against people bigger than she was. "Because he will take you by the ankles and wrap you twice around the nearest tree."

"You're funny," he said in a dull voice.

"For God's sake, Dave. If he dies, we're finished. If he lives, you're finished. Be reasonable will y'?"

"I like it here," he said stubbornly.

"Think about it," she said and started away.

"Hey. Where you going?" He caught her by the arm.

"I'm going home," she answered. With her free hand she peeled off his fingers and pushed his hand away from her arm. "Take forty-eight hours. Decide what you want to do. I don't see you've got much choice. If you're still here in two days—" She shrugged.

Preston swung his flashlight around, cutting wheels through the windy leaves.

"Okay," he said. "I'll think about it. But I'm telling you—"

He stopped. She said, "Tell me what, Dave."

"I like it here," he said again.

"Shit, man, we all like it here." She walked away through the eucalyptus.

Rose startled awake, still upright; she was sitting on the floor by the bunkbed, her back to the frame, and had dozed off. She got up onto her feet, every joint creaking, and went to the window.

Steam covered it. Through the misted glass the first light of dawn was shining. She stretched her arms over her head, her back pulling and loosening with a deep pleasant ache, and worked her shoulders.

"Hey."

Turning, she sat down on the side of the bed. "What are you doing awake?" She laid her hand against Coyote's forehead. "How do you feel?"

"Pretty bad."

His voice was a murmur, his lips hardly moving. Rose took the thermometer from the glass on top of the chest of drawers and shook it down and reached for the bottle of alcohol. "Does it hurt?"

"Like hell."

"You're lucky the bullet went all the way through you, or we'd have had to take you to the doctor." She held out the thermometer, and he opened his mouth for it.

"No doctor. No cops." He spoke around the glass tube.

"Yes, Jim, we're all in agreement on that."

His eyes shut; she thought he was asleep again. But after a moment he said, "Pretty powerful for a squirrel gun. Preston's."

"He must have been within feet of you."

His eyes were still closed, and he made no reply. She made herself busy around the room, straightening the covers and picking up wads of bloody bandage. When she took the thermometer out of his mouth, his eyes opened.

"Hurts."

"I'm sorry. All Peter has for pain is aspirin. I want you to take a tetracycline. Are you hungry?"

"Hurts."

She wrote down his temperature, still a little above normal, and took one of the vials of medicine from Peter's bathroom medicine chest. "I'll get you a glass of water."

"Hurts," he said. "Coke. Get me some coke."

At first she thought he meant Coca-Cola; she eyed him uncertainly, and he said, "Cocaine. Get me some cocaine."

"God, Jim, I don't know if that's a good idea."

"Get me some coke!"

She took the litter of dirty things on the dresser top to the kitchen, filled a pitcher with water, and found a clean glass. Miller was curled up on the couch by the wood stove, his body in a fetal position, his head cradled on a stack of magazines. She shook him awake.

"Mil. Miller, wake up."

"Hunh—hunh?" He lifted his head.

"Coyote wants some cocaine. He thinks it'll help the pain."

Miller sat up, stretching his arms and shoulders and working his neck; he rubbed his neck with his hand. "I guess it would," he said and got to his feet, yawning. "But I haven't got any more." His T-shirt rode up above the curve of his belly, and she put her hand on his golden Russian skin.

"You did a great job last night. How did you know what to do?"

"It seemed pretty obvious to me." Another yawn split his face. She moved inside the arc of his arms and pressed herself to his soft warmth.

"How's he doing?" Miller hung his arms over her and kissed her.

"Pretty good, I think. He's not running much of a fever and he's wide awake and coherent, but he says it hurts."

"I'll bet it does."

"Have you seen Peter?"

"As far as I know, he's still in the living room." Miller kissed the top of her head and walked away down the hall. Rose went into the front room.

Peter was there in the big stuffed chair, his feet on the hearth, his lower back against the seat cushion, his body curved like a question mark. She sat down on the hearth and shook his head. When that had no effect, she pried off one of his heavy work boots and tickled the sole of his foot.

He woke up with a jolt. "Oh," he said, staring down the length of his body at her. "Wha'd'you want?"

"Peter. You remember what happened last night?"

He watched her a moment, unmoving; abruptly his eyes opened wide and he sat up. "How is he? Is he okay?" He swung his feet to the floor and reached for the boot beside her.

"No," she said. "He's still pretty bad off. What are you going to do about Dave Preston?"

He laced his boot up and tied it. "What about Dave? You ask me, Coyote got what was coming to him, raiding the pot field."

"You told Preston—"

He lurched to his feet and walked away across the front room. Rose followed.

"You told Preston you'd kick him out if he brought out the gun again."

"Are you sure it was him?" In the hall he paused; his head turned from side to side, looking down the hall toward the bunkroom, looking up the hall to the kitchen. She knew he was caught between the desire to see Coyote and his need for another drink. She pushed him slightly in favor of the bunkroom, and he went that way.

"It was him," she said, behind him. "He's not pretending it isn't. I talked to him last night—"

"*You* talked to him!" He stopped at the doorway to gape at her.

"Yes. He called up and—"

"Why you? Why'd he call you?"

"He's very traditional. He called me after he shot Hallie's goat." She watched him chew on that for a moment; from the drawer beside the sink she got a big brown paper sack. "I'm going down to the flat to get some vegetables for dinner. I'll be back."

Peter said, "Maybe he split." Turning, he walked away down the hall.

Rose went down to the flat, the paper sack under her arm. The crying of a baby led her over to the fence around Johan's place.

Just inside the fence, the baby lay on her back on a yellow blanket in the grass. With each shrill scream her body stiffened, her legs thrusting out, and she shook her fists in the air. Crooning reassurances, Rose bent over the fence and patted the little brown stomach, bare save for her diaper and a short pink jacket tied at the neck with ribbon. At her touch the baby stopped screaming and turned her head from side to side, questing with her lips. Finding nothing to suck on, she let out a shriek of boundless rage.

"I'm coming," Margaret called. "I'm coming, Gaby."

Rose looked up. Johan's wife was struggling into the yard from the back fence, dragging a goat after her by a rope around its neck. Rose vaulted the fence and went to help her.

"Thanks," said Margaret. She tied the goat to a fence post and went to pick up her child. "She got away. I mean the goat." The baby was nuzzling impatiently at her blouse, and she pulled down her sleeve to bare her breast and poked the nipple into the baby's mouth. With a loud sigh the baby began to nurse.

Rose laughed. "Greedy, isn't she?"

"Oh, yes," Margaret said. "Sometimes I think she's going to eat me alive."

"How do you like the goats?"

Before Margaret could answer, Johan called from the house. Seeing Rose there, he jumped to the ground and came toward them through his orchard of shoulder-high trees. "Hello there, Sister Rose."

"Hi."

The goat bleated. It was the smaller of Hal's two nannies, brown and white with streaks of black on its face and legs. She reared up suddenly and flung her weight against the rope that held her to the fence. Rose grabbed her collar to hold her still. "You milk these things?" she said with distaste.

"I try," Margaret said.

Johan stood astride the goat and slapped his long, thin hands against her sides. "Goats are among the most interesting animals. I'm glad we have goats." He scratched behind the goat's floppy ears.

"Will you milk her?" Margaret asked. "Gaby's so hungry, and the goat's late to be milked."

"Redwood," Johan said, correcting her. "Milking the goats is your job, Sunshine."

"Oh, Jo, just this once?"

"We decided," he said and ended the conversation by turning his back on her. To Rose, he said, "I heard there was more trouble in the pot field."

"Yeah," Rose said. "Preston shot Coyote."

He shook his head, his hands gripping the fence in front of him. "This is very serious news, Sister Rose."

The goat bleated and lunged at her tether; between her

hindlegs the swollen udder hung like the bulging bladder of a bagpipe. Rose grabbed her collar again. "We don't know how bad it is, yet."

"Jo," Margaret said, "please milk her. That's why she's so skittish."

Johan ignored her. He pulled on the fence, watching Rose with solemn eyes. "How much worse can it be? River Ranch is contaminated with violence now; it can never be made pure again."

"Oh, really?" Rose was stooped to hold the goat, bouncing and lunging against the collar. She said, "Well, for instance, if Coyote dies, I'd say that's worse than if he lives."

Margaret's head snapped up. "Is he going to die?"

"I don't know," Rose answered. There was a plastic pail in the high grass beside the gate, and she dragged the goat in that direction.

"It's all the same to me," Johan said. "Any act of violence is as terrible as the worst."

Rose said nothing to that, although her temper bridled, symptomatic of the brainlessness of what he said that he could not say it any better than he had. She pulled the goat around over the bucket. "I've never milked a goat. Let me try."

Margaret was sitting cross-legged by the fence. She tucked her striped skirt over her knees. The baby was hard at work at her breast. "You just—" Margaret freed her hands a moment to pull at imaginary teats hanging in the air. "Don't let go of her—"

Rose had already taken both hands off the goat, to milk her, and the animal leaped away into the orchard. With a yell Rose ran after her, cut off her escape around the house, and tackled her under the apple trees. She hauled the beast back to the pail. Once in Sweden she had seen a farmwife milking a goat while holding it backwards between her knees, so she swung one leg over the goat's back, clamped her legs down around the goat, and reached down over her back for the udder. She pushed the pail under the goat and squeezed.

Jets of milk squirted into the pail. Margaret said, "Perfect. Good for Rose."

"Are you leaving River Ranch?" Rose tugged at the goat's finger-length nipples, warm in her hands. Her back ached from bending over.

"No," Margaret said.

Johan said, "If we have to. We need peace and freedom to raise our child, so that she will enter into her destiny."

"What destiny?" Rose glanced at the little body in the yellow blanket.

Johan watched her, his face grave. "I have known," he said, "from the first moment I touched her that my child came into the world for a very special purpose."

"Which is?"

His shoulders moved, putting that off. "Something not to be lightly discussed."

"But we can't leave," Margaret protested. "It took us so long to build the house, to plant the trees and the garden, and now you want to leave?"

"I know what's right, Sunshine."

Rose worked at the milking, the goat clutched between her calves. Margaret cried, "Watch out, she'll—"

The goat kicked over the bucket. Milk spilled out onto the grass, and Rose let out a yell, leaped away from the goat, and launched a wild, swinging foot at her. The goat bolted away through the orchard.

Margaret rocked with laughter. "She used to do that all the time to me, too."

Johan shook his head with disapproval. "Don't abuse the animals," he said to Rose.

She wiped her hands on her thighs. The tangy odor of the goat clung to her fingers. "I'm sorry about the milk." The bucket had emptied onto the grass; white shone on the blades of the grass and the fringed leaves of the mallows that grew by the fence.

"We have too much of it anyway," Margaret said, "now that Johan doesn't drink it any more."

"Don't like the taste?" Rose asked him.

He gave her another of his measuring looks. "I have given up all dairy products," he said. "I am now on a two-month fast, nothing but fruit juice to clean out my body."

She slid her arms behind her. Lately every time she talked to him she had to struggle with her temper. "That's going to be a little hard on you, isn't it? A two-month fast?"

"I don't need food," he said to her. "When I've cleansed my body, I shall enter into a new state of being, one in which I will require only water and air." Unsmiling, he nodded to her. "I know who I am now, Sister Rose."

"Who are you?"

"I am spirit, Rose."

The tone of his voice suggested a mild surprise that she had to ask. Rose frowned at him, bewildered; he presented a hard, smooth surface, an adamant faith, which repelled her thoughts and words as neatly as a ball bouncing off a wall. She shrugged. "Well, good luck."

"I am fully in control of those influences you call luck, Sister Rose."

"Oh, really?" She bit back the sarcastic retort she longed to throw at him. Useless. She turned to Margaret. "Can I buy some vegetables from you?"

"Sure." Margaret led her toward the garden, the baby cupped in her arm.

While they pulled onions and picked up the enormous leaves of the zucchini to find the fruits, Rose kept an eye on Johan. If he had walked on air, he could not have bothered her more.

He went inside and she gave Margaret a dollar for the zucchini and onions, a tomato, and a head of lettuce.

"Does he mean that?" she asked. "A fast like that could kill him."

Margaret folded the dollar between her fingers. "He's been saying some strange things lately. It's just to get people to listen to him. Maybe I'm not paying enough attention to him, now that Gaby's here." The trouble in her eyes made her look much younger. She brushed back her long, fair hair with a freckled wrist. "We aren't leaving River Ranch."

Rose was stuffing the vegetables into her sack. "Thanks —I'll be down in a couple days for some more."

"I feel silly taking money."

"You'd be silly not to." Up by the willow tree in Sam's front yard, a car was nosing down the ranch road. It was Dave Preston's old black Fairlane. Rose straightened to watch. He pulled into the Viggs' front yard and got out. Across the twenty yards that separated them he and Rose stared a challenge at each other. He was first to look away; he went into the house. Rose walked back up the hill to her brother's.

When she got back to her brother's house, Peter was out on the front porch, leaning on the rail, his eyes fixed on the hazy distance. Rose went over to him, taking a joint out of her pocket, and lit it and handed it to him. For a moment they were silent, passing the joint back and forth.

"You're losing another of your settlers," she said at last.

"Who? Preston, I hope?"

"No, Johan."

"Did you see Preston?"

She nodded. "I don't think he's going to jump ship under his own power."

"God." He turned his face back toward the airy vistas of his ranch. "Why does all this have to land on me?"

"Because this is your place," she said.

His face settled. "Where is Johan going?"

"He says he's leaving River Ranch. For good. Too nasty for him here, he says. He wants peace and freedom, he says."

"What about his share of the dope?"

"Oh, he'll wait until it's harvested."

Peter curled his lips into a grimace. "Fuckin' asshole." He vaulted up onto the porch railing and slung both legs awkwardly across to the deck. "Come on."

She went after him into the kitchen; he went straight to the refrigerator and opened the door.

Rose hung back. He would not let her control him, and

she should not want to, anyway. He turned to look at her, his face expectant.

"Well?"

"Do what you want, Peter."

He stooped, took out a can, and shut the door. It was a red Coke can. Pleased, Rose let out her breath, and went over to him to hug him.

"Easy does it," he warned, fending her off. "You don't have to overreact." He pulled off the pop-top and raised the fizzing can to his lips. "What d'you think I should do about Dave?"

"I don't know." They walked together out of the kitchen, down the hall toward the bunkroom. "It's up to you. Whatever you want."

"God," he said, glancing obliquely at her. "Strike two, sissy."

"Yes, master."

In the bedroom Coyote lay asleep under the blankets, and Miller was gathering up the red bandages and dirty linen in a brown paper bag. He held the bag out to Rose. "Throw this in the fire."

She took it, although it rankled to obey him. Peter asked, "How is he?"

"He's running a fever," Miller said. "I think he's getting sick in the wound."

Peter said, "You give him any antibiotics?"

"Yeah. But it's a long, deep wound, and I might not have gotten everything out of it."

Rose took the bag of dirty rags away to the woodstove and threw it in. She felt prickly all over with tension. If Coyote died—if he died— She put herself furiously to work in the kitchen, her stomach like a knot in her middle.

"Aaarrgh—"

"Easy," she said. "Easy, boy. Easy." At the top of her lungs she shouted, "Miller!"

"Aaaah—" Coyote twisted convulsively. She pressed her weight down on him, to hold him still.

"Easy—easy—"

He howled, throwing her off him with both arms in a surge of sick strength. She banged her head on the frame of the bunk and sprawled over him again, trying to keep him from tearing off the bandage. He pawed at his wound and she struck his hand away.

"Hurts! It hurts! Aaaarrrrgh—"

The door crashed open, and Miller rushed into the room. "What's happening?" He pulled the chain on the overhead light; the room was thrown into its unshielded glare.

"He's trying to get to the wound," she said. "He woke me up, yelling." She struggled to keep him down under her, to hold onto his wrist.

"Jim!" Miller pulled her away from the sick man and sat down where she had been. "Jim!"

Coyote answered with another wordless roar of pain. Miller put his hand on Coyote's forehead.

"He's got a burning fever. Get me some wet rags."

She ran down the hall. Peter's bedroom door opened, and he poked his head out.

"What's going on?"

"Coyote's delirious." She went on to the kitchen and looked for a pail and some rags; her ears were cocked so hard that they ached.

With water and towels she strode up the hallway again. Miller had pulled off the blankets and was holding Coyote's wrists fast in his fists; Peter bent over him, shouting, "Jim! Hey, Jim, come to!"

Miller glanced at Rose and let go of the man in the bed. He took a rag, soaked it quickly in the water, wrung it out, and draped it over Coyote's bare chest.

"Hurts." Coyote pulled at the bandage, and Miller struck his hand away. He wiped Coyote's face with another cool, wet towel. Almost at once Coyote stopped thrashing; unconscious, he lay still while Miller washed him with cool towels.

"There he goes," Peter said.

"Jim," Miller said, "Jim, you there yet, man?"

Coyote's eyelids fluttered. "Hurts."

"Yeah, man, it oughta hurt. Come on, Jim, you gotta try not to lose it, man."

"Is he okay?" Rose asked.

"Hurts," Coyote repeated.

"Yes, yes, yes." Miller threw a towel into the pail at his feet. "It should hurt."

"Sauna," said Jim.

"He's still out of it," Peter said.

But Coyote's eyes opened, and his head turned slightly toward Peter's voice. "Sauna," he said again. "Get me in the sauna."

"Are you kidding?" Peter leaned across Miller's shoulder to talk into Coyote's face. "It'd kill you."

Miller swiveled his head toward Rose. "What d'you think?"

"I don't know," Rose said. "It sure sounds strange."

"Maybe it'd sweat him clean."

She shrugged; she had heard of Indians and Vikings taking steam baths for sickness. This was not a disease, but a wound.

"I know," the man in the bed whispered. "Sauna. Give me sauna."

"He's crazy," said Peter.

Miller stood up, rubbing his hands together. Without moving his gaze from Coyote, he said, "Can you fire the thing up, Rose?"

"Okay," she said.

"You're crazy," Peter said.

She went out to the sauna to build a fire in the woodstove. With Peter's axe she split a chunk of redwood into tinder and kindling, and when that was blazing, she laid chunks of hardwood over it and shut the door of the woodstove.

It was four in the morning; she was tired, and now, waiting for the stove to heat up, she felt the drag of fatigue on her body and her mind. Coyote was getting worse. This sauna was a desperate move. If he died—if. He was strong and fit from hard work, a young man in the prime of his strength; it would take a lot to kill him.

The woodstove was roaring now. She went into the house to help them bring Coyote out.

They wrapped him up in a blanket for the trip from the bed to the sauna. Miller draped one arm over his shoulders and Peter took the other and they carried him out, his feet dragging mostly, sometimes trying to walk. She ran ahead of them down the porch steps to open the door of the sauna.

Inside the little room it was already sweltering hot. Miller and Peter hauled Coyote into it, and while Miller peeled off his own clothes, Peter stayed with Coyote, one arm around him, holding him up. They took the blanket away, and Miller went into the steam bath and shut the door.

"I'm going back to bed," Rose said. "If anybody needs me, call me."

"Wait," Peter said and followed her into the kitchen. "Tell me what you told Dave Preston."

She turned slowly toward him, her limbs aching for sleep, and went to the couch and sat down. "Okay. Basically I reminded him of what you said, that the next time he brought out the gun you would escort him to the door. Then I told him he had forty-eight hours to leave. That was last night about, oh, ten, eleven. I'd say if he's still here tomorrow, he's overstaying it."

"God, Rose." He took another can of Coke out of the refrigerator. "God. I was bluffing, Rose, you know that. I was only bluffing. He's bigger than me. I don't know anything about fighting. He'll want to fight for sure." He drank deeply of the Coke. "Jesus, I wish this was a Rainier."

"Peter, maybe he won't fight. What if—"

"He'll fight. He wants to stay, doesn't he?"

She nodded. Her brother walked aimlessly around the

kitchen, drinking the Coke and cursing it for not being ale. Rose reached around a stack of *Penthouses* for his dope tray and rolled a joint.

"Come on, Peter—you're in pretty good shape, for a drunk—"

"He was in Vietnam. He was decorated in Vietnam."

"Well, what about the wrestling team you were on? Don't you remember any of that stuff?"

He looked around at her, his face hanging as sadly as a hound's. "I wasn't really on the wrestling team. I tried out, but I didn't make it. They let me be the team manager. I spent most of the practice sessions sleeping in the locker room."

"Oh, Peter," she said.

"What am I going to do, Rose?"

She lit the joint and held it out. "Play it by ear, Peter."

"But I'm no fighter." He sat down next to her, taking a hit on the joint, and passed it back to her. "I can't fight, Rose."

"Well, hell, Peter, the worst thing that can happen is you'll lose."

"No. The worst that can happen is I'll get beat up." He shook his head. "And Dave Preston will still be here."

They sat smoking the joint in silence until the pot was gone. Peter's eyes were sunken into the dark hollows of their sockets; he looked ten years older than he was.

"I got to get Preston off my place," he said. "Or it ain't my place any more."

"I got to get some sleep," Rose said. "Is that okay with you?"

"Yeah. I guess I'll go spell Miller." He reached out suddenly for Rose's hand and held it tight. "You're a champ, sissy. You know that?"

She went warm at the praise and the love in his voice. "So are you," she answered. She bent and kissed his cheek, and he stood up, and they embraced. Rose felt the tears burning in her eyes. Momentarily bereft of speech, she thumped him on the back, and he muttered something only half-worded.

"Good night," she said. "If you need me—"

"Get some sleep," he said. "Good night."

She went down the hall to her bed.

A steady thump-thump-thump woke her up. She slid off the kitchen couch, struggling awake, and stood a moment by the woodstove trying to locate the sound. It stopped. She went out the back door onto the porch. It had seemed to come from outside, and now while she stood there, it began again, louder, THUMP-THUMP-THUMP. Somebody banging on the sauna wall. She ran across the yard to the shack.

The stovepipe looked cold. When she opened the door, a moist, warm gust blew into her face. The humidity condensed on her cheeks and her hair.

"What is it? What's the matter?"

"Come on, help me," Miller said, grouchy. "God, I've been beating on this wall for hours. Get him off me. Either the fever's broken or he's dead and cooling off."

Because she could see nothing in the dark room, she went toward his voice, her hands outstretched. With her right hand she touched Coyote and with her left Miller. Both startled under her fingers. She slid one arm around Coyote's waist and hung his arm over her shoulders.

"Come on."

They carried him between them out and across the yard to the house again. In the biting predawn chill Coyote woke up; his feet dragged helplessly after him, but his voice was healthy enough.

"Three degrees right rudder! All ahead full." They negotiated him up the stairs. Rose ran herself into the upright of the railing with a thud. "Back engines. Comin' on a lee shore." His head wobbled, and he gathered his breath with an effort. "Oh, the pins are a little weak."

"Come on," Miller said. "Just a little while more."

They got him into the bunkbed. Rose sat beside him and felt his forehead and held his wrist a moment, feeling his pulse. "God, he seems so much better."

Miller edged her away from Coyote. "I'll do that. Go down and get me something to eat. I'm hungry."

She backed into the middle of the room, her eyes on Coyote's face. His face was as pale as a baby's. "Shall I feed him, too?"

Miller's head swiveled toward her. "What's the matter with getting me something? I know all you care about is him—"

"What are you talking about?" she said, astonished.

"I asked you to get me something to eat! The first thing you think about is giving it to him!"

"For Christ's sake, he's half dead. What d'you—"

"Get me something to eat!"

She goggled at him a moment, shrugged, and went down the hall to the kitchen. He had no business talking to her like that. She sliced a tomato and the leftover beef from dinner the night before and piled it onto a slice of bread. While she was spreading mayonnaise and mustard on the cover slice, Miller came in and, turning on both the sink taps, scooped up the water into his face.

"Here you go," Rose said, putting his sandwich on a plate.

"He's asleep," Miller said. He reached for the sandwich and went over to the couch by the woodstove to eat.

"Come on, sit down with me," he said.

"I thought I'd just go down and—"

"Leave him alone. What's the matter? Why can't I ask you to sit with me while I eat? You can't even give me that much?"

"God, you are in a strange mood." She sat down on the couch.

"I just don't want you in there pawing him, that's all."

"Ooooh," she said. "Are you jealous?"

"I just happen to know how you feel about him, that's all."

She leaned back against the stuffed arm of the couch. "Then you don't know how I feel about you, or you wouldn't be jealous of Coyote."

He was chewing a mouthful of the sandwich. He had been naked in the sauna; he was still naked, and his belly slumped down into his lap. She reached out and patted it.

"How do you feel about me?" he said.

"I love you."

"Really?"

He put down his sandwich and, leaning forward, kissed her on the mouth and on either cheek. She leaned against the back of the couch. The window over the sink was pale with dawnlight.

"When can we harvest our dope?" she asked.

"Couple a days. You been down there since we went to Reno?"

"Yes." She had walked down in the afternoon. The blossoms were fully open, the delicate tendrils tinged with pink and purple, uncurling into the sun like the antennae of an invader from space.

"What are you going to do with your money?" he asked.

"I think I'm going to write a novel."

"You're lucky," he said. "To have something like that to do. Something you like so much."

"Yes." That irritated her. It was not luck; she had worked for what she had. "What are you going to do?"

"First I'm going to Hawaii. I want you to come with me. Then I'd like to go to Peru."

"I've never been to Hawaii."

"Will you come with me?"

As he spoke, he put out one hand to touch her hair. She slid toward him on the couch and slung her arm around him. "Sure." She kissed him, bending over him.

His hand cupped the back of her head; he held her fast through another long kiss.

"What are you going to do when we get back?" she said.

Freeing one arm from the embrace, he reached for the sandwich he had put down. "I haven't thought about it. I don't like making plans that far ahead. Something always happens to mess things up."

"Would you like to live with me?"

His face turned toward her, the wide, blue eyes burning with a new intensity. "Where? Here?"

"Yeah." She smiled at him; her heart was beating hard, and a little apprehension uncurled in her stomach; she crushed it down again. "Come live with me and be my—"

"Okay, okay. Don't beat me into it with words."

"Good," she said.

He ate the rest of the sandwich. Her hand behind his head, she fingered the tight red-blond curls at his nape. He put the plate down and brushed the crumbs off his thighs and the curve of his belly.

"What about Preston?" he said. "Is your brother gonna chase him off?"

"I hope so," she said.

"So do I, but I don't think so."

She did not want to look hard at this knot in the future. She bent down and kissed his shoulder. The smell of alcohol clung to his hair. The smell of marijuana. Divorced old barren reason from my bed and took the daughter of the vine to spouse. Except it was the son of the marijuana seed. She kissed him again.

"How would we know if he did leave?" Miller asked, pressing mercilessly on the unpleasant business of Dave Preston.

"Oh, God," she said. She straightened again, away from him. "I'll go down there tomorrow and sniff out what's going on. Okay?"

"I just don't think it'd be too cool for him to hang around here, now that Jim's getting better."

"I know. I'll go spy it out."

"Good. Give me another kiss."

"A thousand kisses, and another thousand," she said and bent to place her lips firmly on his.

"Hi," Rose said. "A long time ago you asked me in for a cup of coffee—can I take you up on it now?"

Glory Vigg said, "Sure. You just come right in." She stood to one side, and Rose entered the house.

"The guys are in the living room," Glory said. "I was just washing the breakfast dishes. You want coffee or a beer?"

"Coffee's fine." Rose stood looking around the narrow kitchen. The linoleum on the floor was worn through in great patches, and the walls were dark with age, but the place was spotless. A stack of dirty dishes stood beside the sink. The air smelled deliciously of bacon.

Glory brushed by her. A terry robe swathed her enormous body. Under her breath she said, "You here to see Dave?"

"Not really," Rose said, although she was.

She went into the living room, which was so small there was hardly room to walk around the couch and the redwood stump that served for a table. Billy Vigg was slumped on the couch watching television. Beside him Dave Preston was rolling a joint.

They looked up when Rose came in, and Billy crowed. "Well, now! Company! You set down right here, now, Rose." He made a narrow space beside him on the couch.

Rose sat in the only chair in the room. "I think I'll keep my distance. If I were that close to you temptation might overwhelm me."

Billy guffawed. He picked up the tray on the stump in front of him and rolled a joint. On both arms he had the intricate tatoos of someone who had spent a lot of time in jail.

Dave Preston and Rose stared at each other without speaking. He licked his lips, and his eyes shifted. He said, "You come down here to see me?"

"Just being neighborly," she answered. Somewhere outside someone was shouting; she turned her head a little, trying to locate the faint racket.

Billy scratched a kitchen match afire and lit the joint. "This here's not bad weed," he said, "if you can get by the rasp." He held it out to her.

Rose took it. "Where'd you score the dope?"

"Oh—down in Springville," Billy said, but his eyes changed, as if a shield had come down between him and her, and she knew it was Coyote's dope she was smoking. She took a long hit.

Glory came in, sat down, swirled the skirts of the blue robe over her knees, and smiled. Her heavy, yellow hair lay over her shoulders. She smiled at Rose.

"How's tricks?"

"Not bad," Rose said. The shouting in the distance reached her ears again. "Where is Patty staying, do you know?"

"She's down at Sam's house," said Dave.

Rose's head bobbed. She passed the joint on. "This is pretty hard on the throat. Is it cured in something?"

"Just good old Humboldt County homegrown."

Rose turned her head, looking at the open window in the other wall, through which the yelling in the distance reached her ears. "What the devil is that?"

"Oh." Glory smiled at her. Preston offered her the joint, but she waved it off, her gaze still on Rose. "That's Johan and Sunshine. They're always arguing."

The phone rang. Glory leaped up to answer it.

Dave Preston held out the joint to Rose. "What's Peter got to say?"

She shook her head. "Ask him. I'm staying out of this."

"You tell him what I told you?"

"Yes."

Glory screamed. "The sheriff!" She dropped the phone, which swung by its curled cord against the wall, and raced toward the front door.

Rose lunged for the open window. Behind her the men were saying, "What's that? What's happening?" Rose stuck her head out the open window to see down the road.

"The sheriff!"

From here she could see up the road all the way to the gate. As she watched, Patty burst out of the little house there and sprinted up the road toward her. Behind her, at the gate, were a couple of cars, and on top of the cars racks of red and blue lights flashed around and around like mute sirens.

"What is it?" Dave Preston leaned over her, jamming her against the windowsill so that he could see out over her head. She felt his chest expand as he dragged in enough air to shout.

"It's a raid! It's a raid!"

Glory screamed; she ran into the living room, turned, and ran back into the kitchen. Dave Preston's weight left Rose's back, and she swung her leg over the windowsill and jumped out.

Glory's screams filtered through the house to her ears. Rose made for the road; at the Viggs' gate she stopped to look down toward the sheriff.

They didn't even bother to open the gate; they were bulling through it with their trucks. There were a lot of cars and trucks. As she stood watching, a man in a uniform vaulted the fence and started up the road toward her, and another followed him, and another. She ran across the road to Johan's house.

"Johan! The heat's on!" She cupped her hands around her mouth and shouted, "Johan!"

Out of breath, Patty ran up to her, holding up her jeans with one hand. "I gotta get my plants," she said, passing by Rose.

"Patty." Whirling, Rose got her by the arm before she could run out of reach. "Patty, you got to get away. Into the woods. They'll bust you if they catch you. Patty!"

The girl's eyes were glazed; she pulled at Rose's arm, trying to run. Her jeans would not close over the swelling of her body. When she let go of them, they slid down past her hips.

"Patty, run for the woods!"

Johan rushed out of his house, saw the police, and yelled. Behind him came Margaret, the baby bundled up in her arms. Johan shooed her on through the gate.

Patty was staring down the road at the police. "My baby," she said, "my baby," and began to cry.

Beyond her, the Viggs were piling out of their house, Billy leading. They raced through the pasture behind them toward the woods; Billy did not even pause at the stock fence midway there, but put one hand on the post and vaulted over it. Glory had to stop. Rose could hear her screaming for help as she struggled to climb over the fence; she got her foot into one of the wire squares and tried to climb, and her weight bore the whole fence down.

Dave Preston came up behind her. Grabbing her elbow, he hustled her on ahead of him.

Patty was crying. "I don't care any more," she said. "I don't care any more." Sobbing and dripping tears.

The sheriff was moving up the road. Rose gave Patty a shove. "Go hide in the woods."

"I don't care any more!" Patty turned and trotted away over the field. Rose turned along the road and started to run.

Behind her a bullhorn bellowed. "Please, stay where you are. Everyone please stay where you are. This is a raid—"

Rose toiled up the hill, her back cold and tight, waiting for bullets. Her lungs burned from overuse. Not daring to look back, she forced herself up over the crest of the hill and through the grass to her brother's house.

Peter was sitting on the front porch. "What's all the racket?" A plate of bacon and eggs rested beside him on the porch rail.

"It's a raid." Rose gulped for breath. "The sheriff's here."

He let out a yell and dashed back into the house. Rose followed him across the front room and down the hall.

Coyote lay asleep in his bed; Miller was stretched out on the floor beside him. When Rose and Peter clattered into the room, he lifted his head, grouchy.

"Goddamnit, I haven't had an hour's sleep in—"

"The sheriff's here," Rose said. "Hurry. You haven't got much time."

His face tightened, alert now, his eyes brilliant blue. He grabbed her arms. "What about you?"

"I'll stay here," she said. "With him." Her hand jerked toward Coyote. "You get out of here before they catch you and bust you."

Peter grabbed his jacket. Miller held Rose by the arms a moment longer; their eyes met. She put her hand on his stomach. "Hurry." She gave him a push. Miller let her go and ran after Peter toward the kitchen door.

Rose bent down to put her hand on Coyote's forehead. His skin was cool, and when she touched him, his eyes opened.

"What's happening, lady?"

"There's a pack of sheriffs on the road," she said. She pulled the covers around him. "Whatever you do, act sick. Right? Sicker'n hell."

"Sure." He closed his eyes again.

She went through the room picking up the evidence of his wound, the bloody towels, the old stained bandages. The room smelled of alcohol. While she was stuffing the dirty gauze into a paper sack, a knock thundered on the door.

She went out to answer it. Three men in dark green uniforms waited on the porch. Around their waists they wore heavy black leather belts. Guns hung on them, handcuffs, little radios. Their badges gleamed. When she opened the door, the man in the middle said, "Hello, ma'am. We're looking for Mr. Peter McKenna."

"He isn't here," she said.

"Who are you?"

"I'm Rose McKenna. I'm his sister." Her heart was beating so hard she thought they must see it, fluttering her shirt. Down on the flat the whine of a chain saw began.

"Is there anyone here besides yourself, ma'am?"

"There's a man sick down in the bedroom," Rose said.

They all reached up, took off their hats, and started into the house. They were polite, as slow moving as cows, unfrightening, but they were coming into the house and they would not let her stop them. She said, "He's down here," and led them off through the house.

"Who is this man, ma'am?" The leader went with her; the other two split and walked off in other directions, searching the house.

"Jim Wylie," she replied. "He lives down on the other side of the hill." She went ahead of him to the door, put her hand on it, and, facing him, said, "He's real sick. I'm not going to let you bother him." She watched his eyes. "He has the mumps."

"I just want to see him, ma'am. If he's not Mr. McKenna, then I'll leave."

"Do you know what Peter looks like?"

"Yes'm." The man glanced at the door and put his hand over his mouth. "Contagious mumps?"

"Very contagious," she said, opening the door to let him through.

He stayed as far from the bed as he could, way back by the door, and stood up on his toes to see Coyote's face. In a voice crisp with relief he said, "Naw, not with that hair. That's not him." He turned. "Thank you, ma'am. Sorry to disturb you." He left.

Rose pulled the door shut. Her legs were quivering like rubber bands, threatening to set her down hard if she took an unwary step. The sheriff tramped away down the hall. She forced herself calm and went after him.

"What about my brother?" she said, when they reached the front door.

"Well," the sheriff said, "we'll see if we can't serve him with the warrant some other day."

"A warrant."

On the porch now, he paused and looked down at her, a tall man in early middle age, his graying hair cropped above his ears and high on his neck. "For cultivation of marijuana."

"You don't want me?"

"We try not to bother women and children," he said. "We don't want anybody hurt."

"How many raids have you staged so far this year?" she asked.

"Twenty-nine," he said proudly.

He moved off across the porch. Around the outside of the house came the two men he had brought with him.

"They all took off for the trees," one shouted, and the sheriff waved his hand.

"Twenty-nine," Rose said to him. "Do you know that there are probably ten thousand pot gardens in Humboldt? You put on all this action, spend all this money, and all you get is twenty-nine? Not much of a return on your investment, is it?"

He looked down at her, his hat still in his hand, his face molded into the grave courtesy that old-fashioned men still offer to women. "That's certainly true, Miss McKenna. On the other hand, in the five years we've been raiding here, not one person has been hurt." He put his hat on, adjusting the flat brim with both hands. "Think about that," he said and went off down the porch steps.

She watched him go, wondering if he knew how close he had struck to the real crisis on River Ranch. The shrill scream of a dozen chain saws was climbing the air from the flat. They were hacking down the pot. Her heart contracted. She gripped the rail with her hands, wondering if they would take hers as well. Slowly she went back into the house.

She made some soup and took it to Coyote. He awakened when she came into the room; his fever was gone, but he was too weak to lift his head off the pillow. She braced him up with other pillows and Miller's rolled-up sleeping bag and fed him the soup spoonful by spoonful.

"The Man's cleaning house, hunh?" he said.

"I guess so." She thought of Patty, depending on the pot for a living while she had her baby. "God," she said. "If you grow grapes and make wine, everybody thinks you're an aristocrat."

"I'm still hungry," he said, and she went to the kitchen for more soup.

"What a bummer," she exclaimed, while he was eating.

"Well," he said, "live and learn. Did everybody else get away?"

"I think so."

He swallowed. "They didn't take nothing of mine." He lay back on the pillows, and his eyes closed.

The sheriff cut down the whole field in less than half an hour, using chain saws and power scythes. They packed it up in bundles and loaded it on their trucks and hauled it away, to burn later, she supposed, or perhaps to sell it themselves; thinking of the sheriff she had talked to, she doubted that. He was too straight-arrow for that.

She cleaned the house, fed Coyote more soup, and wandered around, wishing she could go down to her field to see if they had taken her pot as well. In the afternoon it began to rain. She stood at the front window looking out at the meadow, the rain splashing on the pipe rhinoceros. Peter's Folly, she thought.

Not long after that, Peter and Miller came back, driven in by the rain.

"Did they come up here?" Peter asked. He went to the refrigerator door and got out a Coke.

"Yes," she said. "They have a warrant for you."

"God," he said. "Jesus God."

Miller had gone down to the bunkroom to check on Coyote. He came back to the kitchen, smoking a joint, which he handed to Peter.

"He looks pretty good. The sauna must have done it."

"Kill or cure," Rose said.

Miller was staring steadily at her, his eyebrows raised a little, waiting for something from her. She was making dinner; she dropped the roast into a pan of water and put it on the stove.

"Stoke that up, will you?" she said to Peter, then went out to the front room.

Miller followed her. Alone in the room, they kissed.

"My brave lover," he said. "Staying here like that. What

a brave lover I have." His hand stroked roughly down over her hair, and he held her so tight she gasped.

"I missed you," she said.

"Of course you did." Letting her go, he looked down at her, smiling. "They didn't get ours."

"What?"

"They couldn't find it. They tramped around down there for half an hour, but they couldn't find the pot field."

Her chest swelled with a jubilant yell. She thought better of it. "Hooray," she said softly and let out the extra breath.

The rain had steadied into an unrelenting downpour. Drenched and downcast, the other settlers of River Ranch straggled into the house and gathered by the fire, closely together, seeking the comfort of a shared misery. Glory Vigg sat down in Peter's stuffed chair and covered her face with her hands and began to cry.

Rose built the fire in the hearth. Glory's sobs bothered her; she felt cut off from the others by her good fortune. Patty came and sat on the hearth in front of Glory and pulled her hands away from her face.

"Come on, Glo, it's all right. We'll get by. We always have."

"What'm I going to do?" Glory wept. "What'm I going to do?"

Sam Overfield and Billy Vigg went to play pool. Billy said, "I knew we shoulda harvested it last week."

"Goddamnit," said Sam, and hit the cue ball so hard that it jumped off the table.

Dave Preston came into the house. He looked warily around the room, saw Peter was not there, and went down to watch the pool game.

"I had flowers this big," Billy was saying, holding out his hands a foot apart. "The best smoke in Humboldt. I told y' we oughta harvest it last week."

"Goddamnit," Sam said again.

Peter came into the room.

Preston was leaning against the wall, his hands behind

him and one foot up. When he saw Peter, he moved forward a step, so that he was standing squarely. Peter faced him across half the length of the room. The others fell quiet, looking on; Sam, who was bent to shoot pool, straightened halfway, his hands braced on the green felt.

Rose held her breath. She forced her hands behind her back, to hide her fists. Peter and Preston faced each other for long seconds, with everyone else in the room watching them, and at the end Peter lowered his gaze, looked away, and, turning, walked slowly toward the hearth.

A little buzz of comment started up all around the room. Over by the wall, Patty stooped down to whisper into Glory's ear. Rose went over to the hearth, where Peter stood, doing nothing, his hands idle, his gaze fixed on the fire.

"You okay, Bub?" she said.

"No."

She turned away, biting her lips to keep from railing at him.

Someone else was coming into the room through the hall door. He paused a moment on the threshold to look around, and as the others caught sight of him, they stopped talking and fell again into an electric hush. With all eyes on him, Coyote walked slowly and painfully into the room, passed Glory and Patty, and, putting his hands on the back of the stuffed chair by the fire, held himself up on his feet and breathed heavily, gathering his strength.

Rose reached out for her brother's arm and turned him. He knocked away her hand, but he saw Coyote and he froze in his place, staring.

Coyote turned around, still leaning on the chair; he would not sit down, Rose guessed, not as long as Dave Preston was in the room. He looked for Preston in the crowd and, seeing him, leaned back on the chair and folded his arms. His face was white with effort.

"Well?" Preston asked.

"If I was you," Coyote said, "I'd be long gone before I get any better."

"I ain't afraid of you!"

"Oh, yeah? I don't see that gun around nowheres. That's the only kinda courage you got."

"I ain't afraid of you."

"Hey, guys," Patty said. "Come on, just knock it off, will y'?"

"Yeah," Sam said. "Everybody's lost it all. Now why can't we at least stay friends?"

Preston and Coyote glared at each other, seeming to hear nothing. The front door opened, and Johan came in, Margaret behind him, covered up in an old army rain poncho; Glory and Patty went over to help her get it off.

"I don't need my rifle," Preston said; his voice rang through the room. "I ain't leavin'. There's nobody can make me. Look at him; he can't hardly hold his head up."

"Maybe not now," Coyote said. "Ain't sayin' nothin' about tomorrow, or the next day—"

"Come on, you guys!" Patty strode in between them. "Shout down! What're you trying to do?"

"One of these days, man—"

"Shut up!" Peter walked into the middle of the room, nudged Patty out of the way, and stood looking from Dave Preston to Coyote and back again. He turned toward Preston. "I tol' you you were supposed to go, and I meant it."

Preston's quick, dark, squirrel eyes ran around the room and back to Peter. "Come on, Pete. Be realistic. He stole the dope. Whyn't you run him off? He's a goddamn thief."

Coyote's jaw clenched, his lips thin and his whole face sharp with temper, but he said nothing to that.

"Shit," Patty said. "The dope's gone anyway. Who cares if he took a little?" She walked back toward the little group of women by the wall. "We blew it all anyway."

Peter went a few steps closer to Preston. "I guess I gotta throw you out, is that it?"

Dave Preston smiled at him, leaning against the wall, his arms folded over his chest. "You can try."

Johan said, "Don't you people think you've done

enough?" He wore an old army jacket, open down the front; he gave dark looks all around the room. "It was your bad karma that got our field busted."

Rose muttered, "Jesus." Miller was in the doorway now, watching, and she went toward him. An angry hum of voices circled the room as people turned their tempers on Johan. When Rose passed by Coyote, he put out his hand. He meant to grab her arm, but his fingers were too weak and he simply slapped her elbow.

She turned toward him, just in time to catch him and keep him from falling. He drooped over her shoulder, his weight like an iron net over her, bowing her down. Miller ran to help her. Lifting Coyote's bulk off her, he helped her get him around the chair and sitting down.

"Damn you," he said to Coyote. "You nearly bought the farm once, you want to make another offer?"

Rose straightened, looking down the room toward her brother. He was still facing Preston. Doggedly he coiled his hands into fists and walked a few steps closer.

"I want you off my place."

"Shit, man," Preston cried, his voice loud in the sudden hush. "Whyn't you throw him off?" His arm thrust out at Coyote. "He's the fuckin' rip-off who—"

"Because I like him," Peter said, "and I don't like you. Get off my place!"

Supremely confident, Preston grinned at him. "Throw me off, Pete. Come on, try."

Peter approached him straight on, slowly. Rose could see how frightened he was, and, as he always had when he was frightened, he spoke again in a loud voice.

"I'm gonna break up your face."

"Try," said Dave Preston.

Peter gathered himself, his body tense, his arms cocked; then once more he scattered his energy in a loud threatening speech. "This is my ranch. Whenever you're here, you gotta do by my rules."

"Make me," said Dave Preston.

Peter jumped him. It was so fast that Rose started up with a yell of surprise. Preston socked her brother in the gut, and he fell over backwards on the floor.

Preston stood over him. "Come on, sucker. Make me."

Pushing himself up on his arms, Peter shook his head once, and without rising to his feet he launched himself at Preston's knees.

Dave shouted; his legs went out from under him and he fell, landing on top of Peter, knocking the breath out of him. They scrambled around on the floor for a moment, banging their elbows on the planks and the legs of the pool table. When Peter rolled away and got up, he came up under the edge of the table and hit his head so hard on the bumper that he sat back down again. Preston stood.

"I'm staying."

Patty yelled, "Kill him, Peter!"

Rose clenched her fists. Her mouth was dry with excitement. She wanted to run in and shield her brother, kick Preston's balls off, shatter the look of contempt on his face. Peter pulled himself onto his feet, one hand on the pool table; wobbling, he went at Preston again.

All around the room the people yelled and waved their arms. Sam was shouting, "Kill the bastard, Peter"; and behind Rose, Coyote whispered, "Jesus, go get him, boy." Nobody shouted for Preston. Even the Viggs were cheering for Peter.

He and Preston grappled. Peter swung his leg around, trying to trip the other man over, but Preston butted him in the face. He cried out in pain and flung his arms up to protect his face, and Preston socked him in the belly again.

"Leave him alone!"

Patty charged across the room, past Rose, past the other settlers, and flung herself on Preston, kicking and scratching. "Leave him alone!"

Rose moved, her arms out. "Patty—Patty—the baby—" The others were moving, too. Overfield and Billy Vigg and Glory and even Margaret, her baby in her arms, rushed in a mass at Dave Preston. He shouted, indignant, and his brother and Sam Overfield hoisted him bodily off his feet. Patty ran on ahead to the door.

"Throw him out! Throw him out, the fuckin' bum!"

The others roared in a single voice. Bearing Dave Preston in their midst, they hurried out through the door onto the porch. The wet, gusty wind swept in behind them.

Patty cheered, "One, two, three—heave!"

Rose put out her arms, and Peter came to her and laid his bleeding head on her shoulder. "I made an asshole out of myself, didn't I?"

"No," she said. "Not at all. In fact I think you just got reelected." She closed her arms around him. "Peter, you were super."

Johan was standing by the hearth, frowning at them. Margaret came back first from the porch and went toward the fire, the baby cradled in her arms. Johan flew at her like an angry rooster. "What are you doing? You see how this place has corrupted you? You would never have done that before."

"I like Peter," said Margaret calmly and she sat down on the brick apron and laid the baby on her thighs.

Sam and the Viggs tramped back into the room, jubilant and laughing. Rain dripped from their clothes, and they left a stream of wet tracks across the floor. Johan gave them all a furious, cutting look. He stooped over Margaret.

"You see why we have to go. Can you envision raising Redwood in a place like this?"

"Go, then," Margaret said. "But I'm not going with you."

She was straightening the baby's clothes; as she spoke, she fussed elaborately with the baby's blanket and jacket and hair. She did not look at Johan. Glory Vigg sank down on the brick beside Margaret.

"Come on, Jo. Don't you ever get tired of carrying around that halo?"

A few people laughed. Johan was staring at Margaret, as if he heard nothing else. Cared about nothing else.

"Sunshine, I am going."

"I'm not," she said.

"We've talked this all through, Sunshine. You know what's right. You know what all this means to me."

She said nothing, nor did she look at him. After a moment he went across the room toward the door.

"I can see now," he said in his preacher's voice, "that this has been a test of me." His gaze raked the other people around the room. "You are all nothing but illusions. Now that I have what I came here for, I shall go on my way." He walked out the door, into the rainy darkness. The door swung shut behind him.

"What the devil did he mean by that?" Coyote muttered to Rose.

She shook her head. Impossible to see what Johan saw. To know what Johan knew or thought he knew. Maybe his blackness, which meant so much to him and so little to the white people around him, had driven him into a perpetual exile. She put her hand up to her eyes, feeling tired.

Miller Tarn was taking a cue stick down from the rack on the wall. She lowered her hand, watching him. As he bent over the table to measure his shot, his eyes flicked a glance toward her. She thought she understood him, yet his inner world was as impregnable to her as Johan's. What she understood was what she needed of him.

He stretched along the cue stick and stroked the white ball down across the table. She walked toward the front door, which the wind had blown slightly open. There was no sign of Johan anywhere. He had melted into the night, that great outlying blackness.

Her own good luck over the pot raid tormented her again. She and Miller alone of them all still had their treasure. She could not stay here and keep from the others that she had survived the raid. If she lied to them and hid the dope, the guilt would rot away her friendship with them. If she told them, it would be worse; they would be jealous and angry, however they rationalized it. She stood before the open door, rubbing her hands together.

The rainy wind touched her face. She went out the door

onto the porch, windswept and wet. The trees on the distant ridge were swaying and dancing to the wind.

She could go, take the pot and leave, and that would be okay; she would have Miller and the dope. But she could not stay on River Ranch and keep the dope. She licked her lips, struggling to decide.

She knew already, knowing herself, what she would do. She also knew that Miller would leave her for it. The rain tapped on the porch roof. The air tasted deliciously fresh. She put out her hand and let the rain fall into her cupped palm. She loved Miller and wanted him, but she needed River Ranch. She understood herself here; she knew how to act.

The door behind her opened, and Miller came out; she knew it was he by the sound of his feet on the boards. He came up behind her, and his arms slid around her.

"We can cut the field tomorrow," he said. "Then we can be gone from here by noon."

She said nothing. He had enclosed her in his embrace, his weight pressing slightly against her back, bowing her head forward a little.

Her silence warned him. Sharply, he asked, "What's wrong?"

"I want to share it with them," she said. "They lost all theirs."

He thrust himself back away from her so hard that she came up against the porch rail and gripped it to keep her balance. Turning, she put her back to the rail and the darkness. "What d'you mean?" he cried. He spun away from her, his arms out, and whirled again to face her. "Why should they get any? They don't deserve it. They were stupid, they put it out there with flags on it, and they lost it. That's just simple justice."

"How can you have lived around here for so long and still hate them?"

"I don't hate them. I just don't care about anybody but me and the people I like, that's all." He put out his hands to her arms and drew her up against him. "I don't want you to care about them, either." He kissed her head, his arms encasing her again. "I love you, Rose." He kissed her again.

"I love you, too," she said. "But that doesn't change my mind about sharing the pot."

He pushed her away. "You don't love me. You don't love anybody but yourself."

"I do love you," she cried, desperate.

"No, you don't. You treat everybody the same. You don't love me."

"Mil—"

She put out her arms toward him, to give him her love, and he recoiled and struck her hands down. Her temper broke; she lunged at him and hit him on the chest, open-handedly, with all her strength. It was like hitting a wall; he hardly seemed to notice it. He stared at her a moment longer, while she struggled with her feelings, and abruptly he turned away.

"Well, see y' around, Rose."

He walked off down the porch. Rose leaned back against the railing, her gaze following him; the space between them seemed like a hundred miles. There was nothing to say to bridge that difference. She was tired. She let that cap off her struggling passions. In the darkness at the far end of the porch, a lighter bloomed; he dipped his face into the light to light a joint. She pulled her gaze away and went into the house.

"Hey, everybody," she said and stopped. The crowd was scattered through the room, some playing pool, and some talking, and some staring into the fire. Rose went up toward the hearth, where Glory, Patty, and Margaret were sitting with Margaret's baby.

"Everybody," Rose repeated, her hands unsteady and her throat clogged. She spoke to the three women, but nearby others looked up as she went on. "I got—I have—the sheriff didn't get mine. I have a field, down in the woods, and they missed it."

Now they were all watching her. In the stuffed chair Coyote pushed himself forward.

"It isn't very much," Rose said, "not divided among everybody. Maybe a pound apiece. But it's something."

For a moment they gaped at her, startled, their mouths open. Then all at once a ragged cheer went up from the men by the pool table, and they came down the room toward her. The three women before her stood. Patty crowed a high, relieved laugh. "Oh, Rose." They gathered around her, laughing and hugging her. She put her head down on Margaret's shoulder and wept.

After a while, they pulled the chairs and couches out of the middle of the floor and turned on the stereo, and Glory Vigg danced. Billy danced with her, but it was Glory who drew the eye. Rose leaned against the wall by the kitchen, watching. She had never been able to dance. The steady beat of the music boomed through the room; it was a Rolling Stones album, rich in weird harmonies, which cut the beat's monotony, made it vital.

Glory was beautiful when she danced. Her small feet moved in neat little steps. Her great bulk seemed airy and light in the rhythm of the dance. A mattress balancing on a bottle of wine. She turned and dipped, her arms over her head, smiling, while around her the others clapped and called encouragement.

Patty came over to Rose and leaned against the wall beside her. "You think Johan will go without Margaret?"

Rose nodded. "He loves his big ideas more than he loves any person."

"Yeah, you're probably right." Patty smoothed the red-and-white-checked blouse over her stomach. "I could live there, with Margaret. In that house. Don't you think?"

"I think you'd better ask Margaret, not me."

"Oh, she asked me."

Rose lifted her head; there across the room Margaret sat,

her baby in her arms. Catching Rose's gaze on her, she smiled back, the mysterious, perfect smile Rose had always thought came with her pregnancy. But it was just Margaret. Rose could not help smiling back.

Other people were going out to dance now. Peter came over to her. "You wanna dance?"

"God, Peter, I can't dance." The thought took her back to the high school dances, her backward youth, when she had never had a date, and had always been made to dance with her brother.

"Come on," Peter said. "I'll show you."

"No, I—"

"Chicken?"

"God," she said, moving away from the wall. "You know how to push the buttons, don't you?"

"Sure. Come on, like this." He showed her a little sideways step, holding her by the hand. Uncertainly she imitated it.

"Okay, good," he said. "Now like this."

Thinking of Miller, she could not concentrate on dancing. She pushed him back out of her mind. And set her mind. And set her feet to the music.

In the morning while she was serving breakfast to Coyote in the bunkroom, Miller came in behind her.

"Come on," he said to her. "Let's go down and cut the field."

She nodded, her back still to him, hunched forward over the tray of food. In the bed Coyote sat up, his attention aimed past her to Miller.

"Well," Miller said, "I'm going. Good-by." He reached over Rose's shoulder to take Coyote by the hand.

"Leaving?" Coyote looked startled from Miller to Rose. He gripped Miller's hand tightly. "Hey, man, I owe you a lot, man."

"It's cool," said Miller.

"No, it ain't. I'd like a chance to make it up to you." Coyote still held Miller by the hand; he looked at Rose. "You taking off, too?"

"No," she answered. She looked over her shoulder at Miller. "I'll be right there."

"I'll be in my car," he said and went out.

She put down the tray beside the bed. "Here, you need more. You can get it, can't you?" She forced herself to meet Coyote's eyes.

He said, "I thought you and he had a thing going on."

"Yeah," she said. "Not any more."

"Why?"

"I gotta go down—" Standing, she wiped her sweating palms on her jeans, avoiding his eyes.

"Because of last night? You giving us all your dope?"

She nodded. Going to the closet, she took out her jacket and put it on. "I'll be back in a couple hours."

"He'll come back," Coyote reassured her.

"Maybe." She went out to Miller's car.

The marijuana blossoms were dying, the long delicate curls of purple and white and yellow turning brown at the tips. They cut the plants down one by one and stacked them beside the field.

"You see this—" Miller held out a stem of the pot, ending in a cola of flowers and buds nearly four inches long. "You trim off all the leaves with nail clippers, dry this out, and smoke it. I guarantee you it will send you through the ceiling."

"Okay," she said. "God, that's a lot of work."

"The whole thing is a lot of work," he said, sounding angry. "Which is why I don't see how you can just give it away like that."

She said nothing. She knew he thought she was a fool.

They divided the plants into two piles and stuffed them into green trash bags, their root ends sticking out. She hid her ten bags of plants under the berry bushes at the foot of the crag and helped him lug his share off through the woods toward the county road.

His car was waiting there, packed with his things, his sleeping bag and clothes and tennis racket. They stuffed the bags into the back seat and covered them over with his shirts and a blanket and some towels.

"Be careful," she said. "If the Man pulls you over, he'll smell that for sure." The rich odor of the marijuana rapidly permeated the car.

"I'll go fifty-five all the way," he said.

They sat together in the front seat and smoked a joint. She asked, "Where are you going now?"

"Back to L.A., to off this dope. Then I'll go to Hawaii."

"Send me a postcard."

He gave her a swift, shy look. "Sure. Do you want me to?"

"Yes. I'll miss you."

She held out the joint, and he took it. Their fingertips grazed. She let her hand fall to her knee.

"Will you ever come back?"

His head swung, turning his face away from her. "You want me to?"

"Yes," she said. "Yes."

"Maybe. I don't like to make plans too far ahead."

"Yeah, I know." She rubbed her hand back and forth over her knee, wishing she could touch him. "Come on back in the spring. We'll plant another garden."

His head bobbed. She reached for the handle of the door, and he said, "Give me a kiss good-by."

She leaned toward him and kissed him, and he slid his hand behind her neck and held her fast, a hard kiss, his tongue sliding fiercely over her lips and her tongue. A long kiss, which neither of them wanted to end. It did end. They separated, looking elsewhere.

"Good-by," he said.

"Good-by."

She got out of the car, and he drove away. She stood

watching him disappear around the curve of the road. Her mind was numb; for a while, at least, she felt nothing. The trees keened in the wind, and a few drops of rain splattered her, not real rain, but water trapped in the high branches. She walked up the road toward River Ranch.

Peter went up to Eureka in the afternoon to see about the warrant; Rose went with him in case he had to spend time in jail. But all they wanted was his signature on a paper releasing him on his own recognizance.

"Well," she said, "that was easy."

They walked down the hall to the public defender's office, and Peter talked to a lawyer there while Rose read a magazine in the waiting room. Finally he came out, frowning.

"Well?"

"He says usually all they do is plea-bargain these things. I'll plead guilty to a misdemeanor, and they'll fine me a couple hundred dollars."

"So what's the matter with that?"

In the elevator several other people joined them, and he kept his mouth shut, but when they got out of the elevator and walked across the lobby of the courthouse, he said, "Well, Jesus, Rose, I don't understand it. They act like it's no big thing; it's all routine for them. So why do they do it at all? Why not leave us alone?"

Rose shrugged. "Because then they'd have nothing to do."

"Yeah? What happened to Miller? He split, didn't he?"

"Yes."

"You guys have a fight?"

"Yeah, more or less. He was pissed off I gave up my dope."

"He'll be back." Peter put his arm around her and squeezed her against him. His lip was still swollen where Preston had butted him in the face.

"Yeah, I think he will," Rose said. And would leave again, time and again. They went out onto the cantilevered stairs that led to the sidewalk.

It had been raining all day, and the air was bitter with the wet cold. A low slate roof of clouds hung over the town. Night was coming. She stopped to snap the front of her jacket and wind her scarf around her throat.

Already she missed him, his challenges and his strength, but she had strength enough without him, if he did not come back. At that thought, even under her lowering mood, she felt better. Ready. She went down the steps after her brother.

A NOTE ON THE TYPE

The text of this book was set on the Linotype in a type face called Baskerville. The face is a facsimile reproduction of types cast from molds made for John Baskerville (1706–75) from his designs. The punches for the revived Linotype Baskerville were cut under the supervision of the English printer George W. Jones.

John Baskerville's original face was one of the forerunners of the type style known as "modern face" to printers—a "modern" of the period A.D. 1800.

Composed by Fuller Typesetting,
Lancaster, Pennsylvania

Printed and bound by American Book—Stratford Press,
Saddle Brook, New Jersey

Typography and binding design by
Virginia Tan